Inseparable

Printed in the United States of America

ISBN: 0-615-30056-1

EAN13: 9780615300566

Visit www.ytaylorbooks.com for additional copies.

ytaylor@ytaylorbooks.com

A special dedication to my children and grandchildren, who are the center of my heart and my inspiration.

A special thanks to my daughters, Tyrica, Jaimie and TyAmber, and my aunt, for their contribution to this book.

And most importantly, I thank **God** for His love and all that has come and will come out of His love. I thank Him for His presence in my life and blessing me even more than I could ever imagine.

I have been crucified with Christ and I no longer live, but Christ lives in me. The life I now live in the body, I live by faith in the Son of God, who loved me and gave himself for me (Gal. 2:20).

Yvonne Taylor

❧

Inseparable

Prologue

*Y*es, she was definitely pregnant. She took two home pregnancy tests and another at the clinic. She just couldn't believe it. "How could this have happened?" she asked the nurse, on the verge of hysterics. After all, her husband had had a vasectomy. Before the nurse could respond, she already knew the answer. "Ah, don't bother. I know the answer, 99.9 percent effective."

"Yep, that's it."

"How am I going to tell Brannon?" She spoke more to herself than the nurse as she paced the length of the examination room. "He won't believe it. Things are already shaky in our marriage."

"I know, Liah," the nurse said understandingly. She put her hand consolingly on Liah's shoulder, ceasing her nervous pacing. "But the sooner you tell him, the better."

"He's out of town at the moment. I'm thankful for that. It will give me some time to process this."

"Well, if there's anything I can do, just call," the nurse offered.

"Thank you. I appreciate that," Liah said kindly, although she knew she'd never take her up on her offer. She left the clinic and went to the park to think. She knew that whatever she was about to face, she would get through it.

A week had gone by, and she hadn't told anyone about her situation. Brannon was due home today. She had fixed his favorite meal, trying to convince herself that it would be easier to tell him. The truth is she knew it wouldn't have any effect on his reaction being the arrogant jerk that he was! However this panned out, she wasn't going to go out of her way to prove that she hadn't been unfaithful, something he had attempted a year ago.

The homecoming was good and dinner was delectable. They had a "Leave it to Beaver" evening. That was until the kids went to bed and she told him the news. She showed him the pregnancy test she had brought home from the clinic and brochures on a vasectomy procedure's effectiveness percentage. "You're pregnant," he said, seemingly calm.

"Yes, seven weeks."

Then he flew off the handle. "See, I knew you hadn't forgiven me for having that affair," he accused, sending his chair flying back as he stood up abruptly. "You not only went out and cheated, but you got yourself pregnant."

"Excuse me? You idiot, you think I cheated on you? I can see why you would say that, being the person you are," she said derisively. "You know—you don't deserve my fidelity." She took a deep breath. "And you know what else? I'm not going there with you. This is your child, and that's all there is to it."

"But I had a vasectomy. I can't produce," he said as he slowly sat back down, abandoning the pretext of her infidelity.

"You're sure not producing any sense right now," she murmured, sure that he'd heard her.

"I don't care what this paper says. That is not my child, and there is nothing you can say to convince me otherwise," he stubbornly declared.

"You don't have to worry about me going out of my way trying to prove anything to you. You are looking for a way out of this marriage and your responsibilities, as you always have. Except this time, I'm not giving you a reason to stay. So if you don't think you already have a reason to stay, you definitely shouldn't. Despite everything, Brannon, I've always been there for you. But if you want to leave, by all means, go. I'm not begging you to stay." She dramatically went to the door and opened it. He grabbed his bags he'd just brought in and walked out.

She closed the door behind him and took a deep breath, not the least bit shocked that he had left. Liah walked over to her recliner, picked her Bible up from the coffee table, sat down, and began reading as tears ran down her face. She had put everything she had into their marriage. Now it was over. After reading her Bible, she noticed Brannon's blazer on the couch next to her. She picked it up then threw it on the chair and a photo fell to the floor. She picked up the picture. It was a photo of Brannon, a female, and a baby. Written on the back was "To Brannon, please keep this picture close to your heart—from your baby girl and me."

Liah was fuming. She could not believe that he would be so careless to cheat and get someone pregnant and now have the audacity to deny their child together. She took the liberty of checking all of his pockets, finding a note written to Brannon, thanking him for a wonderful weekend.

The next day he came back without his luggage this time. He told her that he was leaving for good.

"I just don't believe that the baby is mine," he said. "But if for some reason it is, I don't care to know."

"Brannon I have just one question, retrieving the photo from the coffee table. "Tell me this, who is this female and baby in this picture with you?" She went on to say. "Come to think of it, this baby looks just like Jayde when she was a baby. Now you and I both know it's not Jayde."

"Liah I'm so sorry. I ..." She cut him off.

"Brannon just save it. You and I both know you're in no way sorry. The only reason you're breathing sorry is because you got caught. Now back to our situation."

"I'm a going to only offer you this option once. Do you want to have a paternity test done? If so, we can certainly have one. Not for you, but for the sake of our child. Then it will know that you chose to leave because you wanted to leave, not because you didn't know that it was yours."

"I don't care. I want out," he said simply.

"Then out you will get. You had better take everything today because come tomorrow, the only thing that will be left here that are yours' are the children you're abandoning." She was about to turn and walk away from him, but stopped and faced him for the last time.

"Just tell me one thing, Brannon. What shall I tell our children?" she asked angrily,

"They know I love them."

"But yet, you're abandoning them."

"Tell them whatever you feel you need to." With that, he packed whatever he could fit in his truck and departed, leaving everything else behind. He didn't bother telling the kids goodbye. And she didn't bother to ask him where he was going.

Later, she sat down with all of the kids and explained things the best she could. The kids didn't take it too badly. They weren't used to spending a lot of time with him anyway, as he was always away on his work trips. She also told them about the new baby on the way. They all seemed thrilled.

Liah immediately started planning for their future over the next few weeks. They planned for a huge garage sale. The house was on the market. By the time the divorce was final, she hoped to have an offer on the house. The garage sale went better than she had expected. She sold everything she didn't think she would need. She took all of the money from the garage sale and opened up a new savings account. She called it her "just-in-case-something-happened" money, her "cushion."

A few months later, her divorce was final. With the exception of the house, there wasn't much left for her to get in the divorce settlement. Brannon was a big spender. He had debts she knew nothing about. The majority of their life's savings was used to pay off all debts, mostly his. He tried to negotiate the kids' college fund. But there was no way she would allow that. Other than the house, which most of that would be used to finish paying off debts, and college funds, she was ready to cut her losses and move forward. She did just that. Neither she nor the kids heard from Brannon after that. She supposed he had moved back to Virginia Beach, where his family lived.

About three weeks later, the house sold. They moved into a three-bedroom apartment. The two oldest boys were living in dorms on campus. They were in their second and third years of college. Liah had to go on bed rest the entire last trimester of her pregnancy. She knew the hard times would come soon. There was no way she was going to let them get the best of her. She predicted that she would not be able to work for at least six months. She would just take it one day at a time.

After the baby was born, she only had enough money to sustain them for two months. For the moment, they had everything they needed, but facing hardship was a concern. She never would have imagined that circumstances would force her to apply for government assistance. Two months went by and she had reached the end of her savings. Government assistance had not yet, been approved, and she still wasn't getting any help from her ex-husband, of course. She could have easily picked up the phone and called her mother. She did come from a pretty wealthy family. Liah was always determined to do things on her own: Especially when it came to taking responsibility for her own choices. She wasn't sure what she was going to do. One thing she was sure of, she would not give up. Through all her hard times, she remained a faithful Christian. She always reminded herself of Philippians 4:13, "I can do all things through Christ who strengthens me." She was very spiritually grounded, and that is what sustained her. In addition to that, she would never let her children down.

Another month went by and things were worse than ever. Still holding her head up high, she spent hours standing in free food lines. She had gotten behind on all of her bills, and no one knew how bad she was doing, not even her family and closest friends. One day she reached her breaking point. She fell to her knees in tears for she felt burdened down. She stayed there praying. *I will deal with today because it's a new day and it brings new things*. She told herself this each and every day. Even if things didn't appear to be getting better, she had the faith that they would someday.

She considered going back to her previous job, but it didn't provide the flexibility she needed as a single mom, and with a new baby. She was a Consumer Psychologist and her position was quite demanding.

She decided to take an independent sales job, working for a motor club. This allowed her to work around the kids' schedule and keep the baby with her most of the time. She didn't have the income she was accustomed to having. Nonetheless, she was doing quite well and most importantly, she was finally making ends meet.

About nine months later, she decided to put her talent to work and became a contract chef while she continued her position as an independent salesman. For the next two years, she worked as an IC, an acronym she came up with for independent chef. She was known as one of the best, if not the best, chef in town, turning down numerous job offers.

One day, she decided to treat herself to an expensive lunch while the girls were at school and the baby was in a learning center, part-time. She made reservations at A'Palace restaurant and dressed up for the occasion. Liah was sitting in the restaurant waiting for her food. After waiting for thirty-five minutes or so, she went to the waitress to find out what was taking so long.

"Excuse me, may I ask what is taking so long for my lunch to be served?" She made an effort to be polite.

"The chef quit," she was told.

"You have got to be kidding me. You all have a lot of people here. What are you going to do?"

"Well, we still have the sous chef. He's good, but he doesn't know all of the ins and outs just yet," the waitress explained.

"Where's the person in charge of this restaurant?"

"In an important meeting across town—unreachable."

"How convenient," Liah said sarcastically. "Which way to the kitchen?" The waitress pointed toward the double doors, and Liah boldly walked through them.

"Hello, everyone! My name is Liah Mathis. I'm your chef for the day." Everyone looked apprehensively at Tina, the dining manager.

"You heard her," Tina said, looking at Liah, with an instinctive confidence in her ability to head the kitchen. We need a chef and now we have one. Liah nodded at Tina in appreciation before addressing the others. "Okay, guys, let's get moving before we have an empty room. Now, who's my sous chef?" she asked looking around.

"That would be me," a well-groomed man said, stepping forward. He was about six feet tall, seemingly in shape, dark hair, and fairly handsome.

"Okay. And your name is…?"

"Louis. My name is Louis. Are you really a chef?" he asked unbelievingly. "You look more of the business type."

"Looks can be deceiving, Louis. Let's get to work," Liah said. "Alright, boss," he said in compliance.

16

"Don't call me that, Louis."

"Okay... Ms. Mathis?"

"Liah will be fine," she told him." She fell right into delegating. Everyone liked her right off the bat. Although she was in charge, she was exceptionally easy to work with. Everyone was served and sent compliments to the chef. Some ordered food to go, and the waiting staff even made better tips. Liah thanked everyone for working with her, and they thanked her for saving their hides. "You guys are awesome, but I have to go meet a client now," she explained. "Louis, I took the liberty of jotting down a few important tips for you. And I made some extra sauces for you to help out with the evening crew. You guys have a good day." They all thanked her again and turned to leave after giving Louis her business card.

As Liah was walking out of the kitchen, Bob Rogers, the owner, a tall, average-built, salt-and-pepper head—older man and Percy Thompson, the manager, an average-height and fairly slim man, with light-brown hair were coming in. "Who was that leaving out of this kitchen?" Bob asked.

"That's the woman who just saved this restaurant," Louis said. "What do you mean? And where is Jared," Percy questioned in confusion.

"First of all, Jared walked out a minute before the lunch rush," Louis interjected. "And second, Liah was a customer who sat for thirty minutes waiting for her food. She was gracious enough to take over Jared's duties once she found out he walked out on us. She came in, introduced herself, and took over the kitchen," Louis explained.

"And you let her walk out?" Bob asked in disbelief.

"What was I supposed to do? She's not on the payroll," Louis said.

"Who exactly is this Liah character?" Percy asked.

"That doesn't matter," Bob stated. "She saved my restaurant. We'll make her our permanent chef."

"Well she did leave me her card. But she already has a job and she just left to meet a client."

"I don't care. Where's the card?" Louis handed Bob the business card. He passed it on to Percy and adamantly insisted he call her. "And offer an incentive ... a company car ... with a sign-on and yearly bonus, whatever it takes."

"Well, call her! What are you waiting for? You never know who else's kitchen she might stumble into and save. And Percy!"

"Yeah?"

"Make her an offer she can't refuse."

"I'm on top of it," he said, dialing Liah's number. He called, but was unable to reach her, so he left her a detailed message. Liah got the message, but decided to make them sweat and returned their call a day later.

She returned the next day and reluctantly scheduled an appointment the following day, although she wasn't sure if she would be interested. After all, accepting an hourly job meant that she would probably be doing the very thing she detested, punching a clock and committing to work for someone else. She didn't really need a job, even if it was a good-paying one. She was doing well financially. Most importantly, she liked her freedom and flexibility, working on her own terms and time. *Why should I give all that up,* she asked herself. *Hmm. Though, this could be one of those chances in a lifetime....*"

The next day she arrived for her interview about ten minutes early, thinking that she was meeting with Percy, only. When she walked into the office, Bob Rogers was there as well. "Hello, Mrs. Mathis," I'm Bob Rogers. I owned this establishment. I'm very pleased to make your acquaintance. Thank you for taking the time to meet with us."

"Please to meet you as well. I think," she responded kindly.

"No worry, I'm just here to make sure you get what you want."

"Good afternoon, Mrs. Mathis, I'm Percy Thompson. I'm the manager. Thank you for meeting with us on such short notice."

"No bother, shall we get started?" She was eager to begin the meeting.

"Yes ... indeed, we shall," Mr. Thompson replied. She handed Mr. Rogers her résumé and some letters of recommendation. While he looked them over he said things like, "hmm" and "impressive." "You seem to have an exceptional track record, Mrs. Mathis. All of these recommendations are from people in high places. I see that you've catered for countless special occasions all over town."

"That's right," she responded, with a nod of the head as well.

"Percy," Mr. Rogers called in his deep voice.

"Would you like to take a look?" Percy asked, misinterpreting Mr. Roger's address.

"No, I believe we're ready to make her an offer." And indeed they were. They offered her an outstanding monthly salary, a new company car with an exchange every two years, a sign-on bonus after ninety days, plus a yearly bonus.

"Impressive," she said, but she was in the negotiating zone. "Mr. Thompson ... Mr. Rogers," she responded modestly.

"Please, call me Bob," Mr. Rogers broke in.

"And call me Percy, please."

"Well, Bob and Percy, this is a very kind offer, but I do quite well working independently, and I enjoy my flexibility."

"And you can still have your flexibility," Bob interjected hastily.

"All you have to do is look at these figures and say yes," Percy told her. She looked but showed no indication of being blown away by those figures.

"It was a pleasure talking to you both," she said politely as she stood. "I will get back to you in a day or so. You have a wonderful afternoon," she said and walked out, leaving them both somewhat dumbfounded.

She walked into the restaurant the next day and continued on to Percy's office. "Okay ... you got me," she said.

"Great!" You had us worried there for a moment. But I think you knew that," he chuckled. "I like it."

She spent most of the day making changes. The entire staff was delighted to have her on board.

~Chapter One~

Four Years Later

*L*iah and her children were attending a gospel meeting at the Ridgeview church of Christ. The song that the a cappella group was singing was one of Liah's favorite songs, "The Greatest Commands." They planned to stay for the fellowship dinner afterwards; after all, Liah had no social life. She was a single parent of six. Her two older boys, Joshua and Jacob were married with children. Her oldest daughter, Jayde, was in her first year of college at seventeen. Liah's three youngest still lived at home. Jacqlyne was sixteen, Jessica was fifteen, and Jason was six.

She felt as if she had come such a long ways in such a short time. It always seems to work out that way when God is put in charge and He is allowed to direct one's path.

Finally, the four of them sat down to enjoy a delectable meal, prepared by the 'great chef' at the A'Palace restaurant. Liah wasn't arrogant. Nonetheless, she was that great chef.

Just as she stuffed a piece of chicken in her mouth, barely having time to chew, a handsome, well-dressed, and well-groomed man walked toward her. He had dark-brown hair and gray eyes, and stood about six feet tall, give or take an inch. "Excuse me, is this seat taken?"

His voice was striking, causing Liah to forget to swallow. Jessica looked at her oddly, and she realized that her mouth was still stuffed.

"No, sir, please sit," Jacqlyne said, prompted by Jessica's aggressive nudge. Unfortunately, it was right by Liah. She looked at him and smiled as she continued to swallow. The moment came for her to say something. It felt as if a million thoughts had entered her mind in one second. Taking a shallow breath, she regained her composure, hoping to be ready to answer whatever question he might ask next. "Hi ... my name is Marcus, and I am sorry to have caught you in such an awkward moment."

"That's okay, and I'm sorry. My name is Liah," she said smiling.

"Very pleased to meet you," they said simultaneously.

"The pleasure is all mine," he said.

Breathing a sigh of relief, she quickly uttered, "These are my children," waving toward them, "Jacqlyne, Jessica, and Jason."

"They all call me Jas, that is until someone gets angry with me," looking at his mother toward the end of his statement.

"Well, Jas," he said politely, "I am very glad to meet you. Liah, you have very beautiful children. They all have bright smiles, just like yours."

"Thank you," she said, flaunting that bright smile. "So Marcus, do you have a last name?"

"I do," he said simply.

"And that is?"

Chuckling, he said "Michaels—Marcus Michaels. And you?" "Mathis."

"Liah Mathis," he clarified.

"That's me," she said. "Now that we have gotten the introductions out of the way, are you a member or a visitor?"

"I'm a member and so is my family. My dad is one of the elders."

"Oh really! And are you following in his footsteps?"

"Well, I would have liked to," he said hesitantly. "So, what brings you here?" he asked her, changing the subject.

"I enjoy gospel meetings," she answered without hesitation. "And I really like the speaker and the group singing, and I also helped prepare the meal." He coughed and cleared his throat.

"This chicken is kind of dry," he said coarsely. "I need water." The kids burst out laughing.

"Yeah right, you know this is probably the best you've ever had," she said arrogantly.

"I'm kidding," he admitted with a smirk on his face.

"We know," Jessica said, "but it was funny."

He sobered. "Truly, this is better than my mom's. You're a really good cook. Can I get the recipe?"

"Seriously?"

"Yes, I'm serious."

"Why do you want it anyway," she said, smiling. "Can you cook?"

"Hmm, a little."

"Well, that didn't sound too convincing, but I'll email it to you anyway."

"Really?"

"Really."

"All right," he grinned, pulling out a pen and pad before getting his words out. "So, Miss Mathis," at least he was hoping it was Miss, "are you coming to Sunday service?"

"Are you?"

"Of course I am."

"Well, I'm not sure if I'm coming here or not. Maybe."

"Excuse me," one of the servers interrupted. "Ms. Mathis, we need your help in the kitchen," the server frantically.

"Okay, I'll be right there. I'm sorry, Marcus," she apologized, turning back to him. "I have to go see what's going on."

"Sure, no problem. It was great talking to you. We should do it again soon."

"Right," she responded.

"Don't forget to email me that recipe."

"I won't. Girls, finish up because we're leaving when I'm done in the kitchen."

"Okay, Mom," said Jessica.

"It was nice meeting all of you ... Jacqlyne, Jessica, and Jas, right?

"Yes, sir," Jas affirmed.

"Let me get a high five, Jas." Jas jumped up and slapped Marcus' hand.

Liah smiled pleasingly. "I have to go; I'll be in the kitchen. Marcus, you take care."

"Don't forget the recipe!" he reminded her.

"I won't," she said, sniggling. "I'm beginning to think you just want my email address," she said as she grinned at him. He looked at her and smiled.

"We're done," said Jacqlyne.

"Okay. Goodbye, Marcus," Liah said shyly looking at him.

"Goodbye," he said reluctantly. Marcus walked out of the fellowship room with them. As they walked off, Liah sensed him looking as they walked down the hallway. She didn't dare to look back. He wanted so badly to continue their conversation. But he knew she had to leave. "Man," he said out loud, "Why did I not get her phone number? I'm such an idiot." *Well maybe not*, he thought, *she did say she would email me the recipe. And, I will have to email her, thanking her for the recipe, of course. What is wrong with me? She might be married*, he considered, continuing with his thought as he walked back into the fellowship room. *Although, I didn't see a wedding ring on her finger*, trying to be hopeful. *Besides, someone that gorgeous—a man would be insane not letting everyone know that she's taken*. At this point he's a bit annoyed with himself. *All right, Marcus, this conversation is over. I'll wait for her to email me.*

Stepping into the kitchen, Liah's whole mood changed immediately, watching her chocolate truffles being scooped up off the floor. "What happened to my truffles?" She was irate.

"As they were about to push the cart out of the kitchen, the wheel broke and all of the trays slid to the floor," Louis informed her.

"I don't believe this!" Inhaling deeply, "Okay," she whispered. "What do we have that we can quickly work with?"

"Angel food cake, fresh strawberries, powdered sugar, some ice cream, and some chocolate bars," Louis told her.

"Alright, let's get to work. We have about twenty-five minutes." They quickly prepared another dessert and had it served on schedule.

After she was done in the kitchen, she walked out into the hallway and walked right into Marcus.

"So we meet again, Ms. Mathis," he said to her. You get everything worked out?"

"It worked out fine. Thank you for asking, Mr. Michaels."

"You're welcome." She looked at him, smiled, and shook her head.

"What," he asked curiously.

"Nothing."

"Well, it was a pleasure bumping into you, again," he told her. "I'll be looking for that recipe."

"I'm sure you will," she said smartly. Boldly, he took her hand and kissed it.

"Until then, you take care and have a nice evening."

"Same to you." They walked away in separate directions.

When Liah got home, she went straight upstairs to send Marcus the recipe before it slipped her mind. He was already sitting at the computer when he received the email, immediately responding, thanking her and asking if he could call sometime. She giggled and then responded by telling him she would think about it. They continued sitting at their computers. Not quite five minutes had passed before Marcus sent another message asking her if she had thought about it yet.

Laughing out loud, she typed, "sure, and I will let you know when I'm ready."

His response message was, "I guess that's fair, for now."

She messaged him back saying, "Well, Marcus, you have a good night. I might see you at church tomorrow."

His last response was, "Looking forward to it."

The night was still young. All of the children had gone to their rooms. Liah was left alone to her thoughts. She found herself completely taken by Marcus. She had a strong feeling about where things with Marcus could lead, and not at all sure if she was ready for it. In spite of all the warnings that went through her mind, she could not stop thinking about him. Deep into her thoughts, she was startled by a soft knock on the door. It was the kids coming to tell her goodnight. Jas brought his book in so she could read him a goodnight story. About ten minutes into the book he had fallen asleep. Liah looked down at him and smiled adoringly, then picked him up and carried him to bed.

She went back into her office and stretched out on her lounger. She fell right back into her thoughts. She had prayed that if and when she met a man he would fit perfectly into her family. Her heart simply broke every time Jas asked for his dad or she got a note from the school pertaining to any father-and-child event. Liah centered her life on her children and work to keep her focus off wanting a relationship. Most importantly, she stayed in God's word, which kept her afloat

She was again startled by another interruption. This time, it was her closest and dear friend, Chantel, calling. They were probably the closest out of the four friends, as they had the most in common. They were both divorced with children. Alisha and Shayna, the other two friends, were both married with grown children. They lived in Virginia Beach.

"Hi, Chan," she said excitedly. "What's going on with the DC chic?"

"I'm good. I am just seriously overworked. This second year of residency is kicking my butt. I think I sleep while I'm standing." They both laughed out loud.

"You poor thing! This is only the beginning. But I believe you will survive. After all, you and I both got through school with small children."

"We sure did. And you struggled through two degrees," Chantel reminded her.

"So have you decided what you wanted to do with the other one?"

"Believe it or not, I finally started working on that book. I even have a name for it."

"And what is that?"

"I'm not going to tell you ... yet."

"Hmm ... I like it," Chantel said, kiddingly. "Is this the book you were talking about combining with poems and recipes?"

"Yes, that's what I'm working on, but enough about me. Tell me what happened to the new guy you were seeing."

"Honey, that's the problem. I wasn't seeing him, at least not for what he really was."

"And that was?"

"A pathological liar. Girl, he told me that he was an account manager at the bank, right. Well, I called there one day and spoke to the receptionist, asking for a James Minton, and I was told that no one worked there by that name. As a matter of fact, she said and I quote her, "I believe that's the James who delivers lunch to the second floor, three days a week." She goes on to say, 'you could probably reach him at Coco's Diner on MLK Avenue."

"You're kidding?"

"No ma'am! I called Coco's and asked to speak to James, and guess what? The lady told me that he was on delivery at the moment."

"I know you confronted him. So what did he have to say for himself?"

"He told me that he was embarrassed by his present position and he didn't think I would be interested in him. I said, 'first of all, you didn't give me a chance to make that choice. If you did, we would certainly not be having this conversation. And furthermore, did you think lying would help?' So then I said to him, 'what else are you lying about? Do you drive your own car? Do you have your own apartment?' He says, 'I do have my own car, but sometimes I drive my mom's Chrysler 300 and I live with her."

"Huh, sounds like he's a failure to launch, honey."

Chantel screamed in laughter. "Girl, you're crazy, but you're right and this is a relationship that won't launch." Liah cracked up.

"Okay, so what happened next? Because I know you're not still seeing him."

"I told him it takes a real man to know a real woman and a real woman don't appreciate a man lying to appease her. Then I simply asked him, where was his integrity. Liah, would you believe he had the audacity to ask me 'where do we go from here?'"

"Are you for real?"

"I kid you not. So I did the only thing that a sensible person would do. I laughed and then said to him, 'let me help you go from here. Have a good life and I'll remember to keep you in my prayers.' Anyway, to make a long story short..."

Liah cuts in and asked, "Chantel, did you just tell me the whole story?" Don't be making the story short."

Chantel yawned and then screamed, "I am so tired. Okay, I'll tell you more."

"You need rest, child! But continue on."

"Okay, turns out that his car hasn't worked since last year. He has absolutely nothing to offer. Not only did he lie to me, but he's broke with no car, and no place of his own. At least, Mr. cute Matthew McConaughey, in 'Failure to Launch,' had some class."

"Chan, you're pitiful. And he is cute. But you're right, that's a bad way to begin a relationship. So I take it you haven't heard from him."

"Nope. And I hope I never will. Of course, unless he becomes a real man and get a life. But I still wish him well." Liah heard her email alert. She was hoping it was Marcus.

"Chan, for what it's worth, I think you did the right thing. He should have been honest from the start. But you know you drop a guy quickly." They both burst out laughing. "Seriously, though, you bring a lot to the table and you deserve so much better. Take a breather and give yourself some down time. Before you know it, the right man will present himself. Stop looking and let yourself be found."

"You're right, and I'm going to take your advice."

"All right then, girlfriend. Let's keep hope alive."

"Don't you start with your 'keep hope alive' speech."

"I'm not because I have to go."

"What do you have to do?" Chan asked curiously.

"Return an important email," she answered ambiguously.

"Well, I know it's not a man, so I won't ask to whom."

"Okay, Chan. You take care and try to get more rest."

"I will, dear! Thanks for the ear."

"Anytime, love."

"Talk to you soon, Liah!"

"Yes soon, love!" As soon as Liah got off the phone, she rushed to the computer. She took a deep breath before checking the message. It was indeed a message from Marcus.

It read, "Hi, Ms. Mathis. I was still sitting at my computer thinking and I just wanted to let you know it was great meeting you today. And I hope to see that beautiful smile again. Have a good night."

She didn't bother sending a return email. *Oh, my God*, she said to herself, *what is it about this man?* She couldn't shake the wonderful feeling. She turned off the computer, went to her bathroom, took a long relaxing bath, and turned in for the night. As she lay there in bed, she couldn't help but wonder what it would be like to have finally met the right man for her and her children. She clutched snuggly to her silk body pillow with thoughts of Marcus, until she fell sound asleep.

Though she turned in early, it seemed that morning came quickly. She was briskly awakened by the glare of the sunlight coming through the half closed vertical blinds. Hastily pulling the cover over her head, she was suddenly startled by the sound of the alarm clock. With the cover still over her head, she reached over and hit the snooze button. She always set her alarm to go off fifteen minutes prior to getting up. It allows her time for her morning prayer before her actual arising time. Sometime she woke up even earlier to get a jump on her Bible reading. After finally getting up, she hit the wake call button to the girls' room and then went in to wake Jas. She splashed her face with cold water to finished waking herself, and then hurried down stairs to make breakfast.

On the way to Sunday morning service, Jas asked if they were going to see Mr. Marcus at church. "I don't know, sweetie."

Then Jessica asked, "Does that mean we're going to the same church we visited yesterday?"

"Yes, Jess," she responded.

"He's a member there, right, Mom?"

"Yes, Jacqlyne, he is a member there. Now, would you all stop with the questions" she said in an annoyed way. "I am trying to listen to this song." They all sniggled! "And why are you all sniggling? I don't recall saying anything funny."

As they walked into the auditorium, Liah immediately spotted Marcus. They sat closer to the back of the auditorium, since it was quite packed when they walked in. Sitting in the back didn't bother her, as long as she could hear. Brother Jack Taylor was the guest speaker today, one of Liah's favorite. He was a very powerful and well-known church of Christ minister. He was visiting from Buffalo, New York. Right before Brother Taylor came up, the song leader led one of her favorite songs, "He's Been Good." Jacqlyne whispered to Liah, "I love this song, Mom."

"So do I."

Brother Taylor preached an inspiring lesson entitled "God is Love." After his lesson, he led, "The Greatest Commands" another one of Liah's favorite. Right before closing, all of the guests were announced and asked to stand. When they announced Liah Mathis and family, Marcus looked back. He was pleasingly elated. Liah looked at him and their eyes met. She couldn't sit down quickly enough. The minister also made the whole congregation aware that Liah and her staff from A'Palace had prepared that fantastic meal yesterday.

After service was dismissed, Marcus eagerly tried to make his way to Liah, but kept getting stopped by someone. Liah was hoping to talk to him as well. She visited with everyone she knew, it seemed, except Marcus. She was sorry she had missed him, but she wanted to attend the second morning service with her congregation.

Finally, Marcus made his way to the back and Liah wasn't anywhere in sight. He was exceedingly disappointed. As he was about to leave, he ran into an old buddy of his.

"Jarred ... Jarred Townsend," Marcus exclaimed!

"Marcus," Jared responded, surprised as well as elated.

"Yeah, man, it's me. Where have you been hiding?" asked Marcus.

"Hey, man, I've been around. I've been working hard and keeping busy."

"Man, it's been ages," Marcus said to him.

"Yeah, it has been quite a few years."

"We just got back about six or seven months ago."

"How is Lisa?" Before he could answer, she was walking toward them.

"Lisa," Marcus called out, excitedly.

"Marcus, Marcus Michael, she exclaimed in disbelief," as she hurried to give him a hug.

"Girl, it is good to see you again. And look at you. You look good."

"Yeah, I lost all that weight."

"I didn't want to say that, but yes, you did."

"Hey, Marcus, we're going to try to catch our second service. Why don't you come to worship with us?" Jarred asked him.

"All right, man, cool! Let me just say bye, to mom and dad."

"Okay, we'll wait for you right here."

After the second service, Liah decided she would take advantage of the beautiful day, and take the kids to the fun-park. There were a lot of rides, water slides, games, food, and a barrel of fun things to do. The first thing they decided to do was to drive the bumper cars. As Liah was twirling around, she twirled right into Marcus. Both of them were stunned. When Jas spotted him he screamed from across the way, "Mr. Marcus."

"What are you doing here?" Liah asked him.

"I was in the mood for fun and had nowhere else to go. So here we are, thrown together. Kind of a serendipity thing!"

"Yes, here we are," Liah murmured. "Serendipity!" Suddenly, Jacqlyne crashed into Marcus.

"Yes," Liah, screamed, "she saved me again." She welcomed Jacqlyne's crashed. It gave her a moment to collect herself.

The five of them spent the next couple of hours eating Greek food and having a blast. With all the people around, they acted as if they were in a world of their own. Liah looked at her watch and blurted, "Oh gosh, I didn't realize the time."

"Yes, it happens when you're having fun," Marcus said cynically. "So why do you have to leave if you don't mind my asking?"

"I'm meeting with some perspective clients to discuss a catering gig for my sous chef."

"Well, Ms. Liah, I have had the time of my life with you and your children today. It's been forever since I've had so much fun. So thank you for allowing me to share your day."

"I had a great time, too, and I know the kids did. So thank you for sharing it with us." Marcus hesitantly, inquired about her schedule for the next day.

"Working," she said playfully.

"Do you think you can get away for lunch?"

"Uh, no, well—maybe! It would have to be a late lunch, probably around one forty-five."

"Terrific," he said. "Can you meet me at Jenos? It's on Fifth Avenue about two blocks from the A'Palace."

"Okay, sure," she said.

"Then it's a date, right?"

"If you say so," she responded. He laughed and thanked her again for her day with him."

"You're welcome, Marcus. But I really have to go."

"Okay tomorrow, one forty-five at Jenos," he reminded her.

"I will be there," she whispered.

They all said goodbye and then Liah and the kids left. As they were walking off, Jessica said to her, "Mom I like Mr. Marcus. He's a lot of fun."

"Yeah, he is, Mom," Jacqlyne agreed.

"Mom is going out on a date with him," blurted Jas.

"Wow, Mom, this is like your first date," said Jessica, "I mean ... in like forever."

"Thanks, Jess, I didn't know that. Now enough, guys. I am putting a movie in so you all can calm down and be quiet." She needed a moment to be with her thoughts. The rest of the ride home was semi-peaceful. As soon as they walked in the house, Liah ran upstairs, took a quick shower, got dressed, checked on the kids, and then rushed out the door. She didn't live far from work, though the ride for some reason seemed long. She didn't mind it a bit. It gave her time to reflex on her afternoon with Marcus. If only she could freeze that moment she thought. She arrived about ten minutes prior to her meeting, which was fine with her because she still had Marcus on her mind.

She was sitting in her office when the hostess told her that her appointment had arrived.

"Thank you, Simone. Will you please send them in?"

"Sure thing."

A very handsome older couple walked in. "Ms. Mathis," the tall distinguished older gentleman said. Right in that moment he reminded her of someone.

"Thank you for meeting with us on such short notice. I know you are standing in for Louis. I appreciate it."

"You are quite welcome. I'm glad I could help."

"By the way, dear, I'm Morgan Michaels and this is my wife Lillie."

Oh my gosh, she thought to herself. Her heart skipped a beat. *Could this be Marcus' parents? No way.*

36

She quickly collected herself and then managed to say, "Please to meet you Mr. and Mrs. Michaels. Please, have a seat."

"Thank you," he said.

"Can I get you all something to drink? I have water, of course, coffee, green and white tea, hot or cold."

"Green tea would be lovely, honey," Lillie said.

"I'll have some water please, dear."

She went over to her little refrigerator and took out a bottle of water and a pitcher of tea, then grabbed some glasses from the cabinet and rinsed them. "Thank you," Morgan said, "you're very kind."

"You're welcome. So tell me, how can I help you all?"

"We're planning a dinner party for our niece," Morgan replied. "She will be graduating from college in May."

"I see," Liah responded. "And how many guests will there be?"

"About twenty to twenty-five," Lillie responded.

"Do you have a menu in mind?" Liah asked them.

"The menu, well, we haven't a clue," Lillie acknowledged honestly.

"Let me show you our party menu. If it doesn't look appetizing to you, we can put one together," handing them the menus.

"I think number one looks good," Lillie answered. "Honey, what do you think?"

"I think I like the A'Palace special combo," Morgan responded with a chuckle.

"Now that's a good choice," Liah said. "It includes a combination of all of the party favorites. So, Mrs. Michaels, your choice is included."

"Oh, please, honey, call me Lillie."

"Well, in that case, Lillie, I will throw in the chef's special. Here, look toward the bottom."

"You're going to give us that one!" she said surprised."

"Sure ... for the same price as the A'Palace special party combo."

"How can we thank you?" Morgan asked.

"You already have. You're kind people. Now what date did you all have in mind?"

"Any weekend in May, before the twenty-third," Lillie told her.

"Alright, let's take a look at the calendar. It looks like I have an opening on May tenth and seventh."

"Let's shoot for the tenth." Morgan said.

"Okay, the tenth it is," Liah responded. "Now do you all have a time in mind?"

"What about from six to nine?" Lillie responded.

"Sounds great!" I will be in touch with you all on the final details."

"Well, Ms. Mathis, it was a pleasure to meet such a lovely person with a smile that brightens the heart," Morgan said kindly.

"She does have a beautiful smile, doesn't she?" Lillie stated. "Yes, dear, I just said that."

"Oh, Morgan, stop it." They all laughed.

"Thank you, both, and please call me Liah."

"Then Liah, please call me Morgan," he said with a mysterious grin on his face.

"I will," she responded.

"Well, we had better get out of here. We've taken enough of your time," he told her.

"Yes, we have," Lillie agreed. "And if any changes arise, we would let you know, honey".

"Thanks, I appreciate that. I'll do the same. You all have a good evening."

Finally, she thought, a moment of peace. She leaned back in her chair and closed her eyes and meditated for a few minutes. Opening her eyes, she realized just how exhaustingly tired she was. She then picked up the phone to call home. Jessica answered the phone.

"Hi, Jess, I'm on my way home."

"Okay, Mom."

"How's Jas?

"He's good. We fed him, he said he was sleepy, so he took a bath and got in the bed."

"Is he asleep?"

"Yes, ma'am."

"Ah, I didn't get a chance to say goodnight to him."

"I went in his room to let him call you but he had already fallen asleep."

"Alright, sweetie, thanks anyway. I'll see you shortly."

"Okay, Mom, drive to arrive!"

"I will."

On the way home she was so tired she didn't feel like thinking. However, she couldn't help but wonder if those were Marcus' parents.

When she got home, she rushed upstairs to kiss Jas goodnight. When she kissed him, he slightly raised his head and said, "good night Mom, I love you" and then laid his head back down.

"I love you too, big boy."

She said good night to the girls before heading to her room, hoping to turn in early.

As she lay in bed, she wondered if Marcus had emailed her. Nonetheless, she couldn't force herself to get out of bed to check. But as tired as she was, she was unable to fall right to sleep. She couldn't seem to stop thinking about Marcus. She thought about how easy it was to be around him and how well the kids took to him, and then finally she drifted off to sleep.

~Chapter Two~

Today was the first day of spring break. The kids were sleeping in and Liah slept until eight o'clock. She stayed in bed for about fifteen minutes longer. Energetically, sitting up in bed, she screamed, "I have a date with Marcus today." She jumped out of bed and ran to her closet. As she sat at her vanity pushing the automatic button that spun her clothes around, she pondered over what she should wear on her first date. Finally deciding, she pulled out a casual dressy ivory pants suit with matching shoes and purse. As she carefully put everything in her suit bag, including accessories, she couldn't help but grin like a teenager on a first date. After all, it was the first real one she had had in such a long time.

Around nine, she started getting ready for work. The kids were still asleep when she went in to check on them. She didn't want to wake them, so she went back to her room and wrote each of them a note and stuck them on their doors, before going downstairs to fix hers breakfast. Sometimes if the kids were still asleep when she left for work, she would have breakfast delivered to them. And they were still asleep when she left for work, around ten o'clock.

"I am so glad I came in later, I missed the early morning traffic," she said out loud.

Liah started fixing breakfast for the kids as soon as she got to work. She had Len, A'Palace's personal delivery guy, take it to them. She knew that they were awake because she had received two text messages each, from the girls.

"Alright, guys," she said to her kitchen staff. It's about time for the lunch rush, so let's get moving. Louis, you went beyond prepping duties today. And I am not complaining because this will probably be a busy day, and you know how much I appreciate you."

"I know you do, but you are complaining," he responded. "You're the only boss who complains about someone working too hard."

"You guys do work hard."

"And so do you," Tina added.

"I think we all work hard at making a great team," Liah said.

"Yeah, that's probably why we're the best in town," Tina declared, sounding confident. Mel, the head waitress, walked in and told them it looked like they're going to have a busy Monday. "Liah's words indeed," Tina said.

"And we are ready for it, thanks to Louis," Liah said.

Liah worked non-stop at full speed. She wanted to get out in time for her date, and she wanted to make sure she didn't leave her staff swamped. "Okay, Louis, we are ahead so if you don't mind, I am leaving things in your capable hands. I have to get ready for a late lunch date."

"Oooooh ... sounds interesting," he replied. "Anything I should be happy about?"

"Aaah, I'm not really sure, Louis," she murmured, sounding mysterious. "We'll see."

"Oh, my gosh!" Tina blurted. "She has a date with a man. I mean a real date with a man." They all burst out laughing.

"Tina, I know it's mighty hard to believe, but I can get a date."

"I know that. What's hard to believe is you accepting one."

"Don't give her a hard time, girl," Louis said to Tina. "She might change her mind."

"And we will not accept that mind," Tina responded. "Liah, go get dressed honey, and tell us all about it when you get back."

Liah giggled and said, "You're pitiful, you know that right?" After getting dress, she went back into the kitchen to tell them she was leaving.

"Now that's what I'm talking about, girlfriend," Tina said.

"I sure hope he's able to have a conversation with you," Louis stated. "Cause from the looks of it, I don't know if he's going to be able to do anything but look."

"Oh, stop it, Louis," she said modestly. "I'll see you all later."

~Chapter Three~

She was a bit nervous on her way to Jenos. She arrived at Jenos about one-forty. After taking a deep breath, she walked through the revolving door leading to the hostess station.

"Hi, my name is Mindy. How are you today?"

"I'm great, thank you for asking. How are you?" Liah asked the hostess.

"I'm great. Thanks. Will you be dining alone?"

"No, I'm meeting someone."

"Is there a reservation?"

"I'm not sure."

"What is the first initial and last name of your party?"

"M. Michaels."

"Oh, yes, he's already here! Give me a moment and I'll show you to your seat. He's the gentlemen sitting right over there," she said as she pointed toward him. "I'll walk you to your table."

"Oh … you don't have to walk me down there."

"Are you sure?"

"Yes, thank you."

"Okay, if you look to your right, he's the gentlemen sitting with the blonde and looking toward us."

"Okay. Thanks." As soon as she started walking toward him their eyes met. He then focused his eyes back on the woman he was sitting with. She noticed that he was holding her hands and made no attempt to acknowledge her. She couldn't believe what was happening. Her mouth dropped. *I don't believe he set me up like this*, she thought. She quickly looked for the ladies' room so she could quickly make an exit and save herself from embarrassment. She immediately spotted the ladies' room and gracefully headed in that direction. After she walked in, she sat on the sofa in the lounge area. As bewildered as she was, she remained as calm as possible. Her first thought was to walk out there and tell him exactly what she thought about him. Being the composed person that she was, she wasn't about to make a fool of herself. Even in an awkward situation, she was a master at keeping her composure. However, the more she thought about it, she felt like screaming. She continued to sit there for at least five minutes or so longer, deeply sighed and then elegantly walked back into the hostess lounge.

"Mindy, how long has he been here with the blonde?"

"They arrived about one-thirty."

"Thank you Mindy," she said. She tipped her with a twenty and walked out.

Marcus arrived at Jenos *only* shortly after Liah had. He waited for her about twenty minutes. He finally got up and walked back into the lounge. As he was talking to the hostess, his twin brother and his ex-girlfriend walked up.

"Marcus!" Morgan bellowed. "Hey man, I didn't know you were coming here."

"Well, we don't have to share our daily personal itinerary, Morgan," Marcus declared sarcastically.

"Whatever, man!"

"You guys are twins?" Mindy asked.

"Yes," they answered at the same time.

"Oh, my gosh! No wonder she seemed so upset. She must not have known that you all were twins."

"Who?" Morgan questioned.

"Liah, my date," Marcus replied.

"You had a date?" Morgan asked, utterly surprised.

"I can't believe that," Lisa said reprehensibly.

"Wait a minute," Morgan uttered, "classy, with big brown eyes and a bob-like hairstyle?"

"That would be her," Marcus replied.

"Man, I saw her, she is gorgeous. She was walking toward the table and looked right at me, then took a detour into the ladies' room. Oh no, she thought I was you."

"Morgan, you're so smart," Marcus said sarcastically. "What do you think?"

"Marcus, I am so sorry. I bet when I looked away and kept talking to Lisa it made things worse."

"I know it did," Marcus responded.

"For whatever it's worth, she's really a nice person. And I'm sorry, too, since I'm the one who pointed her toward the wrong Michaels brother."

46

"Thank you for saying that, but it's not your fault, neither is it yours, Morgan."

"Morgan, I'll catch up with you later. Lisa, it was good to see you again."

"Same here Marcus, and good luck!"

Marcus knew he had some apologizing and explaining to do. He just hoped that she would listen. He rushed over to the A'Palace, hoping that he would catch her there. Liah was in her office. She had come in through the side door so no one would see her. When Marcus came in he told the hostess he had a luncheon with the Ms. Mathis at Jenos and missed her.

"I don't think she's back yet. I haven't seen her come in."

"Doesn't she drive the black Chrysler 300, with 'The Chef' on the license plate?"

"You're right. That's her car. Wait here, please, and I'll go check. Who may I say is looking for her?"

"Marcus Michaels."

She went in the kitchen to ask Louis if Liah was back. "I don't think so," he told her.

"Some guy is looking for her name Marcus Michaels and her car is in her parking space."

"Well, let's just go to her office to see if she's back." He knocked on her door then asked if she was in there.

"Yes, I am, Louis," she responded. He opened the door and asked her if she was okay.

"I'm good."

"How did lunch go?"

"It didn't," she said dryly. "And I don't wish to talk about it right now."

"Okay, but there's a Marcus Michaels looking for you."

"You're kidding!"

"No, he's waiting in dining."

"Come show him to me, Louis." They walked out and peeped around the corner.

"Where is he?" Louis told her to take a one o'clock to her right. "I don't believe he had the audacity to come here," she said.

"Was he your date, and if so, what did he do so I can go kick his butt?"

"I'll tell you about it later, and thanks, but I got this."

"Alright but I will be right here if you need me."

She walked over to the table where Marcus was sitting. The first thing he said to her was, "Oh … wow, you do look gorgeous." She didn't bother saying thank you, nor did she even crack a smile. "Will you please sit down and allow me a moment to explain?"

"Five minutes … start talking … time is ticking." And he did just as demanded.

"I have an identical twin brother; his name is Morgan. When you showed up, Morgan was there having lunch with his ex-girlfriend Lisa. The hostess apparently thought Morgan was the M. Michaels you were referring to. So she pointed you toward the wrong person. When I showed up, I apparently was seated by a different hostess and on the other side of the restaurant. And after waiting for about twenty minutes for you, I decided to go to the hostess lounge. A moment later, Morgan and Lisa were on their way out. That's when we un-raveled the mystery. In a nutshell, with thirty seconds left, that's what happened."

48

She couldn't help but smile, after sitting there the whole time not breathing a word.

"So you have a twin brother? How do I know you're telling me the truth?"

"Because I have no reason to lie, and if I want to continue seeing you, I believe you'll eventually find out. Besides, you can ask the hostess at Jenos. She met him and Lisa. Anyway, I would have told you except we have haven't had that much talking time. That's why I wanted to spend today with you. Anyway, I am so sorry things happened this way. So what do you think? Can we pick up from here?"

"Well, I am hungry," she replied.

"We might as well eat here," he suggested. "So, chef, what do you recommend?"

"Depends on what you're in the mood for—seafood, veal, chicken, beef, or pork?"

"Seafood."

"Good choice. But why don't I surprise you with my favorite. Do you like asparagus?"

"Yes."

"Great, I'll be right back."

She went in the kitchen to place their order. And Louis, of course, inquiring mind had to know if they'd worked things out. Especially since he offered to *kick Marcus' butt* everything.

"Yes, it was just a mix up. I'll tell you about it later."

After giving her order to Louis, she went back out to let Marcus know that their meal would be ready shortly. In the meantime, she called to check on the kids and to see what they wanted for dinner.

Of course, they wanted their usual, grilled chicken, shrimp, twice-baked potatoes and haricot vert-French green beans. She told them she should be home around five-thirty. Marcus overheard her conversation with Jacqlyne. "You seem to be such a good mom," he said to her."

"I do my best. So what about you, Marcus? Do you have any children?"

"No, but I wish I did."

"So why don't you?"

"I can't have children. I'm sterile."

"Oh, gosh, Marcus, I'm so sorry."

"No, no, it's ok," he assured her. "You couldn't have known. Besides, if it's okay with you, I'd like to share more with you. Well at least the important stuff." She looked at him and sighed. Before she could respond to his request, their food had arrived.

"Oh, good. Our food is ready," she said with relief.

"And it looks delectable," he commented.

"I hope you like it," Mel said.

"I'm sure I will enjoy it," he said. "Thanks."

"Thank you, Mel," Liah said.

"You're welcome. Call me if need something." Liah looked at her and smiled.

"She's great. She has a very kind spirit," Marcus said.

"She is a great person. Mel is one of the A'Palace's long-term employees and a dear friend. Well, we should eat before our food get cold." He reached over for her hands so he could bless the food.

"So what do we have here?" he asked.

"We have grilled Cajun shrimp kabobs, fried brown and wild rice and grilled asparagus, Liah said. And for dessert we're having the chef's specialty."

"And what is that, if I may ask or is that a surprise?"

"No. It's not a surprise. It is pineapples simmered in a caramelized rum sauce, served over ice cream and pound cake."

"Now that sounds yummy. It sounds good so I know it will be good."

"Trust me—it is. Now if you don't mind—getting back to our previous conversation; that's if you don't mind my asking, how did you become sterile? You know what, never mind. It's really none of my business."

"Liah, it's ok. I don't mind. I want us to get to know one another better, so that means personal things will be shared. I mean if that's what you want."

Yes, I'm all for that."

"I don't want to appear to be moving too fast. It's just that being here with you seems so right," he said to her with a serious look. She looked at him and smiled.

"Well, anyway, my brother and I were sterile at birth due to some complications."

"So how do you feel about not being able to have any biological children?"

"I was disappointed when I first found out, because I really wanted children. But there are so many fatherless children out there who need to be loved, and who need fathers. I know this might sound crazy, but I believe that being sterile is a gift from God. And I also believe that

God will bless Morgan and me both to be fathers to a child or children one day. I realized that a biological connection doesn't determine how much one can love a child. And" then, you know is almighty and powerful; I could might have a biological one day. I mean, look what he did for Abraham and Elisabeth.

"Amen, I know that. I can appreciate your attitude," she responded.

"Seems that you have a story to share," he said.

"Yes, but just the opposite of yours," she murmured. "But please continue on."

"I truly believe that when one loves with the love of the Lord it makes it easier to love anyone. Loving a child is easy. That makes it easier loving an adopted child as one would love their own child."

While she sat there listening, she was amazed. She thought to herself, *he is a real saint.* So caught up in his profession, she was nearly speechless, barley able to force out words. "Wow, I…I feel as if I've been listening to a beautiful inspirational speech. Thank you for sharing that with me."

She was blown away by his openness and honesty. She admired a man with integrity. It was high on her list. He looked up and said, "Here's our dessert, and it looks scrumptious. And by the way, if I haven't told you, I am delighted to be here with you. Thank you for allowing me the opportunity to defend my honor."

Liah giggled, and then said softly, "I'm glad I did, and I'm just as delighted as you. Now please enjoy your dessert."

"Alright … Ms. Mathis, I will."

"Thanks, Mel." Mel shook her head and then walked off.

After he took his first bite, he closed his eyes, moaned and said, "This is really good, Liah. Is this another one of your personal recipes?"

"It is indeed."

"You should publish a cook book."

"Interesting that you said that," she replied. "I am sort of working on something."

"What do you mean sort of working on something?"

"I will tell you but just not right this moment. I would rather be farther into the project before I tell anyone about it."

"Okay, I guess I will have to be patient," he said.

"Thanks for understanding."

"No problem!"

"Will you excuse me for a moment, Marcus? Mel, would you mind taking this order in the kitchen and asking Louis to fix it for my babies?"

"Girl, you know I don't mind."

"So did you enjoy your meal?" Liah asked him.

"From the beginning to the last crumb!" He took out two twenty-dollar bills and a credit card.

"What are you doing?" she asked him.

"About to pay for the meal."

"You don't have to do that."

"Liah, I am not about to let you pay for our meal."

"Marcus, thank you for wanting to pay, but you're eating as my guest, today."

"Are you sure, because I can afford a meal?"

"And I believe you can, but, yes, you are my guest."

"Well I can pay the tip, right?"

"Sure, I have no problem with that." He laid two twenties on the table.

"As pleasurable as this late afternoon lunch has been, I have to be going shortly," she told him.

"I know you have to get home to the children. And it has indeed. It has been a pleasurable day."

"And interesting," she added.

"And satisfying, too," he said. Both of them laughed.

"Alright, Ms. Liah," Mel said, "your order is ready."

"Okay, and thanks again, Mel. Everything was grand. Be sure to tell Louis I said so."

"I will. What about you, Mr. Michaels?" Mel inquired. "Did you enjoy?"

"Everything was delightful, Mel. Thank you for asking."

"Well, I am going to get back to my work. You all have a good evening."

"Same to you, Mel," Marcus told her.

"I have to be going, Marcus. I'm glad you came after me."

"Does that mean I can call you and asked you out again?"

She looked at him and smiled, and then reached in her purse to get a card with her personal number on it and said to him, "Sure, you may call me anytime." He took out his card and told her to please feel free to call him anytime, day or night.

"Do you mind if I walk you out?"

"No, I would appreciate it, but can you give me a moment? I want to let them know I'm leaving."

"Sure, I'll be waiting right here."

When she walked back over to their table, he was standing by the table holding the bag. As they walked out, he caught her hand and held it until they got to her car.

"You take care now, and please, drive home carefully," he told her.

"I will. Thanks. And you do the same."

He stood watching until she drove off. She could see him watching her through her rearview mirror until she drove out of the parking lot.

She was definitely smitten by the handsome Mr. Marcus Michaels. After all, it seemed that he had all the important qualities she admired in a man. But most importantly, he seemed to be a well-rounded Christian man. That was already a plus to her. On her way home she tried relentlessly not be consumed with thoughts about him, with no success. But how could she not think about this gorgeous creation of God's ... this wonderful person she had spent the better part of her afternoon with. A man she barely knew took the time to find her and give her an explanation. This was new for her indeed. A sudden ring from her phone freed her from thoughts.

"Hello," she answered.

"Hi, Liah!"

"Alisha?"

"Yes, and don't be acting like you don't know who I am."

"Whatever, girl!" she responded.

"Hi, Ms. Liah!"

"Shayna?"

"Yes, Liah."

"Hi, Shayna."

"How are you guys?"

"We're good," they both replied.

"So why are both of you calling?"

"Shayna and I were talking and decided to call you and Chantel."

"Have you talked to Chan yet?"

"No, we're going to call her next."

"Right," Liah said.

"So have you met a man yet, Liah?" Shayna boldly asked her.

"I meet men all of the time," she replied, smartly.

"Well, I know that, dear. You practically own a restaurant. Anyway, girl, you know what I mean."

"Uh oh, here she goes," Alisha mumbled, "always trying to rush someone into a relationship. She'll meet someone when the time is right, Shayna."

"So what have you guys been up to?" Liah asked them, turning the heat away from her.

"Girl, you know … husbands, working, and making the best out of married life," Shayna replied.

"We all go out together once a month with some friends," Alisha said. "And Shayna and I visit each other often."

"Liah, when are you going to take some time out of your busy schedule and visit?" Shayna asked.

"Perhaps I will consider it soon. At the moment my schedule is jammed packed. Well, as always, girlfriends, it was good talking to you all. I promise I will work on my schedule. And I am sorry, but Jacqlyne is calling, so I will get back with you all soon. You married people take care."

"You too, Liah," they said. She clicked over to answer her incoming call.

"Hi, Mom, we're hungry! Where are you?"

"In the garage, honey."

"Good, I'm coming out." She hung up the phone and rushed out to the garage. Jas ran out with her as well.

"Mommy," he called out animatedly.

"Hi, my big boy! How was your day?"

"Good, Mom."

"How was your day?"

"Interesting," she replied.

"Hey ... Mom, let me help you with that food," Jacqlyne said eagerly.

"Sure, thanks, Jacqlyne. Where's Jess?"

"She's in her room."

"Jas, will you go upstairs and get your sister, please?"

"Sure, Mom." She heard feet trampling down the stairs.

"Well, here she comes. Stop running down those stairs, Jess, please," she screamed.

"Mom, you're here!" Jessica cried excitedly. "Did you have a good day and did you see Mr. Marcus, is he coming over?" Jessica had a habit of asking several questions within one sentence and one breath.

"Yes and no, take a moment to breathe," she told Jessica.

Jacqlyne took the trays out of the bags. Jessica grabbed some glasses and three bottles of vitamin water, forks, and spoons. They all sat at the bar together to eat dinner. Of course they wanted to know how the date with Marcus went. They weren't too happy when she told them what happened at Jenos. She quickly shifted gears and said that it was his twin brother.

"Really," Jacqlyne exclaimed!

"Oh, my gosh ... he has a twin brother!" Jessica screamed. Now that might be a man for Auntie Chan.

"Yes, he does, and they're identical. And, you might have a point about Chan. But mind your own business girl," she laughed.

"Hey Mom," Jessica uttered, "did you think for a moment that he was trying to do the 'Bachelor of Austin' on you? You remember, right, when Brad had his twin brother make the ladies think that he was Brad." They all laughed.

"There was no time for thinking, honey. I just wanted to get out of there."

"Mmmm, this food is good, Mom," Jason mumbled.

"Yeah!" The girls said about the same time.

"Did you cook," Jacqlyne asked?

"No, Louis did."

"So when are you going out with Marcus again," Jessica inquired?

"Mr. Marcus to you, and I don't know."

"Hey, do you guys want to camp out on the floor in the den, watch a movie, and play Uno?" Liah asked them.

"Yes," they all answered.

"Ok, you all finish your dinner. I'm going to take a quick shower."

"You always take a quick shower, Mom," Jessica said. Liah smiled at her and gave her a big hug.

"Alright finish eating and get some movies." Her phone rang as she walked up the stairs. It was Jayde.

"Jayde, hi sweetie, it's about time you return my call."

"I'm sorry, Mom. I've been strapped with schoolwork and work-study."

"I know, baby. So how's the work study going?

"It's going well, Mom."

"I'm working as an assistant at the Children's Art Museum."

"Honey, I hope you're not overdoing it."

"Mom, I'm good. I'll let you know if I get overwhelmed, I promise."

"Ok, Ms. Jayde, if you say so."

"So, Mom, who is this new guy you finally met? Yeah, Jacqlyne told all, Mom."

"That big mouth girl!"

"Mom, this is good. And if you let him spend time with you and your children, there has to be something pretty special about him, other than his looks. You know how funny you are about that. So come on, give me the scoop. And don't leave anything out, ok?"

"Okay, but I'll have to make it quick. I told your siblings I would play Uno and watch a movie with them."

"Ok, then. Start talking."

"You had better mind your manners, child."

"Sorry," Jayde said giggling.

"Well, as you already know, I met him at church last Saturday." She told her all about Marcus, including the incident at Jenos. When she got to that part, Jayde blurted,

"Nah uh! Are you serious?"

"Yes, but it was his twin brother."

"Oh … my gosh. Well, I thought you left Jenos."

"I did."

"How did you find out it was his brother?"

"He tracked me down at work."

"Really?"

"Yes, really. We talked a lot, had a late lunch, said our goodbyes in the parking lot, and here I am."

"Wow, I think I like him and haven't even met him."

"Please don't get your hopes up too high, honey."

"Yeah, because you're dragon lady when it comes to dating."

"Jayde Mathis, cut it out."

"Ok," she laughed. "Seriously, Mom, he sounds like a genuine good person. I think you should give him a try."

"Why, thank you, dear, for your permission, but I don't think I need motherly advice from my smart-mouth college-student, daughter." Jayde sniggled again and told Liah she was funny.

"Well, Mom, I have to go. My study group is here. Go out with him again, Mom. I love you, Mom."

"I love you too, sweetie."

"Ok later, Mom. I'll talk to you soon."

"You had better." Liah took a quick shower and went down stairs. The kids were already on the floor with sleeping bags, ready for Uno and a movie.

"I'm sorry, guys. Your sister called as I was on my way up stairs."

"We were wondering what took you so long, Mom," Jessica replied. They played cards for about an hour while watching "Ratatouille." Jas fell asleep shortly afterwards. By the time the movie was over, they all had fallen asleep. Liah woke up to turn off the TV and DVD player. She got right back in her comfortable position and went back to sleep.

She woke up about eight forty-five the next morning, just in time to get some quality Bible reading in before work. The kids were going on a road trip to Virginia Beach with Jen and Tim, some good friends and next-door neighbors. Their kids were about the same ages as Liah's. While they were there, all of the kids planned to spend time with some old friends, who moved away about a year or so ago. Liah knew they would have a blast, but she also knew she would miss them. It was her first time without them since Jas was born.

She went in the kitchen to fix breakfast before the kids woke up. As soon as she was done fixing breakfast, the kids came into the kitchen. They all sat at the breakfast bar and enjoyed a fabulous breakfast. When breakfast was over, Liah went upstairs to help the kids get ready for the trip. "I am going to miss you all," she told them.

"Mom, it's only one or two nights," Jessica reminded her.

"I know, Jess, but I'm your mother and I'm used to seeing you every day."

"I'm going to miss you, too, Mom," Jas said. She grabbed him, kissed him, and gave him a big hug. Jas had never spent a night away from her.

"Are you ok spending the night away from me, sweetie?"

"Yes, ma'am. I'll be ok. But if you want me to stay home I will."

"Thank you, baby, but I want you to have fun. Make sure you behave well, Jas, and please listen to Jen and Tim."

"I will, Mom," he said.

"Mom, don't worry. We'll keep an eye on him," Jacqlyne said.

"Yes, please do. Now come on. I'm going to walk you all over to Jen's, so I can go to work." As they were walking up the driveway, all three of Tim and Jen's children ran outside excitedly. Although they saw each other several times a week, they were always happy to see one another. Liah walked up to the door just as Jen was coming out with bags.

"Hi, Jen," Liah said.

"Hi, Liah."

"How are you, and are you sure you're ready to deal with six children?"

"Girl, we will be fine."

"What about you? You know you're not use to being home alone."

"I know, but I'll be fine."

"Jen, thank you all for taking my babies with you."

"Now, Liah, you know those are our children, too, just as ours are yours. And don't worry. They will be fine."

"I know. Where's Tim?"

"He went to the store for snacks and ice."

"Well, tell him hi and thanks."

"I will."

"I wasn't sure how much money they needed, but I gave them a hundred a piece."

"Oh, that's plenty."

"Now do you have the hotel number?" Jen asked. "Oh, what am I talking about, you made the reservation."

"And I still have the number. Well, okay. I have to go to work. You all drive careful."

"We will." She gave all of them a hug and told them she'd see them when they got back and to be sure to call that night.

Liah arrived at work around eleven forty-five that morning, just in time to fall into the lunch rush. She took a break around three o'clock. During her break Marcus went to see if she was free for the evening. He wanted to take her and the kids out for pizza or whatever they were in the mood for. "That's very kind of you to offer. Thanks, you. But the kids are out of town and I do motivational speaking tonight for the women's group at the YMCA."

"What time are you done?" he asked.

"About seven-thirty."

"How about a late dinner?"

"Sure — sounds good, but nothing too heavy."

"Fantastic. Would you like for me to pick you up at the YMCA or at home?"

"Why don't you pick me up at the YMCA. It's about two blocks from here, same street, two blocks down, on the left."

"Ok, I'll see you later," he said.

"Alright, I'll see you later." She hung up the phone before he could say another word. She was thinking it would be a really good time to have him over. In the same thought, she knew it was too soon. Nonetheless, she would just make the most of the time they were going to spend together, no matter where they went.

Marcus showed up about ten minutes before the meeting was over. She saw him walk by the door on his way to the lobby. She was even more eager to wrap up her lecture, now that she had seen Marcus.

When she walked into the lobby, his eyes lit up. Her heart pounded as she stood in the doorway, practically frozen as he walked toward her. He hugged her unexpectedly and kissed her on the cheek. In a whispering but masculine tone, he told her it was very nice to see her again.

"It is good to see you as well," she murmured.

"Wow, you look good," he said, not taking his eyes off her. She was wearing a black denim skinny-jeans outfit with a beige ruffle blouse and a short, above-the-waist jacket.

"Do you always look this good?" he asked cordially.

"No, I don't," she said. "When I'm home I like to wear sweats and old jeans with holes. Sometimes I wear them to the store."

"Really, I don't believe that," he replied.

"It's true."

"Well, I don't mind. I'm the same way. But you do know now that I want to see you in your holes and jeans and warm ups," he winked, with a mischievous grin. "Shall we go?" he asked.

"We shall, Sir Michaels," she replied humorously.

"Hum, I could get use to that," he said.

"Don't," she said quickly. Then they both laughed. They had a casual conversation on the way to the diner. When they arrived, he got out of his black Escalade, opened the door for her, like a gentlemen, and then reached for her hand. She readily took his hand and stepped out of the truck. *He's a real gentle-man*, she thought. And he was exactly what she could appreciate.

They sat in a quiet and private area of the restaurant and talked until they realized all the other customers had left. "Looks like everyone is leaving but us," he stated. They just looked at each other and smiled. The attraction they had for one another was uncanny.

Marcus took out his wallet and left a very generous tip before going up to the register to pay their bill. Neither one of them was ready for the night to end. They left the restaurant hand in hand. While waiting for the valet attendant to bring the truck around, he put his arm around her. She felt at home in his arms. He drove her back to the YMCA to pick up her vehicle. By the end of their date, the relationship had escalated to the beginning of something special. This was indeed a new beginning for the both of them.

They were ready to move on from the fear of starting over. Liah refused to allow the pain and disappointments of a past relationship decide her chance at happiness. She just hadn't met anyone who enthralled her interest past the first conversation. That is, until she'd met the charming Mr. Marcus Michaels.

Marcus parked right by her car when they got back to the YMCA. They continued talking for a few minutes longer before she got out.

"I had the best night, and I'm not ready to say goodnight, Liah," he said earnestly.

"Neither am I. But "

"I know what you're going to say, that we both have to go to work tomorrow, right?"

"*Whoa, that's exactly what I was going to say.*" she thought. "Yes, we both have to go to work tomorrow," she replied.

"There will be many more nights and days, right?" he said in a sort of 'asking way,' hoping that she felt the same way.

"Sure," she whispered. "I had a really wonderful night, Marcus. Thank you."

"No need for thanks, baby. I mean—

"I know what you mean. It's okay."

"Well then, Liah Mathis, so did I and I do believe the pleasure of your company was all mine. Now, if you don't mind, I'd like to say something," he told her. "I don't think we should start evaluating or thinking about how serious this could get. I think we should take one step at a time, enjoying every moment while getting to know each other and dealing with whatever comes up, together. I already like what I see, and I like the person whom I've been spending time with. Now, I know what I'm about to say may be stretching it. But I just want to wake up one morning and know that it's you I want right beside me, or go home one night and come to the realization that I don't want to leave you anymore. I want to say to myself that this is the woman I want to spend my life with. I believe that sometimes when a relationship seems to be getting serious people began to evaluate, and then over evaluate, then here comes fear, and fear causes doubt. And we both know the effects of doubt. I bet you think I've gone psycho. Don't you?"

"Yeah, you sounded kind of scary there," she uttered wearily. Then she burst out laughing. "I'm kidding," she blurted quickly, still giggling. By that time he was at a loss for words. "Seriously, no, I don't think you're psycho. I couldn't have said it better myself." She laughed out again and then said "I'm sorry Marcus, but you set yourself up for that one."

He laughed and admitted, "I really did, didn't I?"

"But anyway, I agree with you. We should enjoy whatever is happening between us and keep making deposits. I don't want to think about whether or not we're moving too slow or too fast. I want to move in each moment without realizing the speed."

"So we're in agreement?" he asked.

"Without a doubt," she responded.

"Alright, partner, he replied wittily." Then he told her to shake on it.

"You're crazy," she said.

"Yes, I've been told quite a few times," he smiled as he gently took her hand and kissed it. So may I call you tomorrow?"

"Anytime," she murmured. He got out and opened the door and walked her to her car. He opened the door for her watching as she gracefully got in and then closed it. They said their goodnights and she drove off. He waited until she was out of the parking lot before he got into his vehicle.

As soon as Marcus started his truck his phone rang. It was Morgan. "What's going on Morgan?" he asked.

"Hey, man, I just came from your house. Where've you been?"

"Morgan, it's none of your business."

"Since when is your business not my business?"

"Probably since I have some now and you don't," Marcus responded scathingly.

"Whoa ... let me guess, you went out with Liah again, didn't you? Hey, man, I'm not hatin,' she's gorgeous. And if she's holding your interest, she must be an extraordinary woman, because you've been slow at getting back in the game. How long has it been man?"

"Morgan," he exclaimed, and then told him to shut up.

"Hey, what did mom tell you about that?" They both laughed.

"Any way, Morgan, I only say shut up to you."

"Yeah," he replied. "So come on."

"What?" Marcus responded.

"Stop being coy. Tell me about the gorgeous Liah."

"Okay ... alright. Well, as you already know she is gorgeous. But most importantly, she is easy to talk to, very composed, funny, and she listens well. She has a kind and gentle spirit. I also like the fact that she is fair and she's a straight shooter. Morgan, man, I've only known her for a very short time and although I've spent each one of those days with her, I thirst for more. She seems to be a great mom too. And guess what?"

"What?"

"She's a Christian ... she's a member of the Church. On top of all that, she's a fabulous cook, a chef."

"Man, all I can say is Mom and Dad would be please," Morgan told him. "And Mom, would want to meet her soon."

"You are so right. Oh, and one more thing."

"What?"

"She has three children at home."

"Man, you're kidding me. She barely looks as if she has one."

"Hold up. That's not all," Marcus said. "And three older children, two boys, married with children, and a seventeen year old daughter in college."

"Man, you know that woman doesn't have all those children. She looks too young and looks too good."

"I kid you not, Morgan. I'm serious. She is just fit."

"Very fit," Morgan replied. "How old is she?"

"She's forty-five."

"Man, at first I thought she might be in her mid-twenties. But since you were dating her I figured she had to at least be in her thirty's. But forty-five, no way! Did you ask her for an ID?"

"You're not serious, right?" Marcus questioned. Morgan started laughing.

"Not really," he replied.

"However, I did have my PI guy investigate her."

"Noooo!" Morgan cried.

"Now you wouldn't believe this. So did she."

"Seriously?"

"Yep."

"You guys are made for each other."

"My thoughts exactly," Marcus responded.

"I have one more question, man."

"What's that, Morgan?"

"Does she have a sister of legal age?"

"I think I remember her mentioning a younger sister. But I know she has a close friend in med school or intern or something. I think she's doing an internship at some hospital in DC."

"Interesting. I wouldn't mind meeting her. You think it's possible?"

"I don't know. Maybe."

"Did she show you pictures?"

"As a matter of fact, she did. She just finished running a twenty-six mile marathon. She looks pretty good and she has three children, two boys and a daughter in college. And I don't think she is married, or maybe she used to, not sure."

"Soooo, do you know when she's coming to town?"

"Not sure, man. Anyway, Liah hasn't told any of her friends about me yet."

"Why not?"

"She said she wanted to savor the moment before she shares the goodness."

"Oh, really!"

"Really."

"I heard that. Kind of like how we feel about telling mom and dad too soon"

"Exactly. But she also wanted to have more insight as to where we're heading."

"I totally understand that," Morgan replied.

"Man, I don't think I'm telling Mom and Dad until we are somewhat committed," Marcus told him. "Do you think it's too soon to give her a promise ring?"

"Not really," Morgan responded. "You're just promising to commit to getting to know each other better."

"Well, I'll give it some thought," Marcus said.

"When are you going out with her again?"

"I'm not sure. Her schedule is pretty tight for the rest of the week. But I'm sure I will be talking to her."

"So, Marcus, what are your feelings? I mean, are you scared?"

"Yes, I am. But I'm ready. And I'm not about to let myself give in to that negative feeling. It feels good and right. And if the love at first sight 'cliché' has any truth to it, then I am definitely at that level."

"Marcus, I have to ask you this question. How do you know she's legit? You said she had you investigated."

"I just know she is. She doesn't look like she's hard up for money. I know what you're thinking. She's not a gold digger."

"Does she know you're a business owner and what about the mansion?"

"Yes, she does. I don't think she's knows how big the company is. And, no, she doesn't know about the mansion. She does know that I'm a homeowner."

"Well, I guess you should go with your feelings. I've never seen you like this before. I can hear the sincerity in your voice."

"Thanks, Morgan, but what about you?"

"I believe I'm ready. I just haven't met that special woman yet."

"I sure hope that happens to you soon, before you change your mind."

"I'm serious, Marcus. I'm ready. There is no changing my mind."

"I know you are, man, and I hope that person comes along soon. Hey, man, I'm home and I'm beat, catch you tomorrow at the office."

"Alright, later man."

~Chapter Four~

By the time Marcus and Morgan had finished talking, Liah was already home and on the phone saying goodnight to her children. They had made it to Virginia safely and were hanging out in their hotel room.

"What did you all eat?" she asked Jacqlyne.

"We stopped at a seafood buffet. It wasn't your food, of course, but it was pretty good."

"Thank you, honey, for sparing my feelings."

Jacqlyne giggled. "For real, Mom."

"I know, sweetie, but I'm glad you enjoyed it anyway. How did Jas like it?"

"Mom, the boy stuffed himself."

"He did. That's my boy. Where is he?"

"He took a shower, and he's in bed now."

"Will you put the phone to his ear so I can talk to him?"

"Sure."

"Jas," she said softly. "How's mommy's big boy?"

He smiled as he whispered, "Hi Mom, I'm good ... I'm just sleepy. I miss you, Mom."

"I miss you too, sweetie, and I love you."

"Okay goodnight, Mom I'm going to sleep."

She hissed, "Goodnight, big boy, see you in a day or so."

Jessica got the phone from him. "Hi, Mom."

"Hi, Jess. How are you?"

"Good, Mom. Thanks for letting us come. We had a blast on the way here."

"You did. How so?"

"We ate snacks, watched movies, cracked jokes, and played Pictionary."

"Who won the game?"

"Mom, of course I did," she said proudly.

"Go figure, huh."

"I'm your protégé Mom. You know that, right?" she declared surreptitiously.

"Whatever you say, honey. My protégé, I have another big day tomorrow and you guys are going to be busy as well. So I am going to take a shower and call it a night, and so should you all."

"Okay, Mom."

"Oh ... I almost forgot, Jen said you all might come back Thursday."

"I know, Mom."

"How does Jas feel about that?"

"He's fine with it, Mom. Stop worrying, your little boy is growing up. He will be okay. Will you?"

"Yes, ma'am, mommy daughter," Liah responded.

"Okay, now. Take your shower and go right to bed, young lady," Jessica told her kiddingly.

"Goodnight, Jessica Alexandria."

"Goodnight, Mommy. I love you."

"Love you, honey."

Just as soon as she hung up the phone, another call came. It almost never fails. Although this was one she didn't mind a bit. It was Marcus. "Hello, Marcus," she said in a merry tone.

"Hello, Ms. Mathis."

"I'm sorry, what did you say?"

"I said 'hello, Ms. Mathis.'"

"No, say it the way you first said it." He started laughing. "What? Why are you laughing?"

"You're silly," he said.

"And you like it."

"No, I just feel sorry for you."

"Yeah, right," she replied. "Anyway, Mr. Marcus Michaels, what can I do for you?"

"Now there's a question ... an unsafe one. Nonetheless, one I have an answer for."

"Well, since you put it like that, it makes the question sound precarious, so I'm retracting that question and revising."

"No, no, it's on the table now."

"Whatever, Marcus!"

"Okay, seriously," he said, "I just wanted to hear your voice and say goodnight. So… goodnight." There was a brief moment of silence.

"Goodnight, Marcus," she murmured.

"I'm sorry. Did I ask if you were busy?"

"No, but that's okay. I had just finished talking to my children."

"How are they?"

"They're fine. They had a good drive. And thank you for asking."

"Have I told you that you have a beautiful voice? You don't have to answer that. You have a beautiful voice."

"Thank you, I think."

"Am I embarrassing you?" he asked her.

"No, not really. I have a question for you! How alike are you and your brother?"

"I would say we're a lot alike, but somewhat different. I'm more laid back and he's more free spirited. I look better, of course."

"Marcus, you're identical twins. You look just alike."

"Yeah, I hear that often."

"I have no doubt."

"Actually, there is a way someone can tell us apart."

"How's that?"

"My dimples usually show when I talk and his when he smiles. My lips are a little fuller and he has a little mole on the right side of his nose. Of course, most people are not aware of this unless it is pointed out to them."

"I sure wish I had known that earlier. I could have saved myself some embarrassment."

"What, the first incident?"

"Of course."

"I know. I'm sorry."

"I know you are, but I didn't bring that up for you to apologize. There is no way you could have predicted it."

"I appreciate you saying that. But as much as I don't want to let you go sweetie, it's getting late, so I don't want to keep you up any longer.

I hope to continue this conversation soon, like maybe tomorrow. That's if you don't mind?"

"Not at all," she murmured.

"If I haven't told you, I had a really nice time tonight," he said in an illuminating way.

"So did I," she whispered.

"Just in case I don't call you tomorrow, I am anticipating a very busy day," Marcus told her.

"I understand. So do I." They both said goodnight.

Wednesday was a very busy day for Liah and Marcus. By the end of the day, they hadn't talked to each other. After work, Liah didn't have time to go home to change. Fortunately, she kept a few outfits in her office closet. She even had a step-in shower.

After Bible class, her plan was to head straight home to rest. Despite how much she would have liked to talk to Marcus, she was equally glad that they didn't have any plans for tonight.

Marcus and Morgan were working on a deadline. Unfortunately one of the blueprints for a big project got destroyed. Since the deadline was on Monday, they both had to work overtime to meet it, in addition to their normal workload. Marcus was furious when he walked into the office and Morgan showed him what had happened to the project they had worked on for six weeks.

He said in a monotone voice, "I hope this is not what I think it is."

"It is," Morgan said dryly. He sat down in his chair and rubbed his head. As exasperated as he was, he placidly asked Morgan what happened.

"Okay, I'm standing by the door, right. Julia," who was their secretary, "was sitting at his desk. There was a big cup of coffee sitting on the desk in one of the cup holders we made, especially designed to avoid spills. Anyway, a client came in with her dog. He ran in and jumped on top of the desk and knocked Julia over in her chair. She was screaming, which made the dog act even crazier, he knocked the cup holder over with the coffee cup in it, and peed on the paper, that is after he tore it up."

"Tore the paper up and then peed on it. I don't believe it. Is Julia okay?'

"She'll be okay. I told her to take the rest of the day off."

"Good, I'm sure she didn't mind. Man, stuff like this only happens on TV," he stated as he laughed.

"I'm glad you're taking it so well because I sure didn't," Morgan mumbled.

"Don't be fooled. I'm not taking this well at all. I really feel like crying. And since I don't curse, the only thing left to do is laugh." They both looked at each other and heaved a sigh.

Marcus was incredibly disappointed. He knew it would be days before he could see Liah again. He also knew there were a lot of work to be done and a short time to do it. *I need to email Liah*, he thought, *perhaps even a brief phone call later.*

"Alright, Morgan, why don't you pull a team together? I'll call the cleaning crew and start on the blueprint. It looks like we're going to pull an all-nighter or, better yet, camp here for the next four days."

About thirty minutes later, the team went back to the drawing board. They worked religiously to recreate the blue print and a new model, for the rest of the day. Marcus and Morgan took off around six-thirty, so they could make it to Bible class by seven o'clock. They rode in Morgan's vehicle. After Bible class, they headed back to work. On the way back to the office, he called Liah but got her voicemail. He left her a message briefly explaining what had happened. He also told her he probably wouldn't see her for a few days.

"Man, it would nice to hear her voice, especially after this day."

"I know what you mean," Morgan responded. He went on to say, "I sure am glad we built those sleeping quarters."

"So am I."

"You know we'll get over this hump, right, Marcus. Even though this is a big one."

"Oh, I'm sure of it. We can do all things through Christ who strengthens us."

"Now those are words to live by," Morgan avowed. "Hey, do you want to pick up something to eat or just wait to see what the guys want?"

"Ah ... we better wait," Marcus replied.

When Marcus and Morgan walked in, the guys were famished. They all decided on barbeque. In the meantime, they continued to work on the project.

After they were done eating, they went right back to work and worked until about one o'clock in the morning. Morgan suggested everyone get rested up for another hard day.

Liah did exactly as she had planned. She went straight home. After talking to her children, she lay on her lounger and closed her eyes. She so wanted to hear Marcus' voice. Unfortunately she never got his message. She considered calling him; however, she calmed her overanxious desire, and decided she probably wouldn't be much for conversation anyway.

Liah was in one of her mellow moods. A mellow mood for her meant doing something she enjoyed doing, which was writing. She lay there for a moment, thinking about Marcus and about the enjoyable time they spent together. She had never been so engulfed by any man, especially so early in the relationship.

She reached over and picked up her cell phone to call Chantel, but quickly put it back down. She then stared at her writing notebook momentarily, before deciding to write. She wrote until her hands could no longer hold the pin firmly. She didn't bother getting into bed. She stayed on her lounger the entire night.

The loud ring of her home phone awakened her about eight-thirty that morning. She didn't get many calls at home, especially early in the morning.

"Hello," she said sleepily.

"Mom, hi, Mom," Jacqlyne said, sounding all chipper.

"Hi, sweetie. Why are you calling me on the home phone?"

"Cause your cell phone goes right to voice mail. Is it turned off?"

"No, I don't think so. But hold on and I'll check. No, it's on. It must be having some kind of network trouble. I'll turn it off for a moment, maybe that will work. I suppose that's why I haven't gotten any calls since yesterday afternoon."

"Did you check your voice mail, Mom?"

"No, I haven't. I'll check it later. Anyway, what's up, honey?"

"Auntie Jen told me to tell you that we will be leaving around eleven tomorrow morning."

"Okay, baby. Where are Jess and Jas?"

"Jess is in the shower and here's Jas." She handed him the phone.

"Hi, Mommy."

"Hi, big boy. How are you this morning?"

"I'm good, Mom."

"Do you remember talking to me last night?"

"Oh yeah, I did talk to you last night. I don't remember what I said."

"Not very much, sweetie. You were tired again last night, too. But so was I. Jas make sure you check around the hotel room to make sure you don't leave anything. I'll see you when you get home, big boy. Now let me talk to your sister, please. I love you."

"Okay Mom, I love you, too."

"Hello, Mother," Jacqlyne said."

"Hi, Jacq. What do you think about you guys going to the Y with me tonight?" The YMCA had a huge recreation center with a theatre, arcade, and Bistro in it. The kids enjoyed hanging out there while Liah attended her Thursday night writing and poetry reading class.

"Mom, we like going to poetry night with you. We always have so much fun. I'm going to tell Jas and Jess. Hey, guys, we're going to poetry class with mom tonight," she exclaimed loudly.

"Stop screaming, child! Now I have to go so I can call Jen before going to work. I'll see to you all tonight. I love you."

"Okay, Mom. Love you, too."

Before Liah left for work, she powered her phone back on, hoping it was working properly. She picked up her home phone and called her cell to see if the call would go through. "Yes," she said out loud. When she listened to her messages, the second message was from Marcus. "Oh, my gosh, he did call," she said, quite pleased, as she strolled to his name, and pushed the call button.

"Well, good morning, beautiful."

"Good morning," she responded. How are you?"

"I'm ... I'm okay, he said hesitantly."

"I'm sorry I'm just getting back to you. I actually just heard your message. My phone seemed to have been having some network problem, so it appears that all of my calls were going straight to voice mail."

"It's okay," he said. "I really didn't have much time to talk anyway. I was just calling to let you know what happened."

"Thank you for thinking of me. So, Marcus, what really happened?" He went through the details just as Morgan had told him.

"Wow, Marcus, I am so sorry. It sounds like something that only happens on TV."

He laughed and said, "I know. I said the same thing."

"How's the project going so far?"

"I believe we're going to make the deadline. The downfall of that is I'm not going to be able to see you for a few days."

"I'm not going anywhere. I'll be here when you're done."

"Well, you better not go anywhere," he said daringly, "and I am holding you to your word."

"Aye, aye, Sir!" He giggled.

"As much as I would love to keep talking to you, I really need to get back to work, babe."

"I know," she hissed.

"Liah," he said in a low but masculine tone. "If I don't tell you I've missed you when I see you again. I've really missed you and I can't wait to see you again."

"Back at you, Marcus. Now go finish that project."

"Yes, ma'am. Have a good day, and I'll talk to you soon, real soon."

"Take care, you," she told him."

After work, Liah swung by home to pick up the kids. She was very glad to have her children back home. Although they had a barrel of fun, they were equally glad to be home. Liah had a very close relationship with all her children, one she cherished dearly.

When they got to the YMCA, Liah went straight to her class and the kids went to the recreation room. The kids immediately made new friends with the three Carrington boys. They were seventeen, sixteen and seven. They all hit it off quite well. After hanging out for a while they discovered that they lived in the same neighborhood and attended the same schools. Their parents were the owners of Carrington Weddings and Events Planning. Their mom, Elizabeth Skye Carrington, was also a member of the YMCA and attended the poetry class.

Liah walked into the Bistro and saw six children sitting at the table eating. "Hi, guys," she said. "Who do we have here?" she asked, curiously. Jessica introduced the boys to her. About five minutes later, Liz, the boy's mom, walked in.

"Hi, Liz."

"Hi, Liah," she replied cordially. "I really enjoyed that poem."

"Thank you, Liz."

"Mom, these are our new friends," Christen said.

"Liah, are these your children?

"Yes, they are mine."

"Hi, Mrs. Carrington, I'm Jacqlyne."

"I'm Jessica."

"And I'm Jason."

"Well, it is a pleasure finally meeting all of you."

"So we've been coming here for quite a while and our children have never met," Liz said to Liah.

"Seems that way. But you know how we are, we all have a short visit after class, then everyone is trying to get out so they can get home."

"You're absolutely right. I am probably the first one to get out of here."

"Then again, this place is so big, a person can get lost in here," Liah added.

"Now there's a scary thought. But you're right. It is huge."

Liah then turned her attention back to the kids. "So I guess you all had a nice time hanging out here together?"

"We always have fun hanging out here," Jessica answered. Then all of the kids told her they liked hanging out together. Liz then suggested that they should plan an outing sometime soon.

"That would be great," Liah replied.

"It's getting late and I had planned on working on some new recipes for tomorrow."

"Indeed, I have a pretty busy day tomorrow and I need to work on a wedding project."

"Alright guys," Liah said. "Say goodnight."

"Come on, boys. Liah, I will see you next week," said Liz.

"Okay, have a good rest of the week."

~Chapter Five~

It was eight o'clock Saturday night. The weekend was almost over and Liah hadn't heard from Marcus since Thursday. However, the night was still young and she hoped he would call before the night was over. The kids were all in their rooms doing their own thing. She decided she needed a distraction, so she took advantage of the time and did some Bible reading, and hoped to get some writing done as well. About forty minutes into reading she dozed off and was suddenly awakened by the phone. It was an unknown caller, the type of call she never answered. As soon as she dozed off again, the phone rang again. This time it was her cell phone. She reached over on her nightstand, picked up the phone, and answered it before opening her eyes. "Yes," she said softly.

"I haven't asked you yet."

"Marcus," she whispered excitedly.

"Hi you," he said in an enchanting voice. "Were you asleep?"

"I was dozing," she answered honestly.

"I'm sorry if I disturbed..."

"Oh no, don't be … you didn't. I was really disturbed by the unknown caller right before you."

"I don't answer those," he responded.

84

"Neither do I."

"Well, sweetie, I'm not going to hold you long. I just wanted to let you know that we finished the project, and I believe it is better than the first."

"Really. That's terrific."

"Yeah, I feel really optimistic about it and so does everyone else."

"So what is the next step?"

"On Monday we will present it to the client, and if he likes it, we will build.'

"It doesn't sound like there should be an 'if', Marcus. But more so, he'll be asking when you all can get started."

"I do like the sound of that," he replied. "You know, you're like the breath of fresh air that every man starves for."

"Hum, why that's sweet of you, Marcus."

"It's true, my dear."

"Yes, I know that," she said arrogantly.

"Ha, ha," he replied. "Soooooo, do you think you will have some time available tomorrow between or after service?" he asked her graciously.

"Sure, we plan to go to the first service and the evening service is scheduled to start earlier. I should be out around three o'clock."

"Well, if you don't mind giving up your evening, I would like to spend some time with you all."

"I would like that. Why don't you go to the evening service with us, and you can come over for a cook out?"

"Serious?"

"Serious," she replied.

"Yes, I would be delighted to. But I'll cook."

"Marcus, can you cook?"

"I can grill."

"Really," she said.

"I'm serious, I can grill."

"That's very kind of you, but you're my guest."

"Okay, I'll come, you cook, and I'm bringing something and that's final."

"Okaaay, I don't have a problem with that."

"Well, I'm looking forward to it."

"So am I. Check your email shortly; I'm going to send you the addresses."

"I'll be waiting."

"Alright, I'll see you tomorrow, have a good night."

"Yes, you will and you have a goodnight as well."

As soon as she hung up the phone, she went right into her office to email him. And soon afterward, he emailed her back. He thanked her for sending the addresses.

A few minutes later he sent another email saying, **"by the way, I'm bringing steaks and something special."**

She just shook her head and smiled. He sent her another email asking her to email him a picture of her. Obediently, she strolled through her online pictures and sent him one.

He sent her another email saying, **"Wow, you're beautiful."** She read his message and decided to leave him hanging. She then went to check in on the kids. They all had turned in early.

~Chapter Six~

Sunday morning was always an early rise in order to be on time for early service. Liah woke up in a very chipper mood. She was excited about Marcus coming over. She told the kids during breakfast, and they were just as excited as she was, especially Jason. He had spent the first six years of his life without having a father figure around. He often asked Liah about seeing his dad. He had even told her that he wished she would get married, so he could have a dad. It pained her heart to see him longing for a dad. But she also knew it took a special man to fill that spot. And she just might have finally found that person. Of course she wanted to see how the cookout went and how he reacted in close proximity with the kids.

She started preparing for the cookout as soon as they got in from morning service.

She had a beautifully designed backyard with a huge playground. It had an outdoors kitchen with a path leading to the dining area. The dining area sat between two ten-foot lighted waterfalls in the design of palm trees. The tables sat on stone flooring with palm tree canopies overshadowing them. Her backyard was a great place for entertaining. There was also an enclosed patio with a beautifully designed fireplace. The patio was also connected to the green room, as Liah called it. It was filled with beautiful plants and herbs, and had a waterfall designed out of stones. She had a fascination with stones, waterfalls, and plants. This was one of her favorite rooms in the house. It was indeed her retreat room: Her place to escape.

Liah and the kids arrived at church about fifteen minutes early that evening. They waited for Marcus in the foyer. He showed up about five minutes later. Jason was the first to notice him. He ran to him and Marcus picked him up. Liah and girls got up off the bench as he was walking toward them.

He looks better than he did the first time I saw him, Liah thought. He was wearing a black Armani suit. She could hardly take her eyes off him, and she didn't want to. However, to keep from appearing obvious and worse, lustful, she did. "Hello, beautiful girls," he said. "And, hello, Mom, you look beautiful as well."

"Thanks and so do you. I mean you look good. I really like that suit."

"And thank you. Shall we go sit?" he asked.

"We shall," she responded. When they walked into the auditorium, it seemed as though all eyes were on them. No one had ever seen her walking in with a man before, a handsome man at that. When service was over, they tried to leave right away. But Liah knew better than that. She introduced him to several of the members. Even though she didn't mention anything about them dating, nor even a hint of being involved, most of them commented on how good they looked together. Some of the members already knew him. The Michaels family was a pretty prestigious family. Morgan and Marcus had even designed some of their homes.

He held her hand as they were walking out, not giving any thought to what conclusion anyone would draw. He didn't have any problem letting whoever was interested, know, that they were involved and neither did Liah. Finally they were outside. "My," he said, "they seemed quite pleased with you having a man by your side."

"Yeah, I know. A few have even tried to fix me up."

"I have no doubt."

"But it's all good. They all have my best interest at heart."

"I can appreciate that," he replied. He walked them to the car, and being the gentlemen that he was, as always, he opened the door for them. "Drive carefully and I will see you all about four-fifteen." She looked at him with a pleasant smile, and told him that she would see him shortly.

When he arrived, the kids ran out to meet him. Liah was in the back cooking. She had already made potato salad, coleslaw, baked beans, and homemade brownies earlier. Now she was grilling burgers, and Italian sausages. She had also planned to grill some vegetables.

Marcus and the kids came out with three bags and a case of vitamin water. He had steaks, fruits, and treats for the kids. "Hi, you're here," she said.

"Yes, and thanks again for inviting me."

"You're welcome. Now make yourself comfortable. Can I get you something to drink?"

"Thanks, but I'm good. I'm going to finish up this vitamin water. Liah, I love this backyard. This is an awesome design. Who designed it?"

"I did it."

"You're kidding."

"No, I designed it myself."

"You should come to work with Michaels & Michaels."

"Nah, you can't afford me."

"Wanna bet?"

"No, thank you."

"Good answer." They both giggled.

"Do you really like it?"

"Yes, I really do," he answered while admiring her modesty. "So what's in the bag?" she asked.

"Steaks and goodies," he replied.

"Yum, I haven't had a steak in a while, a long while." She took the steaks over to the sink to wash them. "Marcus, you don't have to stand around. You can get comfortable." He walked over to the lounger and sat down. Liah got a platter and took the meat off the grill.

"Please, let me help," Marcus said, pouting.

"Okay, you can put the steaks on the grill."

"Alright," he said and happily jumped up and washed his hands and did just as she suggested. While the steaks were cooking, she gave him a tour of the backyard, starting with the dining area.

"Oh, Liah, this is beautiful. Can we sit down and talk for a moment?'

"Sure."

"So tell me," he said. "What other talents can I look forward to seeing?"

"You'll just have to wait and see," she said smartly.

"I knew you were going to say that. Has anyone ever told you that you have a smart mouth?"

"Yes, often," she answered without any hesitation.

"At least you're honest about it." She looked at him and laughed as she stood up and he could only laugh with her. He got up, put his arms around her and said, "You're too much."

"I know. But I haven't been told that before." He coddled her closer.

"I bet this is a beautiful site at night," he said to her.

"It is." She walked over to the jukebox and played one of her favorite slow songs by the Manhattan.

"Look at you. I bet you came up with that idea too—an outdoors jukebox."

"Of course I did, just adding a touch of style. Besides it accommodates whatever mood you're in." she responded. He laughed and shook his head. "Sometime I come out here by myself and listen to my oldies, relax and think and sometime do some writing."

"So what do you write about, if you don't mind my asking?"

"Whatever comes to my mind: Like thoughts, recipes, poems and ideas."

"You are an interesting woman, Ms. Mathis. A bit stand-offish."

"I am not," she said in her defense. "I just like to stand back and observe my surrounding. And besides, I am very talkative."

"I know that. But I'm glad you are, because so am I, especially when the subject is interesting."

"We should go check on the steaks, kindly ending the conversation."

"Oh, yeah, we should do that," he agreed. When dinner was ready, Jacqlyne and Liah fixed everyone's plate and dinner was served on the patio.

"Marcus, would you mind blessing the food please?"

"Yes, absolutely."

"Mom is a good cook, isn't she, Mr. Marcus?" Jas thought he would mention.

"She sure is, and I am honored to be eating it." They sat at the table for about thirty minutes, eating and talking. It was a perfect family portrait, and Marcus seemed to fit in well.

After dinner, Marcus played soccer with Jas. Liah and the girls put everything away then joined them. After playing soccer, they all played on the waterslide. They were having so much fun, they didn't realize the time. Kind of how it had been when they were in the park together.

The kids went upstairs to take showers. Liah and Marcus sat on the patio and talked for a short while. "Do you mind waiting while I get a quick shower?"

"Oh no, I'll be fine."

"Okay, I'll be back shortly." As she was about to walk through the door, Marcus asked her if he would be out of place if he asked to take a shower in the pool house. Marcus just happened to have had an extra outfit in his vehicle."

"No, by all means, make yourself at home." He went out to his truck and took out his jeans and a pullover shirt. After Liah finished taking her shower, she said goodnight to the girls. She went back to her room, picked up her cell phone and sent Marcus a text message, saying she would be down shortly. He immediately texted her back and said "I'll be waiting." She tucked Jas in and read a poem to him.

When she got downstairs, Marcus was sitting in the patio room watching Extreme Makeover. He took one look at her and said to her, "You look stunning."

"Thank you," she whispered. She was wearing a chocolate- brown, satin bell-bottomed lounger, with a waist-length pullover drawstring matching top and a pair of flat chocolate-brown slippers with furry tassels. "I see you made yourself comfortable."

"I hope you didn't mind."

"No, not a bit. I told you earlier to make yourself comfortable. You're the one who was acting uptight. But I understand. You're out of your comfort zone. By the way, I like the shirt. And I was referring to the shirt and jeans when I said you made yourself comfortable. You look good in jeans. Not that you didn't look good in that Armani suit," she said hesitantly, after thinking that she was probably babbling.

"Well, thank you for saying all that in one sentence," he said teasingly. She looked at him and they both laughed. She walked over to sit in her chair, but he reached out for her and kindly said, "Here, come sit by me please. I won't bite." She politely honored his request. He then gently took her hand in his said to her, "Liah, I hope you don't think I'm moving too fast or being too forward. Because I am truly just taking it as it comes. I've only known you for a very short time but it seems like a lifetime. I can honestly say that I believe this has been the best week in my life so far. Before I met you, I didn't think I would ever feel so open and free with anyone. I'm not afraid to move forward with you. I meant it when I told you that I want to wake up one morning and know that I have to, need to and want to have you in my life. Maybe I didn't say it in those exact words but it means the same. What I'm trying to say is that, I am willing to commit myself to ... to getting to know you better, to a relationship, at whatever pace. I feel that we have a good foundation to build on. Now if you're not ready, I totally understand. Liah."

"Yes," she whispered.

"You can speak now." She needed a moment to take it all in. She was seriously caught off guard. In no way was she expecting this.

"I," she murmured, pausing momentarily. "Marcus Michaels, you are an amazing man and that's a tough speech to follow. So I'm just going to honestly agree with you. You're right. We've gotten off to a good start. Well, with the exception of the mixed up.

"There is that." He laughed.

"I know right. Anyway, yes, yes, I want the same. But one step, one day at a time." He then reached in his pocket and took out a ring box and opened it. Her eyes widened. He had sprung another surprise on her. *What is he, an angel?*

He said, "This ring is a symbol for you and me committing to give this relationship a chance, hoping to grow into something inseparable." It was a beautifully cut one-carat diamond white-gold ring.

"Oh my gosh, Marcus," she murmured innocently, "you don't have to give me a diamond to get me to commit to giving this relationship a chance."

"I know. I just wanted to. Please don't think I'm trying to show off. This is just to symbolize our commitment."

She looked at him with her head raised. "I know you're not trying to show off. I'm just ... okay, I will accept it. But I'm not sure at this moment that I am ready to put it on. I need a moment to process all this. Please don't take it the wrong..." He broke in.

"You don't have to explain, I understand. It was a bit sudden." He took her hand and said, "I am just glad to be here with you right now."

She whispered back, "I am glad to have you here with me right now." What she really wanted to tell him was that she wanted exactly what he wanted. But she was not even ready to admit that to herself and certainly not to him. She could not believe what she was feeling and neither could he.

Suddenly, Marcus blurted, "Why don't we watch a movie?"

"Okay," she responded astonished, looking at him, knowing why he suddenly broke the mood. He got up and walked over to the movie rack and pulled out "Transformers."

"Good choice," she said. "But before we watch the movie," lowering her tone, "would you mind putting my ring on?" She could not believe that she just blurted out those words, and neither could Marcus. But he didn't question it. He picked the box up from the coffee table, took the ring out, and slipped it on her finger. "I like it. It's really gorgeous, Marcus. Thank you."

"You're welcome. It looks good on you," he said as he continued to hold her hand. He gently lifted her hand and kissed it proudly.

"Okay, let's watch the movie. She grabbed the throws off the ottoman and gave him one, and then they cuddled, separately, in their own throws.

About five minute later Marcus asked, "What happened to dessert?"

Liah said, "brownies ... right. I'll go get them."

"I'm helping."

"Well, come on then." They went into the kitchen and fixed a big bowl of ice cream and a small basket of brownies. Marcus carried the bowl of ice cream and Liah carried the brownies.

"Don't forget the spoons," Marcus exclaimed.

"Got them," she uttered. They ate ice cream and brownies and talked for the first thirty minutes of the movie. "Okay, we gotta stop talking Marcus; the movie is about to get interesting." They got comfortable, watched the movie, and ended up falling asleep before the movie was over. Liah woke up about one. "Marcus, wake up."

"Oh, my gosh, what time is it?"

"About one."

"Liah, I am so sorry."

"Why? I fell asleep, too."

"I had better go while I am still awake."

"Okay," she said sleepily, "I'll walk you to the door."

"Goodnight, babe, I'll talk to you tomorrow." He gave her a quick kiss on the cheek, and said good night again.

She went upstairs, crawled into her Victorian-style bed, cuddled up with her body pillow, and went right back to sleep.

The next morning she woke up about twenty minutes before the alarm went off. She sat up in bed and stretched, then laid her head back on her pillow. Somehow the ring slightly grazed her cheek. She sat back up in bed and touched her lamp. It all came flowing back to her.

She had committed to seeing only Marcus. It was a commitment she was very pleased with. And she was honored to be wearing his ring. Though she'd only known him for a short while, she was surer in one week than she had ever been in any long-term relationship. *If there were any strikes against him, the good would certainly outweigh the bad*, she thought. Marcus Michaels was the real thing. Still lost in her thoughts, she was startled by the alarm. She turned the alarm off and lay back down, attempting to free her mind of thoughts and steal just a few more minutes of sleep.

~Chapter Seven~

Today was the kids' first day back to school, after the spring break. The routine was back in action. Liah got up and fixed breakfast for the kids and got them off to school. Since Jen and Tim were dropping them off at school, she had some extra time before going to work. She went back upstairs and got back into bed to read her Bible.

When she got to work, she didn't mention anything about the ring. She went on about her day without anyone noticing it. Well, that was until she reached on the shelf to get a bottle of seasoning. That's when the sparkle caught Louis's eyes. "Oh, my word. I know you didn't come up in here and didn't tell anyone about that rock." Everyone in the kitchen ran over to see it.

"Okay tell the story," Tina demanded.

"It's just a promise ring, guys, you know, symbolizing a genuine effort toward the relationship."

"And he gave you a rock for that," Louis exclaimed.

"Yes," she answered smartly.

"Liah, he wants you badly and all to himself," Louis declared.

"Hey, I'll put forth an effort for a rock like that," Mel replied. "What is it? One big beautiful carat."

"Yes, it is," Liah said.

"Yeah, and it's real, too," Tina added.

"It's about time you let a man in your life," Louis uttered, all the way from the other side of the kitchen.

"The next question is, does he like and get alone with the kids?" Tina inquired. "You know what? Don't even worry about answering that. I know you."

"Yes, you do. And, yes, he does like kids and they get along quite well. Jas especially took to him well. He thinks he's awesome."

"There, you have your answer," Louis responded. "Jas has an animal instinct. He knows good meat."

"What?" Tina asked? "Louis, you're crazy?" They all burst out laughing.

"Louis, are you comparing my baby to a dog?"

"No, no, you know what I mean. The boy is gifted."

"Okay, Louis," Liah said. He came over, hugged her and told her that he was happy for her.

"So have you told the other girlfriends about him yet?" he asked.

"No, I haven't. I'm not ready yet."

"Why?" he asked. "You have the first rock. Ring! I meant ring." They all burst out laughing.

"Girl," Tina said, adding her two cents in. "Ain't no man gonna spend that much on a rock for any woman and not be serious. You know that, don't you? Cause most men are cheap."

"What have we started here," Liah asked, "a comedy show?"

"No," Tina said, "but kitchen sink drama is kind of catching. I mean, Liah. Let's get real. The way you all met, and the way he dashed over here after the twin mix up, and you've seen each other almost every day since.

This is like one of those needles-in-haystack lottery- winner kind of deals. He has looks, physique, he's gentle, generous, and he's rich. Shall I go on, Liah?"

"What do you mean, he's rich?" Liah questioned.

"Girl, isn't he an architect, and isn't his last name, Michaels?"

"Yes," she answered.

"Alright then, Michaels and Michaels Architecture and Designs. Remember last week, we passed by that big building on the other side of town that takes up almost the whole the block: The one you like so much?"

"Get out of here," Liah said. "You are for real, huh?"

"Yes, she is," Louis assured her. "She has last month's 'Business Tycoons' magazine to prove it."

"I can't believe he didn't tell you," Tina blurted.

"He told me he owned his own architecture business. He might have even mentioned Michaels and Michaels. It just didn't dawn on me. But he certainly didn't expound on it. So I just assumed it was something small," she said in disbelief. You know what … it is probably in the missing page from the investigator's report, which is now in an unopened package on my desk. He had it delivered to me. Her phone rang. It was Marcus. "Marcus," she said softly. "Hi."

"Hi, baby. How are you?"

"I'm good. How are you?"

"Splendid! I wanted to share some good news with you."

"What?" she asked.

"Remember that project we had to recreate last week?"

"Yes," she answered, still thinking about Tina's enlightenment.

"We got the contract," he exclaimed excitedly. "It is a fifty-million dollar deal."

"Wow, are you serious?"

"Yes, babe. I'm serious."

"Marcus, that's great. I am so happy for you all."

"I'm kind of glad the dog destroyed the original project," he said.

"See, things do happen for a reason," she said to him.

"Yes, it does," he agreed. "We should go celebrate tonight. Bring the kids."

"I would love to, except this evening the kids have a martial arts class and probably homework."

"Why don't we meet for lunch?" she suggested.

"Yes, let's do that," he agreed. "Can I pick you up about one forty-five?"

"Sure, I will be ready."

"All right, I'll see ya then," he said and hung up. She walked back over to the table with her mouth half opened in somewhat of a shock.

"What?" Louis and Tina asked.

"You're right, Tina, he's rich. And they just signed a fifty-million dollar contract. If he wasn't rich before, he is now."

"Say what?" Louis screamed out. "Girl, you better go for it. But I know you, and money doesn't seem to impress you a bit. Hey, ya'll remember when that guy fell for Liah and he thought he could buy her. So he sent all that stuff to her."

"Yeah," Mel replied. "I tried to convince her to give it to me, but she sent it all back to him."

"Wait a minute," Tina exclaimed, "she sent it all back with a nasty note. Come to think of it, Liah, that was your first date between divorce and Marcus. Guys do fall for you on the first date."

"Hey, that guy and I didn't really have a date. We had lunch twice and talked mostly about him putting in a new pool for me."

"And if memory serves me correctly," Louis said, "he was wealthy too. A little psychotic, but he seemed like a good guy."

"I think he got married, too," one of the kitchen assistants added. "However, I heard he was unhappy, because all his wife does is shops all day, then goes home and drops her lazy self to that couch Liah sent back."

"And don't anyone laugh," Liah warned. "That is sad, not funny."

"Whatever," Tina said. The whole kitchen staff started laughing. Liah felt compelled to laugh herself. They didn't know if she was laughing at them or with them.

"Just so you all know, I am laughing at you all, not him. And you all are mean. By the way, did I tell you all that I am going to lunch with Marcus?"

"No, but have a good rich time," Louis told her.

She just shook her head and said, "Pitiful. I am going to freshen up."

Marcus arrived on time. On the way to lunch, they talked about the deal Marcus and Morgan had closed. He told her exactly how the meeting went and the type of building they were going to build.

They only spent about forty minutes at the pub. They talked about their busy week and made plans to see a movie Saturday night. Marcus asked if she would like to take a tour of the Michaels building and meet his brother and the guys.

"Sure, I would like to meet your brother and the guys, of course." Before they got to the building she could see the big sign 'Michael & Michaels Architecture & Designs.' When they drove up, he parked in the reserved space with 'Marcus Michaels' on it. She was in visual shock. She couldn't believe how big and beautiful the building was.

"This is your business?" she asked him looking surprised.

"Mine and Morgan," he replied.

"Wow, I knew you had your own business, but I had no idea..."

He cut in, "I thought you had me investigated," he said curiously.

"I did, but I didn't read the entire report. Anyway, I wasn't interested in knowing how much money you had. And apparently you're pretty loaded. I guess that explains this ring."

"I hope this won't be a problem for you," he said.

"As long as it's not for you."

"It's not," he responded, "Money doesn't make me any different, or better than anyone else. Though, it is necessary. Shall we go in?"

"We shall," she said in a sweet mockery kind of way. They walked into Morgan's office, he wasn't there.

"We'll come back later," he said. "Let me give you a tour. And if you don't mind, I would like to show you my house."

"Sure, I don't mind," she replied. As they were walking down the hallway, they ran into Morgan.

"Well, hello there, you must be Liah," he uttered, cheesing from ear to ear.

"And you're Marcus' double."

"Yes, and it's about time I met you."

"It's a pleasure meeting you too, Morgan."

"So what are you guys doing here?" he asked. "I thought you had a lunch date."

"We did and we've already had lunch. Now we're here so Liah can meet the man who wrecked our first date."

"Oh, yeah," Morgan said. "I am so sorry about that."

"No apology needed. It wasn't your fault."

"You're too kind," Morgan said.

"Morgan, I'm going to give Liah a tour and then we're out."

"Alright," he replied. "Liah, I'm glad to have met you. It was a pleasure indeed." She smiled. "And a beautiful smile too," he added. Marcus and Liah started to walk off. "Marcus," Morgan called out. "Hold back for a moment. Man she's gorgeous."

"Thanks, I know that. Gotta go," he said. "I'll talk to you later."

"Everything okay?" she asked.

"Oh yeah," he responded. "Morgan is just being silly."

When they drove up to Marcus' gate, she couldn't believe her eyes.

"This is home sweet home, baby."

"This is your house!" she said unbelievingly.

"Yep," he said.

"And you live here alone?"

"With the exception of my butler and the cook. The housekeeper comes in every day and she brings in a cleaning crew once a week. And before you ask, I built this house after I was divorced."

"Okay, so it was my next question." They drove into the three-car garage and right next to a Silver Dodge Charger.

"Ooh, I like the Charger," Liah said, "Although, I was expecting a Mercedes or something."

"No, it's too fancy for me. I really prefer the Charger," he assured her.

"I guess I can see that. You don't really seem like the flashy type."

"I'm really not," he agreed.

"But why such a huge house?"

"I don't know," he said. "I guess I've always dreamed of having a big house, filled with kids and, of course, a wife."

"Yes, of course," she responded. "You're kidding, right!"

"No ... I'm not. I truly hoped that I would meet someone just like you."

"Well it's good you met me instead," she said, breaking the mood.

"Come on. Stop trying to make me laugh. I'm serious, Liah." And he went on to say. "You are genuine and I am blessed to have met you."

"The feeling is mutual, Marcus," she assured him. They got out of the truck and he opened her door. He then took her into arms and embraced her tightly.

When they walked into the kitchen, Liah was bowled over. "Oh Marcus, this is ... this is my dream kitchen." It had a double stove with a grill, a butcher's table, breakfast bar, a long island, and a joining breakfast room. If she didn't know better, she would think it was designed just for her. "Did you design the kitchen?

"Yes, I did, but Morgan and I designed the rest of the house together."

"I haven't seen the rest of the house, but considering how this kitchen looks, I bet you guys did an outstanding job."

"Well, let's go see the rest of it, Ms. Mathis."

"Lead the way." He showed her the rest of the house. *Oh my gosh*, she thought to herself. "Was I married to him in another life?" It was as if the house was especially designed for her. *Someone pinch me, but please don't wake me from this dream, just let me know that I am still among the living. This man is too good to be real ... business owner ... home owner ... full of integrity, and most importantly, godly.*

"Liah, are you okay?" Not really. But as long as he was in her world, who cares.

"Yes, I'm fine." I'm just blown away by the design. You all did an amazing job, Marcus."

"Thank you, baby."

"I know you designed it, but don't tell me you decorated it, too."

"Hum, I did do most of it."

"But it's not even done in all masculine tones."

"That's because I took into consideration that I would have someone like you here, one day"

"Yeah, right. But that was a good try." She laughed out loud and so did he. They went back downstairs and he offered her green tea. While waiting for her tea, she sat in the den. She picked up a photo album from the coffee table with pictures of Marcus and Morgan. They were so cute and some of the pictures were even funny looking. She couldn't help but laugh. She looked up and saw an older gentleman with salt and pepper hair walk in.

"Hello," he said. "That album cracks me up, too."

"Hi, how are you?"

"Wonderful dear. You must be Ms. Liah."

"Yes, I am." Marcus walked in with two glasses of tea. "Jeffrey, I thought you had gone out."

"I did. I'm back. Ms. Liah, I'm Jeffrey. It's a pleasure to meet you, dear. I hope I see more of you."

"It was a pleasure meeting you as well, Mr. Jeffrey."

"Oh please, dear, call me Jeffrey."

"You take care, Liah."

"You too, Jeffrey."

"Should I be jealous?" Marcus asked.

"Yes," they both answered at the same time, then Jeffrey winked at her and she smiled.

When Jeffrey was walking out of the room, he whispered in Marcus' ear, "I like her, she's beautiful and it's about time."

"Thank you, Mr. Jeffrey," Marcus uttered. "So what do you think about Jeffrey?"

"Interesting, but I really like him."

"Good, you'll probably be seeing a lot of him."

"Okay," she replied. He sat down beside her.

"So why haven't you married again," he asked her randomly. He seemed to have a way springing surprises on her, even if it was just questions.

"Simple, I've never met you before."

"Good answer."

He got up and pulled her into his arms, looked into her eyes and, said, "I'm glad I met you, love. I'm glad you're in my life. Now I had better get you back to work."

"Yes, I do need to get back."

"Why don't you and the kids come over Saturday for dinner?"

"Okay, I think they would like that."

"So what would you like to eat?" he asked her.

"How about something Italian, and maybe strawberry cheesecake for dessert?"

"Fantastic, I think my cook can handle that."

On the ride back, he asked her about the kids' father. "This ride isn't long enough for that story. Not even the short version. Can this hold until a later date, maybe even Saturday?"

"No problem. Why don't you all come spend the entire day with me on Saturday?"

"You want to spend the whole day with three children?" she asked surprisingly.

"Love to. Besides, I want to get to know them better, too."

"I think that's a good idea. I assume you have a backyard?"

"Ah man, I forgot to show you the backyard. It's not as nice as yours, but it's pretty big."

"Marcus, why don't you and Morgan live together?"

"Well, for one, we didn't want to go through the trouble of moving if one of us got married, and we preferred having our own space. Morgan lives a street over from me."

"Don't tell me his house is as big as yours?"

"Not quite. He has five bedrooms, whereas I have six. However both houses are pretty similar. His kitchen is black and chrome."

"Wow, I bet it is really nice."

"It is. I almost wanted to change mine. I'll take you by there one day, soon, probably."

"Oh, yes, definitely," she replied.

"Liah, what do think about introducing Morgan to your friend the doctor?"

"The intern doctor and I just might do that. She might be here this weekend. When I find out for sure, I'll let you know."

"Okay, babe, I'm sure Morgan will be thrilled."

After they made it back to the restaurant, Marcus walked her in. They went in through the side door. He lifted her hand to his chest and said to her, "I miss you already." While bringing her hand down, the ring caught his eye. "You know, this ring really looks good on your finger."

"It does, doesn't it?

"Well, I'm going to let you get back to work." He took her into his arms and whispered in her ear, saying, "I've had such a wonderful time with you, I don't want to let you go. But, I know I have to. Soooo, I will call you later, baby."

As soon as Marcus left, Liah heard knocks at her door. At least half the kitchen staff piled in her office. "Okay, Tina and Louis both demanded. "Tell us what happened and don't leave anything out."

"There is nothing to tell."

"Whatever," Tina said! "Give it up girl, okay."

"So he does own the business that takes up nearly an entire block. He took me on a tour. I met his double and the design team. And you know how big you guys think my house is?"

"Yeah!" Louis said impatiently.

"Well, you can probably put my house inside of his."

"Get out of here!" Louis responded.

"For real, Liah?" Tina said.

"Yes, Tina, I'm serious. He has a beautiful home and the kitchen is spectacular. But on a more serious note, if he didn't have a humongous successful business or that beautiful and gorgeously designed, house, he would still be this gorgeous, wonderful, caring, and loving gentleman. Honestly, I can't help but 'thirst' for getting to know him better."

"I heard that, Liah," Tina said.

"Yeah, but when you marry that rich man, don't forget about us working class," Louis uttered.

"I don't know about all that, Louis. We are taking it one day at a time."

"From where I'm looking," Louis added, "I'm thinking a proposal before the year is up. Probably even marriage!"

"All right, all right, all right, enough," Liah exclaimed. "It's time to get ready for dinner rush. Louis, will you get started for me, please? I need to call the kids."

"Shall do, chef," he said.

"Thank you, Louis." When she came back into the kitchen, she had the most pleasing smile on her face. Marcus had sent her a text message saying, "You are my shining star." She replied by saying "and don't you go away." Both were lines taken from the song "Shining Star" by Manhattan.

"What is with the smile?" Tina asked.

"Tina, stop being nosy," Liah told her.

"Liah, if you don't want me asking questions, stop grinning like the Cheshire cat." They both laughed.

"It's really nothing. I just received a text from Marcus."

"Whatever," Tina replied. "It was enough to make you smile like that." She just sighed. Mel came into the kitchen.

"Liah," she called out.

"Yes, Mel."

"Do you know a Morgan and Lillie Michaels?"

"Yes. Why?"

"They're in dining."

"Really?

"Are they Marcus' parents?" Tina asked, curiously.

"Honestly, I really don't know. I believe they are. I mean, how much of a coincident could it be: Young Morgan Michaels, older Morgan Michaels?"

"Maybe we should look in the phone book and see just how many Morgan Michaels we can find in there," Louis suggested.

"Now there's a thought," Liah said. "A crazy one, but it is one. I could just call Marcus and ask him."

"Even better," Tina said. "I can't believe he hadn't told you about them," she went on to say.

"Well, we did talk about his parents and a sister."

"But no names ... right?" Louis questioned.

"Nope! I didn't even tell him my parents' names. I suppose we didn't want to spend time naming relatives," Liah stated in their defense.

"All ... we rubbed off on you, didn't we?" Tina blurted. "Listen at you saying nope."

"Bad habits are easy to pick up and hard to lose," Liah replied. "Ha, ha," Tina said giggling.

"Mel," Liah called out. "What are they ordering?"

"Oh, I'm sorry. They said let the chef surprise them."

"I know just what to fix them."

"What?" Mel asked.

"The Chef's Monterey Chicken Dinner."

"Oh, that's a good one," Mel agreed. "What about dessert?" she asked.

"Hmmm—they seem like the carrot cake type people," Liah said.

"I just made a fresh one today. As a matter of fact, tell them that they're getting a complimentary meal from the chef. If they ask what do you mean. Just tell them it's for allowing me the pleasure of choosing their meal."

"Will do, boss."

"Don't call me that, Mel."

"Ooops, sorry, boss"

"Girl — don't make me bring harm to you."

"Yeah, Mel, cause you know she believes in beating people real down," Louis inserted wittily.

Mel starting laughing and then went back to the Michaels' table to tell them that their meal would be out shortly.

"You know Liah, "If they are his parents, they're going to love you." She went on to say. "You know what they say ... food makes the heart grow fonder." The whole kitchen crew burst out laughing. "What?" What are y'all laughing at? Tina asked.

"It is absence makes the heart grow fonder, Tina," Liah said shaking her head.

After Tina realized she had the old saying wrong, she started laughing and then mumbled "It sure is. Well what is the food saying?"

"It's the way to a man's heart, Tina," Louis said.

"Okay, heart, growing fonder. It all means the same thing."

"It kind of does, Louis," Liah said. "Anyway Louis, remember the meeting I took for you?"

"Yeah, I do remember you telling me about them. So they are the Michaels?"

"Yes, and we're catering their party," Liah told him. "Actually, they're having the party here in May. I'll bring you all up to speed on the Michaels' party soon."

Liah packed them a to-go box. "They look like good tippers," Tina uttered.

"Tina, have I ever told you that you are crazy?" Liah asked. "All the time," Tina responded.

"Is the Michael's order ready?" Mel asked.

"Yes, it is, dear," she said.

"All right, it may be your time to shine in front of Marcus' maybe parents," Mel said. The Michaels were totally impressed with the way everything looked.

"Well, it looks scrumptious, dear," he said to Mel.

"And well prepared," Mrs. Michaels commented.

"Enjoy your meal, Mr. and Mrs. Michaels. It's complimentary from the chef."

"Oh, no, we can't allow her to do that," he said.

"Mrs. Mathis wouldn't have it any other way."

"Will you ask her if she has time, to please come out to say hi?"

"I will give her the message, sir," Mel said politely.

"Thank you very much," he said. "You're very kind."

"Liah, the Michaels would like for you to come out to say hi if you have time."

"Really? Okay.

After Mel picked up their plates, Liah came out with their dessert.

"Oh here she is, dear," Morgan said to Lillie. He stood up to greet her. "Well hello there, Ms. Mathis. It's so nice to see you again," he said.

"It's good to see you all as well."

"Liah, hello. It's wonderful to see you again, darling," Lillie said. "Do you have a moment to sit down and join us?" she asked.

"Oh sure. I hope you all like carrot cake."

"Oh, honey, please. I like it quite well," Morgan avowed, "though, it is Lillie's favorite."

"Yes, it is," Lillie agreed "and thank you for choosing it."

"By the way, that meal was delightful," Morgan expressed.

"It sure was. I enjoyed it very much," Lillie told her. "And now we have this delightful-looking carrot cake. I don't know how you knew it was what I wanted. But, honey, thank you, thank you," she said pleasingly excited.

They both picked up their forks to have their first bite. "Oh, my," Morgan said. "I think carrot cake is going to be my favorite. Liah, this is by far, the best carrot cake I've ever put in my mouth."

"And you have put a lot in your mouth," she laughed, and so did Morgan and Liah. But he's right, Liah. This is the best." Mrs. Michaels picked up another fork and said to Liah, "Here, I have an extra fork. This is a big piece. Don't let me eat it all by myself. Because I will! So come on eat," she insisted.

Liah willingly took the fork and cut off a small piece. "It is good," she moaned, though she already knew that.

"Yes, it is," Lillie said. "Now eat more."

They talked for about ten to fifteen minutes. They even invited Liah out to lunch the following week. And she accepted with pleasure.

"Well, I have to get back to the kitchen. It was a pleasure seeing you all again. Thanks for sharing your cake with me Lillie. You all please come back soon."

"Oh, we will, and thank you very much," Mr. Michaels said.

"You are quite welcome," she said. "Would you like to take ...?"

Before she finished the question, Mrs. Michaels cut in and said, "Yes, we will." She knew Liah was offering them carrot cake to go.

"I will have it sent right out to you." She left the table and went back to the kitchen.

"Well," Tina questioned. "You still don't know if they are his parents, do you?"

"No, but I have a lunch invitation next week."

"I think they're his parents, Liah."

While the Michaels were waiting for their take home trays, they contemplated how they could get Marcus and Liah to meet. Lillie said to her husband, "What if she's a better fit with Morgan?"

"No, she is definite Marcus' type. I have an idea, honey. We could invite Marcus to lunch the same day we invited Liah."

"Oh, that's an excellent idea, Morgan. Let's do it. If it works out, he'll forgive us."

Mel brought the bag of food out. "My, this is a mighty big bag for a couple pieces of cake," Lillie said.

"Oh, she took the liberty of packing you all an extra meal as well."

"Well, please tell her thanks a bunch, and we will call her early next week."

"All right, honey, where's our bill?" Morgan asked.

"It's complimentary from the chef, remember?" Mel reminded him.

"Oh, yeah, you did tell me that. Tell her thanks again for us, please. And you have been very kind, too, Ms. Mel."

"Please, Sir, call me Mel."

"Mel, thank you." He reached in his wallet, pulled out a fifty-dollar bill and gave it to her. Have a good evening Mel," he said.

"I will sir, thanks. You all have a good evening to, and please come again." He picked up their bag and they left. She went back into the kitchen and told Liah thank you.

"Why? What did I do?"

"I got fifty dollars tip."

"Really! Good for you, Mel. I don't know what I did but I'm glad I could help."

"Liah, do you know that every time you give a customer a complimentary meal, I get a rather large tip?"

"Oh, you do, don't you?"

"Uh huh."

"Liah, what time are you leaving?" Louis asked.

"About six, I have to take my children to their martial arts class." "Why? What's up?"

"I really need to leave about six, something important came up."

"Well, why don't you leave now and pick the kids up and drop them off at class."

"For real?" he said.

"Yes, you've earned it. I'll stay here until eight."

"I'll be back around eight."

"If you want to you can, but you don't have to. We'll be closing an hour later. I doubt that there'll be a lot going on."

116

"You're the best," he said.

"Louis, you always have my back." He started walking toward the clock so he could clock out. "Oh, don't bother clocking out," Liah told him. "I'll clock you out when I leave."

"The best!" he said.

"You had better go before I change my mind. And thanks for picking up the kids."

"Okay, I'm gone."

Liah did both her job and Louis'. She even prepped for the next day. By eight she was beat. "All right, guys, I am out of here. Have a good night." She went by to pick the kids up from martial arts class. They were all pretty tired when they got home. They weren't hungry because Louis fed them before he dropped them off. They took showers and went right to bed. As soon as Liah laid her head on her pillow, the phone rang. It was Chantel.

"Hi, Ms. Thang," Chantel said, with her usual vivacious attitude.

"Hi Chan," she barely murmured.

"Are you in the bed?"

"Yes, I am."

"Are you sick?"

"I don't know," Liah replied. "I'm too tired to feel anything."

"Well, you sound pitiful."

"Yeah, I know," she agreed with a fading tone.

"I'm going to let you go. Call me tomorrow when you're back among the living."

"Goodnight, Liah. Get some rest." Liah hung up the phone. About ten minutes later the phone rang again. She looked at the caller ID. This time it was her mom.

"Honey, are you ill?"

"No, I'm just exhausted, Mom."

"Why are you so tired, child?"

"I work, Mom. I am a single parent and I have somewhat of a life."

"When did you get a life?"

"Mom, I've always had a life. I just wasn't dating."

"Do you need me to come help you out?"

"Thanks, Mom, but I'll be ok ... if only I could just get some sleep."

"Did you meet someone?"

"Mom, can I please call you back later? I love you, Mom," she said quickly and smoothly.

"I love you too, baby. Kiss my grandkids and tell them I said hello."

"Okay, Mommy. Goodnight."

"Good night Sweetie."

"Finally," she said out loud. "Man, that woman can talk." She laid her head back down. About thirty minutes later her cell phone rang again. She reached over and picked it up. She didn't bother looking at the caller ID this time. She answered the phone in a sleepy whispering like voice.

"Hi, baby. Were you sleeping?" he asked.

"Yes. Wait a moment. Who is this?"

"Who else calls you baby?"

"Marcus," she murmured surprisingly.

"It is I, love. You were asleep. I'm so sorry I disturbed you."

"It's okay. Mom and Chan called shortly before you."

"What's wrong, babe? Do you need me to come over?"

"I would love that, but then I probably wouldn't get any sleep."

"You're probably right. I'm going to let you get back to sleep. I promise to call you earlier tomorrow."

"Ok, Marcus," she whispered. "Thanks for calling." She kept the phone in her hand and fell asleep.

Tuesday was another busy day. Marcus called around noon to check on her. Even though he had a pretty full day himself, he wanted to see her. Liah had planned to work through lunch. However, Marcus insisted she take a break. The kitchen staff agreed and practically pushed her out the door. They grabbed a healthy, but hefty, salad and a natural fruit slush to-go at a little shop just up the street, from A'Palace. Then they went to a cozy little park close by. After eating their salad, they didn't talk very much. They just cuddled up on the bench together for about thirty minutes.

"Thanks for insisting that I take a break. I really did need it."

"You're welcome, Liah, but you sounded a bit burned out last night."

"I know. I felt a bit burned out."

"Maybe you should take some time off."

"No. I can't right now."

"Liah ... if you need help with anything please let me know."

"Okay, Marcus. Thanks, but I will be fine."

"I care about you, baby. I care a lot."

"I know, Marcus, and I appreciate it." They got up off the bench and he put both his arms around her and slightly pressed his forehead against hers. He then lifted his head and continued to hold her closely in his arms. She said in a whispery voice. "I wish we could stay here longer, but I have to get back to work." They walked back to the car hand in hand.

Wednesday morning before going to work, Marcus called her. "Good morning, beautiful," he said in his to-die-for morning voice.

"Good morning, Mr. Michaels. I've never talked to you this early in the morning. I like your morning voice," she said.

"Oh really," he responded.

"Uh huh."

"So what do you like about it?"

"I rather not say. Let's just leave it there for now." He chuckled in a low tone, making his voice sound even more appealing.

"How are you feeling today?" he asked.

"I'm better. How about you?"

"I was good until I got a call about a new proposal."

"What's not good about that?"

"Well, I have to fly to Austin, Texas."

"When?"

"In a couple of hours."

"When will you be back?"

"Friday night or Saturday morning. I promise I'll be back for our day together. I'm looking forward to that."

"So am I."

"Will you call me when you get there?"

"I wouldn't have it any other way, baby."

"Okay, honey. Hope everything goes well with the new proposal."

"So do I. Well, babe, I have to pack."

"Okay," she said, reluctant to let him go.

"Liah ... I, I will call you when I get to the hotel. I'll see you on Saturday."

120

They both pushed the off button and held their phone in their hands for a moment. Both of them had it bad for each other. She closed her eyes and thought about how he made her feel. She couldn't believe she had met such an incredible, loving, passionate, gentle, and caring man, who overflowed with integrity. She couldn't believe he wanted her regardless of how many children she had. She knew it would be easy to fall in love with him. After all, what was not to love about him? But she wasn't ready to fall in love with him, though she knew there was nothing to shield her from it. It was just a matter of time and she would be overtaken by her emotions. *Goodness, let me pull myself together, so I won't look like a loved-stricken teenager when I walk into work,* she said to herself.

Marcus was reluctant to pack his bag. He could not shake the feeling that he should not leave her, not even for a day. He picked up the phone and called Morgan to tell him how he was feeling. Morgan offered to go in his place. Marcus said, "Thanks, but I'll go. Besides you have a proposal here and they're expecting you."

"Why don't we have a prayer together before you leave," Morgan suggested. They prayed on the phone.

As soon as he got to the hotel, he called Liah. They didn't talk long because he had a meeting downstairs in fifteen minutes. He told her he would try to call her back later but it would probably be late. She told him whenever he could call would be fine.

When she got home, she sent him a funny text message. He received it during his business meeting. He was very discreet when answering it. He couldn't help but crack a smile.

He didn't wait until he returned to his room to call her; he called as soon as he stepped out of the meeting room. "Hi babe, I know it's late but I wanted to say good night, and I can't believe how I miss you already."

"I miss you too, Marcus. I wish you didn't have to go out of town."

"I know, and I really didn't want to go. I even called Morgan to tell him I couldn't shake the feeling that I should be there."

"Are you okay now?" she asked.

"I'm better. Morgan prayed with me before I left."

"That's good. Prayer always helps."

"Yes, it does!"

"Well, baby, it's late and I have an early meeting tomorrow and you sound kind of sleepy as well."

"Okay, honey, I hope everything goes well and please hurry home."

"Thanks, babe, and I will be back as soon as I can."

Shortly after they hung up, Marcus sent her a silly picture of him with a miss you message. With that thought in her mind, she caressed her pillow and fell asleep.

Chantel called early that morning to check on Liah. "Hi Chan, how are you and what do I owe the honor of this early morning call?"

"Did you remember that Alisha and Shayna are coming this Friday?"

"Yes."

"Just thought I'd check."

"Actually, you guys are coming at a good time." She knew that would be a good time since she wasn't expecting Marcus until Saturday. She figured it would even be a good time to tell them about the new man in her life, whom she'd kept all to herself.

"Hey, Liah, I have to go, I'll call you back tonight."

"Okay, Chan, you have good day."

"Same to you, hon!"

~Chapter Eight~

Thursday after her class, Liah and the kids hung out in the Bistro with Liz and her boys. While the kids were playing games, Liz was hoping that Liah would indulge her by looking at wedding dresses. "Hey, Liah, check out this wedding dress. Or you could just dream for a moment. If you were going to pick out a wedding dress, which one would you choose?" Liah looked through the book. She chose a beautiful satin champagne dress. "Oh that's a good one."

"Actually it is one of the most gorgeous dresses in this book," Liah responded.

"Yeah, I think so, too. So what color will the groom's tuxedo be?" Liz asked, urging her on.

"Chocolate brown with a beige or champagne shirt."

"Now that will go good together," Liz said.

Liah held her head down and shook her head. "Are you okay, Liah?" Liz asked.

"I just feel a little light-headed."

"Do you think you can drive home?"

"Yeah, I'll be ok."

"I don't know Liah. I don't feel good about you driving home."

"I just think it's the new allergy medicine plus some antibiotic." She had gone to the doctor earlier that day.

"That's it," Liz insisted. "Leave your car here. It will be okay. I'm taking you guys home. I'll pick up my husband and have him drive your car home."

"Okay, Liz, I really appreciate it." Liz got the kids and told them what happened. She drove them home and made sure Liah got upstairs to bed.

"Do you have an extra set of keys?"

"Yes, I do."

"Good. When we bring your car home I'm going to lock your keys in the trunk."

"Okay, Liz, thanks." The girls made sure Jason got his bath and tucked him in bed. Liah went right to bed. Right before she fell asleep she got a text from Marcus telling her goodnight.

The next morning she still wasn't like herself, but she still went to work. Chantel called her on her way to work to tell her she wasn't sure she would make it in on Friday. The conversation was very brief. Liah didn't have time to tell her what happened the night before, because Chantel got paged and had to hang up suddenly. Liah tried to reach Alisha and Shayna, but was unsuccessful. She practically pushed herself to get through the day. Her staff knew that she wasn't feeling well, and knew that she would not go home so they tried to lighten her load.

When she got home from work she took her medicine and lay down. Chantel called around seven that night to apologize for rushing her off the phone. Chantel could hardly understand what Liah was saying. She finally heard her say she didn't feel right and then she heard the phone drop. Chantel called her name several times and didn't get a response. She picked up her home phone and call Jacqlyne's phone. She told her she was talking to her mom, she heard the phone drop, and then everything went silent. Jacqlyne rushed into the room, the phone was on the floor and Liah was unresponsive. Chantel told Jacqlyne to pick up her mom's phone and call 911.

Jacqlyne checked Liah's pulse. She told Chan she could barely feel a pulse. Chantel asked her if she knew CPR. When the paramedic arrived she was barely hanging on. "Make sure you take your phone to the hospital and call me as soon as you get there. Remember to take whatever medicine she's been taking with you and give it to the doctor." After Jacqlyne hung up the phone she called Tim and Jen to tell them what happened. The kids met them outside as soon as Jacqlyne had finished talking to Jen. Tim and Jen both took the kids to the hospital.

When the ambulance arrived at the hospital, Liah's pulse was very faint. They immediately rushed her to a room. Tim, Jen, and the kids walked in right after they took her in. About thirty minutes later, the doctor came out and told them she was breathing a little better, but she was unconscious. He went on to tell them that the next twenty-four hours would be crucial. He couldn't assure them of her recovery or how long she would be unconscious. However, he did tell them the longer she was unconscious increased the chance of her slipping into a coma. He asked them if she was taking any medication. Fortunately, Chantel had told Jacqlyne to take the medicine with her.

"We will let you all know something as soon as we get the test results back."

Several hours later, the doctor came back and informed them that Liah had a bad reaction from a combination of the medications. "She is blessed to be alive," he said. "I'm sorry to say, but I still can't give you any indication as to how long she would be unconscious. She seems to be a fighter. That's a good thing," he uttered. "I know you all don't want to leave her. I'm going to let you visit with her briefly and then I suggest you all go home to get some rest. We will call, if there are any changes."

Jacqlyne called Chantel to give her a report on Liah's condition. She then called her brothers. They all agreed not to call Jayde until they had better news. They knew she would be worried, and will drop everything and be on the next flight home, and they knew Liah would not want her to do so. They also decided not to call Liah's mom and sister, Paige, they would be frantic. They did not have any news to report, at least not any good news.

Tim and Jen took the kids home to pack their bags. They had planned on keeping them until their brothers got there.

Marcus called shortly after Liah was taken to the hospital. He called both Liah's cell phone and house phone and no answer. His uneasy feeling immediately returned. He paced the floor most of the night. After spending time in prayer and Bible reading, he finally fell asleep, with the Bible cuddle in his arms.

Another unsuccessful call early that morning before catching his plane, took him right back to the night before. He called her job but Louis told him that she wasn't scheduled to come in. However, he had been trying to reach her and was unable to as well.

Marcus had reached the stage of frantic when he called Morgan. "You sound upset, man. What's going on?" He told Morgan he had been trying to reach Liah since last night and she wasn't answering either of her phones. Morgan told him that he was coming to pick him up at the airport. Coincidentally, Marcus was at the airport, the same time Chantel, Alisha, Shayna and the boys were there. As a matter of fact, they were sitting together talking while they were waiting for their rides. They left the airport right before Morgan showed up to pick up Marcus.

When Alisha, Chantel, Shayna and the boys arrived at the hospital, Tim, Jen and the kids were already there. They were all glad to see each other. They only wished it was under different circumstances. Tim, Jen, and the kids left, so the others could visit with Liah. After a short visit with her, the nurse came in and told them that they had to get her ready for more tests. She told them that the doctor would speak with them shortly after he gets the result, to give them an update on her condition. They all seemed pretty worried. They knew the longer she stayed unconscious, the higher the risk was for her slipping into a coma. Everyone sat around talking while waiting for the doctor to come back with an update.

Finally the doctor came back and informed them the test results were all good and she should be waking up at any time. He told them to keep talking to her, read, sing or whatever it took to bring her back. They all thanked him. Then they went back into her room and prayed together. After they were done praying, all of her children sang "God's Amazing Grace." It was another one of her favorite songs. All of Liah's children had beautiful voices just as she did.

"Why don't we all check into the hotel and get something to eat," Jacob suggested.

"Good idea," Joshua agreed.

Jen and Tim went home and the others checked into the hotel, including the kids. They knew Liah wouldn't have it any other way. After getting settled in, they ordered up room service and hung out before going back to the hospital. Jason got a bit anxious and told his brothers that he wanted to go back to the hospital to wake up his mommy. They all wished that it was that easy.

When they got back to the hospital everyone but Jason and Jessica stayed out to talk to the doctor again. Jason went in and laid on Liah's chest while Jessica was talking to her. She told her how sad Jas was, and he needed her to wake up. While she was talking, tears rolled down Liah's face. Jessica didn't notice it until Jason said, "Mommy don't cry."

"What are you talking about, Jas? Mommy can't cry. She's unconscious?"

"Yes, she can! Then why is her face wet?" he asked. Jessica touched Liah's cheek and looked at her eyes. She noticed her trying to open her eyes. "Jason, stay in with her. I'm going to get the doctor."

"Jess, what's wrong," Alisha asked.

"Mommy has tears in her eyes and she was trying to open them." The doctor went in and asked Jason to wait out with the others. About ten minutes later, he came out and told them she was coming to. He allowed four of them to go in at the same time. The three boys and Chantel went in together. When they got in the room, Liah's eyes were still closed.

"Maybe you all should sing to her again," Chantel suggested. They harmonized "It's Not About Us" a song by one of Liah's favorite a cappella groups." Toward the end of their song, Liah asked in a whispering voice, "Why are the angels singing to me? Am I in Heaven?" She then faded back out.

"She would be the one to ask if she died and gone to heaven, wouldn't she?" Chantel mentioned.

"Yep, that's my mom! And if anyone is going to Heaven, it would certainly be her," Joshua said.

"Yes, it would be," Jacob agreed.

"No, I don't want her going to Heaven yet. I'm not old enough to cook for myself or get a job," Jason murmured. They all burst out laughing.

"Why is everyone laughing?" she asked. Everyone's eyes widened.

"Mommy!" Jason exclaimed. He was the first person she noticed.

"Hi, Jas. Where am I?"

"In the hospital Mom. Mom, are you going to live now?" Jas asked her.

"Yes, baby," she whispered. Why am in the hospital?

"Mom, you could have told us you wanted to see us. You didn't have to scare us like that," Jacob said humorously.

"Jacque and Josh, what are you all doing here?" She tried to sit up but was too weak.

"Liah, honey, stop trying to get up," Chantel warned her.

"Chan," Liah whispered. "Hospital! Why?" They explained to her what had happened. She apologized for having everyone worried and taking them away from their lives.

"Mom, you're our mother," Joshua told her. "We might not call you every day like you want us to, but when you need us we are just a phone call and a flight away."

"Yeah, Mom, we will always be here for you and it's never a problem."
They all gave her a hug then left out so that the others could come in.

She was delighted to see Alisha and Shayna. And the feeling was mutual. "I'm so sorry I scared all of you. And, Jacqlyne and Jess, thanks for being so brave." They stayed in the room until the doctor came in and told them he needed to check Liah's vitals again, and she needed her rest.

Later that evening when everyone came back, Liah was sitting up in bed eating jello. Shortly after her visit, the doctor came in. He told them Liah would make a full recovery but had to stay in the hospital for a few more days and he would be running more tests on Monday. They were all very pleased with the good news.

Joshua called Jayde to tell her what happened. Though she was upset because they didn't call her sooner, she understood. She was just glad her mom was better and on her way to a full recovery. While he was on the phone with Jayde, Jacob called her mom, and she was ready to jump on a plane, but he talked her out of it. She was much calmer after she heard Liah's voice.

"When are you all leaving?" Liah asked.

"Since you are better I guess we will go for that ten forty-five flight out tomorrow morning," Jacob replied. "But we can stay longer if you want us to."

"No, no, that's not necessary. You all have families and jobs to get back to."

"Mom, jobs can wait and we can always send for our families," Joshua told her.

"Thanks honey, but you guys can come for a visit soon … like when I am not in the hospital." They all left the hospital by eight thirty. Liah fell asleep right afterwards.

Morgan worked relentlessly at keeping Marcus distracted the whole day with work, and later that evening at the tennis court. However, Marcus did manage to slip in four calls to Liah that day. No matter how hard he tried, he couldn't seem to take his mind off Liah, at least not for long periods of time. Finally the day had to come to a close and Morgan took Marcus home. He hoped that Marcus was so burned out that he wouldn't be able to do anything but fall asleep. He was burned out indeed. As soon as Marcus got home, he took a long shower, went straight to bed, and fell right to sleep.

Sunday morning, the nurse came in to give Liah a sponge bath. Liah flat out refused to be bathed by the nurse. She told the nurse that she appreciated her, but she was getting out of that bed and taking a shower by herself. The nurse didn't bother arguing with her. "Okay, Ms. Mathis, whatever you say. But I'm helping you to the bathroom and back in bed. But, you have to promise to push the nurse call button if you feel the least bit lightheaded."

"Okay, I promise." After she was done taking her shower, she put on the lounger that Jen brought her the night before. She made herself presentable then crawled back into bed. As she lays in bed thinking about Marcus, she wished she could remember his phone number. She was sure he had called and knew he would be wondering why she was unreachable. She had planned on calling Jen after church and asking her to go by her house and bring her purse and cell. To her knowledge, no one at her job even knew she was in the hospital.

The boys came by at nine to see her before leaving for the airport. She was sad to see them leave, though she hid it quite well. She knew they would want to stay if they knew how she really felt.

Chantel, Alisha, and Shayna came by about ten-thirty. "Where are the kids?" Liah asked.

"Believe it or not, they are still in bed," Chantel told her.

"Yeah, they stayed up really late with their brothers and talking to Jayde," Alisha said."

"Even Jas?"

"Not as late as the others, but I'm sure it was way past his bedtime," Chan responded.

"Well, usually on Saturday I try to keep them on the same schedule as a school night because we go to early worship service."

"Yes, you do," Chantel said. "So, anyway, did you have a good night?"

"Yes, I did. I slept well and I got up and took a shower by myself."

"I bet you gave the nurse a hard time when she came in to give you a sponge bath," Alisha said.

"Yes, well, not really a hard time. Would anyone like to watch a movie?" she asked quickly, before someone proceeded with a topic she wasn't quite ready to approach.

Marcus and Morgan went to second service on Sunday morning. The person who was opening the service mentioned that he had received a call that Liah Mathis's daughter, had found her unconscious in her room on Friday night, and she was rushed to the hospital. He also mentioned that when he checked on her Saturday morning, she was still unconscious. Marcus' heart dropped. He couldn't believe what he had heard. "Did I hear that right, Morgan?" Marcus asked.

"Yeah man, your intuition was right." They abruptly got up and walked out of the auditorium. Marcus told Morgan to find out what hospital Liah was in and he would get the truck.

They rushed right over to the hospital. When they found out what room she was in, they practically burst in through the door. As soon as the door opened Marcus said, "Liah, baby, I just heard the announcement at church."

"Marcus," she whispered. She was lying in bed and the other three were sitting next to her on the bed. She was both shocked and delighted to see him.

"What happened?" he said, walking toward her bed. Morgan and I practically ran out of church. I just had to see you. Do I need to come back?" he asked.

"Marcus, it's okay." Alisha, Chantel and Shayna were totally shocked.

"Wait a minute," Chantel exclaimed. "No, no, you certainly don't need to leave. Come on over here," she demanded. They all got off the bed to let him sit down.

He gently lifted Liah and put his arms around her. "Baby, I just heard the announcement at church. I'm so sorry I wasn't here for you. I was so worried when I couldn't reach you. Why didn't you call me?"

"Marcus, you have no reason to be sorry. I'm sorry for not calling you. I didn't have my cell phone with me and that's where the numbers are."

"I'm just glad you're okay. I was really worried out of my mind."

"He sure was." Everyone looked around.

"Two of them," Shayna exclaimed.

"I'm sorry guys. I haven't properly introduced you all."

After the introduction, Alisha blurted out, "Liah you want to tell us why we know nothing about Marcus?"

"Yeah, and a handsome brother who looks just like him," added Shayna.

"I was going to tell you all this weekend. But don't act surprised. You all know me."

"Yeah, she's right," Chantel agreed.

"Well, for what it's worth, she talks about you all often. And I am pleased to meet all of you," he stated with optimal satisfaction.

"Yes, it is definitely a pleasure, ladies. And you must be the Doctor Chantel Harris?" Morgan asked boldly.

"I am she."

"And she's unmarried," Alisha blurted.

"Lisha, no one asked you for that piece of information," Shayna uttered.

"Is anyone hungry," Liah asked. "I sure am."

"Liah, has the doctor told you that you can eat solid foods?" Lisha questioned?

"No, but someone please go check?"

"I'll go find out," Marcus volunteered.

"I'll go with you, Marcus," Morgan said.

She knew she was in the hot seat. So as soon as they left, she started telling her friends about him. "I only met Marcus less than a ago. We met at a gospel meeting where he worships."

"Well, good. He might be a Christian man," Shayna stated.

"Most definitely! And he's not just a man in a Christian suit. He's a genuine godly man who overflows with integrity. He is more than even my wild imagination could imagine. And this is in just a short time. I am without any doubts, absolutely sure about him. He and Morgan own an architecture and design company. He owns his own home. Actually, you can sit my house inside his."

"Seriously!" Chantel cried, for confirmation.

"Yes."

"What about that rock on your finger?" Alisha inquired

"It's a symbol of our promise to give our relationship a genuine effort to flourish."

"And he bought you that?" Chantel asked.

"Girl, yeah. Stop acting dumb," Shayna stated. "You know Liah wouldn't go and buy herself a promise ring."

"I know that, Shayna. I'm just tripping. I'm stunned, girl. This is a lot to take in, in such a short time."

"It sure is," Alisha commented.

"Anyway, as I was saying, he and Marcus both are genuine, ordinary, down-to-earth, hardworking Christian men. Any woman would be blessed to be in their lives. But, most importantly, he loves children and has no problem with how many I have."

"He is a gem," Shayna commented.

"Shall I continue?"

"You shall," Alisha said giddily.

"He gets along well with the kids and they really like him."

"Even Jas?" Shayna asked.

"Jas is ready for us to get married already."

"He must be good," Chantel uttered. "Because Jas is quick to see a red zone."

"Girl, yeah, that boy is gifted," Alisha agreed. By the time the conversation was coming to an end, Marcus and Morgan walked back in.

"I'm sorry, sweetie." He said no solid foods right now, but maybe later this evening or tomorrow morning. Sooooo, I brought you yogurt."

"Wow ... yogurt, thanks Marcus, you're so kind," she said apathetically.

"Liah, honey, you have to follow doctor's order. He is looking out for your best interest," Marcus told her.

"Yep, he is certainly the man for you," Chantel told her. "I guess he told you. Huh?"

"I guess he did," Liah responded.

"He also said you need to stay off your feet and rest when you're released from the hospital."

"Now that's near impossible," Liah responded.

"I knew you were going to say that," he replied. "So, I have an idea."

"And that is?" Liah asked.

"You and the kids can stay at my house until you're better. I have a cook and a butler that will be at your beck and call. I will stay with Morgan while you all are there."

"Marcus, I can't let you do that."

"Honey, it's no problem. Tell her guys."

"She'll be there," they all practically harmonized.

"There!" he blurted, pleased. "So what do you say?"

"When are you all leaving?" she asked her harmonizing friends.

"Maybe a few days after you get out of the hospital," Chantel responded.

"Why don't you all stay at my house with Liah?" They all agreed with pleasure.

"Can you all at least stay until Saturday?" Liah asked.

"I don't have a problem with that," Chantel said.

"Neither do we," Alisha answered, for her and Shayna.

"Well, okay then, Marcus. I guess you have some house guests," Liah murmured. "But when I leave here, I need to go by my house to pack some clothes."

"Liah, why don't you let me take care of that," Marcus said, stepping in and handling things. "Now before you answer, let me just say this. I am not trying to take control of anything. I just want you to take the time to give yourself a full recovery."

"O…kay," she said hesitantly.

"I'm hungry. Are you all hungry?" Morgan asked randomly.

Everyone answered yes, but Liah. "Would you mind checking on my children before you get something to eat?"

"That was my next question," Morgan said. "We'll go by and get the kids and take them with us. Marcus, I know you want to stay here, so would you like me to bring you something back?"

"Yes, bring him yogurt," Liah said smiling.

"I'll eat some yogurt. Just get me some food to go along with it," he laughed.

"Haha, so funny," Liah said shaking her head.

"Time to go ladies," Morgan bellowed, "before a new conversation starts."

"Finally, I have you all to myself."

"Yes, you do. But I'm afraid I'm not going to be much company. I feel as if I've been running a marathon." He kissed her on the cheek and cuddled up with her. They both fell asleep.

They slept until the nurse came in to check her vital signs. After the nurse left, Marcus confessed to Liah how he felt, when he was unable to reach her. "I felt lost and helpless. For a moment, I didn't think that I would ever see you again. It took some sincere praying to get me through that moment." He paused briefly. "That's when I knew that I loved you. I'm not trying to change the pace that we're moving at. We should still just take things as they come and deal with it at that appropriate time. I just wanted to share that with you. And you don't have to say you love me back. Whenever you feel you're ready, I know you'll tell me. I just needed you to know that."

"Marcus," she whispered.

"No, you don't have to say anything. I am just so grateful that you are okay and I am here with you." He kissed her hand and held it close to him.

When they all walked back into the room, Marcus and Liah were gazing into each other's eyes. It was like watching a beautiful early-morning sunrise over a beautiful ocean.

"Alright, break it up," Morgan exclaimed, in his usual playful way. All of the kids huddled around Liah and Marcus. They were glad to see both of them. Marcus got off the bed and Jason climbed into bed with Liah.

"Mom, how long are you here for?" Jessica asked.

"I think a few more days."

"Are we going to stay here, too, Mom?" Jason asked.

"No, honey. You don't want to stay here anyway. The food is not so good. Do you all want to stay with Jen and Tim?"

"We like staying with Auntie Jen and Uncle Tim, Mom, but we want to stay close to you," Jacqlyne stated.

"But if you stay here you won't have a ride to school."

"Why don't you have the limo pick them up and drop them off?" Morgan suggested to Marcus.

"Good idea, Morgan,"

"Liah, what do you think about that?" Marcus asked.

"Mom, that would be cool," Jas shouted.

"The driver has an excellent driving record," Morgan told her, "with a spotless criminal background."

"Yeah, he's been with us for many years," Marcus added.

"Okay, okay, that would be fine," Liah agreed. "By the way, guys, Marcus has invited us to stay at his house until mommy is better. He will be staying at Morgan's while we're there," she quickly added.

"Really?" Jessica replied.

"Hmm, that's mighty nice of you, Mr. Marcus," Jacqlyne mumbled with a Mona Lisa smiled.

"Mom, I think it's a great idea. It would kinda be like taking a vacation," Jessica smiled. "But only if you have a pool."

"I do," Marcus responded. "And I have a big game room, too."

"Oh, yeah, we are there. Right, Mom?"

"Yes, Jessica Mathis."

"Am I in trouble or something? Cause you always call me Jessica Mathis when I'm in trouble."

"No, sweetie, you're not in trouble."

"Now that we have all that settled," Chantel uttered. "Where's the mall?"

"We can show you," Morgan blurted quickly.

"Liah, can the kids go?" Chantel asked.

"Sure, I don't mind. But I don't have my purse with me, so they don't have any money."

"That's not a problem," Morgan answered delightfully. "We'll treat everyone to a shopping spree."

"Is that okay with you, Liah?" Morgan pouted.

"I suppose so," she said hesitantly. "Okay, have fun. I need to get some rest anyway."

"Marcus, are you going, man?" Morgan asked.

"Yeah, I'll catch up with you."

"Okay, Ms. Mathis, your answer was a bit hesitant," Marcus said, "sure you're okay with the shopping spree?"

"No, I don't mind. It will take their minds off me."

"Okay, try to get some rest and we'll see you later, baby." He gave her a smooch on the cheek. As he was about to walk out of the door, he looked back and said to her, "You know ... you look good for a bedridden woman." She just looked at him with those big brown eyes that he loved gazing into, and smiled, and then he walked out the door.

She finally had a moment to make some phone calls. First on her list was calling her job to let them know what was going on. She knew that Percy would be in his office doing paperwork. It was usually how he spent his Sunday afternoons. She told him what happened and she would probably need to take a leave for recovery. "I can assure you that my staff is well-trained and they will do well, even without me. If Louis needs any input on anything, I'm just a phone call away."

Percy was very understanding. He knew that the restaurant was the best in town because of Liah. So he wanted her at her best. He graciously told her to take all time she needed. Then he wished her a speedy recovery. "Will you have Louis and Tina to come by the hospital tomorrow? I have some things I need to go over with them."

"Yes, I sure will, Liah. You take care and get well soon."

"Thanks, Percy."

She decided to make her other phone calls later. She took a deep breath, sunk down under the covers, and cuddled with her pillow. As she lay there, thoughts of Marcus crept into her mind. She thought about how generous it was of him to invite all of them to stay at his house doing her recovery. She never imagined that she would end up meeting such a wonderful person. But she certainly considered it a blessing. For some reason unknown to her, she knew that she could trust him. And trust was something that didn't come easy for Liah. As admired as she was by many people, she had a small circle of people she trusted.

After she had finally fallen asleep, about an hour later the nurse came in to check her vitals. *They have really good timing*, Liah thought to herself. *I think they're watching a monitor, waiting until I fall asleep so they can come in and wake me up. It must be a nurse conspiracy.* Soon after the nurse left, she went back to sleep. She slept until the gang came back.

Jason could hardly wait to tell his mom about the trip to the mall. He tried to be as quiet as possible, being as excited as he was. In spite of their effort all of the whispering woke her anyway.

"Hi," she whispered. "You guys are back. Have you all been shopping all this time?"

"Oh, no, hon, we left the mall and went to church," Alisha replied.

"That's good. Where did you all go?"

"We took them to church with us," Marcus answered.

"Girl, we had a blessed time, too," Shayna avowed.

"Liah, how are you feeling?" Chantel asked.

"I feel much better. I got a lot of sleep while you all were gone. With the exceptions of those trained and devoted to disturbed tranquility."

"Nurses, huh," Chan snickered. "Yep, gotta love'm!"

Jason couldn't wait any longer. He climbed into bed with her and told her everything he had gotten. After he was done, the girls told her about their shopping spree. Chantel suggested they take everything back to the hotel.

"That would good. Thanks Chan. So what's in the bag?" Liah asked.

"Oh, this is for you," Marcus said.

"For me," she responded. "Thank you, Marcus." He bought her a heart-shaped pillow with "my love" embroidered on it. He also bought her a couple of plants. He knew how much she loved them. "Marcus, these are gorgeous and I like the pillow. Thank you so much." Morgan and the kids bought her cards and a pair of slippers. The others bought her some Danielle Steel and Barbara Taylor Bradford books, and Taste of Homes and bon appetit magazines. "Thank you all so much for everything. You all are very thoughtful. Morgan and Marcus, thank you all for the kids' shopping spree." They assured her that there was no need for thanks, because they had just as much fun as the kids. "Now what did you ladies get?"

"You name it and we got it, Shayna replied. "But we'll have to show you when you get sprung from here."

"I bet you bought a lot of shoes, Shayna."

"Jacqlyne bought more than I did. Girl, you know she's just like you, a shoe fanatic."

"Guys, Morgan and I are going to step out for a moment," Chantel whispered; as they were about to gracefully make an exit.

"So you're a shoe fanatic, huh, Liah? Marcus asked, curious."

"I'm pleading the fifth."

"And particular," Alisha added. "I mean, very particular."

"Whatever, I am not that bad."

"Yeah, right."

"But most importantly, Marcus," Shayna informed him, "she has the heart of a saint and a contagious spirit."

"Finally, someone has my back—alright my sister."

"Ah, you know we'll always have your back, girlfriend," Alisha said."

"Always Liah," Shayna confirmed.

"Guys, I know that," Liah replied giggling.

"You all seem really close? Like inseparable" Marcus inferred.

"Just like butter," Alisha responded."

"I can see that."

"Alisha," Liah, uttered. "Butter …." Everyone burst out laughing. "Anyway, girls, it's time to take Jas back to the hotel so he can take a shower. Are you all sure that you have everything you need for school tomorrow?"

"We're sure Mom," Jessica answered. They hugged her and said goodnight. "Make sure you all call me before you go to bed."

"We will, Mom," Jessica murmured.

"I love you all, babies." They told her they loved her, too. "I am so sorry I am stuck here. I will slow down and take better care of myself."

"Wishful thinking my friends, Shayna said. But the only thing that's slowing you down is death, and you will try to move around then."

They all looked at Liah with that quizzical expression on her face and then at Shayna, and then they burst out laughing, including Liah. "She got you Mom, said Jessica, because you know, the only thing slow about you were dating." Everyone screamed. They knew it was true, even Liah.

"Wow … you all are on a role. Okay mouth, Jas and Jacqlyne, leave, leave now. I am ill for God's sake. And now I am being emotionally abuse." In the effort of fake crying, she laughed out loud. "Man—that would have been good! But I couldn't hold it."

Marcus looked at her and said "you are crazy. She's crazy. I thought you were serious for a moment."

"Marcus, my dear," Alisha said, you have yet, a lot to learn."

"So true," Shayna agreed, "a lot."

"Okay, serious now, you guys need to go get ready for school tomorrow. I am so glad the hotel is adjacent to the hospital," Liah said. "It's very convenient."

"It sure is," Marcus agreed. "You don't even have to go outside of the hospital to get to it."

Morgan and Chantel walked back in. Chantel had a wide grin on her face.

"What's with that grin Chan?" Alisha inquired.

"What? I always grin."

"Yeah, but that's a different kind of grin, Chan," Liah avowed.

"Y'all, leave me alone."

"Okay, but it's only because I want to see the rest of Extreme Make-over," Liah told her.

"Yeah, I want to watch the rest, too," Chantel said, appreciating Liah's save.

"Uh huh, but I bet it's because you don't wanna tell us about that grin," Alisha asserted.

"You all don't give each other any slack," Marcus said.

"That's the way butter is, Marcus," Shayna told him. "No slack." They all watched the rest of Extreme Makeover together.

"Marcus, do you think you can do my backyard like that?" Liah asked.

"Oh, that is beautiful," Alisha commented. "But, Liah, your back-yard is beautiful, too. You don't need anything done to it."

"I agree with her, Liah," Marcus confirmed. "I honestly think yours look better."

"I really like that wrap-around bar," she said. "And check out the sauna."

"It's nice," Marcus agreed. "But you have a wrap-around bar to, honey."

"Okay, I give up."

"Hey, Marcus, remember, we need to work on the Austin project," Morgan reminded him, very aware that he didn't want to leave Liah.

"Right, we do need to get started on that." He stood up. "Well, la-dies, it was a pleasure meeting you all, as well as shopping with you. Are there any requests you all have for your stay at my house?" They all told him no, not at the moment. They thanked Morgan and Marcus for the shopping spree.

"You all are quite welcome," Morgan said. "It was indeed a pleasure meeting you all and hanging out with you. We must do it again."

"Yes, we must," Chantel replied.

"Ms. Harris, Morgan said. "I will see you tomorrow for lunch," he told her trying to be subtle.

Everyone looked at Chantel and Morgan and said, "Oooooh."

"That's why she was grinning like a Cheshire cat," Alisha noted.

"Come on, guys, leave her alone," Morgan told them. They all walked out so Marcus could say a proper goodnight to Liah. He knew he had to leave, but he didn't want to, especially after almost losing her. A few minutes later Morgan peeked in to tell Marcus to come on. He finally managed to detach himself from her and said goodnight.

~Chapter Nine~

They all hung out a while longer, after Marcus and Morgan left. "So what do you think about Morgan?" Chantel asked.

"I like him a lot," Shayna responded. "If I wasn't already married I'd date him. You know, well, if I met him first."

"Well, I think he's awesome," Alisha told her.

"You already know how I feel. He's a lot like Marcus," Liah told her. "But this is your decision Chan. He's really a great guy."

"I think I will. I certainly see potential," Chan said with a glowing smile.

"Well, alrighty then!" Liah responded, briskly.

"Good choice, Chan," Alisha said.

"I am so happy for you guys," Shayna sang. "I think you both made really good choices."

"Well thank you, mom, for your approval, Chantel uttered, in her usual silly playful way. "Now Liah, seriously, I think Marcus is definitely the one for you. He is all that you said he is and probably more. Those type of men are few in numbers and already taken," Chantel conveyed.

"Did you all see how Marcus was with Jas at the mall?" Shayna asked.

"Yeah, they have that father-and-son relationship already," replied Alisha. "It was as if he knew exactly what Liah would say when Jas asked for something he shouldn't have."

"Liah, does he have any children?" Chantel inquired.

"No, Marcus and Morgan were both born sterile."

"In a way that's kind of sad, because I think the both of them will make great dads," Alisha expressed.

"Yeah, it is," Shayna agreed. "But God knew what he was doing. Those are special men. The Lord knew there would be some fatherless children who needed them."

"That is so true," Liah replied. "And mine are some of those children."

"Mine might as well be, too, Liah," Chantel responded.

"Then we all will bless each other through God's bountiful blessings," Liah stated, sincerely.

"Now, Liah, I have to ask this question." Alisha said. "And I'm only asking you this because I know you."

"Okay, go for it."

"Did you have the man investigated?"

"Girl, you know I did," she answered innocently.

"I knew it."

"I'm glad he knows I'm not a gold digger because since I'm camping at his house, he might have thought that."

"Liah, we all know you run from men with money," Chantel blurted.

"Now you don't even have to go there," Liah said laughing, and the others joined in. "Actually, I wouldn't let the investigator tell me anything that was too personal or would interfere with my decision to date him. So I didn't know about his successful business or his mansion until last week. I did know he didn't have a criminal background and he was debt free. Those two things say a lot about a man these days. I'm depending on God's blessed wisdom to do the rest, and, of course, Jas."

"Now that's funny," Chantel blurted, laughing. "True, but funny, because we all know little Jas is gifted."

"However," Liah went on to say, "I found out from one of my friends and co-worker. Not about the house, but the business and wealth. She reads "Business Tycoons" magazine. By then, I had already fallen for him. Believe it or not, I fell for him when I first met him."

"Now that's rare for you, Liah," Shayna responded. "But then again, Marcus is an exceptional man."

"Yes, he is," Liah agreed. "And the exception was made." They all double up. "Did I tell y'all that Marcus also had me investigated?"

"Did he really?" Alisha asked.

"Yep."

"Were you offended?" Chantel asked.

"Oh no—not at all. If I did, that would make me a hypocrite, because I did the same thing. Considering the way people are these days, I would say if you can afford it, do it. My most important concern was the criminal background. I have children, so I needed help making that decision: Common sense, Godly direction, and much observation. You know, I have two things to thank Brannon for—my children and the

150

Brannon Mathis lesson. Now, he wasn't a bad person. He just never grew up."

"So, Liah, these guys are in their forties? Have they ever been married?" Alisha inquired.

"Yes, they both have. "Marcus' wife couldn't accept the fact that he couldn't produce children, even though she knew before she married him. So she cheated on him and got pregnant. I'm not sure about Morgan's situation. If memory serves, I believe Marcus said something similar happened to him or maybe it was that Morgan's wife found out that her marriage to her first husband was never resolved. I think the divorce papers weren't filed. I don't know, let Morgan explain. As a result, Marcus went in dating seclusion and Morgan just dated. Marcus said he just came to a halt and stopped dating. So, Chan, you will be a welcome change for Morgan, unlike those who were only out for his wealth."

"Hey, remember those cheapos who took you all out?" Shayna reminded Liah and Chantel.

"Are you talking about the guy Chan got all dressed up for and he took her to McDonalds?" Alisha questioned.

"Yeah, that's him."

"That was hilarious. She got all dressed up in her black and gold outfit. She thought she was going to some place extravagant." She burst out laughing. "And she went to McDonalds! I'm sorry Chan, but that still cracks me up." They all started laughing, even Chantel.

"Liah, I know you're not laughing," Chantel blurted. "You got all dressed up just to go to Church's Chicken and he used a dollar and ninety-nine cent coupon." They really laughed at that memory.

"I know right. Chan, at least your meal, cost more than mine."

"I can't believe we went out with those cheapos."

"I think my date lasted a good thirty minutes," Liah said. But I ate that chicken, because I was hungry like a stray dog on a fresh bone."

"Oh, my gosh, Liah, that is too funny. Girl, you still crack us up," Alisha said.

After Chantel finished laughing, she said "My date was thirty-seven minutes—to be exact. And that was only because it was a long line at McDonalds' drive thru. And twenty-three of those minutes were in the line."

"Yep, I remember," Liah said. "The other fourteen minutes were in the car, transition and getting out of the car. I think you came in with a wrinkled McDonald's bag."

"Girl, you are so right, Shayna said. She was boiling— mad as an angry cat."

"And it was raining that night. Her hair looked like a wet cat," Alisha threw in. They cried laughing.

Okay, I have to stop this laughing," Liah told them. "But you know, Chan?"

"What?"

"Now that I think of it, maybe they weren't cheap. Maybe they were just broke," Liah conveyed. They laughed out loud again. They were laughing when the nurse came.

"Okay, I hate to break up all of this fun, but visiting hours are over and I need to check vital signs."

"Thanks you all for hanging out with me."

ᏇᎧ

Tuesday morning, Liah received a beautiful plant and a fruit basket from Lillie and Morgan. She called them to thank them and also reschedule her luncheon for the following Wednesday. She had a pretty busy day. In addition to her regular visitors, her co-workers came by.

Wednesday, she was released from the hospital with instructions to follow for the next few weeks. The doctor wanted her to take a month off for some rest and relaxation. He told her that she needed to give her body time to recuperate completely. Marcus sent the limo to pick up Liah and her friends from the hospital. He wanted to come himself, but he got stuck in a meeting. Nevertheless, all went well. Marcus had given Addie and Jeffrey specific instructions.

~Chapter Ten~

Alisha, Shayna and Chantel were all blown away when the limo drove through the gate. "Liah, this is a mansion," Chantel raved.

"I know that, Chan. I told you that."

"No, you didn't. Well, maybe you did. I don't know."

Jeffrey met them at the door. "Good to see you again, Ms. Liah."

"It's good to see you, too, Jeffrey."

"How are you feeling?" he asked.

"I'm much better, Jeffrey. Thanks for asking."

"You're welcome, dear. And who, may I ask, are these beautiful ladies?"

"These are my friends, Alisha, Chantel and Shayna."

"Well I am pleased to make your acquaintance, ladies. Please allow me to show you to your rooms. Ms. Liah and Ms. Harris are in the downstairs guest rooms as Mr. Michaels requested, especially for Ms. Liah. He didn't want you climbing the stairs. The elevator is out of order at the moment."

"Now, Jeffrey, if you expect us to have a good relationship, we're going to have to be on a first-name basis," Liah insisted. "Is that cool with you?"

"It is indeed, cool with me, Liah," he said smiling. She snickered. He was glad to have her there. He liked her the very first time he met her. He knew he would like her friends as well. He especially took well to Chantel. They all settled into their rooms. Jeffrey knocked on Liah's door shortly afterwards.

"Come in. Oh, hi, Jeffrey. What's going on?"

"What would you all like for lunch?"

"Let me call and ask the others. Can I get back with you?"

"That would be fine, dear."

They decided to go with chunky chicken salad sandwiches and Caesar salad. "What about dessert?" Chantel asked?

"How about a brownie surprise?" Liah replied.

"Is that with the ice cream, brownie and topped with bananas, straw-berries and cool whip, and roasted pecans?" Chantel eyes widened.

"Yes, Chantel Harris," Liah mumbled.

"I don't know if I like the way you said that. But oh, yeah, bring it on," she responded.

"Girl hush. You are a junky."

"Me too," Shayna said.

"Wait, add me there," Alisha screamed. My name is Alisha, and I am junky." Chan, Shayna and Liah laughed at her.

"Crazy, crazy. Okay junkies, we might as well make our dinner menu," Liah suggested. I can order something from work if you all like."

"Look at you," Shayna uttered, "handling your business."

"Girl, it's food. It's my specialty."

"Liah, you know we're not choosy," Alisha told her.

"I wonder if the cook would be offended," Liah said out loud. "I'll be right back guys ... I need to ask Jeffrey something." Just as she was opening the door, Jeffrey was at the door. He almost knocked on her face.

"Oh dear, Liah. I'm so sorry."

"No problem, Jeffrey. I have a question. Would the cook be offended if I ordered dinner from work?"

"Certainly not, dear. As a matter of fact, she would welcome any input you would like to share with her."

"Really?"

"Scouts honor," he replied.

"Awesome. Well here's our lunch menu. And here is the dinner menu."

"What are we having for dinner?" he asked.

"We're having grilled amberjack with white dill weed sauce, twice-baked potato, strawberry and spinach salad, and peach cobbler for dessert. Would you please tell her if she has any questions or needs any help, don't hesitate to ask?"

They all piled up in Liah's bed and watched a movie until Jeffrey came in with their lunch. They thanked him and continued watching the movie while they ate. Marcus and Morgan came in just as Jeffrey was bringing in dessert. "Yea, we showed up just in time," Morgan said.

"Shall I bring you all some dessert, too?" Jeffrey asked.

"Yes, Jeffrey, please. That would be great," Marcus answered. "Thanks. Are you ladies making yourselves comfortable?"

"Yes, we are, and thanks for having us here," Liah answered.

"Is Jeffrey treating you all well?" he asked, already knowing the answer.

"Yes, he is. He's a sweetheart," Liah replied. They all sang Jeffrey's praises. Jeffrey went back into the kitchen and got Addie to fix Marcus and Morgan dessert.

"Wow, these brownies are delicious," Chantel mumbled.

"That's not fair. You all are supposed to wait until we get our dessert," Morgan told them.

"Oh, stop whining, Morgan," Marcus told him. "Let them enjoy their dessert."

"Good, here's Jeffrey with our dessert," Morgan exclaimed. "Thanks, Jeffrey, you're the best."

"You're quite welcome, sir".

"Cut the sir out, Jeffrey," Morgan told him. "I'm too young for that."

"Jeffrey, just call him Morgan and be done with it," Marcus told him. You all always go round and round.

"I do call him Morgan sometime. Maybe if he came around more, I could remember it"

"Don't worry, Jeffrey, I'll be happy to remind you," Liah volunteered.

"Thank you, Liah. I appreciate that. It's good to have you here."

"Likewise, Jeffrey."

"I'll see you all at dinner," Jeffrey.

"What are we having for dinner?" Morgan inquired, inviting himself.

"We!" Marcus mimicked. "What do you mean, we? Who invited you?"

"I invited myself."

"Well, I guess you're coming to dinner. So what are we having Chef? Marcus asked. Liah told them what was on the menu, all the way down to the dessert, and they couldn't have been more pleased. "Sounds like a chef's special!" Marcus replied.

"It is," Alisha responded.

"Marcus, who is picking Jas up from school?" Liah asked.

"The driver is going to pick him up and drop him off and then pick up the girls."

"Thank you, honey. I really appreciate everything you're doing."

"I know you do, sweetie. So stop thanking me," he said kindly but wittily.

"It makes him uncomfortable," Morgan told her. "So what do you all have planned for tonight?"

"We're just going to hang out, maybe watch movies," Shayna responded. "

"Have you ladies had a tour of the house yet?" Marcus asked.

"No, not yet," Chantel answered.

"I'll take them," Morgan volunteered.

"Thanks, man. I'll stay here with Liah."

"I can walk, Liah cried."

"Liah, walking around is not bed rest."

"Liah, stop being hard headed. A few more days is not long", Shayna scolded.

"Okay, Mom."

"She's right, baby. You need to take it easy," Marcus told her. He sat beside her and put his arms around her. She gave them her word that she would follow doctor's order.

"Come on troops," Morgan uttered, humorously.

"Oh, I forgot to call Louis. Will you pass me the phone, please?" When she called, Tina answered the phone. She talked to Tina for a moment, then Mel and, at last, Louis. After she hung up, Marcus said to her,

"You better hope my mom and dad don't come over here while that carrot cake is here."

"Why?"

"They are carrot cake fanatics. When you feel up to it, I want you to meet them and my little sister. They're going to love you."

"I would like that, very much. I think. I hope they can accept how many children I have.'

"I can promise you that they will. They love children and they've always wanted grandchildren."

"What about your sister?"

"Lecxa is a sweetheart, but no babies.'

"Okay. So, Marcus, do you get lonely in this big house?"

"Yes, a lot. That's why I work a lot. But if you and the kids visit me often I won't be lonely."

"Don't be trying to use that as an excuse to get me over here."

"I'm not," he said laughing.

"Anyway, Marcus Michaels, I have the best reason for frequent visits."

"What's that?"

"You," she whispered.

"Good answer."

"Marcus," Chantel called out. "You have an awesome house. Liah, I bet I know which room you like."

"Well, that's not hard," she responded. Everyone yelled, "The kitchen."

"It is gorgeous?" Liah responded. Liah looked at her watch and said, "Oh, Jas should be here in a moment."

"And there he is," Morgan announced.

"Mom, you're home, I mean you're here. Mom, the limo is awesome," Jas said excitedly. "It's a stretched Hummer. Oh, hi everybody," he said politely. They all laughed at him. He was on a roll. He turned to Marcus and thanked him for letting them stay at his house. "It's really cool and huge," he said.

"How was school today, Jas?" Liah asked. He told her all about his exciting day at school. After he finished telling her about his day, he wanted to know what the doctor told her. He feared that she would get sick again. She assured him that she was much better, and she would be back to her old self in no time. "Sweetie, are you hungry?" she asked him.

"Yes, ma'am,"

"Come on, champ, I'll take you," Marcus volunteered. "Do you want to see the game room, too?"

"Yes, sir," he replied, animatedly. After Marcus and Jason left, Morgan and Chantel went out on the patio. Alisha noticed Liah was looking a bit tired, so she and Shayna left, so she could rest before Jas and Marcus came back. Liah had planned on just lying down for a moment to rest. However, she fell asleep. After all, it was her first day out of the hospital and she hadn't taken any time to rest.

When Marcus and Jason came back to her room, she was still asleep so they went back to the game room. The girls had made it home by the time she had awakened. She went in the game room and found everyone hanging out there.

"Well, sleeping beauty has awakened," Marcus stated. The girls were glad to see her, especially out of the hospital.

"Hi, girls, how was your day at school?"

"It was good," they both replied. They were in the middle of finishing up their game. So a brief answer had to suffice.

160

"Why did you all let me sleep so long?"

"Because, Liah, if you slept that long, you must have needed the rest," Alisha responded.

"I know, Lisha, but don't start." She didn't like people fussing over her.

"Honey, were you okay walking up the stairs by yourself?" Marcus asked with frown, grateful that she didn't fall from being too weak.

"I'm fine, Marcus," she murmured. "Thank you for asking. Besides, Jeffrey made sure I didn't fall down the stairs."

"Good for Jeffrey," he replied.

"Jas, did you do your homework?" she asked.

"Yes, Mom, Mr. Marcus helped me."

"Really! Thank you Mr. Marcus."

"You're welcome, Ms. Liah."

"Does anyone know if the order from A'Palace has arrived?"

Jeffrey had just walked in to tell her it had just arrived. "It just arrived a few minutes ago, dear," he told her. "And dinner will be served in about fifteen minutes."

"Thanks, Jeffrey. Will you tell Addie that we'll be right down?"

"Come on, Jas. Let's go wash up," Liah told him.

They ate in the formal dining room. Marcus didn't usually have dinner parties at his house, so Addie wasn't used to serving that many guests. Jeffrey was kind enough to help her serve. Jeffrey and Addie worked quite well together. I guess you could say they had each other's back.

"Marcus."

"Yes, Liah."

"Do you ever invite Addie and Jeffrey to sit down and eat dinner with you?"

"No. I hardly ever eat dinner at a decent time. So I've really never giving it any consideration. But now that you've mentioned it, I rather like the idea. They are just like family." When Jeffrey came back in the dining room, Marcus said to him, "Jeffrey, why don't you pull up a chair and come have dinner with us?"

Jeffrey was somewhat surprised. He and Marcus talked often, and had even shared pizza and popcorn. But they'd never actually sat down at the table together to have dinner. Jeffrey thanked him, and told him that he had already offered to help Addie in the kitchen and help with serving.

"Maybe another time, though."

"Anytime, Jeffrey," Marcus said kindly. He looked at Liah and said, "Thank you. You're good for me, you know."

"What kind of fish did you say this was, Liah?" Morgan asked.

"Amberjack."

"This is good," he replied. They all agreed that it was good.

"What's for dessert?" Morgan asked. They all laughed at him.

"What?" Morgan asked. "I am not a shame to admit that I am not used to eating this good and healthy," he openly stated. "So I am taking full advantage of it now."

"I told you we're having carrot cake and peach cobbler," Liah said.

"Oh yeah, right! If my mom and dad came by, they would want to take that cake home."

"Marcus said the same thing."

"I really like the strawberry and spinach salad," Shayna commented.

"I do to," Chan agreed. "At first I couldn't put the strawberry and spinach together, but they really blended well together."

"Why, thank you, Chantel. They blend well with walnuts too," Liah told her.

"Well, we'll have to try that the next time."

They all continued eating and talking like one big happy family. After dinner, they all watched a movie together in the family room. Liah observed the whole evening. She was pleased how the evening turned out. *I couldn't have planned it better myself*, she thought. It was a memorable evening for all of them.

Chantel volunteered to tuck Jason in bed after the movie was over. The girls said goodnight and they went to their rooms. So did Alisha and Shayna. "Well, it looks like it's just the three of us," Morgan said.

"No, it's just the one of you, Morgan," Marcus responded. "We're going out on the terrace." They told Morgan goodnight.

"So how are you feeling, babe?" Marcus asked her again.

"Do you realize you call me 'babe' often?

"Yes, it sort of flows. And it feels right. Now, how are you feeling?"

"I'm okay."

"Good. I'm not going to stay too long. I know you need your rest."

"Marcus."

"Yes."

"You don't expect me to stay through my complete recovery, do you?"

"You can stay as long as you want and need to stay."

"I do hope you will give it at least a week or two."

"I don't like the idea of putting you out of your house."

"Honey, it is no problem. Believe me." She leaned over on his arm. For a brief moment neither of them said a word. They sat there admiring the uniqueness of the stars. Suddenly Liah said to him, "I feel as if I am in a dream."

He took her hand and placed the palm of it on his face. Then he said to her, "This is real; I am real; and we are real, baby. But if you're dreaming, so am I, and I never want to stop."

"Look, there's a falling star," she exclaimed.

"Where? Oh, there it is. I see it. It is such a beautiful moonlight tonight." He looked at her and said, "You are so beautiful." She looked at him shyly and smiled. "Are you shy?" he asked.

"What do think?"

"No," he replied.

"Actually, I am sometimes."

"I think you just have a problem accepting compliments."

"Yeah, I'm pretty sure I do."

"Why do you think that is so?"

"I think I only have a problem when the compliments come from non-relative males. And probably the reason for that is guys seemed to be drawn to me for my looks rather than my brain. I had a problem with that in school, and so when guys complimented me on how I look, I wasn't that impressed. In fact, it was a bit of a turn off. My ex-husband used to compliment me quite often while we were dating. And after we were married, the compliments began to fade unless we were around his friends or coworkers. He sometimes made me feel like a showgirl."

"Sweetheart, that was then and this is now. You are indeed a beautiful woman. And any man, who can see can't help but notice. I think a blind man can see what I saw in you when I first met you. The inner beauty complements the outer beauty. Let me tell you a story about my first wife. She was a beautiful woman with absolutely no inner beauty. It was the worst decision I've ever made. She used that beauty to manipulate and use people. She didn't care who she hurt, as long as she got what she wanted."

"How long ...? Never mind. Continue."

"In a way, I'm glad there weren't any children involved. I was able to make a clean break."

"Our children, at least for me, were the best things that came out of my marriage to Brannon. It was tough on them at first, but one day at a time, they were able to get past the fact that their dad walked out on us. Jas never knew his father, so he didn't have to bear that pain. However, he was cheated before he was born, so he bears a different kind of pain. Brannon didn't believe Jason was his and he didn't care to stick around long enough to get verification."

"Why didn't he believe?"

"He had a vasectomy—which is said to be 99.9 percent effective. When I told him I was pregnant, he just lost it. He said even if the baby was his, he didn't want to know. To make a long story short, he left without saying goodbye to his children. My children have a sister they've never seen before." Marcus' eyes widened.

"Seriously," he asked, totally shocked.

"Yes, she's not much older than Jas.

"Wow, Liah. I am so sorry you and the kids had to endure such un-necessary hardship. So has he ever ...?" She broke in. She knew what he was about to ask her.

"No, he's never seen Jas before."

"That is so unfair to him, and you. What do you think about me spending time with Jas?"

"Why? Look Marcus, I didn't say that because I want your sorrow."

"Now, Liah, you know that's not why I said that. It's so many children who are fatherless, because of men like Brannon. And yet there are so many men without children who want to be fathers. If each one of us can save just one fatherless child, so many children would have dads."

"I understand where you're coming from. Jas craves for a dad. I don't mind you spending time with him. But I'm not sure I'm ready to risk him getting too attached to you when we're not entirely sure where we're going. We're in a really good place right now. And I believe that the both of us know where we want this relationship to go, but the truth is we don't really know. We are moving faster than both of us realize. Look where we are right now. We are in your home. I am staying in your home. Don't get me wrong, I am liking the speed, and I am committed to seeing where it will lead. I just don't want Jas caught in something that's not definite. So I encourage you to get to know the kids. But you can't see Jas as this fatherless little boy that you want to reach out to and smother with fatherly love. I appreciate how you feel, however, your relationship with Jas has to move at a slower pace until you and I know where we're going."

"You're right, and I understand what you're saying. I just know how it feels as a boy, growing up with a dad. So I couldn't imagine my life any other way."

"You can spend time with him while we're here. Then let's just go from there."

"Sounds fair. Liah, I promise you I won't let him down."

"Marcus, I really believe you mean that. But let's just see what happens. You have to understand that I've worked endlessly to get my children to where they are now. Nonetheless, I do understand that when I allow someone to come into my life, I'm allowing the same for my children as well. But, with them, I have to use caution."

He took her into his arms and told her that he just wanted the best for all of them. He went on to say, "I have the utmost respect for you. I don't know what all you've gone through to get to where you are now. I can only imagine how tough it was with six children. You could probably write an inspirational book and make it a best seller."

"Hum, now there's a thought."

"How about a subject change?"

"Okay."

What are your thoughts on premarital sex?" he boldly asked. She was astonished that he asked that question. "Maybe I should give you mine first."

"Sure," she replied. "I'm okay with that. You and I both probably feel the same way"

"Probably," he answered. "If so, then that will make dating you even easier."

She looked at him and said, "And your answer is?"

"It's simple. It's wrong because God said it is."

"Yep," she replied. "God said it in 1st Corinthians 6:18, Ephesians 5:3, and 1 Thessalonians 4:3 to name a few."

"Good, we are on the same page, then. This is the first time I've dated someone who respected God's teaching on premarital sex. Most females thought I was gay." She giggled. "I'm serious. Anyway, it might be challenging with us spending so much time together and the attraction. Now I will admit that I have wanted to take you in my arms and kiss you passionately. But that's just my fleshly man's desire. My spiritual man is striving to please God, and that's where I find my strength. So I pray. And it really helps."

Is this man real? What planet did he drop from? Liah had practically stopped breathing, from a sudden shock of spiritual integrity. No wonder she wanted to be pinched, so she could know she was still among the living. *He is a rare man.* Liah didn't know if she should comment on what he was saying or just continue to give him her undivided attention. Marcus laid it all on the table. He went on to say, "So whenever we're faced with that temptation, we just have to take ourselves from among that temptation. Liah, I don't want sex to be a part of our relationship before marriage. I want to enjoy and appreciate the beauty of that blessing without anything being between us, like sin. I just needed that to be up front."

"I am with one hundred percent. I feel the same way. Intercourse is sacred. It is designed for husband and wife, not dating couples. So, since we're both striving for that perfection, we should have no problem resisting or finding a way out." They agreed that if and when the passion started to heat up, they would separate. This talk perhaps took their relationship to another level. Both of them had a new-found respect for one another. They just sat there together—quietly. Moments later, they said goodnight.

Morgan and Chantel walked through the door as they were walking into the foyer. "Where have you all been?" Liah asked, curiously.

"Morgan showed me his house."

"Uh huh," Liah responded.

"Sweetie, I'm going to go," Marcus told her. "You sleep well." He told Chantel goodnight and told Morgan he would see him at home.

"Goodnight, Marcus." He walked out, quickly.

"Yeah, I'm going to say goodnight too," Morgan said. "I'll see you tomorrow beautiful lady," he said to Chantel and then told Liah goodnight.

~Chapter Eleven~

"Okay, Chantel, give it up. What's the story with you and Morgan?"

"We're just getting to know each other. We're going to see how a long-distance relationship is going to work out and just take one step at a time. And guess what?"

"What, Chan?"

"I had planned on telling you when I got here. But of course, you being in the hospital and all pushed it to the back of my mind."

"Okay, Chan, get to the point."

"I got two job offers here."

"For real, Chan?"

"Yes."

"Well, are you going to accept?"

"I don't know."

"What do you mean you don't know?"

"Well, I'll have to move in two months."

"Is it a good job offer, Chantel?"

"Yes, one is at the same hospital you were in."

"Well, now, there you have it, and you'll be close to me. And, you won't have to have a long-distance relationship." She thought she would throw that in as an incentive. "Of course you can't make your decision based on Morgan. But he is a good incentive," Liah said laughing. "Anyway, up-rooting your family is a serious step. I'm babbling, aren't I?"

"Yes, hon," Chantel said, giggling. "I'm going to give it some more thought. I've prayed about it. But I really think it will be a good move. Of course I need to talk it over with the kids."

"Did you mention it to Morgan?"

"Girl, no."

"Good call. He'll be worse than me. Well, on that note, I need to make some phone calls before I go to bed. So good night, dear."

"Good night, hon! I need to call my children, anyway."

Thirty minutes or so later all of the adults in the house seemed to be in the mood for a late night snack. Coincidently, they all arrived in the kitchen only a few minutes apart. Jeffrey and Addie were the first to arrive.

"Well hello dear," Jeffrey smiled. "I thought you had gone to bed."

"I wanted tea, and on my way to the kitchen I decided that I might as well have a slice of carrot cake."

"Same here," Alisha and Shayna exclaimed. They all looked around and saw Alisha and Shayna walking in. Shortly afterward, Chantel walked in. The whole gang sat at the bar, ate carrot cake, and talked. Liah's cell phone rang. It was Marcus.

"Hi, Marcus," she said.

"Hi. Why are you so chipper?"

"We're all sitting at the bar talking and eating carrot cake."

171

"The kids, too?" he asked.

"No, they're in bed. It's just us grownups. You wouldn't believe that we all arrived in the kitchen only minutes apart."

"No kidding?" he replied.

"No! For real."

He chuckled. "Well, I'm not going to keep you. I just wanted to hear your voice and say goodnight. Don't stay up too late. Remember, you're supposed to be recuperating."

"I know, and I won't be up much longer." He told her goodnight and to sleep well, and she wished him the same.

"Liah, didn't he just leave a short while ago?" Alisha asked. "What are you doing, keeping watch?" Liah inquired.

"No," she replied politely. "I just said that to give me an opening to say something else."

"What's the name of that song?" Alisha asked. "Something about when he hang up, he calls right back."

"You got it bad," Jeffrey replied.

"Huh," Addie chuckled. "Who would have thought you would have known what she was talking about, Jeffrey," she stated as she continued to chuckle. They were all surprised and laughed.

"Hey, I listen to the radio," he said in his defense.

"Well, he got it bad for you, Liah," Shayna added.

"She's right," Jeffrey confirmed. "He never invites any females over and certainly not to stay at his house. I would say you're definitely an exception dear."

"She's Ms. Liah."

"Addie, please call me Liah."

"Well, Liah, I'm glad you're here," she told her. "You all have been here for one day and it has already given life to this house."

"That's a very kind thing to say, Addie." She thanked her and said goodnight to everyone.

~Chapter Twelve~

On Friday, Liah, Marcus, and Morgan had planned a farewell night for Liah's friends. Liah and Addie planned to bake cookies. Jeffrey was Liah's assistant, since Addie agreed to let her help, if she promised that she would sit down. They baked chocolate chip, banana peanut butter, and James' doodle cookies. James' doodles were a gourmet cookie recipe that Liah created for one of her favorite clients when she was a salesman. The main ingredient in James' doodle cookies is oatmeal. Liah liked to refer to them as a special kind of oatmeal cookie. The three of them made a great team.

Liah had also planned a surprise fashion show for Jacqlyne on the patio so she could choose her prom dress. She decided to throw in some surprise dresses for Jessica, Addie, and the others as well. Alisha, Chantel, and Shayna thought the whole night was planned for Jacqlyne. They were all surprised, especially about the fashion show. Finally Jacqlyne chose two dresses she couldn't part with, after looking several others. Addie, Alisha, Chantel and Shayna were ecstatic about the dresses they chose. After the fashion show, they all gathered around the Chinese- style table and enjoyed a Chinese feast. Jeffrey and Addie were invited as well.

Liah made sure of that. At the end of the festive night, they all camped out on the floor in the family room in sleeping bags. They enjoyed delicious cookies, played Uno, and watched movies until they fell asleep.

Saturday morning, the limo picked up Alisha, Shayna, and Chantel to take them to the airport. Saturday seemed to have moved at a super speed. Liah's best friends hadn't been gone long, but she missed them. Jen picked the kids up for a play-date with her kids. Marcus and Liah practically forced Jeffrey and Addie to take a day off. However, they didn't stay away too long.

Liah and Marcus sat on the terrace for hours talking and enjoying each other's company. They were so engulfed by each other they didn't realize that they had talked through lunch. They went in the kitchen and made lunch together.

Marcus had an interesting, yet unexpected idea. He wanted him and Liah to record an answering machine message together. Liah thought he was kidding. "I'm not kidding," he said to her. She reluctantly agreed. He wrote a quick script. "Okay, this is what it's going to say. 'Hi, you've reached Marcus. I can't take your call at the moment' Then you say 'Come on, Marcus, what are you doing?' And I will come back in and say 'And that's Liah. You can leave a message for me if you like or perhaps Liah and your call will be returned as promptly as possible.' Then we both will say 'have a wonderful and blessed day.'"

"Marcus, you're insane."

"Alright, that's a wrap," Jeffrey exclaimed, totally surprising them.

"Jeffrey, how long have you been standing here?" Liah wondered.

"Oh, just long enough to hear the new voice message. Don't mind me, I like it." Marcus and Liah looked at each other and laughed.

"You don't think it's too much, Jeffrey?" Marcus asked.

"Not at all," he replied smiling as he left the room, "not at all."

"I think it's insane."

"Maybe it is a bit over the top. But that's okay."

"Well, my work here is done," Liah said. "I think I'm going to take a nap before the kids get back. They want to go swimming later."

"That's sounds like a good idea," Marcus. "We might as well top the evening off by having a small cookout," he suggested.

"Yeah, sounds great. Let's do it."

Liah went to her room to take a nap. Marcus worked on some blue-prints in his office. Liah slept until Alisha and Shayna called to let her know that they had arrived safely. Chantel called shortly afterward. "So what have you all been doing since we left?" Chantel asked. Liah told her that the kids were out, and she and Marcus had been hanging out together. She told her about the new voice mail recording and how insane she thought it was.

"Girl, that man already knows he's going to marry you."

"It's not that serious, Chan."

"Liah, get real! He rushed out of church when he heard you were in the hospital. Not only did he invite you to stay at his house during your recovery and including your friends, he moves out because he knew that was the only way he would get you to stay there. And of course, it was the Christian thing to do. Now you're on his voicemail. He's insane or he is one in a million. And insanity has been ruled out. I predict a proposal sometimes in the near future. Very near future!"

"Well, you're right about one thing. He is one in a million."

"I'm right about everything, and you know it. You're just being Liah.

You used to tell us all of the time, "you name it—you claim it—it becomes a part of you."

176

"I still believe that. I just don't want to jump ahead to the proposal."

"Now that's my Liah."

"So, Chantel Harris."

"Uh oh! Here it comes."

"What? I was just going to ask you if you had called Morgan."

"No, but I'm about to."

"Well, don't let me hold you. Call me later, Chan."

"I will, Mrs. Michaels."

"Cut it out, already! Talk later!"

Liah lay in bed for a few minutes longer. She got up when she heard the kids outside. Marcus was outside talking to Tim when she walked out there. She and Jen spent a few minutes talking. "Liah, I really like Marcus. I think you all are the perfect match for each other. Jas says he thinks he's the best. Girl, he found his daddy. You know he is gifted."

Liah couldn't help but laugh. "I tell you the truth. All of my friends are just alike. You all think the same."

"I guess that's why you chose us. Huh?"

"I guess."

"How long are you all staying?"

"I think, probably, until next week."

"Girl, I can't believe he temporarily gave up his house for you all. Now that's a true godly man. Those types of men seem few."

"Girl, that's because those men who are of age are already taken." They both chuckled.

"Come on, Jen, we have to go," Tim called out.

Liah thanked them for taking the kids out. Then Marcus and Liah walked them to their car.

"I really like them, Liah. And their children are quite well-mannered, like yours. We should all go out together sometime," Marcus suggested.

"They are good people. And I like that idea," Liah replied.

Jas ran up and asked if they could go swimming. "Yes, Jas. Why don't you guys go get suited up," she told them. She and Marcus waited for the kids in pool room.

"Mom, are you and Mr. Marcus getting in?" Jessica asked.

"I'm not. Are you, Marcus?"

"Ah ... sure. Let me get change." Liah watched while they splashed and played in the pool. She sat back and observed how good Marcus was with the kids. He was much better with them and more attentive than their father had ever been. He was never home long enough to even know the pool stilled existed, let alone play with them in it. As she thought to herself, she wondered if this could be the life she wanted for her children. She had beaten herself up for choosing Brannon Mathis as her husband and the father of her children. But she was far over that. She accepted her bad choice and was moving on with her life. She knew that the time to make that decision again could be approaching quicker than she realized. *No, no, I will not let myself be overtaken by fear* she scolded herself, on the verge of having a tinge of doubt creep into her mind. She quickly changed her thought process to more pleasant thoughts. She knew they were blessed to have Marcus in their lives. And they will continue to take one step at a time.

"Liah, Liah," Marcus was calling out to her. Suddenly, she heard him.

"What? Yes! I'm sorry Marcus. What did you say?" She totally zoned out for a moment.

"Honey, where were you?"

"I was thinking about something," she answered.

"Apparently deep in thought. Any thoughts you would like to share?"

"Not at the moment," she said with a sigh.

"Mom, we're done," Jacqlyne said.

"Okay, Jacq. You all can go take a shower before dinner."

"Mom, did you see Mr. Marcus' dive?" Jason asked. "He's incredible."

"I know, sweetie." The kids went in to take showers.

Marcus sat down beside Liah. "You know I'm falling in love with your children," he said randomly. Then, he got up and told her he would see her at dinner. It was good that he left because he wasn't expecting that, and wasn't sure how to respond.

After sitting there for a moment, the only thing she was compelled to say or think was "okay."

When she walked into the kitchen, Addie had already grilled the burgers and fixed Liah a plate, including a hefty salad.

"Wow, thanks Addie. You didn't have to do this"

"Honey, it was my pleasure. And you're welcome," she responded. "I didn't make any dessert because we have lots of cookies left over from last night.

"That's fine, Addie. After last night's cookie feast, we probably don't need any sweets anyway. However, since there are two more pieces of carrot cake left, I'm having one of those pieces. Feel free to have the other one, Addie."

"I will be delighted to, dear," Addie said mimicking Jeffrey. Liah laughed. She told her that was a good imitation of Jeffrey.

Marcus and the kids came in together. "What are we eating?" Jason asked.

"Cheese burgers," Addie responded.

"Can you handle a big cheeseburger, Jas?" Marcus asked.

"Yes, sir! I eat a big burger every time mom makes them."

"Alright, Champ. It's time to show me what you're working with," Marcus replied.

"Maybe after that, we can go hang out in the game room," Liah suggested.

"Good idea Mom, but I need to get started on homework," Jacqlyne said.

"Me too, Mom. I'm sorry."

"Honey, there's no need for an apology. Schoolwork is important. We can do it another time."

"Jess, it's still pretty early. We can spare about thirty minutes before we get started on the project," Jacqlyne said. They thanked Addie for dinner and then went upstairs. Marcus played pool with Jason and Liah, and the girls played driving games.

The girls played for thirty minutes as planned then went to work on their project. After Jason and Marcus finished playing pool, Liah read Jason a book and then tucked him in bed. "Goodnight, Mom, and you too, Mr. Marcus," he said. They said goodnight and then went back to the game room to watch a movie.

"So why were you in such a daze earlier?" Marcus asked Liah.

"Honestly."

"Yes, please."

"I was thinking about you and how good you were with my children."

"That's not a hard task. They're quite pleasant to be around. I commend you for your extraordinary work. I appreciate you for letting me spend time with them."

"Marcus, I appreciate you for spending time with them. You have made a big difference in a short time. For that, I am grateful."

"So have you all, in my life," he replied. "By the way, I have a question. The young men who were with your friends, were those your sons?"

"If you're talking about when you all were at the airport. Yes!"

"They are some handsome young men and well-mannered, too. I can't wait to be properly introduced to them."

"Thank you, Marcus. I think they will like you. And so will Jayde. They will be back in May."

"Your birthday is in May, isn't it?'

"Yes! It's May fifteenth."

"Hum! May is a good month."

"Why do you think so?"

"It's your birthday month." he said playing it down. "Sweetie, I had better be going. Come walk me down please." Before he left, he reached into his pocket and pulled out a set of keys. "Here, these are for you. I even got them personalized."

"Really? Thank you, that was very kind. I'll be sure to give them back to you before we leave."

"No, these are yours to keep. This is your home away from home. So you might as well have keys to the place. That's if you don't mind." Liah was rendered speechless momentarily. She staggered over a brief response.

"Ah ... sure ... okay," she slowly responded as she was thinking about her next answer, which was a simple thanks.

"Not a problem. Thank you. Will you tell the kids I will pick them up around nine o'clock in the morning?" He kissed her on the forehead and said goodnight. She went to her room and got ready for bed. She was still a bit astounded. He seemed to have been the only one who could render her speechless. *What's next?* she asked herself out loud. *I should call Chantel,* but then decided she wasn't really in the mood for conversation. She just wanted to lie down, cuddle with her body pillow, and recap her day.

~Chapter Thirteen~

Tuesday was the first day she had been out since being released from the hospital. The girls were having a rehearsal for a school play after school. She invited Marcus to come with them. All of the kids did an awesome job. The girls were naturals. The Carrington boys were also in the play. "Liah," Liz screamed. "How are you feeling? And should you be out so soon?"

"Hi, Liz. I am feeling much better. Thanks for asking. And, yes, I'm allowed to come out and play now." They both sighed. "I am still under doctor's care, of course."

"Okay, don't scare us like that again."

"I will try my best not to," Liah responded. "Liz, your boys are good. Are they interested in acting?"

"Honey, that's the highlight of their conversation. So are your girls. Girl, they are good enough to be on Broadway right now."

"I know, right! You should see Jayde. She's a choreographer. I think they all should be in show biz."

"Yes, ma'am! I agree." Liz and Liah fell so quickly into a conversation; she forgot to introduce Liz to Marcus. "Oh…my…gosh! Marcus, honey. I am so sorry. Liz Carrington, this is Marcus Michaels."

"Yes, it is. Hello, Mr. Michaels. I've heard a lot about you. I mean you're quite known around town, the architect legend."

"I hope that is good," he replied.

"Every word," Liz responded.

"Then it's a pleasure to meet you, Liz Carrington."

"Liz, thanks again for getting me home."

"No need for thanks, honey. We have to look after each other. So Liah," she whispered. "Is this what I think it is? If so, then it's about time." Marcus put his arm around Liah.

"Well, I guess it is," she said.

"Good choice, Liah. So, honey, when are you coming back to class? You're our best poetry writer."

"Probably next week."

"Looking forward to it. Liah, I got to go. I'll talk to you later. Marcus, it was good to meet you."

"Same here, Liz."

"Is she a party planner?" Marcus inquired.

"Yes, all type of events."

"Is she good?"

"The best. Here come the girls."

"How did we do?" Jacqlyne asked.

"You all did a great job," Liah told them.

"Girls, you all were awesome and so were the Carrington boys," Marcus complimented.

"Are you all done, girls?"

"Yes, Mom, we're ready," Jessica answered.

Marcus had the limo driver drop them off first. He called shortly after he got home. He wanted to find out what Liah was doing for lunch the next day. She told him that she had a luncheon engagement. He told her that he was having lunch with his parents, but wasn't sure what time.

"I guess I'll see you tomorrow evening," he told her. "I need to call them, so I will talk to you tomorrow, baby."

What a coincidence, she said to herself. *Marcus is having lunch with his parents the same day I'm having a luncheon with the people who have the same last name as his. Why aren't there any pictures around here of his parents?" she asked herself. "It is obvious that they're pretty close. Well, I am certainly going to find out tomorrow."*

Liah was elated about her lunch with the Michaels. She put on one of her business suits. Her business attire was fitting for almost any occasion. The limo showed up just as she was walking down the stairs. Marcus made sure that she didn't have to do any driving. Therefore, he gave her unlimited use of the limo. On her way to Jenos, she couldn't help but think about her first date with Marcus. After all, it was where their first date was supposed to take place, but went sour instead.

Liah was the type of woman who made an impression wherever she went. When she walked into the lounge, she was immediately recognized. "Ms. Mathis, hello, it is great to see you again, Mindy smiled. I hope that situation work out with you and the *right* Mr. Michaels?"

"Yes! Better than ever. Thanks for your concern. That's very kind of you."

"Okay, I know you don't really know me, but I am curious as how," Mindy stated.

"I would love to, but I am meeting some clients who just might be his parents. How about we do lunch soon and I will tell you all about it. You can come by my restaurant, and it's on the house."

"Oh my, really? Ms. Mathis, I am going to accept that invitation."

"Please, Mindy," call me Liah.

"Well, Liah, I am looking forward to it. Now who are your guests?"

"Michaels. Lillie and Morgan Michaels."

"Oh, yes, they told me they were expecting guests." *Guests*, she thought. *Hmm ... interesting.*

"Come on, Liah. Let me show you to your table."

"Thanks, Mindy."

"Ms. Mathis," Morgan Sr. complimented, "you look beautiful as always."

"Oh, she looks stunning," Lillie added. "How are you feeling, honey?"

"Actually, I am feeling much better. Thank you for asking."

"Now tell me where you got that outfit?" Lillie demanded. "I need to shop there."

"My twin aunts, Aurie and Ariel made it." Aurie and Ariel are her mom's younger sisters. "They are fashion designers. They design most of my business attires. Tell you what, let's get together so I can take some measurements, and I will have them tailor make you some outfits."

"Oh yes, darling. I accept, and you are an angel. Now come on, honey. I need to go to the ladies room."

"Morgan, will you excuse us, please?"

"By all means, dear. You all hurry back." While they were in the ladies room, Marcus showed up.

"Hi, Dad."

"Marcus, son, how are you?"

"I'm good, Dad, really good."

"There's something different about you, son."

"What do you mean, Dad?" Marcus asked, knowing for certain what he was referring to. After all, he hadn't told them about his relationship with Liah.

Morgan Sr. went on to say, "Well, son, if you were a woman, I would say you're downright glowing. Since you're a male, I don't know what to say. Nevertheless, I only recall glowing like that when I met your mother." His father knew him too well. Marcus knew this would be the day he told them about Liah.

"Well, Dad," he murmured, "There has been an incredible change in my life ... a promising one, actually."

"Is that right?"

Marcus looked at him smiling with that glowing look and said, "Yes, sir, that's right."

"Well, are you going to tell me about it or do I have put your mother on you?" he asked as he chuckled.

"Wait, Dad. I thought I was meeting you and Mom."

"She's in the ladies room. Oh, here she comes."

Marcus couldn't see because he was sitting with his back facing them. As they got closer, he slightly turned around.

"Marcus," Liah whispered, totally surprised. "What are you doing here?"

"Liah, honey," he exclaimed, surprised as well.

"Oh my God, so these *are* your parents," she declared with relief.

"I take it that you all know each other all ready," Morgan uttered under his breath. Marcus got up and hugged Liah, and like the gentlemen his father taught him to be, he pulled Liah's chair out so she could sit down. His parents looked at him pleased.

"Okay, Mom and Dad, explain."

"Well, son, we felt you have been out of the loop far too long and you needed a nudge. When we met Liah, we thought she was perfect for you. And now we find out that you've already met her. We think she's a wonderful person and we're very fond of her already. And son, this is a big one, your mother loves her clothes."

"Morgan, I don't think this is the time for jokes," Lillie whispered.

"Well, you do like her clothes."

"That's for sure. But get serious," she responded.

"Liah, why didn't you tell me you knew them?"

"Although it seemed very likely and I definitely entertained the thought, I honestly did not know they were your parents. I have a lot of customers with the same last names, you know. Anyway, what difference does it make? I'm delighted to know that they're your parents."

"She's right, Marcus. It makes no difference. Now I can safely assume you two are involved. But what I really want to know is this, were you going to marry her before you told us about her?"

"No, Mom, I was going to tell you today."

"That you are going to marry her?"

"Of course not Mom, I didn't tell you all because we wanted to take the time to get to know each other better."

"I bet Morgan knows," Morgan Sr. declared.

"Yes, Dad. Of course he does."

"Well, at least you told him," he replied.

"I should go and let you all talk," Liah suggested. She felt a bit out of place. Marcus noticed and took her hand. "I'm sorry, honey. I shouldn't have assumed you knew and kept it from me," Marcus said apologetically.

"Liah, dear, don't you even think about leaving," Morgan Sr. said to her. "You're practically part of the family now."

"Oh, Liah, that is a beautiful ring."

"Thank you, Lillie."

"You might as well know that I gave it to her. It's a promise ring."

"Have you all *talked?*" His dad was referring to his sterility.

"Yes, Dad, she knows everything," Marcus responded, slightly annoyed with his parents, though he knew they always had his best interest at hand.

"Well, I sure hope you have lots of children," Morgan Sr. blurted.

"Oh yeah, the more the merrier," Lillie added.

Marcus took Liah's hand into his again. He looked into her eyes as he was talking to his parents. "Mom and Dad, I love her, and I can truly say that I've never felt this way before. If anyone had told me that love could become so strong in such a short time, I probably would have told them they're crazy."

Talk about an awkward moment. She couldn't believe he was saying this to his parents and in her presence. "For once in my life, I'm not afraid to love. So Liah Anginette Mathis ... I love you." Liah could barely swallow.

"Are you okay?" Marcus asked.

"Yes, I just I need some water."

"I'm sorry, I know this whole day caught you off guard," Marcus said to her.

"Yes, a bit, but it's all good. I am glad I finally got confirmation that these are your wonderful parents."

"Thank you for saying that," Marcus said, quite pleased with the outcome of the surprised." Morgan and Lilly just sat there observing there.

"You're welcome. About what you said earlier, I would like to say Marcus, there is no time frame on love. The beauty of love began with God and he taught us how to love one another. People often get caught up in all the formalities of a relationship, which makes things a bit problematic. I think once there is a separation of physical and emotional attraction from spiritual attraction or connection, one is able to see what's real and what isn't. Who we are drawn to and why is the just the nature of each individual. Physical attraction is just a contributor to a relationship—it will not sustain one. But the spiritual connection is through God, I believe. It has a greater chance of surviving. Everything else is about choice. I've felt love for you and I was drawn to you since the first day I met you. I think a glimpse past the physical attraction we a made an immediate spiritual connection. I made a choice to get to know you. And now that I've gotten to know you better, I love who you are. Oh my gosh, I am sorry! I tend to get carried away sometime." An indeed she does, especially with conversations she is passionate about. She inhaled deeply and sighed, a much needed sigh after that speech. He reached over and hugged her. Lillie had tears in her eyes and Morgan Sr. was speechless. They both knew that Liah Mathis was indeed the perfect match for their son.

The waitress came over to ask them if they were ready to order. "Sure, we're ready," Morgan Sr. answered. "Liah, would you like to go first?" he asked.

"Yes. Sure. I'll have the grilled fajita platter. Will you please make sure that the cilantro and the guacamole are put on the side? I would also like a medium raspberry decaf tea, if you have it."

"That sounds good," Morgan Sr. said, "I'll have the same." Marcus and Lillie ordered the same as well.

"Will you all be having dessert?" the waitress asked.

"What about key lime cheesecake?" Liah asked.

"I say, let's try it," Lillie answered.

If it's not a problem, would you please asked the chef to dice a small bowl of strawberries, add a tablespoon of water, sprinkle a teaspoon of raw sugar on top, and send out a small bowl of whipped cream?"

"I will be glad to."

"Thank you very much," Liah told her. The waitress started to walk off. "Wait a minute," she said. "Aren't you the chef from A'Palace?"

"Yes, I am."

"Oh, my gosh! He is not going to believe this. I'll be back with your order." She briskly walked off, leaving them in suspense.

"Liah, we should eat out with you more often," Morgan Sr said "We can assume things will be just as we like it," he chuckled.

"So, honey, do you know who the waitress was referring to?" Marcus inquired.

"I have no idea." She reached in her purse and took out a bacteria wipe then started wiping off everything on the table. They all looked at her. "I have a little bit of obsessive compulsive disorder going on."

"She does this every time we go out to eat," Marcus informed them.

"Well, you don't know where hands have been before they touched these items."

"I think she has a good point," Morgan Sr. said chuckling. "You can't be too careful."

Marcus looked at Liah, smiling. "Have I told you how stunning you look?" She sighed and thanked him.

"Lillie, I have the final plans for the party," Liah said.

"You're doing a party for them?"

"Yes, she is, for your cousin's graduation," Morgan answered.

A handsome middle-aged man came over to the table. "Liah Mathis, I knew it was you."

"John Usher," she said, surprised. "Oh, my gosh! I didn't know you worked here." She got up and hugged him.

"Still looking good, girl,"

"So do you! Are you ever going to age, John?"

"Nope." They both laughed.

"John, this is Marcus Michaels. Marcus, this is John Usher."

"Wow, you said that with a big smile on your face." She smiled even wider.

"Mr. Michaels, you are a blessed man."

"Yes, I am, indeed."

"And these are Marcus' parents, Lillie and Morgan."

"I am delighted to meet all of you. Tell you what— the tab is on the house. Liah, let's get together sometime soon. I'd like to introduce you to my wife."

"Ooh ... and you're married! Congratulations!" She reached in her purse and handed him a card. "Call me soon," she told him.

"I will. Good to see you again, sweetie. You all enjoy your lunch."

"It was great seeing you again as well John, and thank you."

"You are welcome," he smiled and walked off.

"John and I used to cook together when I was an independent chef. We lost contact when he moved away. It was good seeing him again."

He seems to be a kind gentleman," Morgan said."

"Oh, he is and a great chef." Morgan noticed the waiter walking toward them.

"Good, here she comes with our food," he said.

"It looks delicious, thank you," Liah said. Then Liah continued talking to Lillie about the party. "I'm going to have Liz Carrington do the decorations."

"I think I've heard of her," Lillie replied. "Good choice."

"Son?"

"Yes, Dad."

"When can we expect a visit from you all with the kids?'"

"I don't know, probably soon. Liah, what do you think?"

"Soon is good."

"Okay," Lillie said. "We're holding both of you to that."

"So, Liah. Did you grow up here?" Morgan asked.

"No. I grew up in DC."

"If you don't mind my asking, dear, how long were you married?"

"Dad, let's not get too personal."

"It's okay. I don't mind."

"Now you don't look old enough to have been married that long. You've either got good genes or you've taken good care of yourself."

"I'd like to say both."

"Marcus, I think you found a jewel. God's word says: "When a man findeth a wife he findeth a good thing."

"Morgan, leave him alone. You're embarrassing the child." The waitress came over to pick up their dishes.

"I'll be right back with your dessert," she told them.

"Thank you," Liah said. "So how long have you all been married?" she asked Morgan and Lillie.

"Seems like forever," Morgan teased.

"Oh, Morgan, stop it," Lillie told him. Forty-five years, honey."

"And she still has my heart."

"Morgan always knows how to get his self out of hot water when he says something he shouldn't say."

"This time I was kidding, dear, I know exactly how long we've been married."

"Yeah, I knew you knew better," she responded.

"Dad, have you talked to Morgan?"

"Not since last week. Why, has he met someone, too?"

"Now, Dad, you know if he has, I'll have to let him tell you."

"He'll probably date for a month before he tells us like you."

"I'm sorry, Dad."

"He's just messing with you, Marcus," Lillie said. "You have my permission to ignore him," she laughed. "Anyway, Liah, when you get back into the swing of things, will you bake us a carrot cake? That was the best carrot cake I've ever eaten."

"And I believe she ate all of that you sent home with us."

"That is not true, Morgan. I gave you a little piece." They all laughed.

"Lillie, I will make you a carrot cake anytime."

"Thank you, dear."

"What about me," Morgan Sr. pouted?

"You too, Morgan."

"Seems like you all are enjoying yourselves," the waitress said to them when she brought their dessert.

'Yes, we are," Marcus replied. The waitress had everything just as Liah had requested it. "How do you want me to serve this?" she asked Liah. Liah got up and showed her.

"You take six pieces of strawberries and slightly pressed them into the cheesecake, drizzle it with the strawberry sauce, scoop whipped cream on top, a strawberry then a little more strawberry sauce. Now you can really heighten the look with a mint leaf. It's all about presentation." She did each of their cheesecake the same.

"Wow, now that looks good," the waitress said.

"Now, dear, a good presentation would make you want to eat it before you know you like it," Lillie said to her kindly.

"I don't think I like key lime cheesecake, but this presentation is tempting," the waitress whispered.

"And this is good cheesecake," Morgan exclaimed nodding his head. They all agreed that it was good.

"Will you tell John he did an awesome job?" Liah asked her

"I will be delighted to, Ms. Mathis. You all enjoy the rest of your dessert. Thanks for the presentation tip."

"You bet!"

"Liah, if you don't mind my asking. Are you going to be okay financially, being off work for a while?" Morgan asked.

"Yes, I will. Thank you, Morgan, for asking. That was very kind of you."

"Yes, darling," Lillie said, "anything we can do just let us know."

"I appreciate your offer. But really, I'll be okay. I am on paid leave and I have lots of sick and vacation time."

"If you were in need, would you tell us?" Marcus asked.

"Honestly, it would probably be my absolute last resort."

"She reminds me of you, Lillie," Morgan mentioned. "She was too proud to ask for help."

"Yeah, and I have learned better."

"I am really okay. Honestly! Now I really must be going. I need to make it home before my son gets there. It has been a pleasure spending time with you all. We should do it again soon. Lillie, please call me so we can get those measurements. And I am going to give Liz your number so she can discuss some party ideas with you."

"Yes, please do and thank you, Liah."

"You're welcome."

"Do you need me to take you home?" Marcus asked.

"No, no Marcus. Finish visiting with your parents. Besides, I have the driver waiting."

"Okay, I'll be by later." They all hugged her.

"Now you take care dear," Morgan told her. Marcus walked her out.

"Are you tired, baby?" he asked her.

"I am a little."

"Maybe you should rest when you get home."

"I will. I'll see you later." Marcus went back in to join his parents.

"I don't know how you did it, Marcus, but you landed a beautiful woman—inside and out," his dad told him.

"Don't forget intelligent and stylish," Lillie added.

"And she can cooks too," Morgan said. "Don't let her slip away, son."

"I won't Dad." By the way, Mom, Liah's birthday is May fifteen. I want to give her a surprise birthday party. Can you help me out? Maybe you can talk to Liah's friend, Liz, to see if she can pull something together for the seventeenth. I can talk to her friend, Jen, and also get the girls to help out."

"I will be honored to help out Marcus."

"Thanks, Mom. Well, I have to be going. I need to stop by the office before I go home."

"Hold on, Marcus," Morgan said. "Does she know about your financial status?"

"Yes, she just recently found out."

"I bet you had her checked out."

"I did and she knows it."

"She wasn't upset?" Lillie inquired.

"No. She also had me investigated."

"Smart lady. But how did she not know about your financial status?" Lillie asked.

"She could have. The investigator presented her with the file. She wouldn't let him show it to her. She wasn't interested in how much money I had. She was only interested in a criminal background report, homeowner, credit history, and if I was among the working class. Here top priority was to confirm the safety of her children."

"I had to ask, son," Morgan told him. "But I didn't think for a moment that she was a gold digger. She seems quite honest and straightforward. I like her."

"Well, I think she's perfect for Marcus."

"Thanks, Mom. You know, Mom and Dad, I just want the best for her and her children. They've been through a lot. Liah practically raised six children by herself. Her husband walked out on her before Jas, her six-year old, was born. She's a strong and well-rounded woman. And she is a good mom. All of her children are well-mannered and smart, too. I have so much respect for her and most importantly, she is a genuine and dedicated Christian."

"I think my respect for her just rose to another level," Lillie reevaluated.

"Mine too," Morgan added.

"Mom and Dad, I love you all, but I gotta go."

After Marcus left, Lillie and Morgan continued talking for a while. "Morgan, I think he's going to asked her to marry him soon," Lillie predicted.

"Well, I sure hope so. He's like his father. He doesn't believe in wasting time. My motto is if you know what you want and it's within your reach, grab hold of it."

"You sure didn't waste any time asking me to marry you."

"And here we are forty-five years later," he said. "Did you notice how Marcus lit up when he talked about her children?"

"Yes, finally we can have some grandchildren. And I think Marcus is good father material. I think Morgan would be a good father too," she declared.

"Speaking of Morgan, did you see how they looked when I asked if Morgan had met someone?"

"I sure did, and I hope he has."

"Well, honey," Morgan said, "we had better get out of here."

"Don't forget to leave a tip," Lillie said. "That was a helpful young lady and sweet too." He left her a fifty dollar bill.

~Chapter Fourteen~

As soon as Liah got home, she put on her lounger and crawled into bed. As she lay there, she reflected over her luncheon. Her day was much more eventful than she had expected. Not only did she find out the Michaels were Marcus' parents, but they had planned a scheme to get them to meet. She thought that was a plus. In addition to that, they weren't at all bothered by how many children she had. Now that was a super plus. And to make the day even better, embarrassing, but better, nonetheless, he opened his heart right up to her in front of his parents. *This day couldn't get any better*, she said out loud. *Nah, I wouldn't say that. Perhaps it can.* She finally calmed her mind down and fell asleep, but was awakened by the doorbell. It was Jas. He came in her room excited to tell her about his day at school. "Hi, big boy. How was school?"

"It was awesome, Mom. I won a spelling bee and I get to have a pizza lunch with the teacher. And guess what?"

"What?"

"I have all fours on my report card. Here, Mom, here's my report card and you have to come to my award ceremony next Tuesday."

"Wow, you did have a good day. Jas, I am so proud of you. Maybe we can take you somewhere special. You can pick the place."

"Thanks, Mom. That would be cool."

"Come give me a hug. Okay, go upstairs and change your clothes and I will have Addie or Jeffrey fix you a snack. She lay back down and closed her eyes and fell back to sleep. Being the light sleeper that she was, she felt a presence in her room. It was Marcus standing in the door. She rolled over and sat up in bed. "Hi, baby, I'm sorry if I woke you."

"No, it's okay. I was talking to Jas before I dozed off just a moment ago."

"I can come back later.'

"No, please stay."

"Okay. I feel I need to apologize for blurting to my parents about my feelings for you, without talking to you beforehand."

"It's okay, honey. I mean, it did feel a bit awkward and it was definitely unexpected, but it's really okay. Your parents are awesome."

"Liah, I do love you."

"I love you too, Marcus." They embraced each other. "I just..." he cut her off before she could finish.

"No honey, no negative thoughts. No buts. Let's just let it happen. I don't want us to fight what we're feeling. Okay?"

"Okay," she whispered.

"I'm going to go say hi to Jas and have a snack with him."

"He would like that. Ask him to tell you about his exciting day at school." As Marcus walked off, she couldn't take her eyes off him. He was an exceptional man. It was the first time Liah had ever been involved with a man whose first priority wasn't sex. Marcus Michaels held firm to his belief on premarital sex. And that made Liah respect him all the more.

Marcus and Jason sat at the bar and had a snack together while Jason told him all about his day at school. They even made plans to go horseback riding.

Liah tried to fall back to sleep. But Chantel called. "Hi, Mrs. Michaels," she said, kiddingly.

"Hi, Chan. How are you?"

"I'm good. I just wanted to see how you're doing. So how are you doing?"

"I am much better."

"Have you been out of the house?"

"Yes, twice. Today I had lunch with some clients"

"You're supposed to be resting, not working."

"I was sitting, Chan — not cooking. And believe it or not, my clients turned out to be Marcus and Morgan's parents."

"Liah, are you for real?"

"As a Benjamin! It gets better, Chan. It was their intention to have Marcus and I meet. So they invited him to the luncheon as well." Chantel screamed in laughter.

"Did you already know them?"

"Yes, I met them a day after I met Marcus. I'm planning a party for them at A'Palace. Now listen to this, Marcus confessed his feelings for me in front of his parents. Right in that moment, I wanted to leave. I even offered to leave. Nevertheless, it all turned out well."

"See, we told you a proposal is in the making."

"Mom," Jason called out.

"Chan, I have to go. Jas is calling."

"Okay, I'm calling Lisha and Shayna so I can tell them about this."

"Okay, talk soon, Chan!" Jason and Marcus came back in the room.

"Mom, Mr. Marcus offered to take me horseback riding soon. May I go?"

"When?" she asked.

"We haven't set a date," Marcus responded.

"I guess it would be fine, Jas. But why don't Marcus and I discuss a good day, and we will let you know. In the meantime, why don't you get started on your homework? If you need help with anything, please let me know."

"Okay, Mom. Thanks, and thank you too, Mr. Marcus."

"Would you like to sit out on the terrace, Marcus?" Liah asked him.

"Sure." He took her by the hand then slipped his arm around her, pulling her closer to him. "So what do you think about my parents?"

"I think they're meddling busy bodies," she said jokingly.

"What?" he asked, shocked by her answer, his eyes widening. She burst out laughing and told him she was kidding.

"I'm sorry, Marcus. You should have seen your reaction," she said as she continued to laugh. He started laughing with her.

"That was really good. You're good. You're in the wrong business, you know."

"I know," she said animatedly. "Seriously, honey, they're awesome and funny. I liked them the very first time I met them."

"You still do after that stunt they pulled? You know, they really are meddling busy bodies."

"No, they're not. They had your best interest at heart. Besides, it says a lot about yours truly. After all, they wanted me to meet their wonderful son."

"I know. I love my parents and they are the best. But I can't believe they set you up like that. But what I can believe is the impression you made on them, which was big. I mean ... look what you've done to me."

"And what is that?"

"You captivated my heart. I'm usually the slow snail—don't-fall-too-quickly kind of guy. At least I was until I met you."

"Maybe it was because you are more than physically attracted to me."

"Physical attraction is what drew me to my first wife."

"Surely, you loved her."

"I did love her. And I was attracted to her. But there was something missing. I believe if you took the agape love away and the attraction, there wouldn't have been much left. However, I vowed to stay with her until death, and I believe I would have, had she not cheated on me and gotten pregnant. It was like a stab in the heart. She will always have my unconditional love. But I couldn't continue being married to her. It was obvious she didn't want to be married to me anyway. Nonetheless, I do understand that she wanted a child and I couldn't give her one."

"Did she know how blessed she was and still is to have you in her life?"

"I don't know."

Liah wanted to break the mood so she invited Marcus to attend her next lecture. She noticed him getting a bit emotional.

"What is the topic?" he asked.

"A Love Not Broken."

"Interesting topic," he replied.

"I like to think of it as a well-needed topic. Hey, maybe you can invite Morgan."

"We will be there. Just let us know when. Well, it sounds like the girls are here."

"I guess we should go inside," she said.

"Yes, after you, Madame," he said trying to sound French.

"That was pretty good. Can you speak French?"

"Yes, I can and three other languages."

"Oh, really? This conversation must continue," she told him. The girls met them as they were walking in. "Hi, girls," Liah said joyously. "How was school?"

Both of them said, "Good," as they often say. Liah knew by their actions that they wanted to ask her something. "What do you want, girls?"

"What makes you think we want something, Mom?" Jacqlyne asked.

"Don't toy with me, girl," Liah responded seriously.

"Okay, Mom. May we go to the movie with Ian and Brandon on Friday?" Jacqlyne asked.

"On a date? Have you graduated from high school yet?" she said sarcastically.

"No, Mom and no ma'am. It's just a movie. And Mrs. Carrington is going to drop us off and pick us up. She also said she might stay out there the whole time. But we won't know, so we had better stay in the movie theatre the whole time." Marcus chuckled. Then Liah raised her brow.

"I'm sorry," he quickly said.

"Mom, you don't trust us?" Jessica asked.

"You know better than that, Jess. I don't trust your surroundings. I'll think about it and talk to Liz."

"Liah, if it will make you feel better, I can have my driver take them and stay there. He can also act as a body guard," Marcus told her.

"I don't have a problem with that," Jacqlyne blurted.

"Neither do I," Jessica added. "It will actually be pretty cool."

"Why don't you all go in the kitchen to get a snack, girls? I'll get back to you all."

"Mom, can we play pool now?" Jason asked.

"I'll take him up if you want to call Liz right now," Marcus volunteered.

"Thanks, Marcus. Jas, I'll be up shortly." She went into her room and called Liz. They decided they would let the kids go to the movie. Liah told her about Marcus' offer to send them in the limo and have the driver watch out for them. Liah spoke very highly of him. But she also thought it would be a good idea to send a trusted sitter she had often used. When she finished talking to Liz, she went in the kitchen to tell the girls. The girls would be fine with whatever. They knew how she was and knew she was looking out for their best interest. Although, sometimes they thought she could be a bit overbearing. Liah was also very much aware of that. She made it upstairs just in time to see Jason make a good shot. "Mom, did you see how smooth the ball went in?" he asked.

"Yes, I did and that was a good shot. You're getting good."

"Can you play pool, Liah?" Marcus asked.

"Somewhat," she responded nonchalantly.

"Jas, do you mind if I show your mom a few moves?"

"No, good luck," Jas told him. Marcus didn't take heed as to what Jas meant. He gave her the first shot. She didn't get one ball in. When Marcus' time came around, he nearly cleared the table. He felt sorry for her, so he told her he would close his eyes so he could miss.

"Marcus, please do not do that. If I don't think you're doing your very best, I will not play. Play fair, okay?"

"Okay, I will." He missed his next shot.

"You better not have done that on purpose," she told him.

"Honestly, I didn't."

"Okay, don't say I didn't warn you." She picked up her pool stick and said, "Now stand back please. I gotta show you what I'm really working with." He stepped back looking curious. She cleared the table and put the stick behind her back and cleared the rest of his balls.

Jas started screaming, "Ooh, Mom that was awesome!"

Marcus couldn't believe his eyes. "I thought you said somewhat. You play like a professional. Where did you learn to play like that?"

"My uncle Arthur was a pool player legend. He taught me."

"You are bad," he told her.

"I know," she said and winked at him. "Well, I'm going to let you guys get back to your pool. I'm going to play Pac-Man. Marcus looked at Jas.

"She's good at that, too."

"By the way, Marcus, you play really well," she told him. The girls came in, and then Marcus asked them if they knew how well their mom played pool.

"Oh sure," Jessica answered, "She's the best."

"Why," Jacqlyne asked. "Did she whip you?

"Yes, she did."

"Don't feel bad. You didn't know what you were up against. She always wins. She plays the nonchalant act, and then they let her go first. They even give her extra shots and she won't put one ball in. Then they feel sorry for her. She begs them not to throw the game for her or she will not play. Then the black widow goes in for the kill," she dramatized theatrically. "She whips the pool stick behind her back. And all the mates disappear." Everyone looked at her and burst out laughing.

"She's good," Marcus said.

"You haven't seen anything yet," Liah told him.

When they finished playing in the game room, they went downstairs and had dinner together. Marcus invited them to go to Bible class with him. Liah asked the kids if that would be okay, and of course, they all agreed. "Mr. Marcus, do you have parents?" Jason boldly asked.

Marcus laughed then answered, "Yes, I do, Jas."

"Well, why don't we ever see them?"

"You didn't see them on Sunday because we went to the late morning service. And they don't come by because I'm not usually home. But I did tell them about you all and they want to meet you."

"Okay, that's cool. I want to meet them, too."

"Mom, are we still going back home this weekend?" Jacqlyne asked.

"Yes, Jacq, that is the plan."

"Man, I'm going to miss being here."

"Me, too," Jason said.

"Me three," Jessica followed.

"Mom, are we still going to see Mr. Marcus?" Jason inquired.

"Yes, Jas. Now, you all go get ready for Bible class." After the kids had gone upstairs, Marcus asked Liah if she was sure she was ready to go home. "No," she answered, "but it's time. I've already overstayed my welcome."

"Liah, you have not. I don't want you all to leave. I can stay with Morgan."

"Marcus, you have been more than kind. I'm not going to keep you out of your home any longer. Besides, I don't want this to get to confusing for the kids."

"I know, baby. But you have open access here."

"I do have keys, don't I?"

"Yes, you do," he said, pulling her out of her chair and putting his arms around her.

"I love you, Liah Mathis."

"I love you, Marcus, and, honey, this doesn't change anything. We can still see each other as often as we do now. That's if you don't mind the drive."

"And I don't."

"I am going to miss Addie and Jeffrey. And Jas is going to miss that pool table. I think I'm going to have him a pool table put in soon."

"He's going to really think that's cool."

"Marcus, I do have one request?"

"Anything, sweetie."

"I need to borrow your cleaning crew, so I can have my house thoroughly cleaned tomorrow. And I think I'm going to talk to Addie about that temporary cook she had mentioned."

"Not a problem. I'll send the cleaning crew over tomorrow. And, honey, don't worry about hiring a temporary cook. You can borrow Addie and Jeffrey anytime. I'm sure they wouldn't mind. As a matter of fact, why don't they stay until you go back to work?"

"For real? I can't do that, Marcus. You need them."

"I'll be fine, Liah."

"Marcus, they might not want to leave this big mansion to stay at a regular house."

"Girl, you're crazy. They'll stay with you if you lived in an apartment. And your house is far from being a regular house. I don't even have a garage apartment. And Jeffrey will love the backyard."

"Well, if they want to come, I will be delighted to have them. And you'll have to come by to eat anytime."

"And I will have to come by to see you all of the time," he responded. "Did I tell you that I love you?"

"I don't know," she whispered. "Let me hear you say it and see if it jogs my memory."

"No, I did tell you." He then kissed her forehead and said, "I love you." Then he kissed her cheek and said I love you again. They then heard Jeffrey speaking to Morgan. He was a welcomed interruption. Before they could walk out to see him, Morgan came in the kitchen.

"Hi, Morgan," Liah said with a cute little grin on her face.

"Hi, Liah, it looks like you're feeling better."

"I am feeling much better."

"Now maybe someone we know and love can stop being a worry wart," Morgan said.

"Someone we know and love should get someone to worry about," Marcus responded.

"I might already have someone to worry about," Morgan countered.

"Who is that sir?" Jeffrey inquired. "Ms. Chantel Harris," he stated, answering his own question. Morgan made no response.

"Speaking of Chantel," Morgan announced, "I just talked to her. She told me that she had a job offer here. Did you know about that, Ms. Mathis?"

"Yes, I did."

"Did you encourage her to come?"

"No, but I'm sure she will. It's a big step for her and the kids, and she has to find a house. However, she could move in with me and put her stuff in storage."

"Yeah, she could do that," he replied.

"Morgan, did you come over to tell us about Chantel?" Marcus asked.

"No, not really. I came to see if you all wanted to ride to Bible class with me."

"Yeah, man, that would be cool," Marcus answered.

"I'm going to get the kids because it is time to go."

After Liah walked out Morgan saw a great opening to question Marcus' feelings for Liah. "You got it real bad, don't you?' I think you're falling in love."

"Whatever it is, it feels good."

"She is a great person," Morgan complimented. "And if you hadn't met her, I wouldn't have met Chantel Harris. By the way, I talked to her boys last night. They seemed pretty cool."

"I hope things will work out well for you and Chantel," Marcus told him before Jas walked in.

"Hi, Mr. Morgan."

"How about Uncle Morgan," he suggested before picking him up. He looked at Liah. She gave him a smile that said "okay."

"Hi, Uncle Morgan," the girls said animatedly.

"Come give me a hug, girls," he told them.

"Alright it's time to go," Liah told everyone. "Jeffrey, are you and Addie riding together?"

"Yes, we'll see you all there."

"Okay, Jeffrey."

On the way to Bible class, Marcus told Morgan about the stunt their parents pulled. He thought it was the funniest thing.

"What's so funny?" Liah asked, teasingly, as if she was offended by the stunt.

"Mom and Dad crack me up," Morgan said. I'm glad it was you and not me, Marcus."

"Oh, don't worry, they inquired about you. They wanted to know if you had met someone."

"Marcus, you all didn't rat me out, did you?"

"You know I wouldn't do that to you, bro."

"Yeah, I know. Hey, remember when they pulled that same stunt with Lecxa?"

"Yeah, I remember."

"Oh, I want to hear this," Liah insisted.

"Wait, Marcus, let me tell this one. They met this nice young man and they really liked him. So they invited him and Lecxa to dinner at the same time. Now when he showed up, he brought his girlfriend with him to meet them. Turns out that he, Lecxa, and his girlfriend were all tight friends in college."

"But I have to give them credit, though, 'cause Mom and Dad played it off good. He never knew what they had planned, but Lecxa knew. And to this day, she never lets them live it down."

After Bible class, they stopped by a little ice cream shop. Morgan and the kids got out and ordered ice cream. They ordered Liah and Marcus a pint each of butter pecan ice cream. While they were ordering, Liah notice Liz's husband cuddled up with another woman. Liah gasped then turned to whisper to Marcus, "Don't look now, but you see that guy in that black Hummer?" He lowered his head and then looked to his right.

"Okay, I see him. What about him?"

"That's Liz's husband and that's not Liz he's cuddled up with."

"Are you sure?"

"Positive."

"What are you going to do?" Marcus asked.

"Stay out of it. It's not my business."

"That's probably the best thing," he said.

When Morgan and the kids got back in, they left and he took them home.

The kids went straight to their rooms when they got home. Liah went up shortly afterward to help Jason get ready for bed and read him a short story. Marcus waited for her downstairs. While Liah was tucking Jason in bed, he made an unexpected request.

"Mom, I want Mr. Marcus to be my dad."

"Jas, do you know the only way Marcus can be your dad is if he and I get married?"

"Yes, Mom, I know that. I'm six years old and you've explained it."

"Okay, I'm just making sure that you remember that. Jas, would you like to spend more time with him?"

"Yes, Mom!" He answered, excitedly. "Can I Mom?"

212

"I think that's very possible, Jas. Marcus would like to spend more time with you as well."

"Mom, Mr. Marcus is awesome."

"I think so, too, Jas. I'll talk to Marcus and find out when he wants to take you on a horseback riding outing. But right now you have to go sleep."

"Okay, I didn't say my prayer." After he was done saying his prayer, Liah tucked him in bed again and said goodnight. She went by the girls' room and told them goodnight before going back downstairs.

Marcus was reading when Liah came downstairs. "Hey, you," he said to her, motioning for her to sit by him.

"Can we talk?" she asked him.

"Sure, what's on your mind?" She hesitated momentarily.

"Honey, what's wrong?"

"Oh, I'm sorry, Marcus. It's not anything alarming. Jas just asked if you could be his dad."

"He did?"

"Uh huh."

"How do you feel about that?"

"Marcus, I think you will be an incredible dad. Nevertheless, I don't want to give him any false hope." What she did not know was this was just the opening Marcus needed, to ask the question he had been pondering about.

"I have a question," he stated. "Do you think there is a time frame a couple should date before they get married?"

"I don't think so," she responded.

"Care to elaborate?"

213

"First of all, some people are together for years and they don't know each other. I think it depends on the individuals, because marriage is for people who understand the commitment in its entirety—and how they feel about one another; where each person is in their lives and what they bring into each other's life. I would also take into consideration the physical, emotional and spiritual connection they have. But most importantly, they need to understand God's love and his blueprint for marriage. Need I go on?"

"So basically, there is no timeline, because it varies with each individual."

"I would say so," she replied.

"Now back to Jas's question."

"Marcus, we can't allow Jas to change our course. His request depends on where we end up. We can't move any faster because he wants you to be his dad. He understands how this process works."

Marcus put his arms around Liah and told her he loved her and she reciprocated he feelings as well. As they both sat there in each other's arms, neither of them spoke a word. They were both thinking about what a blessing it would be to spend the rest of their lives together. Marcus thought to himself how much he would love the chance to be a father to her children. He already loved and adored them. Liah was thinking about what a wonderful dad he would be. Any child would be blessed to have Marcus as a father. They were so deep in thought they didn't hear their cell phones ringing. Finally, becoming aware that their phones were ringing, they quickly grabbed them off the table. "It's Morgan," Marcus uttered.

"What a coincidence, it's Chan," Liah said. Morgan called to get Marcus' input on a project. And Chantel called to tell Liah that she accepted the offer. Marcus told Morgan he would be there shortly. Although Liah was elated about Chantel's news, she practically rushed her off the phone after telling her that Marcus was there. Chantel demanded she call her right back.

"Baby, Morgan needs my help on a project," he whispered, not at all ready to leave her.

"Okay … I understand. Guess what," she said, excitedly. Not giving him time to respond. "Chantel accepted the offer."

"I bet Morgan is happy about that," Marcus said.

"I don't believe she's told him yet."

"Well, I won't mention it to him either. Sweetheart, I have to go so I can help Morgan with the project. I'll see you tomorrow."

Liah walked him to the door. Just as soon as she closed the door, she called Chantel back. "Okay Chan, I'm back. So when are you moving?"

"When I find somewhere to stay."

"Chan, you all can stay with us until whenever."

"Are you sure?"

"Honey, yes!"

"Well then, I guess we'll be there around your birthday."

"House guests for my birthday! That better not be my birthday present."

"Liah, birthdays don't get better than that. Well, unless Marcus proposes to you."

"There's a thought! Anyway, have you told Morgan?"

"No, but I'm going to call him when I'm on break. So I will talk to you later. And, Liah, thanks for inviting us to be your houseguests."

"Anytime, love. You have a good night at work."

Liah went to the kitchen to fix herself a cup of tea. She noticed a jewelry catalog lying open on the bar with a gorgeous ring circled. *Now this is an awesome ring*, she thought. She wondered if Marcus had left it there. *I'm certain that it's not Jeffrey's. Well, even that could be a possibility. He is pretty good-looking and quite charming, even for his age*, she thought. *Or it could very well be—Nah, I'm not going to let myself go there.* She was thinking that it had to be Marcus. She fixed her tea and went back to her room. Marcus called to say goodnight to her. He also told her that Morgan had talked to Chantel and he was on cloud nine.

~Chapter Fifteen~

Liah spent the next day packing and making calls to her other children and family members. In between making calls, she received a call from Lillie, inviting them over the following Saturday to a cookout. Marcus also called to say hi and tell her that he would be tied up most of the day. After he left work, he met Jeffrey so they could pick out a pool table for Jason. He had called Jen earlier to schedule a time for him and Jeffrey to meet her and the delivery guys there. He was glad Liah had mentioned to him that Jen kept an extra set of house keys.

Though Liah's house was not quite as big a Marcus', Jeffrey fell in love with it instantly, especially the backyard. He hinted to Marcus about letting Liah redesign his backyard."

"Funny you should say that, Jeffrey. I've been thinking about that. Did I tell you that I am planning to give her a surprise birthday party in May?"

"No, I believe you failed to mention that."

"Sorry. Any input you care to contribute? I know you and Liah are pretty tight."

"I would be honored to contribute, Sir! Who, may I ask, will be catering?"

"I don't know. I'll probably get with Addie."

"Good choice, Sir."

"Jeffrey, have I told you that "sir", coming from you, makes me feel older?"

"From me," he replied.

"I don't mean because you're older. You look good. It just feels weird, Jeffrey."

"I'm sorry, Sir—I mean, Marcus. I didn't know you felt that way."

"Neither did I."

"Perhaps Ms. Liah is rubbing off on you."

"She's done more than that, Jeffrey. I can't imagine my life without her."

"I believe she feels the same way about you, son."

"Now that sounds better. I do think of you as a second father, Jeffrey." Jeffrey was elated even though somewhat shocked.

"I am honored you feel that way. Because you are like a son to me, you know."

"Yeah, I know. Now back to our prior conversation. I love her children as well. She told me last night that Jas said he wants me to be his dad."

"Have you told her how you feel?"

"I've told her I love her but that's it. I don't want to scare her away. It's just that I know what I want. She is the person I've prayed to have in my life. I don't need time to tell me that."

"Sounds like you have some thinking to do and some serious decisions to make."

Jen walked into the room. "Is it safe to come in here or am I interrupting your conversation?" Jen asked.

"No, no, Jen. I'm sorry," Marcus told her. "Please come on in."

"Wow, Jas is going to be ecstatic over this pool table," Jen said. "Is Liah still having the house cleaned tomorrow?"

"Yes, I believe she is," Marcus answered. "Jen, I have a question."

"Okay."

"Do you know what kind of flowers Liah likes?"

"Oh sure. She would really appreciate a well-chosen soft colorful arrangement, with a mixture of greenery. And she loves akito roses, you know, the white ones. She's not impressed with a bunch of roses. She would prefer one red or white rose versus a dozen." Her saying is "a dozen roses don't take a lot of thought but a well-chosen arrangement shows a genuine effort. She's also really crazy about plants. If you stick a rose or combine flowers with a plant, you can't go wrong. She's particular."

"Now that, I've learned," Marcus said. "Jeffrey, you wanna go with me to the floral shop?"

"I'll help you," Jeffrey answered.

"Jen, thanks for your help. I just have one more favor. Can you help me with her surprise birthday party?"

"You're giving her a surprise birthday party?"

"That's the plan. So will you help?"

"Yes, of course I will."

"Fantastic. Thanks, Jen. I'll be in touch. Come on, Jeffrey, we're going to the floral shop."

They went straight to the floral shop. Marcus put together a beautiful arrangement containing daffodils, tulips, carnations, and lilac mixed with a philodendron. The florist told him that the arrangement was very impressive. He scheduled them to arrive on Saturday morning.

Marcus went back to the office and Jeffrey went home. When he made it back to the office, Morgan and the guys were working on a project for a proposal. Marcus delved right in. They were so into their work, more time seemed to have flown by than Marcus' realized. Marcus politely excused himself and dashed into his office to call Liah. She had just finished reading her Bible, when the phone ranged.

"Hi, beautiful," Marcus said.

"Hi, handsome."

"What are you doing?" he asked.

"I just finished studying a lesson on the Oneness in Christ."

"Let me guess, you're preparing for a class."

"I am. So what are you up to?"

"I'm still at work. I'm helping Morgan out with that project."

"Are you guys working all night?"

"Yeah, I'm sorry, baby. I'm not going to have time to come by tonight."

Liah yawned. "I'm sorry, honey. I'm a little tired."

"Have you taken the time to rest today? And tell the truth."

"No, not really," she mumbled reluctantly.

"I'm going to let you go so you can get some sleep."

"Alright," she replied. "I love you, Marcus."

"I love you, too, baby. Now get some rest."

"Yes, sir!"

Saturday morning had arrived. It was the day for Liah and the kids to go back home. When Marcus came home, he didn't seem as high-spirited as he usually was. "Marcus, what's wrong?" Liah asked him.

"Nothing, I'm okay."

"Okay, now tell me what's really wrong."

"It doesn't really make sense. I'm just being silly."

"Well, let me be the judge of that."

"I'm just going to miss you all being here. It feels as if you're leaving me."

Liah took his hand and said, "Come here and sit down for a moment, please. Marcus, there is nothing changing but my location. I love you, and me going home will not change that. I am committed to this relationship. You and I are good together and we really work. I appreciate you, not just for what you do for me, but for whom you are and what you bring to my life. Marcus, I love you and that love grows each day." She laid her head on his arm, allowing him a moment to let her words savor. She then said, "Marcus, please don't ever let me go."

"After hearing those words, I'm sure I won't. So you're stuck with me, baby." He tried to reposition the arm her head was lying on causing her head to fall in his lap. She then tried to raise her head, realizing her earring was caught on his zipper. She said to him, "Marcus, I'm stuck on you."

"I'm stuck on you, too, sweetie."

"No, honey, I'm serious. I'm really stuck on you."

"I am serious, too, baby. I'm really stuck on you. You know, like white on rice!"

"Marcus," she said, raising her voice. "I think my earring is stuck on your zipper."

"What? My zipper?"

"Yes," she repeated, "your zipper."

"Oh, okay. I'm sorry."

"Marcus, honey. No sorry. Just take off your pants."

"Liah, I'm not taking off my pants. Take your earring out."

"I can't take it out, Marcus," she said a bit agitated. "Do you have on underwear?"

"What? Yes."

"Okay, I'm going to put my arms around your waist and you have to ease up off the couch. When you get up, walk slowly into my room and open your pants and I will take it from there. And, Marcus, please don't let me fall."

"I won't."

"And, Marcus, when I take your pants down, please hold on to your boxers."

"You're crazy, you know. But I love you anyway." He slowly started to get up.

"Wait," she cried.

"What is it now, Liah?"

"I hope you're not wearing any wild and weird-looking boxers because I don't want to hurt myself laughing."

"I was kidding at first when I said you were crazy, but you really are," he said laughing.

"Marcus, would you stop laughing. You're jarring my head."

"Oh, I'm sorry, baby."

"Come on. Let's get this over with before the kids come back down." He followed her instructions to the T. She pulled his pants down to his feet—going all the way down with them, and then told him to sit down so she could take them off. She took off his pants and then was able to get the earring loose.

"Man, the things women do to get men down to their boxers," he teased, chuckling. She grabbed a pillow and started whacking him with it. She then jumped on him, pulling both his arms behind his head. Suddenly it dawned on her that he didn't have his pants on.

"Oh, my gosh, Marcus, you don't have your pants on." Liah quickly jumped off him and ordered him to put on his pants. She walked out and left him lying on the bed clueless. He put his pants back on and walked out.

Jas came downstairs dressed in his new horseback-riding outfit that Marcus had bought him. He'd even bought him cowboy boots and a hat. "You look like a real cowboy, champ. Marcus picked him up and lifted him in the air.

"Wow, Jas, you really look cool," Jess complimented.

"Thanks, Jess!"

"Champ, we had better get going," Marcus told him.

"Marcus, please don't let him fall," Liah said.

"I will guard him with my life, dear." He leaned and kissed her on the cheek, then said to her, "I'll see you later, crazy woman."

"And you love every bit of it," she replied. "Jas, come give mommy a hug. Take care of my baby, Marcus."

"I will."

~Chapter Sixteen~

After Jason and Marcus left, Liah, Addie, Jeffrey and the girls packed up the limo so they could go back home. When Liah walked in the house, the first thing she noticed was the floral arrangement, which was sitting on the table in the foyer." She stood there for a moment, admiring the beauty of the carefully chosen arrangement. "Hmm," she said out loud. "Shows style and effort."

"Why don't you read the card, dear!" Jeffrey suggested.

"I am—I am." She opened the envelope and read the card, but there wasn't a signature or name on the card. Nonetheless, she knew it was from Marcus by the wording. She had a big smile on her face.

"If smiles like that could light up the sky, there wouldn't be much need for sunlight," Jeffrey commented.

"Does it show that much, Jeffrey?"

"I'm afraid it does, dear." They walked into the living room, and Liah immediately noticed the immaculate cleaning job.

"Wow, it's spotless," she stated.

"It was near spotless before they started, dear Jeffrey avowed." She snickered. "By the way, Ms. Liah, you have a nice home."

"Thank you, Jeffrey." Addie walked in the living room. "This is beautiful, Liah," she said.

"Thanks, Addie. Have you and Jeffrey decided between the guest room and the garage apartment?"

"Jeffrey is going to take the guest room, and I'm staying in the apartment."

"Jeffrey, I think you will like the guest room. It's just as big as the apartment. Why don't you take a look at it," Liah suggested. "Come, let me show you. And, Addie, you're going to love the apartment. It's really cozy. It has everything but a stove."

"You're right, dear, it's awesome."

"Awesome, Jeffrey!"

"I got it from little Jas." She smiled and shook her head. "Who's the designer?" Jeffrey inquired.

"You're looking at her."

"So you're an interior designer?"

"No, I just play around."

"Could have fooled me," Jeffrey said.

"Girl, you should go in business. You really did an outstanding job on the design," Addie attested.

"I'm not that good."

"Right!" Addie replied.

"Mom, come here!" Jessica called out. "You gotta see this."

"What is it Jess?"

"Come up here and see."

"Okay, Jess. Coming."

Liah was speechless when she walked into the game room. "Jeffrey, do you know anything about this?"

"You'll have to talk to Marcus, dear."

"I told him that I was thinking about getting a pool table for Jas. I should have known he would do something like this."

"Mom, Jas is going to love this," Jacqlyne avowed.

"Yes, he is! Where's Addie?"

"Probably getting familiar with the kitchen," Jeffrey responded.

"Ah, my other favorite place," Liah whispered. "Come on let's go find her." She was right where Jeffrey said she would be.

"Liah, I love this kitchen. I like how everything is so accessible. This is nice. Don't tell me you designed it, too."

"I did."

"Look at you, Ms. Chef/Designer," Addie murmured. She sighed.

"Girls, you all show Jeffrey the backyard while I show Addie her apartment." They were delighted to show it to him. They loved to see expressions when they showed their mom's backyard art.

"Breathtaking," was Addie's first expression. "This is a beautiful luxurious suite, Liah ... very nice." The living room was very cozy and had an elegantly designed fireplace, signifying a romantic ambiance. The bedroom had a touch of a Vera Wang designed suite, which Liah very much made her own with own style and sophistication. The deep espresso and buttercream designed bedroom, with a spray of lime accent extended quite the invitation for a peaceful night rest. This fifteen hundred square foot apartment would be the place to escape for some alone time for individuals or a couple.

"Liah, I may never leave here," Addie told her.

"Fine by me," Liah responded.

Liah and Addie joined the others in the backyard. "I heard you designed the backyard, too, dear," Jeffrey stated.

"Yes, and I am proud of this backyard. Now this is my place to escape."

"I can see why," Addie replied.

"Ms. Addie, you should see it at night," Jacqlyne said.

"I'm going to take advantage of that invitation," Addie told her. "Liah, what would you all like for dinner tonight?"

"We should all just get settled in, and I will order dinner, from A'Palace, for the next two nights," she suggested.

"Sounds good to me," Addie responded. Addie and Liah went inside to plan the menu for the next two days and Jeffrey stayed out with the kids. Liah showed Addie the rest of the house after she had finished placing the orders. "Liah, how do feel about having a full-time housekeeper?" Addie inquired.

"Do you have someone in mind?"

"Honey, yes. Marcus has more than enough. How many people do you think you'll need?"

"I think two can handle the job. They won't have to clean our bedrooms. The kids have to clean their own rooms. I might have them clean Jas's room once a week. But I think I'll have his bathroom cleaned every day. And it's up to you and Jeffrey if you want your rooms cleaned."

"I'll call them after I'm done touring the place."

"Sounds great," Liah said. After Liah finished showing Addie the house, she went in her room to finish unpacking. She lay on her bed for a moment, realizing how good it felt to be home. Even though she would miss being at Marcus' home, there was still no place like home.

Addie came up to help her put Jas's things away. She was still lying on the bed when Addie came in. "Liah, are you okay?"

"Yes, Addie, I'm fine. I just realized how much I missed being at home."

"I know what you mean. No matter how much fun you're having, there is no place like home."

"My thoughts exactly. But I guess I'll get up and unpack Jas's things."

"That's why I came up here," Addie told her.

"Addie, I really appreciate you and Jeffrey being here. Please make yourself at home."

"Girl, we are delighted to be here, just as we were having you back at the house. You all were like a blossom. You brighten up the place. And I know Marcus felt the same way. Seems to me a proposal is in the making because, honey, he treats you like a wife already."

"Now here you go, Addie, sounding like Chan."

"When is she coming back? I like her. She has a feisty spirit."

"She does," Liah replied.

After putting Jas's things away, Liah went to the patio room. She put in a movie and cuddled up on the couch and Addie went back to her apartment. She was dozing when Jeffrey and girls came in. "Liah, are you alright, dear?" he asked.

"Yes, I'm fine, Jeffrey. I'm just a little tired. Please make yourself at home and if you need anything, don't hesitate to ask."

"Thank you. I will do just that. And if you need anything, please let me know."

"I will, Jeffrey. Thanks. Girls, why don't you all put your stuff away?"

"We will, Mom," Jacqlyne said. "When we're done, we will be next door."

"Alright. Will you tell Jen I'll be over later?"

"Sure, Mom," Jessica answered. Liah fell asleep almost immediately. She slept until Jas and Marcus came back. The house was pretty empty when they walked in. Jeffrey came out when he heard them.

"Hey, Jeffrey, where's everyone," Marcus inquired.

"The girls are next door, Addie is in her apartment, and the person you're really looking for is cuddled up on the couch in the patio room."

"Thanks, Jeffrey. Jeffrey, would you mind helping Jas get cleaned up?"

"Not at all."

"But I'm not dirty."

"I know, Jas. But a shower will make you smell fresh, instead of like the outdoors. And when you're done, Jeffrey can show you your surprise."

"A surprise! Awesome! Mr. Jeffrey, can you help me?"

"Sure, little champ. Marcus, you might want to get a shower, too."

"I am, Jeffrey. I'll see you shortly, champ," Marcus said. He went to the pool house to take a shower. Afterwards, he went to the patio room. He kissed Liah on the cheek and she immediately woke up. "Hi, sleeping beauty."

"Hi. When did you all get back?"

"A short while ago."

"Where's Jas?"

"Jeffrey is helping him get cleaned up. I brought him back in one unscratched piece."

"Thank you. Jeffrey didn't have to help him. Why didn't you all awake me?"

"Honey, Jeffrey can handle it. That's why they agreed to come, so they can help you out."

"Okay! So how did Jas do?"

"Baby, I'm telling you he's a natural. I videotaped him so you all can see his progress."

"You did! Marcus, thank you. You have got to be the most thoughtful person I know. I love you."

"Back at you, baby," he said giddily. She sat up and put her arms around him.

He said to her, "Just don't lay your head in my lap because I'm not taking my pants off for you anymore." They both laughed.

"Shut up, Marcus, that's not even funny."

"Then why are you laughing?"

"So you won't feel bad," she said as she continued laughing.

"Yeah right! Come on so we can see if Jas likes his surprise," he told her.

"Marcus, it was very kind of you to buy that for him, though you know you didn't have to."

"I know you can afford to buy whatever you want. But I just wanted to surprise both of you. So please don't make me take it back."

"Okay, it's a nice gift, Marcus, and very much appreciated."

"Oh, by the way, since we're on the subject, I bought all three of them horses."

"You're kidding!"

"No, I'm serious. But I haven't told Jas the horse he road was his," he quickly added. "Soooo ... is it okay? Can they keep them?"

"Yes, Marcus, but you're not spoiling my children."

"I bought you and Jayde one, too."

"Really?" Well I think that will be fine with Jayde, but I don't know about me. I'm not ready to bust my butt. I'm not as brave as Jas."

"Tell you what. I'll ride with you until you feel comfortable."

"I'm holding you to that,' she said as they went upstairs to the game room.

Jeffrey and Jas walked in only minutes before they did. As a matter of fact, Jas was still in shock. He was standing there with his mouth open.

"Breathe, Jas," Liah said to him.

"Mom, this is awesome," he cried out. He ran over to her and gave her a hug while saying "thank you, thank you, thank you, Mom." He was over the moon.

"Jas, Marcus bought this for you."

"Really?"

"But only because your mom told me she was going to get you one. And I just wanted to surprise both of you," Marcus said, not wanting to take the credit. Jas went over to Marcus, thanking him.

"This is really cool. I have my own pool table. Mom, Mr. Marcus will be a good dad. Not because he bought me a pool table, though. I just think he would be." Marcus looked at Liah.

She avoided making a comment by saying, "Come on, Jas, how about you and I challenge Jeffrey and Marcus in a game?"

Marcus and Jeffrey played a good game but they still lost. "Marcus, why didn't you tell me that she plays like a pro?"

"Jeffrey, I wanted you to see that for yourself."

"Mom is the best, Mr. Jeffrey."

"I believe that," he responded.

"Well, I think I've worked up an appetite," Marcus said.

"We ordered dinner from A'Palace," Liah told him. "It should be here shortly."

"I guess I'll just have something to drink," Marcus said. Just as soon as they got downstairs, the doorbell rang. Liah was about to answer the door. Instead Jeffrey insisted he do so. It was Tina from A'Palace.

"Hi. I have a delivery for Liah Mathis."

"I'll be glad to take it, dear."

"Is she here?" Tina asked. "I would like to see her."

"Yes, let me help you with those bags."

"Thanks. Ah," she sighed in relief.

"Jeffrey. My name is Jeffrey."

"Now who may I tell her is inquiring?"

"Tina."

"Come in and have a seat, dear. I'll let her know you're here."

Thanks, Jeffrey!"

"My pleasure." He took the food into the kitchen and told Liah that a Ms. Tina was waiting for her.

"Tina delivered our dinner?" she asked, surprised.

"Yes, she sure did," Jeffrey answered.

"Okay. Well, you all can go on and get started eating, and I will join you shortly. Addie, would you mind fixing Jas a plate?"

"Not at all, honey. Go on and visit."

"Thanks, Addie." She briskly walked out. "Tina," she yelled. "It is so good to see you."

"Girl, come here and give me a hug," Tina cried, "I have missed you like something crazy! And look at you. You look good."

"So do you. And who told you that you could lose weight, Tina?"

"Girl, I'm trying to look like the rest of ya'll."

232

"Well, you wear it well."

"Yes, I do. So, Liah, when are you coming back to work? It has been too quiet around there."

"Now I don't believe that Tina, not with you and Louis around."

"Yeah, but we were the three musketeers."

"And we still are, sweetie. I might be back next week. I'll find out after my doctor's appointment next week."

"So who is the handsome and polite gentleman?" Tina asked.

"He's the butler. Marcus loaned his cook and butler to me for a while."

"Girl, that man is ready for marriage. First he invited you to stay at his house after you got out of the hospital. Then he temporarily moves out, being the Christian man that he is. And now he is loaning out folks. You know his help, the cook and butler. Honey, we got a lot of catching up to do. But I gotta get back to work so I can clock out."

Liah didn't bother defending herself, denying anything, nor did she make any comments. She simply said, "Okay" and went on to the next conversation.

"Hey, are you working on Tuesday? I had planned on coming by there after my doctor's appointment."

"Girl, you know I'll be there."

"Okay, I'll see you on Tuesday. Tell everyone they better not have my kitchen out of order."

"Not while Louis is around. He reminds them of that every day. You take care of yourself now. And we will see you on Tuesday. We miss you, but we want you completely recovered before you come back."

"I will and thanks for coming by."

When she went back into the kitchen, everyone had nearly finished eating. "This is good, Liah," Marcus told her. "Let me fix you a plate."

"No, no. Thank you, Marcus, but I got it. Let me call the girls first."

After they were done eating, Liah, Marcus, and the kids watched movies in the family room. Jeffrey and Addie walked out to the outdoors kitchen area. Liah and Marcus told the kids about the horses, after the movie. They were all ecstatic, especially Jason. He already knew what he was going to name his horse.

"I gotta call my friends to tell them about the horse," Jacqlyne uttered.

"Me too," Jessica said. "Wait. When do we get to see them?"

"Whenever you all have some available time," Marcus responded. "But I'll have to bring you all your riding outfits before you can take the horses out."

"Look out, cowgirl," Jacqlyne said. The girls thanked and hugged him again and then off to their rooms to call their friends.

"Mr. Marcus, thank you for being so thoughtful," Jason said, before he went upstairs. Jas came right back down and asked if he could lie down on the couch by her and Marcus.

"Sure, honey." Fifteen minutes hadn't gone by before he fell asleep. Marcus picked him up and took him upstairs. After he tucked Jason in bed, he came downstairs and told Liah that Jason wanted to say goodnight. "Okay, I'll be back in a moment," she told Marcus. Jason was nearly asleep when she walked in. She stayed in his room until he was sound asleep.

"Marcus, I want you to know that I truly appreciate everything you've done for us. I feel like I should be giving you something."

"Why, baby?"

"I just do. You're always so giving."

"Liah, those are only things. You've given me something much more valuable—time with you and your children, something money can't buy." She was aching to tell him that she wanted to spend her life with him. Instead she told him that he was the best thing that had happened to her and her children. Though they'd only known each other a short time, their relationship was quite intense. She felt as if their hearts were intertwined. It was apparent to her that they were soul mates.

"As much as I want to continue being in your presence, my love, I need to go so I can get ready for church tomorrow."

"I know." Yet, she was reluctant to let him go.

"Are you going to church tomorrow?" he asked.

"Yes, I plan to."

"Where are you going?"

"I need to go to our worship service tomorrow. Would you like to go with us?"

"Sure, I would love to. Are you going to early service?"

"Yes, I plan to."

"Good, I'll pick you all up around seven thirty.

"Then I will see you in the morning. Let me walk you to the door." He got up and then pulled her up. "Hey, I forgot to ask you. Are you all going to the cookout next Saturday?"

"Yes, I told Lillie we would be there. I hope that's alright."

"Are you kidding? I wouldn't have it any other way. Anyway, Mom told me that she invited you, and I am looking forward to it. I can't wait to see the kids open all their stuff. Ooops," he whispered.

"What are you talking about? What stuff, Marcus?"

"Ah, I wasn't supposed to tell you."

"Come on, Marcus, spill."

"No. I can't tell."

"Marcus Adrian Michaels."

"Okay, alright. They bought them laptops, iPods with wireless head-phones, games, and electronic gadgets. And I know what you're going to say, Liah, but they haven't had the opportunity to spoil children. And she knows that I pretty much think of your children as mine."

"Do you really feel that way?" she asked him.

"More and more each day." She just stared at him with those beautiful brown eyes that seemed to take his breath away. He pulled her close to him, not aware that lips were pressed against her ears. She quickly pulled back, repositioning how they were embracing. Before she knew it the words flew out, "I love you, Marcus, more than you know."

"What? What was that?"

"I said I love you."

"I love you, too, baby. But I'm talking about the words that came after I love you."

"I don't know it probably was an echo."

"Yeah, right, woman."

Good, he didn't hear me. She thought. *At least not well enough to make sense of the words.*

"Okay, for now, but I want to know about the 'more than you know' tomorrow."

Liah giggled. "I thought you didn't hear me." She opened the door and whispered good night to him. "What if I say I'm not ready to go?"

"Then I must insist that you do. It's time to depart, Marcus. Good night."

He inhaled deeply and agreed. "Yes, it is. Okay, goodnight, love." She said good night back then closed the door. He sat down in the chair that was right outside the door for a moment. He thought to himself, *if there were ever a particular time to pray, this is it.* He was in need of strength and so was Liah. She stood by the door with her head bowed, praying.

~Chapter Seventeen~

Sunday after service, Liah and Marcus took the kids to pick out riding outfits. Marcus said to them, "I have an idea. I'm going to give Morgan a call to see if he wants to meet us at the ranch."

"Oh, that's a good idea," Liah agreed. After they were done shopping, they stopped by a little Greek restaurant for a quick lunch. The kids were excited about going to the ranch. Marcus briefly shared the history of the ranch on their way there. The ranch had been handed down to Morgan Sr. from his father's side of the family. After Marcus finished telling them the story, he offered to take them to the ranch to spend the weekend when school was out.

"Whoa, that would be awesome, Mom," Jason said excitedly. "Hey Mom, are you and Mr. Marcus getting married?" he asked, randomly.

"Good question, Jas," Jacqlyne said.

"Well, are you?" Jessica asked. Marcus and Liah looked at each other. Marcus deflected the question to Liah and said, "Liah, this question is for you."

"How about we let you all know when we know."

"Okay, Mom, if that's the best answer you got."

"It's all I got, baby."

When they got to the ranch, Morgan was already there. He was waiting for them out by the barn. The kids were happy to see him as always. He picked Jas up and lifted him in the air. He and Marcus had a habit of doing that. "Be careful, Morgan," Marcus warned.

"He's fine, Marcus," Liah said. "His brothers do it all of the time."

"Well, alright now!" Morgan said, "Are you all ready to go riding?"

"Yeah," they all screamed. They were all excited about seeing their horses. Marcus and Liah watched the kids ride before they took their horses out.

"The girls are natural-born riders like Jas," Marcus affirmed.

"I'm glad they are," Liah said, "because it has been a long time since I've been on a horse and I'm pretty sure I stink."

"Well, I guess it's time to find out," Marcus replied. Liah wasn't as bad as she thought she was. She actually did really well. That is until she was getting off the horse and her boot got caught in the stirrup and she fell into some horse manure. "Nooo," she screamed.

Marcus came running to her rescue. "Liah," he called out. "Are you okay?"

"Yes, I just fell in horse poop, and now I'm stinking."

"I distinctly remember you using that exact word before you got on the horse," Marcus reminded her.

"Marcus, this is not the time to remind me."

"I'm sorry, baby. Can you stand? Are you hurting anywhere?"

"No, I'm not hurt. Just please get me to a shower quickly."

"Come on. I'll take you back to the house."

"I need to get my clothes out of the truck," she said.

"Let's take the cart and we'll drive by the truck." Liah was flabbergasted, when she walked in.

"Oh, my gosh, Marcus, this is gorgeous."

"Who is the designer?"

"My mom and her friend Ariana."

"They did a spectacular job. Okay point me toward the shower."

"There are three showers in here. You can take the one second door on the left." She went in the bathroom got her towels out and then got undressed. She then turned on the shower water. As she was about to get in, Marcus opened the door about to come in.

She screamed, "Marcus, what are you doing?" She quickly grabbed her towel to cover herself. Marcus immediately turned around and profusely apologized. "What are you doing in here, Marcus?"

"I didn't know you were in here. I told you the second door on the left."

"And I counted, one then two and ended up here."

"Did you count the small door?"

"Yes."

"I meant excluding the small door."

"You should have been more specific! Did you see anything?"

"No. Not really."

"What do you mean by not really?"

"Honestly, it happened so fast, all I remember is the towel."

"Marcus, just go please."

"I'm going."

I can't believe he saw me or maybe or whatever he saw or perhaps what he didn't see," she babbled out loud. Oh my gosh, this is so embarrassing. I think I'm ready to go home, she said, as she continued to babble.

Marcus, on the other hand, made it to the right bathroom. He sat down on the stool for a moment to collect himself, perhaps taking a moment to pray again. He then stood up and asked himself out loud, *did I see anything? I don't think so. If I did, I am certainly not ready to remember.* I do not *need that thought in my mind.* He briskly sat back down, looking as if he was still experiencing a moment of shock. He bowed his head again momentarily, taking another moment to pray. Finally he proceeded to prepare for his shower.

After Liah's shower, she waited for Marcus in the living room. She passed the time by looking through an old photo album. She ran across some pictures of Marcus with his ex-wife. *Hum, she is pretty,* she said out loud. *Too bad she didn't hang on to Marcus.* She flipped through the pages and came across some pictures of Marcus and Morgan when they were about two years old. They were in their birth suits. *Awe— looky here, they are so cute and funny looking,* she said out loud. *Why did parents take picture of their children naked back then? I suppose for moments like this, it's a way to embarrass them in front of the girlfriends.*

As she continued to look, she started laughing. The more she looked, the more she laughed as if it was the most hilarious thing. She was still laughing when Marcus walked in. He was more than pleased to hear her laughing. He thought maybe she wasn't so upset with him after all.

"What are you laughing at?" he asked.

"Pictures," she replied.

"Oh no, you didn't see the pictures of Morgan and me naked, did you?"

"I'm afraid I did. I thought you guys were cute."

"Yeah, Mom, I'm paying you back for this one," he said out loud.

"Don't feel bad, it's all parents' trademark."

"I supposed you saw the one of my ex-wife as well."

"Uh huh. I thought she was cute too. Where is she?"

"She's around. She just moved here last year around Thanksgiving."

"Have you seen her?"

"Yes," he answered hesitantly. "Actually, I had lunch with her right before I met you."

"Really," she replied.

"I think she's involved with someone."

"I didn't ask you that."

"I know. I just thought I'd tell you since we had lunch together."

"Marcus, I'm not bothered by what you've done with your ex-wife before you and I met. Neither would I mind you having lunch with her now. However, should that happen now, I do expect you to inform me of it."

"And I will."

"I don't know about you," she stated, but "I don't see this conversation going anywhere good at the moment, so shall we just drop it?"

"Done," he replied quickly. He then sat down and took her in his arms and apologized again.

"Marcus, honey, thanks, but it's okay. I'm over it."

"I love you, baby."

"I love you, Marcus." Just as she was about to embrace him back, Morgan screamed Marcus' name.

"We're in here, Morgan," Marcus answered loudly.

Then the kids ran in frantically asking Liah if she was okay. "I'm fine, Jess. Why?"

"The ranch attendant told us that you fell off the horse," Morgan, replied.

"I'm sorry you guys were worried, but it really wasn't that serious. My boot got caught in the stirrup as I was getting off the horse, and I fell," she paused, "in some horse manure."

"Ugh, Marcus, you're sitting by a horse poop lady," Morgan laughed.

"Morgan, just hush, you're not funny," Marcus told him.

"Yeah, kind of funny. But okay."

"Anyway, did you all enjoy horseback riding?" Liah asked them. They all told her it was a lot of fun and they wanted to come back soon. Morgan sang praises about how well they all did. He was quite impressed, he told Marcus and Liah. "Okay babies," Liah said, "it's time to get cleaned up."

"Talking about me, too, Mommy?" Morgan asked animatedly.

"Sure, Morgan."

"Okay, I will, after the little ones are finished," he responded. "Is anyone hungry?"

"I am," Jason said. "I think the riding drained me of all my food." Horse riding apparently drained everyone because they were all famished.

"I don't know about you all, but I have a taste for barbeque," Liah stated.

"Oh, yeah," Morgan said, "that sounds good. And I know just the little shop to get it from."

"Oh, yeah, Morgan," Marcus exclaimed. "The little shop about a mile away, just at the bottom of the hill."

'That's it. Some good old-fashioned down-home cooking," Morgan said."

"Yes, it is. Marcus agreed"

"What do you all know about some good old-fashioned down-home cooking?' Liah asked.

"Girl, we used to live next door to an African-American family," Morgan answered. "As a matter of fact, we were all close friends."

"Yeah, they moved away right after our graduation," Marcus said. "Trey went in the military and we lost contact with him after about a year. But his mom could cook good and his dad. Oh, man, his dad was the king of barbeque."

"Man, we had some good times back then," Morgan stated. "Okay, this conversation is making me hungry. I'll be back shortly."

"Alright, hurry back," Marcus said. Morgan hurried out the door. "When the kids are done getting cleaned up, I will give you all a tour of the place," Marcus told Liah.

"Okay, but in the meantime I'm going to cuddle up with a blanket. Marcus, do you have any bottled water?"

"I believe so. Let me go check. I'll be right back."

'Okay."

"Yep, as I thought. There was plenty of bottled water and sodas. One for you and a soda for me."

"You know, you're just drinking sugar, right. That stuff is full of high-fructose corn syrup and that stuff is very unhealthy for you."

Marcus sat the can on the coffee table. "Liah, you just had to mess it up for me. That soda was nice and cold and ready to hit the spot. And you had to go and bring up health issues."

"Just trying to save you, honey." Marcus got up and put the can back in the refrigerator and got a bottle of water instead. "Marcus, may I use your phone? I need to call Addie, and mine is in the truck in my purse." He handed her his phone.

'Thanks." She told Addie and Jeffrey to take the day off.

"You're not trying to match-make, are you?" Marcus asked her.

"Not really. But they do already seem kind of sweet on each other."

Maybe they do need a little encouragement."

"Alright, cupid." They both giggled.

The kids came out one after the other. "Did you leave the bathroom clean?" Liah asked them.

"I did," Jacqlyne answered.

"So did I," Jessica said.

"And what about you, Jas?

"I laid my clothes on the hamper. My towels are lying on the seat inside of the shower."

"Okay. Marcus, do you have a washer and dryer here?"

"Yes. Why?

"Because after I'm done cleaning the bathrooms, I'm going to wash the towels."

"Really?"

"Yes, really. Why does that surprise you?"

"Because, my ex asked if I could have the maids come in to do it."

"Maids, I think being called a maid is a belittling word. It's just like being called retarded when someone is mentally challenged. Just a pet peeve!"

"I don't like referring to anyone as maid either. Anyway, honey, you don't have to clean up. We do have a housekeeper on retainer who comes in to clean up the place. But I do appreciate your kind offer. So, let's take a quick tour of the ranch before Morgan gets back with the food."

"Marcus, you and the kids go. I forgot I have on heels and they are not ranch walking shoes."

"Come on. Let's go look in Mom's closet. It looks like you both can wear the same size." He took Liah into the master suite and showed her the shoe closet. His mom had a shoe fetish as well.

"Whoa ... look at all of these gorgeous shoes."

"Come on, Liah—pick out a pair of walking shoes. You can admire the shoes when we have more time."

"Okay, alright, Pops, I'm picking."

He chuckled, and then said, "You are something else, Ms. Shoe Fanatic." She just happened to pick the pair of shoes Lillie wore when she walked around the ranch grounds.

"Oh, now these have got to be the most comfortable shoes I've ever worn. It feels like my feet are in a bed of fur."

"I need to try those shoes on," Jacqlyne said.

"You can, when we get back," Liah responded.

"Mom, be ready to release them."

"If I'm not mistaken, those are the ones my mom likes also. Okay, I'm taking you all to the ground floor first," Marcus said.

"Did you say it has a ground floor?" Liah asked.

"Yes, and it has three bedrooms down there."

"Can't wait to see it," she responded.

"Come on. The kitchen is this way. We have to go through it in order to go downstairs."

"Ooh, this is a really nice kitchen. And I love this country-style stove with the grill," Liah said.

"So does my mom. She just had to have it," Marcus commented. "Look at this pantry. My parents keep it stocked, and also the fridge and freezer, too."

"Why? Are they up here often?" Liah inquired.

"Not really. They just want to make sure when someone does come, they have everything they need."

"Makes sense," Liah said.

"I don't think I told you that I converted my basement into a small apartment. Or did I?"

"No, I don't recall," she responded.

"I still have some minor things to do but it's pretty much done. Morgan converted his as well. He has a little more to do than I do."

"Oh, really? Well I would like to see yours when I'm over again."

"Okay, remind me to show it to you."

"Do you have one in your house?" he asked her.

"Yes, I guess it could be called an apartment. It has a huge family room, a small kitchen, a bedroom, and a bath and a half. We only use it for a safety escape when there's bad weather."

"Liah, it sounds like an apartment to me." He chuckled.

"If you say so, Michaels" He showed them every room. "It is really nice down here. It looks like one of those cottages I stayed in on my last vacation. It's quite well-designed. They did an awesome job."

"Sounds like I hear Morgan driving up," Marcus announced. "How about we finish the tour when we come back to the ranch again?"

"Sure, that would fine. I'm ready to eat anyway."

"So am I," Jason seconded.

"Come on, Jacqlyne," Jessica cried out. "The last one up has to give something new away, like that new top you bought last week."

"No," Jacqlyne screamed, and then sprinted up the stairs. They made it up around the same time, so no one won.

"Yeah," she yelled. "It's a tie, so I don't have to give up my top."

"Whatever, Jacqlyne," Jessica frowned. "You took off before I even got the words out. But I'm gonna be nice and let you slide, because I know how much you like that top."

"Okay, sorry, but thanks," Jacqlyne said to her.

Morgan came back with enough food to feed a little league team.

"Alright, come on everyone. I got food."

"I have an idea. Why don't we take the food out on the patio," Marcus suggested.

"Good idea," Liah agreed. Liah and girls set the table in a buffet style. After Morgan was done blessing the food, Jason insisted he say grace as well.

"Go for it, champ," Marcus told him.

"Okay, thanks. Good bread—good meat—good gosh—let's eat— in Jesus name, Amen." Morgan and Marcus thought it was the funniest thing. Liah just shook her head.

"Wow, this is really good barbeque," Liah said. "Maybe one of the best I've had."

"I'm with you on that, Liah," Morgan agreed. They all had an enjoyable time, laughing, and talking. When they were done eating, Marcus and Morgan cleared the table. Liah and the girls packed to-go bags to share with Jeffrey and Addie.

"Thanks for today Marcus. I'm going to gather our things," Liah told him.

"It was my pleasure. Hey, Morgan, are you going back to evening service?"

"Yeah, but I'm going to take a shower before I leave."

"Alright, man. We're going to get out of here and we'll see you at church."

"Are you going to the cookout next Saturday?" Morgan asked.

"Yeah, we planned to. Hey, we gotta run. Catch you later, man."

"I'm really glad we came to service with you, Marcus. It was a great inspirational lesson."

"It was indeed," Marcus agreed. "Oh no, here comes Mom and Dad, and they're bringing people with them. Hi, Mom and Dad."

"Hi, son, it's good to see you," Morgan said looking proud. Lillie and then hugged him and Liah.

"Mom and Dad, Morgan told me to say hi. He had to leave about five minutes earlier."

"Alright, thanks, son," Morgan said.

"And, everyone, this is Marcus' beautiful lady friend, Liah." Lillie introduced them.

"We're very pleased to meet you," said an older salt-and-pepper haired gentleman, with a deep voice. "Marcus, I hope this means what I think it means," he blurted.

"Depends on what you think it means, Mr. Sandler."

"Ah, now you know what I mean. It's about time you tried it again."

"Well, in that case, it means exactly what you thought."

"Oh, leave him alone, Frank," Lillie told him.

"I'm just making sure he's moving on in life," Frank said, chuckling. Liah's children walked up.

"Liah, these must be your darling children, "Lillie presumed.

"Yes," she responded and then introduced them. "Liah, Mr. and Mrs. Michaels are too formal," Lillie said. "You all are practically part of the family now. Come on, babies. Give your Nana a hug."

"Does that mean we can call you Nana?" Jason asked.

"You bet it does, sweetie. And you are a handsome one too."

"Let me in on this hugging," Morgan Sr. insisted. "You all can call me Poppy, never grandpa because I don't look anything like a grandpa yet. Say, Marcus, why don't you and Liah attend the benefit with us on Friday? It starts at seven-thirty."

"Liah, what do you think?" Marcus asked.

"I don't have anything planned, so, yes, let's go."

"Wonderful," Lillie answered. "Then we'll see you on Friday. And, babies, we'll see you on Saturday."

"It was nice to meet you, Nana and Poppy," Jason said angelically. The girls gave them both hugs.

"Liah, we're looking forward to spending time with these children on Saturday," Lillie said. "And, Morgan, Honey, did I tell you the ball is black and white?"

"No, but I'm glad you remembered Dear. Morgan chuckled"

"I am, too, Honey. Liah I'm sure you have something gorgeous in your closet."

"I don't know, Lillie. I think an occasion like this is a reason to go shopping."

"So do I, so do I" Lillie replied. "Call me and we'll go together."

"Oh, my goodness, Marcus," Morgan Sr. said. "You have one, too."

"One what, Dad?'

"A shopper."

"Right! Yes, sir, I know."

"Marcus, we had better go. The kids need to get ready for school," Liah told him.

"Okay, honey. Mom and Dad, we'll see you all on Friday."

"Alright, baby," Lillie said, "you all have a good week."

"We're looking forward to seeing you all on Friday."

"Same here, Morgan," Liah agreed. "Lillie, I'll call you before Thursday."

"Alright, Dear."

By the time they were on their way home, everyone was tired. Marcus and Liah had very little conversation. When they got to Liah's house, the kids got out and went inside. Liah and Marcus stayed outside and talked briefly.

On Monday afternoon, Marcus called Liah to tell her that he had to go out of town on Tuesday morning, and should be back by Thursday evening. He also told her that his schedule was pretty tight, so he didn't think he would be able to see her before he left.

Tuesday morning Liah went to her doctor's appointment as scheduled. She was very pleased with the results. He gave her a clean bill of health and released her to go back to work the following week. However, he warned her not to overdo it.

She stopped by A'Palace after her doctor's appointment just as she had told Tina she would. She went in through the side door like she usually did, walked in her office, and put on her apron. She then crept into the kitchen. "What have you all done to my kitchen?" she asked in her serious tone, trying really hard not to laugh. They all looked around and started screaming her name. She burst out laughing. "How did you all know I wasn't serious?"

"Cause we know this kitchen is in top health inspection condition," Louis replied.

"That's because you all know better," she responded.

"We sure do. We didn't want to hear your mouth," Tina said.

"Am I that bad?"

"Only when your kitchen is not up to par," Tina answered. "Anyway, honey, we are glad to see you again." They all came over and gave to give her hugs.

"Well, boss, are you ready to get back to work?" Louis asked.

"Don't start, Louis," she said to him. He chuckled. "I will be back next week."

"Alright, we're back," Tina exclaimed. "Time for some more kitchen drama!"

"Alright girls, ya'll know what time is! Louis said. Liah, Louis, and Tina had a little trio skit that they sang and danced to, followed by a handshake. One, two, three, hit it— "bump to the left...bump to the right...bump, bump, bump, cause it's all right...um, uh huh." The temporary sous chef, Joedi, came back in and interrupted them.

"Oh, Joedi," Louis said. "Liah, this is Joedi, my assistant. Joedi, the one and only ... Chef Liah Mathis.

"Chef Mathis, it is a pleasure to finally meet you."

"Well, thank you, Joedi. So how is it going here for you?"

"I think it's going really well. I've learned a lot from Louis. I like working here."

"Good. I'm glad to hear that. Well, Louis, do you think we should keep him?"

"I think so. He's been a great help. After he passes Liah's initiation, he'll be tight."

"Tight, Louis?" she responded.

"One of Joedi's words."

"Alright, Joedi, the moment of initiation has arrived," Liah told him. "Are you ready?"

"As I will ever be," he responded.

"Okay, Joedi, I want you to create me a grilled chicken sandwich. Don't be sparing with the toppings. Create a sauce to drizzle over the meat, and make it original. No yellow cheese, please, no basic white sauce. I would like a twice-baked potato and surprise me with the toppings and a green salad. Also a glass of freshly brewed green tea, and bring some fruit into it. I am looking for taste, creativity, and presentation. Are there any hot-baked potatoes?" she asked.

"Yes, there are," he answered.

"Then you have fifteen minutes. I'm going to sit in my office so you won't feel pressured."

"Thank you, ma'am."

"And, Joedi."

"Ma'am?"

"You can cut the ma'am out. A simple yes and no will do fine. Tina and Louis, would you all like to sit in here with me?"

"Girl, yeah," Tina answered, "Come on Louis."

"Okay, in a minute," he replied. "I need to speak with Joedi for a moment."

Liah and Tina went in her office. "So how's things really been going since I've been away?" Liah asked.

"Things have been going well. It was a bit of a struggle at first, but thanks to you, we survived."

"Yes, we did," Louis responded as he walked through the door. "But we need you back. I'm not as quick on my feet as you. Honey, I don't know how you prep and cook at the same time."

"It's a gift, Louis," Tina said.

"Hey, Chef," Liah said to Louis. "Come on in here and join us. So here's what I'm thinking Louis. When I come back, I'm going to make Joedi your assistant. Therefore, I'm changing your title to SSC."

"SSC?" Louis replied, looking puzzled.

"Yeah, Louis, Senior Sous Chef. And Joedi will be the JSC. The Junior Sous Chef."

"Huh," Louis chuckled. "I like it."

"It does have a catch to it," Tina said.

"It also makes you responsible for Joedi, Louis."

"Alright, I can handle that." Joedi, knocked at the door. He and one of the servers came in.

"Your lunch is served, Madam," Joedi announced, in a Frenchman's voice. "Hmm, not bad for presentation," Liah said. "Okay let's see what you have here. The ice tea glass is not chilled and lemon or lime wedges are missing."

"Snap, I totally forgot that," Joedi responded.

"Hold on now. Let's get to the important stuff. Tell me about the sandwich." He explained everything that he prepared step by step. Liah took three bites before she said a word.

"The sandwich is good, Joedi, very tasty. However, it's missing two of my favorites. What are they, Louis?"

"Did you add sautéed mushrooms and spinach?" Louis asked. "Ah, man! No, I didn't."

"Don't sweat it, Joedi," Liah told him. You did an awesome job on the sandwich and the baked potato looks delectable. I'm giving you nine out of ten on presentation, an eight out of ten on creativity and nine out of ten on taste."

"Now that's good man," Louis said. "I told you he was good, Liah."

'Yes, you did. You all take a piece and tell me what you think," she told Tina and Louis. They both took a piece of the sandwich.

"It's pretty good," Louis mumbled.

"I second that pretty good," Tina said.

"Here's a pen and a piece of paper. You all only need to rate on taste." They wrote their numbers down and handed her the paper. "I don't believe it. Both of you rated nine."

"Well, Joedi, welcome aboard," she told him. "You are now a full-time permanent. Hey guys, I've got to get going. I need all three of you to be here Monday morning at eight thirty. Louis and Tina, we will do catch-up on Monday. Joedi, keep up the good work, and I am looking forward to working with you. And by way, the tea was really good. Even without the wedge and blended fruit. Remember now, you have to think on your toes when customers make specific requests." She packed up the rest of her food and took it with her.

After she left, she picked Jason up from school. She thought it would be a good time to spend some quality time with him before the girls got home. When they got home, she helped him with his homework and then they played pool until the girls returned. By then Addie was summoning everyone to dinner.

By the end of their meal, Jacqlyne randomly yelled out, "Mom, we have to go to rehearsal at six thirty." Liah looked at her, displeased.

"Jacqlyne, please don't do that. I thought something was really wrong. My goodness, child! And I know that you have to go to rehearsal." They all knew Liah couldn't stand it when Jacqlyne randomly yelled out as if something was really wrong. For a moment everything got silent.

"I'm sorry, Mom."

"I know you are, Jacqlyne," Liah whispered. Addie got up and started clearing the table. "I'll help you, Ms. Addie," Jacqlyne volunteered, taking advantage of the opportunity to escape the chill from her mother. They cleared the table and came back with servings of cheesecake.

"You made cheesecake, Addie!" Liah excitedly exclaimed. "You deserve a raise."

"Come to think of it, I have one coming up soon."

"I'll remind Marcus when he gets back," Liah said. Jeffrey cleared his throat.

"You too, Jeffrey." He smile and dug into his cheesecake. "This cheesecake is delectable, Addie," Jeffrey told her. "Wouldn't you agree Liah?"

She had just stuffed a piece in her mouth. After she finished swallowing, she said to him, "It is indeed, delectable, Jeffrey."

"Ms. Addie, it really is delectably delightful," Jacqlyne avowed.

Jessica, then followed in her British accent saying, "It is scrumptious, Ms. Addie.

Jason wasn't about to allow himself to be left out of the complimentary loop. So he looked at Addie and said, "It is stupendous, Ms. Addie."

Addie looked at them, shook her head while smiling and then said to them, "You all are a bunch of crazy folks."

"But yet you feed us anyway," Liah murmured. They all started laughing. "Addie and Jeffrey, do you all have any plans after dinner?" Liah inquired.

"I don't have any," Jeffrey responded.

"Neither do I," Addie said.

"Would you all like to go to the girls' rehearsal this evening?"

"We'd love to," Jeffrey answered, answering for them both.

"Good deal. I'm going to take Jas upstairs so he can take a quick shower and get his clothes ready for tomorrow. We'll be leaving around 6:10. Addie, thanks again for dinner and dessert. Everything was really wonderful."

"You are quite welcome, dear."

Liz spotted Liah as soon as she walked in. Liah immediately thought about what she had seen at the ice cream shop. Nonetheless, she was sticking to her decision to stay out it. "Addie and Jeffrey, would you all excuse me. I need to speak to Liz for a moment? Jas, honey, stay with Addie and Jeffrey."

Liah and Liz walked toward each other. "Hi Liah," Liz cried, energetically.

"Hey, girlfriend, how are you?"

"I'm good. How are you feeling these days?"

"Getting back to myself. I'm going back to work next week."

"Does that mean the doctor released you, Liah?"

"Yes, it does."

"Alright, now. Because you know how you are."

"So I've been told by many." They had a moment to chat before the rehearsal started. "Anyway, has Lillie Michaels called you yet, Liz?"

"Yes, she did. And thank you for sending her to me. I like her, and I know I'm going to enjoy working with her."

"Good. If you like, we can schedule a date for you to come by next week to check out the ball room."

"Oh, yes, that would be great," Liz said. "You know I like to see what I'm going be working with."

"I know. I'll be in Monday."

"Why don't I swing by there around two o'clock?"

"Sure. That's a good time. We'll be slowing up by then."

"So, honey, come on tell me how things are going with you and Mr. Michaels. Do I hear wedding bells ringing?"

"I don't know about that, but things are really good."

"Girl, what do you mean you don't know about that? I saw that look when he looked at you. He was glowing like a pregnant woman."

"Liz, you're funny! You know that right?

Liz laughed and said, "Girl you know I'm right."

"Okay, the kids are going on stage," Liah blurted. "Conversation over!"

"It is for now," Liz mumbled.

"Come on, Liz, Addie and Jeffrey are holding seats for us."

"Oh good. There are a lot of people here. Liah, are you staying for the entire rehearsal?"

"No, we're leaving after their set. What about you?"

"No. We're leaving too. Their dad is supposed to be home tonight. Their dad! What about your husband?"

"Girl, I am a single married woman. He's gone most of the time."

"Are you okay with that?"

"Not really. But I'm not going to let it get me down."

"Anytime you need to talk, please don't hesitate to call."

"Thanks, Liah. I'm sure I'll be taking you up on that." They sat quietly for the remainder of the rehearsal set. Liah felt a bit uncomfortable since she knew Liz's husband was cheating on her. She knew that she had a right to know. However, she feared telling her might not be such a good idea. She was adamant that she was doing the right thing by not interfering. She hoped that he would do the right thing and tell her himself. But what was the chance of that happening? Nevertheless, she was a firm believer in hope. So she kept quiet and remained ever hopeful.

After the first rehearsal, there was a short intermission, which worked out well for Liah and Liz. They didn't want to appear rude by walking out during the rehearsal. All four of the kids spotted them immediately and came rushing over.

"Mom, how did we do," Jessica asked.

"You all were fabulous as always, sweetie."

"I think they're ready for the performance already," Liz commented.

"They are, and it's good because the performance is on Monday," Liah said.

"I'm with you on that, Liah," Addie added. "These stars are ready. Don't you think so, Jeffrey?"

"Yes, and I want a front-row seat."

"Well, Liah, as always it was great seeing you and I'm glad you're feeling better. But we gotta go."

Liah hugged Liz and whispered in her ear. "Remember what I said."

"I will, honey. I'll see you on Monday," she responded

"Okay, you all take care," Liah told them.

The girls said goodnight and went upstairs as soon as they walked through the door. "Addie and Jeffrey, thanks for going with us tonight."

"It was no problem at all. We enjoyed it," Addie said.

"We certainly did, dear," Jeffrey agreed. "Thanks for inviting us."

"You are welcome."

"Anyone for cheesecake?" Addie asked.

"I'm in," Liah answered."

"So am I," Jeffrey responded.

"I'm going to tuck this big boy in bed first."

"We'll be waiting in the kitchen," Addie told her. Like the Golden Girls," she laughed, and so did Liah and Jeffrey. Liah practically drugged Jas up the stairs and put him in bed and then joined Addie and Jeffrey in the kitchen. Addie had already cut her a slice of cheesecake and made her a cup of tea.

"Addie, you are a sweetheart." The three of them sat at the bar and chatted until Marcus called. Then Liah said goodnight and went upstairs to her room. Addie and Jeffrey watched a movie together in the patio room. They seemed to be spending a lot more time together, thanks to Liah. She would have been tickled pink had she known.

After Liah finished talking to Marcus, she called and chatted with Jen briefly. Jen was a little under the weather, so Liah offered to take all of the kids to school the next day. Just as soon as she hung up the phone, Alisha, Chantel, and Shayna called. Shayna was usually at Alisha's when they all talked on the phone together. "So what are you guys up to?" Liah asked.

"We just wanted to see how your doctor's appointment went today," Alisha replied.

"And to find out what you're doing for your birthday," Chantel added.

"My doctor's appointment went well. I am released to go back to work on Monday."

"And?" Chantel inquired.

"And I have to take it easy and not overdo it. As far as my birthday, I haven't made any plans yet."

"Good, we're having a girls' night in," Shayna said. "We'll be there on the fifteenth and sixteenth."

"Really!" Liah responded happily.

"Really," Alisha replied. "Now tell us what's been going on with you and Mr. Michaels," she demanded. Liah told them all about the visit to the ranch, including Marcus walking in on her and falling off the horse in horse manure. They thought that was hilarious. Chantel continued to snicker, after everyone else had calmed down.

"Chantel, you can stop now," Liah told her.

"Okay, alright. I'm sorry. But I do wish I could have seen your expression. I bet you showered for an hour."

"Not quite. Anyway, Lillie and Morgan invited Marcus and me to a black and white ball on Friday, and the kids and me to a cookout on Saturday. She went on to tell them about the gifts Marcus' parents bought the kids. Then she said. "And you won't believe this. They want the kids to call them Nana and Poppy."

"Are you serious?" Shayna asked.

"Uh huh. You know Marcus and Morgan are sterile and their sister doesn't have any children. "So I guess for now, mine are as good as it gets."

"Girl, Marcus is as good as it gets, for you and the kids," Chantel declared.

"Liah, she's right about that," Alisha seconded. "He is a God-send."

"He sure is," Shayna added. "Where is he anyway?"

"He is out of town on business."

"How often does he go out of town?" Alisha asked.

"I believe he's been gone at least twice in the last two months."

"I hope that's the only thing he has in common with Brannon," Shayna stated.

"Believe me, he's is no Brannon Mathis. He has a totally different aura."

"I don't think you have anything to worry about, Liah," Alisha told her.

"He's a real man. Now, Chan, what about you and Mr. Morgan?" Shayna inquired.

"We're getting to know each other. We talk pretty often."

"I think he's a good man, too," Alisha said.

"Oh, he is," Liah agreed.

"That's right, Liah, should know," Shayna blurted.

"He's really good with children, too, Chan," Liah told her. "But dating him is your decision."

"We'll see," Chan replied. "Hey, guys, I have to get back to work. Let's continue this conversation at a later date."

"Wait, Chan," Liah said. "When is your last day?"

"The end of April. I've got to go. Let's talk on Saturday, after Liah's weekend with the Michaels. Maybe it will influence my decision." After Chan hung up the others talked for a moment longer.

"Liah, I can't wait to hear about your weekend," Shayna said. "I just feel like something juicy is going to happen."

"Shayna, you really need to get a life," Liah replied.

"Uh, I know Ms. went-without-a-life-for-six-years, is not telling me to get a life," Shayna stated.

"Yes, she is," Alisha replied. "And she's right."

"Ooh, that's a low blow, Lisha," Shayna said. "I think I'm hurt."

"Right, Shayna." She laughed.

"Okay, ladies, I will talk to you all Saturday," Liah said. They all said goodnight. The phone calls had taken up the time Liah had planned to do something else so she decided to turn in for the night. *I suppose I can get some reading and writing done tomorrow night*, she said out loud. *Oh no, I can't go to bed just yet. I need to call Jayde and the boys.* She called all three of them and was unable to reach either of them, so she left messages.

Thursday afternoon, Liah met Lillie at the mall. They spent hours searching for the perfect ball dresses. Finally, they found the dresses they couldn't resist. "I can't believe we've gone to nearly every formal wear store in this mall and we have finally found dresses," Lillie said.

"I was about to think that we would have more luck wishing for a fairy godmother." They burst out laughing.

"Honey, I hear that. You and me both." Liah found in many ways she was like Lillie, especially when it came to shopping.

They took a break and went to the food court. Liah got a salad at one place and teriyaki chicken at another. Lillie got salad and orange chicken. The both of them ended up eating off each other's plate. The two of them talked as if they were old friends. Lillie suggested that they get dessert so they could finish their conversation. The conversation got deeper during dessert. Lillie even told Liah that she thought she was the best thing for Marcus.

"I'm not trying to meddle in your business. We have made it a point not to interfere in our children's relationships. Well, at least after the initial introduction."

"You mean like the surprise luncheon you and Morgan planned?"

"Child, yes. But Marcus is slow to move on. However, in his case I'm glad he didn't because he might not have met you."

"Yes, I am thankful for that."

"Honey, you have had some profound effect on him. He's never opened up his heart like that about anyone in front of us."

"I was quite thrown with that one," Liah whispered, tersely. "But it was okay. Marcus is an extraordinary man. I considered it a blessing to have met him."

"Now look at you. You're glowing like he does when he talks about you." Liah looked at her and sighed. "Come on, honey," Lillie said. "Let's go search for shoes." Now she was really speaking Liah's language. She was a shoe shopper at heart. They found the perfect shoes to match the perfect dresses. Not only did the store have gorgeous shoes, they had a buy-one-and-get-one-at-half- price sale. They took full advantage of it. Liah even bought shoes for all the kids and Addie. Lillie told Liah that she had had the best time with her and was looking forward to doing it again soon.

"Lillie, any time you want to shop or just have a ladies day out just let me know."

"Don't worry, I will. I have found my soul-mate. None of my friends can keep up with me when it comes to shopping"

"Looking forward to it. Well, Lillie, as much as I've enjoyed this day, I have to go pick up the boys from school, so I will see you tomorrow evening."

"Alright. I'm going to walk out with you. I've shopped enough for one day. I'm gonna have to leave some of these shoes in my trunk so Morgan won't talked about me." They both laughed.

Liah drove up just as soon as the car riders were walking out the door. "Hi, boys. Did you have a good day at school?"

"Yes, Mom. Let me tell you what happen." Both of the boys took turns telling her about their day at school. "Mom, are you picking up my sisters?"

"No, sweetie, Liz is picking up the girls."

"Okay, Mom. Mom, I'm starving. May I have a big snack when I get home and go next door to play?"

"Of course you can have a snack, but you can't go next door, remember Jen is not feeling well. You guys can see each other tomorrow. Liah went right in and fixed her and Jas a snack. After their snack, she helped him with his homework. "Jas, finish up the last problem. I'm going outside to get some bags out of the car. If you finish before I get back in, you can come out to help. There might be a surprise in there for you." He hurried up and finished, then ran outside to help her.

"Mom. Do I really have a surprise?"

"You might. Let's go in so we can check the bags." She told him to close his eyes.

He closed his eyes, and at the same time he was laughing and saying, "What is it?"

"Okay, open your eyes."

"Roller-skate-shoes! Thanks, Mom. These are so cool!" He couldn't wait to put them on. "Mom, may I go outside to play?" he asked animatedly.

"Sure, Jas, remember to stay in the circle so I can see you and if you want to play with Timmy, you need to come in to get permission. I will call Jen to see if he can come outside." She walked him outside. Timmy and Jen were already outside.

"Can he come over to play, Liah?" Jen asked hollering across the way.

"Are you feeling better? Timmy can come over here to play."

"I am just going to sit out here, I will be fine."

Okay, thanks, Jen." The boys played together in Jen's driveway. Liah went upstairs to try on her dress with her new shoes. When she looked in the mirror, she said out loud, *when Marcus sees me in this dress he's going to be speechless*. She turned to the side to get a side view.

She walked out of the dressing room into her bedroom to look at the jewelry she had just bought. She noticed a gift bag lying on the bed. "Hum, was that there when I first walked in?" she asked herself. "Probably so. I did go straight to the dressing room." She knew it had to be from Marcus. She picked up the card and indeed it was. It read, *"Diamonds are 4-ever and so are we. Diamonds are a girl's best friend and you are mine. I love you, Liah."* She closed her eyes and held the card close for a moment. Then she whispered. *I love you, too, Marcus*. She took the jewelry bag from the dresser and walked back into her dressing room. She didn't want to look in the gift bag right away. She wanted to give her emotions a moment to calm down. Marcus' gifts seem to always have an emotional effect on her. She took another look in the mirror. *Yes, Lillie was right. This dress does look good on me*, she said out loud.

She walked back in her bedroom. She couldn't wait any longer to look in that gift bag. So she walked over to the bed and picked it up then took out the box and opened it. She couldn't believe her eyes. "Oh...my... gosh," she exclaimed. "This has got to be the most beautiful necklace I've ever seen. It was a beautiful white-gold diamond choker with a dangling emerald in the shape of a heart and with matching earrings. It was both exquisite and elegant. *It is ironic how it matches my dress so well. It's as if he had already seen it*. She walked over to the mirror and held the choker around her neck. She didn't put it on because she wanted Marcus to have the honor of doing so. As she was putting the necklace back in the case, she noticed the price sticker. *Oh—my—goodness, she exclaimed. I cannot believe he paid ten thousand dollars for this jewelry set. What's wrong with that man?"* *she said loudly. I know he can afford it.... But I can think of a lot of worthy things* *to do with that much money.*

She put the necklace back in the box then quickly stuck the case in the bag. She took off her dress, got dressed, and went downstairs. "Jeffrey," she called out. Jeffrey came running into the living room to see what she wanted. "Jeffrey, I'm sorry for yelling. But why would he spend so much money on a piece of jewelry? Well, actually three pieces. "Why," she whispered, before Jeffrey broke in.

"It's okay, dear. I know what you're thinking. But he gives generously to the needy and to many causes and especially to church missionary work. Although, he's never spent such a large amount on jewelry for anyone before...." Jeffrey paused and smiled. "Nonetheless, I do know he thinks you're priceless." Liah still looked quite puzzled. "Liah, dear, let me put your mind at ease. He also donates a million dollars to children's homes every year. In addition to that, he and Morgan have built several children's homes at no cost. He has a very generous heart."

"Really? I know he does. Why didn't he tell me about it?"

"He's not the kind of person who boasts about what he does. Much like you, dear." She looked at him curiously. "Yes, he knows how generous your giving is as well."

"Let me guess, the investigator."

"Actually, no, dear. He's a board member at some of the children's homes. And he just happened to stumble across the name Liah Cunningham."

"You're kidding!" she said.

"No, I'm pretty serious. And he didn't mention it because he thought you felt the same as he did."

"He was right. Well, okay, point is well-taken. But it is still expensive jewelry."

"Yes, it is, but remember, you're priceless."

Liah hugged Jeffrey. Then she asked him, "How did I get along without you all these years?"

"A guardian angel, perhaps," he replied. They both chuckled. "I love you, Jeffrey, and thanks."

"I love you, too, dear."

"I'm going to go next door to get Jas. Thanks again."

"Anytime."

On her way out the door, the girls were coming in. "Hi, girls, I'll be right back. I'm going to Jen's to get Jas."

"Okay, Mom," Jessica answered.

Liah stood outside and talked to Jen for a moment. They made plans to go to an earlier movie the next day. "Jen, I'll see you tomorrow. Thanks again for watching Jas."

"Anytime, honey. See you tomorrow." Jas ran all the way home so he could show his sisters his new roller skate shoes.

"Hi, Mr. Jeffrey," Jason said.

"Hi there, Jas. How's it going?"

"Good. Mom bought me roller shoes."

"I see."

"Mr. Jeffrey, do you know where my sisters are?"

"I believe they're in the kitchen, Jas."

"Thanks, Mr. Jeffrey. He hurried and went in the kitchen. Jas was in the kitchen before Liah made in the house. "Look, Jess and Jacqlyne, watch me roller skate."

"Boy, you can't skate in here," Jess told him.

"Yes, I can. Watch this." He started rolling around in the kitchen.

"Wow, Jas, I guess you can skate," Jessica said.

"They're roller-skate shoes," Jacqlyne noted excitedly. "Jas, where did you did get those rolling shoes?"

"Mom bought them."

When Liah came in she was looking for Jas. Since Jeffrey was still in the living room, she asked him if he had seen which way Jas went. "He's in the kitchen showing off his new shoes to his sisters."

"Go figure. He's trying to show off his shoes. Thanks, Jeffrey." Liah walked in the kitchen.

"Mom I like Jas's shoes," Jacqlyne told her, hoping that she had a pair of shoes as well.

"I bought you all some shoes too, Jacqlyne." She knew that's why Jacqlyne said she liked Jas's shoes. Although, she really did think Jas's shoes were cool.

"Yes!" Jacqlyne, yelled. She liked shoes just as much as Liah.

"Girl, you're always getting excited about shoes," Jessica told her.

"Hush, Jess. You know you want some shoes, too."

"You all are pitiful," Liah told them. "Let's go upstairs," she said, giving each of them a bag of shoes.

"Whoa, it's two pair of shoes," Jacqlyne exclaimed.

"Mom, I just want to say thanks—before I take a look."

"Yeah, me too, Mom," Jessica said.

Jacqlyne took her shoes out of the bags first. "Mom ... these are the same shoes I was looking at in a store at the mall," she yelled. "I can't believe it. And you got the right color. Mom, you are totally awesome."

"Jacqlyne, look at my shoes," Jessica said. "Mom, these are so cool. Thanks, Mom. You are so cool."

"You are so cool, Mom," Jacqlyne told her.

"Yeah. You say that now."

"Mom, we've always thought you were cool," Jacqlyne said. They both got up and gave her a hug. Then Jessica said to Jacqlyne, kindly, "You know Jacqlyne, these shoes go well with that new top I was trying to win from you."

"Uh huh, sure does. Well, Jess. You may borrow my top, as long as you check with me first to see if I'm going to wear it."

"Alright, sure," Jessica said gladly. "I'm going to try them on with the shirt."

"I'm going, too," Jacqlyne said. Jacqlyne was about to walk out, but noticed the gift bag lying on the bed. "Mom, who gift is this?"

"Mine, Jacqlyne."

"I bet it's from Mr. Marcus," Jessica guessed.

"Is it, Mom?" Jacqlyne asked.

"Yes, it is, nosy children." She took it out of the bag and showed it to them. Both their eyes and mouth widened. They moved in for a closer look.

"Those are real, Mom," Jacqlyne declared.

"Yes, they are," she whispered.

"Wow, Mom, I bet they had to cost at least ten-thousand dollars," Jessica stated.

"You're right, Jess. At least."

"Mom, I bet you think he paid too much money for it," Jacqlyne said, shaking her head, knowing exactly what her mom thought.

"Way too much."

"I sure hope you keep them," Jessica said to her. "These diamonds are blinding."

"I'm not really sure, honey. Now come on. Let's go down for dinner."

"Wait, Mom," Jacqlyne said. "Where's your dress?"

"It's in the closet and you can see it later. I'm going to go to poetry class tonight. You all can come if you like."

"Oh, yeah, we're there," Jessica responded."

"Okay, but you all need to take a shower after dinner, so you won't have to when we get back."

Liah invited Jeffrey and Addie to poetry night. "Jeffrey," Addie said, looking directly at him.

"What?" he replied. "I like poetry too. As a matter of fact, I was known as the 'poetry guy' in school." They all looked at him. "I used to write poems for students and teachers during Valentine's Day."

Liah looked at him and said, "Jeffrey, we have got to talk … soon. But anyway, for now, I need you to please call the limo because I really don't feel like driving."

"Sure, I'll get right on it," he said.

"Thanks, Jeffrey. Oh, and we'll be leaving around six-thirty. Addie, before I forget, you don't have to cook tomorrow. The kids are spending the night with Jen and Tim, and I'm ordering them dinner from the A'Palace."

"You're sure?" Addie responded.

"Of course, yes I am. This would be a good time for you to visit your family."

"And I'm going to do just that. Thanks, Liah."

"Addie, you do know that whenever you need time off, you can take it."

"Yeah, I know."

"Good. Now while I'm upstairs getting Jas ready for tomorrow, will you please check to make sure I have the ingredients to bake chocolate chip cookies and a carrot cake? I'm taking dessert to the cookout Saturday."

"Girl, they're going to like you even more, because those folks love carrot cake. Well, you know that. Marcus and Morgan warned you about that."

"Yes, they did. And I sent some home with them when they ate at the A'Palace."

"Right. So anyway, tell me about you and Lillie's day out."

"We had a marvelous time. We shopped, talked, ate, and shopped some more. I really enjoyed spending time with her."

"She's really an easy going person and easy to talk to. Kind of like Marcus," Addie told her."

"You know," Liah said, "I thought so as well. I also found out that we have a lot in common."

"Maybe that's one of the things that drew Marcus to you. I don't know how true it is, but there is a saying that men are drawn to women who remind them of their mom."

"Yeah, I heard something like that. But I don't know how true it is either. Anyway, I know one thing. She is a shopper at heart and you know that's me."

"Honey, yes!" Addie responded. Jason started giggling. "Jas, what are you giggling at?" Addie asked.

"The way you said, 'honey, yes'!"

"Boy, you are something else," Addie told him.

"And he needs to go upstairs so he can get ready to take a shower," Liah said.

"Alright, I'm going, Mom."

"I'll be up there in a moment. I'm going to help Addie put the food away."

"No, no, Liah, I'll get it," Addie told her.

"Are you sure?"

"Yes, go."

"Okay, I'm going." She went right upstairs and got Jas's clothes ready, while he was taking a shower. "Jas, are you okay in there?" she called out.

"I'm good, Mom." She heard her cell phone ringing, so she rushed out of Jas's room, and ran into her room. She didn't have time to see who was calling before answering. It was Marcus. "Hello, Gorgeous," he said.

"Marcus," she murmured, joyfully. "Are you back?"

"No, baby, I'm not. I won't be back until tomorrow."

"Really," she said, disappointed.

"I know you're disappointed and I'm sorry. But the meeting was re-scheduled for seven o'clock tonight. So I'm disappointed as well. I've been looking forward to seeing you all day."

"And I you, Marcus. I miss you."

"I miss you, too, Sweetheart, and I will definitely be home tomorrow. But for now I'm here and you're there. So ... did you get my gift?"

"Yes, I did and it is beautiful—and expensive."

"But you're priceless, my love."

"Marcus, I'm not kidding."

"Neither am I, baby. I had it specially made for you. And I was really surprised when they called to tell me that it was ready," he mentioned quickly, hoping to slightly change the subject. "I thought it was perfect timing. You can wear it to the benefit tomorrow night. Did you get a dress?" He went on, not really giving her a moment to speak.

"I forgot to leave you a credit card."

"Yes, I got a dress. And that was a very kind thought, Marcus, but I paid for my own dress. And no, you may not reimburse me. And, Marcus," she whispered softly. "It goes perfect with my dress."

"What color is it your dress?"

"I'm not telling you. You'll see it, when you see me in it."

"Don't be mean," he told her.

"I'm not being mean. I'm just not telling you," she said smartly.

"I love you, Liah."

"I love you, too, Marcus, but I'm still not telling you. Now what time will you be back tomorrow?"

"Before noon and I promise I will be back unless it's out of my hand, excluding another meeting. However, I don't think I will see you until I pick you up tomorrow evening. I have to go straight to the office as soon as I land. You know, you could meet me at the office."

"I can do that. Oh, no. I can't. I have plans tomorrow afternoon."
"What kind of plans," he asked curiously.

"I am going to lunch, and to see a movie with Jen."

"Oh ... okay ... with Jen," he replied, sounding as if he was relieved.

"Why do you sound so relieved? Did you think I had a date or something?"

"No," he answered after he bit his tongue.

"Honey, I have to go. I'm going to poetry class tonight."

"I wish I was there to hear your poetry reading. But since I'm not, you have to give me a private reading."

"I will be delighted to serenade you with poetry, Mr. Michaels," she said animatedly."

"I'm looking forward it, Ms. Mathis," he whispered.

"Okay, honey, I' really got to go. I'll talk to you later." After hanging up, she made sure that Jas was dressed, and then hurriedly took a shower. Before she got dressed, she sat on her bed and took another look at the jewelry set. She felt better about accepting it after talking to Marcus. Especially, after he had told her that he had them specially made, just for her. She put the jewelry back in the bag, got dressed and went down stairs.

"Jeffrey is the car here, yet?" she asked.

"About ten minutes ago," he replied.

"Good. Where's Addie?"

"Outside talking to the driver."

As usual, the kids hung out in the recreation center with the Carrington boys. Everyone was glad to see Liah back in class. Liz was the first one to welcome her back, followed by Richard, the instructor. He called Liah their inspiration.

"Welcome, honey, let's hear some poetry," he told her.

"Richard, can you put me at the end?" Liah asked.

"Sure. You must have something good. You usually do."

"We'll see," she responded, modestly. She then went to take her seat beside Addie and Jeffrey.

Everyone did a great job reading their poetry, but when Liah finished reading hers, which was entitled, "The Wings of a Dove," many were touched by her creativity.

"Liah let me be the first to congratulate you on an outstanding poem," said Richard as he hugged her compassionately. "I was really impressed with that title."

"Thank you, Richard. That means a lot coming from you." Addie and Jeffrey walked up to congratulate her as well. "Richard, these are my dear friends, Addie and Jeffrey."

"Any friends of Liah are certainly friends of mine. She has an awesome circle of friends," Richard, conveyed. He told them it was a pleasure meeting them, before he walked off to congratulate others.

"Addie and Jeffrey, will you all excuse me for a moment?" Liah noticed that Liz wasn't her usual talkative self, so she thought she would see if she could be of some help. She had an idea what might be the problem. "Honey, are you okay?"

"Yes, I'm fine," Liz answered.

"Liz, come on now. You don't look fine.

"I just need a moment. I'm going to the ladies room."

"Would you like for me to go with you?"

"Thanks, Liah, but I need a moment alone. Would you mind getting the kids together for me?"

"No, not at all. We'll wait for you in the Bistro."

"That would be fine. Thanks."

"Not a problem. But if you change your mind and want to talk, just call me."

"Okay." Liah hesitantly walked off.

"Is she okay?" Jeffrey asked.

"Yes, she's fine. It's just an emotional time for her. Let's go gather up the kids. Liz is going to meet us in the Bistro.

They were all sitting in a booth when Liz came in. "Thanks for round-ing up the kids, Liah."

"You're welcome. Hey, Liz, Jen and I are going to the movie tomor-row. Would you like to go with us?"

"Yeah, I can do that."

"Awesome. We'll pick you up around noon."

"Alright ... looking forward to it." Liah hugged her, and then whispered in her ear, telling her to hang in there.

"I will. I'll see you tomorrow," Liz told her.

"You all are quite talkative tonight, girls." Liah told them.

"They just left those cute little Carrington boys," Addie stated.

"Ms. Addie," Jessica cried out, feeling somewhat embarrassed.

"I'm sorry, Jess," Addie said. I'm just messing with you." Addie held her head down so Jessica wouldn't see her smiling.

"Okay. We're not talking about them anymore, Mom," Jessica said.

"If you say so, Jess."

"Changing the subject," Addie said. "So, Liah, I wanna see that dress when we get home."

"Me too, Mom," Jacqlyne said.

"And you should see the jewelry that Mr. Marcus bought her," Jessica blurted.

"Liah, why am I just hearing about this?" Addie asked. "Oh it doesn't matter. Ooooh ... I bet it's gorgeous and expenses, girl."

"It is and I'm selling tickets at the door for everyone who wants to come to the diamond and dress show." Addie burst out laughing and told her she was real crazy.

"Now ... I've been told that before. Can we stop at that little ice cream shop?" I need to get ice cream for the show."

Jeffrey chuckled and then said, "sounds like a good idea to me."

"When we get home we're going to stuff ourselves with ice cream and then I will showcase you all," Liah told them.

"Sounds like a plans to me," Addie said.

They did just as Liah had suggested when they got home—sat at the bar and stuffed themselves with ice cream. "I think this ice cream is better than it was the first time I had it," Jeffrey noted.

"Mmmhmm," Addie mumbled. Her mouth was so stuffed, 'mmm hmm' were the only sounds she could utter. She looked up in distress from trying to swallow quickly. They all stared at her and laughed. "Look, I can't help it, this is good and cold. Look at Jas, he is falling asleep."

"Poor baby! Jeffrey, will you take Jas up and put him in bed when you're done," Liah asked.

"I will, dear."

"Thanks, Jeffrey. They all finished up and rushed upstairs, leaving Jeffrey behind.

Liah brought out the dress and shoes.

"Oh—my—goodness, Liah, you are going to be a knock out. Now where's the jewelry?" Addie asked.

"Right behind you," Liah told her. Addie took the case out of the bag and opened it. Her mouth dropped and she was almost speechless.

"You can say something, Addie," Liah said. "Breathe."

"Oh my, Liah ... these are—oh, my, gosh! Liah ... Girl. Okay, these are beautiful," she murmured, finally completing a statement. "I've never been this close to so many diamonds. And on one necklace, like never. And, Liah, it comes with matching earrings."

"Honey, don't sweat it. Neither have I," Liah disclosed. "It's a cluster of diamonds."

"Mom will probably give them back," Jacqlyne stated.

"Liah, you better not give this gift back," Addie, told her. "He bought it because he wanted you to have it. It looks like he even had it specially designed just for you."

"He did, but enough about the jewelry. Girls, it's time for you all to go to bed." The girls said goodnight.

"I'm out of here, too, Liah. I am a bit tired."

"Okay, goodnight, Addie."

After a full day she was more than ready to have some alone time to reflect on her day.

She went straight to her lounger and closed her eyes momentarily and heaved a sigh. *What this expensive jewelry really means*, she thought. *Things are definitely moving at a faster pace—more than I realized. I believe it's time to reevaluate this relationship,"* she said to herself out loud. *"What am I talking about? I haven't evaluated yet. Oh, my God, I am having a real conversation with myself. What is wrong with me?"* she continued talking to herself. *"I love him. I'm in love with him. Okay, I've gone temporarily loony. I should take a shower and go to bed."* She did just that. Just as soon as she dozed off, Marcus called to say goodnight. The conversation was brief because the both of them were tired.

~Chapter Eighteen~

Friday Morning, Liah was in a more chipper mood than usual. When Addie came in to make breakfast, Liah, had already made it, and had everything on the bar. "I knew I smelled breakfast food," Addie said."

"Good morning Addie."

"Good morning, chef. Are we expecting company for breakfast?"

"No, I just woke up early, so I thought I would make a big breakfast."

"You're excited about Marcus coming back, aren't you?"

"That to," she replied. "But I won't see him until he picks me up for the ball."

"What will you do with yourself all day?"

"Remember, Liz, Jen and I, are going to the movie, Addie"

"Oh, yeah, right."

"Addie, why don't you come with us?"

"I believe we're seeing 'Meet the Browns.'"

"Yes, ma'am, I'll go. I've been wanting to see that movie."

"Alrighty then, we'll be leaving around noon or shortly before."

"You know what, Liah?"

"What?"

"You're an unusual person."

"Why do you say?"

"Because you treat employees like friends or better yet, family."

"You and Jeffrey are like family."

"But even the people you work with."

"They're like family, too, and we are all friends. It's just about having a genuine respect and appreciation for each other. Besides, being in an authoritative position doesn't make anyone better than the other person. We are all cut from the same God. I wouldn't work with anyone who lacks respect for other people, whether in authority or not. And besides, you and Jeffrey are Marcus' employees, and my friends and extended family."

"You want be able to say that when you all get married."

"Now there you go, sounding just like Chan."

"I like her," Addie smiled, "she's crazy."

"That—she is," Liah responded. "Anyway, if we get married, I'll still be the same person I am now. I'm not doing any changing. I don't want you all having any reason to leave because, for me, there's only one Addie and Jeffrey in the world. So, honey, marrying Marcus means I'm marrying you and Jeffrey, too, until death do us part. Now I gotta go get my baby up. Will you take the fruit salad out of the fridge for me, please?"

"Yes, ma'am, wise one." They both looked at each other and sighed. As Liah turned to walk off, she almost ran into Jeffrey.

"Oops. Jeffrey I'm sorry. I didn't know you were there. You have got to make a little noise. Well good morning, Jeffrey."

"And a good morning to you too, Ms. Chipper." Addie and Jeffrey looked at each other and at the same time they said, "Marcus is coming home today."

Liah threw her arms up in the air as she walked off and screamed, "Yes, he is."

Jeffrey and Addie burst out laughing. "I haven't seen her carry on like that before," Jeffrey said.

"She couldn't hold her peace," Addie replied, still giggling. Jeffrey noticed the spread on the bar.

"My ... are we having guests for breakfast?" he asked.

"No. It's Ms. Chipper's mood," Addie responded. "She was done fixing breakfast by the time I came in."

"Well, we might as well sit down and enjoy this wonderful breakfast, Addie, dear," Jeffrey chuckled. Both of them ate breakfast in the breakfast room. "Well now, do you think he's ready to pop the question?" Jeffrey inquired.

"He might do it at the birthday party he's giving her," Addie responded.

"I think she's really good for him," Jeffrey conveyed, right before he stuffed a big strawberry in his mouth.

"I agreed with you, Jeffrey. I've never seen him so happy. Honestly, I think she's good for all of us."

"You know, Addie—that was my thought exactly. I guess great minds do think alike."

"I guess." Liah and the kids came down. "Whoa, Mom, you made breakfast?" Jacqlyne asked.

"How do you know it was me?"

"Mom, I've been eating your food for sixteen years. I know exactly how your food looks and how you display it."

"Who cares? I'm ready to eat," Jessica said.

"Me, too," Jas seconded. Liah and the kids joined Addie and Jeffrey in the breakfast room.

"Are you all enjoying your breakfast?" Liah asked Jeffrey and Addie.

"It is delightful, dear, if I may speak for Ms. Addie as well."

"You may, dear," she said trying to sound like Jeffrey.

"That was pretty good, Ms. Addie," Jessica told her.

"What, you don't like my accent?" Jeffrey asked.

"Everyone likes your accent, Jeffrey," Liah assured him. "That's why we're always trying to talk like you. Now come on, kids, eat up. This is a school day."

Liah spent the rest of the morning in her room. She did some Bible studying and spent some time writing and making phone calls. She even took some time to exercise and shower before Addie came knocking on her door. "Come in, Addie, I'll be out in a moment."

Liah and Addie picked up Jen and Liz shortly before noon. They stopped by an old-fashioned hamburger shop before going to the movie. After the movie, they stopped by the mall and went a little crazy with great sales. They barely had enough room to sit, because they had to put bags inside of the car, since the trunk was full with shopping bags. Liah even bought Marcus, Jeffrey, and Morgan necktie sets. Shopping certainly had Liz in a more upbeat mood, more so, than the night before. Liah was pleased to see her acting more like herself. "Liah, I had a fabulous time," Liz told her. "Thanks for inviting me."

"I'm glad you came, Liz. I think it was good for all of us."

"I sure had a good time," Addie announced. "Haven't had a girls' day out in a long time."

"Well, that's it. We should do this at least once a month," Jen voiced.

"I'm in" Liz cried.

Liah and Addie looked at each other and said, "So are we."

"Alright ladies," Jen asserted, "we are on." They all agreed to make it a once-a-month ladies day out.

"Okay, ladies," Liah said, I have plans this evening, so I'm taking you all home now."

"You're just trying to hurry up to get home, because Marcus is coming home today," Liz said.

"She's gotta hurry home and get in that dress and those beautiful diamonds Marcus bought her," Addie announced.

"Diamonds," Liz exclaimed.

"Yes, diamonds," Addie said, not giving Liah a moment to respond.

"I will show you all whenever you're over again. But actually, I'm supposed to be meeting Marcus at his office."

"Well, honey, by all means—take us home. We can barely fit our bodies in this vehicle anyway," Jen declared.

"You got that right, girlfriend," Addie agreed.

"Okay, Liz, I'm taking you home first, since the rest of us practically live together."

"Yeah, that makes sense," she responded.

Before Addie and Liah left Jen's house, Addie called Jeffrey, to tell him they would need help with their shopping bags. Jeffrey was waiting outside when they drove up.

"Did you leave anything in the store?" Jeffrey chuckled.

"We left a few things," Addie answered, "although, they might have to restock very soon." He chuckled and shook his head, then took most of the bags.

"Jeffrey, thank you for helping us take these bags in," Liah told him. Addie and I probably would have had to make two trips out here."

"Three—but who is counting? And I didn't mind a bit, my dear."

"Funny Jeffrey," Addie said.

Addie helped Liah take all of her bags upstairs.

"Addie, those bags go in Jayde's room. Liah had kept Jayde's room just as she had left it when she went off to college.

"You miss her, don't you?" Addie asked.

"Yes, I do, very much and the boys, too. They will be home next month. Speaking of next month, we're going to have a house full.

Chan and her children will be here as well, and I believe Alisha and Shayna are coming, too."

"Girl, we're going to need a hotel," Addie said. "Or you can ask Marcus, if someone can bunk at his house."

"Yep, I could, but he just got his house back. By the way, I wonder if he's back yet. He's supposed to be calling me so I can meet him at the office."

"Did you take your phone off silence?"

"No, I forgot," she admitted shamefully. "My phone is downstairs. I'll check shortly. Addie, didn't you used to be a hair stylist?"

"Yes. Why?"

"I need one of those pin up styles and I don't have time to go to the beauty shop."

"Sure, I can do that. Just let me know what time to come over, down, or whatever," she laughed.

"Okay, awesome." They went downstairs so she could check her phone.

"Mommy," Jason yelled.

"Hi, baby. I didn't know you were home."

"I just got here."

"Are you ready for a snack?" Liah asked him.

"No, ma'am. Our class won a pizza party and it was right before school was out."

"Where did you all get the pizza?"

"I'm not really sure, but it was good."

"Okay, well go upstairs and look on your bed." He didn't bother with saying okay or asking why. He just took off and hurried upstairs. Liah took her cell phone out of her purse and saw that Marcus had called.

"Yep, he called alright." She checked to see if he had left a message, and he had."

"Ooooh," Addie teased, "you're in trouble."

"He'll be alright after a sincere apology. If not, he certainly will be after he sees me in that dress."

"Girl, he'll be apologizing to you then." Liah sniggled and then asked why.

"For not calling twice," Addie replied. They both laughed out loud.

Addie went into the kitchen and Liah went in the study to return Marcus' call. When he picked up the phone, he bypassed addressing her like he usually did. He was more interested in why she hadn't called him earlier.

"Liah, Honey, what happened to you? I called you hours ago," he stated, sounding somewhat annoyed.

She knew then that he was upset. "Marcus, I'm so sorry. I just got your message. I forgot to take my phone off silent after I got out of the movie theater."

"Please try to remember the next time; you could have missed some important calls. Maybe you should put your phone on vibrate. Anyway, I apologize for sounding harsh. It's just that the last time when I couldn't reach you, you were in the hospital."

"You do know that I really am sorry. Even more so, now that I know I scared you. And I did miss a very important phone call," she whispered.

"Well, don't worry about it;" he said sincerely. "I've been pretty busy since the moment I walked through the door. So I guess I'll see you later."

"You guess?" she responded.

"I will see you about six-fifteen, babe."

"Marcus?"

"Yes, Liah?"

"I love you."

"I know, and I love you, too, baby. I'll see you in a couple of hours." She sighed and walked back in the living room.

"Girls, you home! How was school?" They hugged her and then gave them a brief recap of their day.

"Mom, where's Jas?" Jacqlyne asked. "He's supposed to be playing pool with me."

"He's probably in his room trying on his new stuff."

"He got new stuff again today." Jessica stated.

"Yes, and so did you all."

"Really?" Jacqlyne responded, excitedly.

"Really!" Liah replied. They thanked her and then rushed upstairs. "Addie let me help you take your bags home," Liah offered, as Jeffrey was walking in.

"I'll help her," Jeffrey offered.

"Okay," Liah, said quickly looking at Addie smiling. "Well, I'm going to try to take a nap. Jeffrey, will you wake me in about an hour if you're around?"

"Will do, dear."

"Addie, I'll see you around five thirty." She checked on Jas before going to her room.

Just as soon as she lay down, she fell right to sleep. Jen called right before Jeffrey came in to wake her.

"You're already awake."

"Yes, Jen just called. Thanks anyway Jeffrey." She got up and went in to help Jas pack his overnight bag. He was lying on his bed playing with his Rubik's Cube. "Hey, Mr. Man. Are you any good at that?"

"Well, I only have two colors left."

"That's pretty good. Maybe tomorrow we'll work on it together. I used to be pretty good when I was younger."

"They had these when you were younger, Mom?"

"Yes, Jas," she answered, not sure what he was implying. "Come help me pack your bag, Jas."

May I take my Rubik's Cube?"

"Sure, Honey."

"Thanks, Mom, for all the cool stuff."

"You are welcome, Mr. Man."

"Did your transformers shoes work?"

"Yes, ma'am, and they're really cool."

"Now look in the closet and get your transformer backpack."

"I don't have a transformers backpack, Mom."

"Well, just look in the closet and get me a backpack, please." He walked in the closet and saw the transformers backpack hanging in front of the others.

"Whoa...a Transformer backpack! Wow, it's awesome, Mom. Thanks. You tricked me."

"I did. Didn't I? I'm getting pretty good at that."

"Uh huh?"

"Sweetie, I have to take a shower and do my nails before Addie comes to do my hair. Don't forget to pack your toothbrush. I'll see you shortly."

"Okay, Mom."

Liah was just finishing up her nails when Addie knocked on the door. "Addie, is that you?" she yelled.

"Yes, it's me."

"Come on in. I'm in the dressing room."

"I'm in. Alright, Chef, let's get started on your hair."

"Tonight, Addie, I'm just Liah Anginette Mathis."

"I heard that, girlfriend. Liah came out and took a seat right in front of the vanity. "Alright, let's get started," Addie told her. Pass me two pins, please. This is an easy style; it should only take me about ten minutes. Addie was quite pleased with herself when she finished. She yelled, "Yeah ... I still got it."

"I know you still got it, but let me see how much. Okay ... I can't see it."

"Okay, I'm turning you around. I hope you like it. I really think you will like it."

"Addie, this is fabulous. You should be doing this on the side. Why did you stop doing hair anyway?"

"I had an offer I couldn't refuse."

"So did I, Addie. But it's a story we'll have to share over lots of dessert one night. For now, I need to get in this dress."

Addie looked at her watch and said, "Yes, you do. So come on." Liah put on her dress, and the diamond earrings, Marcus, bought her. "Liah, you look like a queen, but without her diamond necklace."

"I'm waiting for my king to put it on."

"Good idea." They heard the doorbell rang.

"Addie, will you go peek to see if it's Marcus?" The girls were coming in as Addie was on her way out.

"Mom, you look beautiful," Jessica told her.

"She looks like a princess," Jacqlyne, replied.

"You guys are so sweet." But babies, I'm the queen tonight." Addie came back in to tell her that Marcus was waiting downstairs and Jeffrey was keeping him company.

"Okay, thanks. Would you tell him I'll be right down, Addie?" Liah took a last look in the mirror and headed out the door.

"Mom," Jacqlyne exclaimed. "Shoes ... shoes would be good."

"Shoes! Right, I do need shoes." Jessica took several pictures of her before she could get out of the room.

"Okay, I'm done. Madame, your prince awaits—no, your King awaits," Jessica corrected herself.

"Will you get Jas, Jessica, so you guys can walk out with us?"

"Jas," she screamed.

"I could have done that, girl. Stop screaming."

"Sorry, Mom."

When Marcus heard voices, he got up and stood at the bottom of the stairs. He seemed as nervous as she did. She paused when she saw him at the bottom of the stairs. *Wow, he really looks like royalty*, she thought.

Marcus couldn't take his eyes off her, as she continued down the stairs. How did I get to be so blessed, he asked himself. "Whatever the answer is, I'm just glad I am." They didn't realize just how much they had missed each other until they embraced.

"Wow ... you look stunning and I've really missed you," he told her.

"I've missed you too, Marcus," she whispered passionately. She handed him the necklace.

"Are you not going to wear it?" he asked.

"Yes, I just wanted you to put it on." That was a relief to hear. He actually was expecting her to put up a bigger fight. Though he wouldn't mentioned that to her. He carefully took the necklace and fastened it around her neck, and then said to her,

"This necklace really looks beautiful on you."

"Thank you Marcus. But this necklace looks beautiful off me. Now, where's your tie?"

"I wanted you to help me tie it."

"I will be delighted to, Mr. Michaels." Jacqlyne took more pictures, making sure that she got several shots of the necklace.

"Okay, we have to go," Marcus said.

"Don't forget the corsage," Jeffrey reminded them.

"Oh ... right," Marcus said. "Thanks, Jeffrey." After Marcus pinned the corsage on Liah, she was completely accessorized. The only thing left was to be on the arm of her king, just like in a fairytale.

"Addie and Jeffrey, thanks for all your help," Liah said. "And remember you have the evening off and you might as well take off tomorrow, too."

"If you all don't have anything planned, you might as well go to the cookout with us," Marcus kindly offered.

"That's a great idea, Marcus," Liah agreed. She was pleased that he asked them. "Yes, you all should come with us."

"Well, what about it?" Marcus asked?

"I'd love to," Addie replied.

"Yes, I would be delighted to join you all," Jeffrey said.

"Then you all have a good night and I will see you all tomorrow," Marcus told them. They all walked out together. Addie walked the kids over to Jen and Tim's house.

The limo driver stepped out of the car to open the door for Liah. Marcus said to him, "No—no, thanks, but I got this." He wanted to open the door for her himself. On the way to the ball, he could hardly take his eyes off her. They talked all the way there. *A fairytale has nothing on this*, she thought to herself as she walked in the ballroom on his arm. She was indeed one of the most blessed women in the world. And she knew it.

Morgan and Lillie spotted them almost immediately.

"Liah, here come Mom and Dad," Marcus warned.

"Well, hello there, my most favorite couple," Lillie conveyed. After they all greeted each other, Lillie complimented Liah on her dress. "Liah, darling, you are wearing that gown and you look lovely in it. And ooh, those diamonds are beautiful."

"Can I get a compliment in, woman?" Morgan Sr. asked.

"Oh, I'm sorry! Go ahead, dear."

"Liah," Morgan Sr. said as he took her hand in his. "You look marvelous, dear. And you look good, too, Son."

"Yes, he does," Lillie seconded, "just like his father."

"Sweetheart, I thank you for Marcus and myself," he said. Liah, thanked both of them, before she complimented them on how well they looked, especially Lillie. She knew that she looked good in that dress, certainly, for her age, and was proud of it.

"Marcus, I'm going to steal Liah away from you for a moment," Lillie told him. I want to introduce her to some friends. I promise to bring her back shortly."

"Okay, Mom," he replied, like an obedient child.

"Well, Son, I guess it's just you and me."

"Oh, here it comes," Marcus thought. "Dad is going to give me the speech — 'Son, you made a good choice. A woman like her is hard to come by.'"

"Son—," Morgan said, and then Marcus mumbled under his breath.

"I knew it."

"You say something, Son?"

"No, sir."

"Well as I was saying, you made a good choice, choosing Liah. You know, Marcus, a woman like that is hard to come by. Don't let too much time get away from you, Son, before you make it final."

Marcus knew his dad well. "Don't worry, Dad. I won't. "But I know what Liah and I have is real."

"As long as you're sure, son. Now let's go find Liah and your mother because she's not bringing her right back." They both laughed. It took about two minutes to find them.

"See that crowd over there, Marcus," Morgan Sr. pointed out. "That's where they are." They found them surrounded by a group of people. Liah and Lillie, both were a natural at working the room. Liah just happened to glance to her right and saw Marcus staring at her. She told the crowd that she would continue their conversation later and then politely excused herself. Both Marcus and Liah made their way to each other.

"Hi, sweetheart," she said to him.

"Well, hello, gorgeous. I see you know how to work a crowd and steal all the attention."

"No, I shared a bit with your mother." She looked at him innocently and smiled the smile that usually left him near breathless. They turned and walked away from the crowd with his arm securely around her waist.

Suddenly, their moment was abruptly interrupted by Marcus' ex-wife, Faith. She marched up to him as if they were best friends, and said, "Marcus, it is so good to see you." She then threw her arms around him and gave him a 'not just a friendly kiss' practically forcing Liah to take a step back, if not intentionally pushing her aside. She did the very thing that Liah detested. She was rude and disrespectful. Liah raised her brow. She was about to help Faith correct her attitude. But by the time she opened her mouth, Marcus quickly pulled her back into his arms.

"Honey, I'm sorry," he said.

"Sorry," Liah snarled. "Honey, you have no reason to be sorry. On the other hand, you, my dear, were tacky and rude. And..." Faith broke in with her phony apology, before Liah could continue.

She said, "I'm so sorry. I didn't mean to. I was just surprise to see Marcus." Marcus cleared his throat.

"Sweetheart, this is my ex-wife, Faith. Faith, this is Liah." Faith looked at her and said, "Liah, it is good to meet you."

"Faith," she said without even a glimpse of a smile on her face. "I am pleased to finally meet you. I've heard so much about you."

"I hope it wasn't all bad." Liah looked at her with her head raised, and with a cute little smirk on her face and said, "No ... not all bad." And that was only because of the person Marcus, was. There really wasn't much good to Faith.

Lillie saw Faith with Marcus and Liah and then punched Morgan and said, "Look what the cats dragged in."

He looked up and said, "Trouble." Liah does not look happy," Morgan said.

"We had better see if we can do some damage control," Lillie told him. They walked over to where they were.

"Lillie and Morgan, how nice to see you," Faith professed. Then she stepped over and gave them a bogus hug. She never did like them. She envied the relationship Marcus had with them. Of course they didn't mind. They never liked, nor trusted her anyway. Nevertheless, they always treated her kindly and respectful.

"So, Faith, how've you been?" Morgan Sr. asked.

"Quite well. Thank you for asking."

"Faith, what brings you here tonight?" Lillie asked, curiously.

"I came with a friend."

"Oh," Lillie responded cordially.

"Speaking of friends," Faith said, "I had better go find him. You all have a good evening. Marcus, we should do lunch soon." Then she walked off.

As soon she walked off, Liah stepped away from Marcus, then looked at him and said, "Don't ever do that again." Lillie and Morgan looked at Marcus and then at Liah, not knowing what to expect. "Lillie, I need water," Liah expressed. "Would you walk with me, please?"

Before Lillie could answer, Marcus volunteered to get her some water. "No, thank you, Marcus," she said unfeelingly, "I can get my own water." Then she walked off.

"Wait up, honey," Lillie called out.

"Lillie, I'm going to the ladies room instead."

"What happened?" Lillie asked.

"Okay, not only did Ms. Thang, practically knocked me out of Marcus' arms, but she threw her arms around him, and then planted a kiss on his lips. And let me just add, she didn't bother saying excuse me. And why would she anyway ... she did it on purpose. Now she was tacky, disrespectful, and rude. But, I have to say, she had nerves.

However, it's Marcus who I'm really upset with. He didn't bother pushing her off his lips quick enough. One could have thought she was stuck there. Anyway, he did not check her rude behavior, nor did he introduce me as his girlfriend. It was just Faith, this is Liah. And to make it worse, when I was about to put her rude behavior in check, he practically shut me up and apologized to me, for her. How dare him!"

"Honey, I know exactly how you feel. I would have felt the same way. But keep in mind how Marcus is. He really tries to avoid personal confrontation. Now I'm not trying to excuse his behavior, but you know how he feels about you."

"Yes, Lillie, I do. And I know what Marcus and I have. Still, I will not tolerate disrespectfulness. And if Marcus doesn't keep in his mind what he has and allow this to happen again, he won't have it."

"Come on, baby, you and Marcus need to talk."

During the time Lillie and Liah, were talking, Marcus was telling his dad what happened.

"I knew when I looked up and saw her, there would be trouble," Morgan said. "Here comes your mother and Liah, Son. Good luck smoothing things out. Are you alright, dear?" Morgan asked.

"I'm better. Thank you, Morgan, for asking."

"We're gonna let you two talk," Lillie. "Come on, Morgan. Let's go fine some seats in the dining area."

"Good idea, Honey. We'll save you all some seats."

"Thanks, Mom." They left them alone. Marcus and Liah went to the lounge to talk.

"Morgan, did Marcus tell you what Faith, did?" Lillie asked.

"Yes, he told me."

"Well, Liah is pretty upset," she told him.

"I know. I could tell. And she has every right to be."

In the lounge, Marcus was profusely apologizing to Liah.

"Marcus, exactly who are you apologizing for? You, for being such a jerk, or Faith, and I don't even use the words that describe her?"

"Both."

"Then I guess you should stop apologizing. You are not responsible for Faith's actions, so please don't apologize for her. However, you may apologize for yourself."

"Honey, Liah, I'm truly sorry. Faith was out of line and I handled the whole incident wrong. I promise that I will talk to Faith. I love you, Liah, and I'm with you. Sweetie, you are the only woman that I want to be with."

"I know, Marcus, and I love you, too." He put his arms around her and then she embraced him back. When he attempted to kiss her forehead, she put her hand between his lips and her forehead.

"You will not be touching my lips, not after that kiss from Faith. I don't know where her lips haven't been."

"Haven't been, honey?"

"Yeah, Marcus, haven't been. You had better go sterilize your lips."

He looked at her and said, "You're serious, aren't you?" She reached in her purse and took out a toothbrush set, and then handed it to him. Then told him, she'll see him at the table," and walked off. At that point, he knew that she was serious. She joined Lillie and Morgan in the dining room. They asked her where Marcus was. She told them he was in the men's room brushing his teeth and washing his lips.

Morgan and Lillie looked at each other. They tried hard not to laugh, but with little success. "What?" she asked. "You all think I'm exaggerating?"

"No—no we don't," Lillie said. "Marcus had it coming."

"But it is funny," Morgan uttered and then chuckled again."

"Yes, it's funny, but there's no telling where that girl's lips have been," Lillie stated.

"My thoughts exactly," Liah said. "Besides, that was a kiss for married folks and for her and Marcus...that one is long over."

A young lady came up to Lillie and whispered in her ear. It was the food coordinator. "Are you for real?" Lillie asked the lady.

"Unfortunately."

"What's going on, Honey?" Morgan asked.

"The chef took sick and had to leave," she whispered to him. "Oh, no," he responded.

"I heard someone mention something about a great chef was here. I heard she's the town's best. Do you know her? I think her name is Liah something." Liah looked up with a distressed look. She was thinking, not again and certainly not in this dress.

"Liah Mathis," Lillie responded.

"Yes, yes. That's her name," the lady avowed. "Please say you know her."

"I know her, but I don't think she's dressed for cooking."

"I will provide her with a chef outfit or whatever she needs." Lillie pointed her hand toward Liah. "That's her?"

"In the flesh," Liah responded.

"Wow ... you are beautiful," the lady observed.

Liah stood up and said, "Show me to the kitchen please."

"Thank you, Ms. Mathis. You are an angel."

"Now I don't know about all that. But I will do my best," Liah said. "Would you all make sure Marcus knows I'm still here?"

"You know we will, dear, and we will save your seat as well," Lillie told her.

"Thanks, I'll be back soon." Right after Liah left, Marcus showed up.

"It took a long time for you to brush your teeth, Son," Morgan said, teasing him.

"And he had to wash his lips, too," Lillie followed, teasing him as well.

"Ha, ha. Alright, Mom and Dad—please stop with the teasing. Did she leave?"

"No, son, she's in the kitchen," Morgan Sr. told him. Marcus was relieved to know that but was curious as to why she was in the kitchen.

"What is she doing in the kitchen?"

"Cooking," Morgan Sr. answered.

"Dad, can you please be a little more specific?"

"The cook got sick and had to leave. They heard Liah Mathis was here and found her. You might as well take a seat. She'll be back. What took you so long anyway?"

"I had to find Faith."

"Did you?" Lillie asked.

"Yes, I did, and I told her about Liah and me. I also told her how I felt about her behavior. And she apologized. Hopefully she will not pull another stunt like that again."

"What do you think?" Lillie asked him.

"I don't know, Mom. But can we move past this?"

"Certainly." Moving pass. I thought Morgan was coming." Just as soon as she inquired about him, he showed up.

"Well it's about time you showed up, Man," Marcus said.

"I've been here for about ten minutes. Long enough to hear what Faith did," Morgan mentioned. "Man that little...."

Morgan Sr. broke in and said, "Don't go there, Morgan."

"Okay, Dad. Where's Liah. Did she leave?"

"No, she was asked to fill in because the cook got sick," his dad told him. "Oh, here she comes right now." Liah came out to apologize for the delay and announce that the meal would be served in about fifteen minutes. She walked over to speak to Morgan.

Lillie said to her, "Liah, I am sorry you got volunteered to fill in for the cook."

"No apology is necessary. Actually, it has been the best part of my evening so far," she said modestly. She looked at Marcus and smiled, then said that she would be back shortly.

"Marcus—man," Morgan uttered, "you are in the dog house," he said hilariously.

"Morgan, no one asked you anything. So don't start"

"Alright—okay, Marcus. But only because Mom and Dad gave me the look. Man, she sure did change quickly," he blurted.

"Who?" Marcus asked.

"Liah, Marcus." Marcus turned around. "Yeah, that was fast."

She didn't come right over. She was instructing the servers.

"Okay, Ms. Mathis," one of the male servers, responded. For the first time, she didn't bother telling him not to call her Ms. Mathis. She continued instructing them.

"I thought that was Chef Liah," one of the guests said, not realizing how loud he was talking. Then he said to the guy sitting next to him. "She is gorgeous. I wonder if she's involved with someone."

He was only sitting a few chairs down from the Michaels' party. Morgan looked at Marcus and said, "I hear competition."

"It was a compliment, Morgan," Marcus blurted, and shook his head.

"Wondering if she's involved, sounds like more than a compliment," Morgan replied.

"I'm just messing with you man. I know Liah is a faithful woman. But that was just a compliment. I mean she is gorgeous and other men are going to admire her."

"That is true, son," Marcus Sr. added. "But like Morgan said, she is a faithful woman."

"I know."

After Liah was done delegating, she made her way back to her table. Marcus stood up to pull out her chair. "Thank you," she whispered softly.

He seemed a bit relieved, more so than he did the first time she came out.

"So Chef Liah," Morgan Sr. said. "What are we having?"

"You have a choice between lamb, baby back ribs, or grilled salmon with a red pepper and pineapple salsa and a variety of sides. And for dessert, well that's a surprise."

"What do you recommend?" Lillie asked.

"It's all about preference, Lillie. They're all good. I did make a sample tray. So if you like, you can try all three before you make your final choice."

"Then I will just do so, sweetie," Lillie said.

"Well, here's the meat tray." She told the server, for everyone who was having trouble deciding that they wanted, offer them samples.

"I will, Ms. Michaels," the server replied.

"Mathis, sweetie, not Michaels," Liah politely corrected her. "Sorry," she responded.

"It's okay. Thanks for during such a great job." She finished serving their table, and then moved on to the next table in her section.

"Let's blessed the food, please," Morgan Sr. said. The whole table got quiet for a moment. Well, at least until Morgan told Marcus that he hoped he was as blessed as he was.

"What do you mean?" Marcus asked.

"To meet someone as beautiful as Liah, that can cook."

"I am blessed," Marcus responded, "better than blessed."

The gentleman who inquired about her earlier whispered to the gentleman next to him again saying, "I guess she is involved." He then sighed and continued eating his food.

"Can we have second?" Morgan asked.

"Sure, after everyone have been served, including the staff," Liah told him.

"I see why everyone likes you," Morgan remarked. "Most chefs don't treat the staff like guests."

"I'm just treating them like humans," Liah stated.

"Well, just pack me a doggie bag," he told her.

"I'll let the servers know," she responded.

"Morgan, you and Lecxa are just alike," Lillie told him. "You're always trying to leave with a doggie bag."

"Uh uh, Mom," Morgan quickly responded. "That girl is worse than a homeless person."

Liah looked at him and shook her head. "I'm serious. It can be nothing left and Lecxa will still leave with a doggie bag."

"Now, Morgan, you know that was low," Marcus declared, "Especially since she isn't here to defend herself." They looked at each other and laugh out loud.

"Are they always like this?" Liah Lillie asked.

"Always," Morgan Sr. said, answering for her.

"By the way," Lillie said. "Did I tell you all she was coming tomorrow?"

"She is?" Marcus responded.

"Yes, she called this morning."

"Alright, my little sister is coming home," Morgan cried out, happily.

"That is great," Liah said. "I'll finally get a chance to meet her. Isn't she an instructor at Richmond?"

"Yes. This is her second year," Marcus answered.

"I wonder if she knows Jayde." Liah whispered, curiously.

"I don't know. But we'll find out tomorrow," Marcus replied.

"I guess we will," Liah mumbled, "and then she asked Lillie if there were anything specific she wanted her to bring.

"Honey, just bring yourself and those babies."

"Okay, but if you change your mind, just give me a call."

"Believe me, I will."

"Marcus, on your way to pick us up, would you mind stopping by the store to pick me up a case of vitamin water?" Liah asked him.

"Sure I will. What flavors?"

"You can call me when you get to the store."

"Alright," he replied. "Alright," he said again.

"Here comes dessert," Lillie said. "These desserts look divine and they are prepared so nicely, almost too good to eat. How did you do this so quickly?"

"With years of practice and much delegation."

Dinner was an outstanding success. Afterwards, everyone gathered in the ballroom to mingle and for speeches. Faith made her way over to their group again.

"Look honey," Lillie said to Morgan Sr. "Here she is again."

She came right over to Morgan. "Morgan, it is nice to see you again."

"Faith ... hello, you haven't changed a bit." They all knew that he wasn't exactly referring to her looks, although she did have looks going for her.

Faith then turned to Liah and said, "Liah, right?" calculatingly.

"Yes, Faith," she answered as pleasantly as she could. "What can I do for you?"

"I just wanted to sincerely apologize for what happened earlier."

"Are you telling me you didn't sincerely mean it the first time?"

"Yes, I meant it. It's just—"

Liah broke in and said to her, "Then there is no need for another one. Though, in the future I suggest you choose a better approach."

Faith gracefully bowed out of that conversation, with an attempt to start another one. "I thought the food was spectacular," she said to Lillie. I believe it's was the best I've ever had. I wonder if the cook has a restaurant."

"I agree, Faith," Morgan responded. "What did you all think?" Everyone in their group responded with one single word.

Morgan Sr. said, "It was delightful."

Marcus, said, "The best."

Lillie said, "Wonderful."

Liah said, "Divine."

The food coordinator came over and said to Liah, "Darling, you saved the night. Everyone is going on and on about the fantastic job the chef did. Come with me, please."

She took Liah by the hand and led her up front then call to everyone's attention. Faith couldn't believe that the hands of her rival had prepared such a meal. She was flabbergasted.

"Everyone," she exclaimed, "Let's raised our glasses to this wonderful person, Chef Liah Mathis. She is responsible for that delectable feast that you partook of this evening. And just let me warn you. What's in your glasses is not an alcoholic beverage. It's a unique champagne-like beverage created by Chef Liah. Thank you and drink up every one."

Just as soon as Liah stepped off the platform, she had a crowd of people surrounding her handing her business cards and inviting her to lunch. She was in no way interested in accepting any of the offers. She was pleased with her current position at A'Palace. Whenever she did decided to leave there, she had every intention of becoming a self-owned business woman. And she had all the capital she needed to do just that. As she talked to the guests, it dawned on her that she hadn't really spent any time with Marcus that night. Apparently Marcus felt the same way, because he fought his way through the crowd to get to her.

"Ms. Mathis, he called out to her. "Is it possible to have a moment of your time?"

"Excuse me, please, I've been waiting to talk to Mr. Michaels all night," she said to the group of people she was talking to. "Call my office and we will schedule lunch." She reached in her purse and handed everyone a business card.

Marcus took her by the hand and then said to her, "Ms. Mathis, I believe your popularity has just escalated to another level."

"Marcus, I'm sorry we haven't spent any time together."

"It's okay, baby. We have the rest of our lives together. Besides, the night is still early."

"I love you, Marcus Michaels."

"And I love you, Liah Mathis." They didn't leave each other's side for the remainder of the night. Despite the encounter with Faith, the night still ended like a fairytale.

~Chapter Nineteen~
The Cookout

Bright and early Saturday morning, Addie and Liah met in the kitchen to start baking for the cookout. They baked and talked for a couple of hours before realizing they hadn't eaten breakfast. They had a bite to eat and then decided they would watch a movie in the patio room, but instead they fell asleep and slept until the kids came home. The kids, of course, were interested in how her night had gone. She didn't bother telling them about her encounter with Faith, only the best part of her evening, including having to fill in for the sick chef. Addie knew Liah was leaving something out. She knew it must have been something she didn't want the kids to know.

"Addie, we need to go box up the dessert," Liah said. "We only have a couple of hours before Marcus comes to pick us up."

"Mom, we can help you all," Jessica offered.

"Good idea. Come on, let's box," Liah said. "Thanks for volunteering, Jess." She finished telling them about the ball while they boxed dessert. "When we're done I'm going to take a shower and get dressed. If anyone needs to change clothes, you all need to follow suit."

"We all took showers last night, Mom," Jacqlyne responded.

"Okay, good. After they were done everyone, but Jason went to their rooms. He went to the game room.

Liah reflected over her night while taking an extended shower. She first thought about the best part of her night. The time she spent with Marcus and even the enjoyable time with his family. She even took a moment to reflect on the incident with Faith. She was still not sold on her so-called sincere apology. She had a feeling that she would try something else. But she wasn't about to dwell on it. She knew Marcus loved her and she didn't in any way, feel threaten by Faith. However, Liah Mathis didn't like trouble and she knew Faith breathed it. She switched back to the best part of her night.

Still deep in her thoughts, she was startled by the ringing of her phone. She hurried out of the shower, knowing that she was expecting Marcus to call her when he got to the store. It was Alisha, Chantel, and Shayna. She didn't spend much time talking to them. She told them that she had to call them back when she got in from the cookout. As soon as she walked back in the bathroom, her phone rang again. This time it was Marcus.

"Hi, my fairy princess," he said to her. "Are you well-rested? I know you were tired last night."

"Hi, Marcus," she said, with a smile so big it glowed in her voice. "Yes, I am well rested. How are you?"

"I am doing wonderful. And I am looking forward to the cookout. I get to spend the day with you and the kids."

"That is pretty wonderful. We all get to spend the day together."

"So tell me what Vitamin Waters you want, babe."

"Why don't you get two of each flavor."

"Alright, I will be there shortly."

"Okay, see ya in a bit." Instead of him getting two of each flavor, he bought a case of each.

Jeffrey helped him unload the cases when he got to Liah's. When Liah came down stairs, she saw all of the cases sitting on the floor, she said, "Marcus, I said two of each, not a case of each."

"Well," he said hesitantly. "I didn't want you to run out."

"Okay, but when we get back, you're taking half home with you."

"I don't mind. I won't have to go out to buy you any when you're there. By the way, Honey, when are you coming back home?"

Liah patted him on his back and then kissed on the cheek. "Come on, Marcus and Jeffrey," she said, "help us take the desserts out to the truck. And kids grab some bottles of vitamin water please."

"Okay. Where are the desserts?" Marcus asked.

"In the kitchen." Marcus and Jeffrey, both, took a couple of cookies for themselves before they took them out.

"Liah did you bake all of these this morning?" Marcus asked. "Yes, Addie and I did."

"Well, I know you all did, I remember you saying you were going to be baking this morning. But after last night, I didn't think you would feel like it."

"How did last night go?" Jeffrey inquired.

"Why don't we tell you all about it in the truck, Jeffrey," Liah suggested? "Well, not all of it—the interesting past has to be later. We need to leave." Everyone loaded up in Marcus' truck. Jeffrey was serious about knowing how things went at the ball. As soon as Marcus drove off, Jeffrey reminded him that he was supposed to tell him about the ball last night.

"Okay, Jeffrey, there were some unpleasant encounters. But it turned out to be better than a fairytale night," Marcus told him.

"What do you mean unpleasant encounters?

"Faith was there."

"Enough said."

"Okay, and Liah had to cook."

"Cook," Jeffrey exclaimed. "Why? Surely not in that dress she had on last night."

"No, I took it off, Jeffrey. Anyway the cook got sick."

"It's like history repeating itself, Mr. Jeffrey," Jason said. "That's how Mom got her job at A'Palace. It's quite a coincidence, isn't it? Except, the chef walked out."

They were all surprised by the way he was talking. "Did he say, it's quite a coincidence, isn't it?" Liah asked.

"He did," Jeffrey answered, "quite plainly."

"What? Did I say something wrong?"

"No, you didn't, champ," Marcus responded. You're just a smart boy."

"You sure are, Mr. Man," Liah said.

"Okay, then thanks."

"You're welcome, Champ," Marcus said.

"Marcus, what are you eating?" Liah asked. He didn't answer right away. He knew he was busted.

"Gum, Liah."

"Smells like Jeffrey is chewing the same gum," Addie said. "And his gum is brown and has raisins."

"Jeffrey, you got us busted," Marcus laughed.

"I believe you were caught before me now, Marcus."

"Okay, I just wanted to get a taste before you let Mom and Lecxa loose."

"Okay, I hear that," Liah said.

"Are we almost there?" Jason asked.

"In just a few minutes, Champ," Marcus answered.

They pulled into a beautiful gated community. "Liah, will you open the glove compartment and pass me that key pad, please?"

"Sure, Honey." When they drove through the gate, Liah was astounded by the landscaping. "Wow, this landscaping is phenomenal."

"Yeah, my mother is much like you when it comes to her yard."

"A woman after my own heart," Liah mumbled.

Lillie must have been standing at the door waiting for them because just as soon as they drove up, she was already walking outside. She was indeed elated that they were there. The kids ran to her as soon as they got out of the truck. They were just as excited to be there, as she was to have them there.

"Look at my sweet babies," she exclaimed. "Liah and Marcus, I don't care what you all do, but these are my grandbabies."

Lillie, hugged Marcus and Liah, then Addie and Jeffrey. "I am happy you all could make it. Come on, everyone is outback. We're going to walk through the house to get to the backyard. It's quicker."

"Oh Lillie, this is gorgeous," Liah told her. "I love the fireplace." "You should see the kitchen," Marcus told her. "Mom, we'll catch up with you all outside. I'm taking Liah to see the kitchen."

"Okay, Son."

He took by her hand and led her to the kitchen. "Marcus, it's almost like your kitchen, with the exception of the colors." He admired her passion for the simplest things.

"Liah," he whispered.

"Yes, Marcus?"

"Have I told you how much I love you?"

"Not since last night," she answered, softly.

He gently pulled her into his arms, looked into her eyes, and then said to her, "I want to spend the rest of my life with you." She wasn't expecting that and was pretty much, unsure how to respond. So she blurted the first thing came to mind. "That's good. I feel the same way."

He held her closer and told her he was glad that she felt the same way. In that moment they continued to hold one another. Suddenly, the sound of a clearing throat broke the mood. It was Morgan Sr. "Are you all going to stand there or are you all planning to join us soon?"

"Morgan, Liah whispered, smiling innocently. Hi. How are you?"

"I couldn't be better. Come here you and give me a hug. Marcus is trying to keep you all to himself." She walked over to give him a hug. "Now that's more like it," he said. "Marcus, you might as well give me a hug too. Wouldn't want you to feel left out. Come on, son. Stop acting embarrassed. Are you trying to keep this young lady to yourself?"

"Yes, sir."

"Well, from what I've just observed, you have plenty of time. It doesn't look as if she's going anywhere," he said chuckling. "Now, Liah, Lillie asked me to ask you, if you will take the potato salad out of the fridge and taste it to see if it needed anything else, and then bring it outside."

"Aye, aye, Sir!" She did as was asked. "Did Lillie make this, Morgan?" she asked.

"She did," Morgan responded. "Why? Is it that horrible?" They all laughed.

"No. It's fine. It's really good."

"Good," Morgan responded. "Now if you all would stand back, I need to take the baked beans out of the oven."

"Marcus, will you asked Jeffrey to help you get the dessert out of the truck?"

"Alright."

"You brought dessert?" Morgan Sr.

"I sure did."

"Hope it is carrot cakes."

"Could be," Liah said, with a sly grin on her face.

"Well whatever it is, I'm sure it would be good and well appreciated. Now let's take this food out before Lillie Michaels come in here."

"Okay." Liah followed behind him.

"Hi. You must be Liah," a pretty medium-height, dark-haired young woman said to her. "I'm Lecxa. I feel like I already know you."

"Hi, Lecxa. Yes, I am Liah and it's a pleasure to meet you." They hugged as if they already knew each other.

"I met the kids, Liah, and they are darling."

"Thank you for saying that."

"Come on, so you can meet some of Mom and Dad's old buddies." Lecxa led her to the dining area.

"Well, hello there, beautiful lady."

"Hello, Mr. and Mrs. Sandler, it's good to see you all again."

"Marcus is a wise man to keep you around," he said.

"Be careful, Frank," his wife told him. "That statement can be taken negatively."

"Well, it's wasn't meant to be negative. I'm just saying that Marcus is a blessed man."

"I know what you meant, Mr. Sandler," Liah told him. "Y'all leave him alone. He' knows what he's talking about."

"Thank you, dear! See ... I told you Marcus was a blessed man. She even has my back." They all laughed.

As Marcus and Jeffrey were walking in with the dessert, Liah said to them, "it sure took you all a long time to take the desserts out."

"They were probably eating some more cookies," Addie stated.

"We did not eat but one cookie," Marcus said in their defense.

"Marcus," Jeffrey said, "sometimes you are too honest." Everyone burst out laughing. Marcus put the boxes down and went over to Lecxa and lifted her off her feet.

"I have really missed you, baby sister."

"I've missed you, too, Markie."

"Lecxa, don't start with the Markie."

"Well, keep me on my feet, then." He just smiled and kissed her on her cheek.

"You all seemed pretty hyped when Jeffrey and I came up," Marcus stated. "What did we miss?"

"Just be glad you weren't here," Mr. Sandler responded.

"He's right, Son," Morgan Sr. told him.

"Liah, is that what I think it is?" Lillie asked.

"Yes, ma'am!"

"Come here, you!" She jumped up and hugged Liah as if she had given her a million dollars.

314

"All of that for a carrot cake," Morgan Sr. uttered. "Lillie, can we eat now?"

"I was trying to wait for Morgan, dear."

"Oh yeah, right. Morgan, just called and said he would be here shortly," Marcus told them.

"Let's give him at least five more minutes," she said.

"While we're waiting, I'm going to round up the kids," Liah said. "Where are they anyway?"

"I think they're on the golf course," Lillie replied.

"I'll help you," said Marcus. "We'll take a golf cart."

"Okay, great," Liah said. "Marcus there's your twin. Hi, Morgan."

"Hi, Liah. What's up Marcus? Where are you guys going?"

"Rounding up the kids," Liah said.

"Cool! Catch y'all in a moment. Lecxa!" he cried out, excitedly. He lifted her off the ground.

"Morgan, why are you always lifting me up?"

"Because I can and I'm glad to see you, little sister."

"I'm glad to see you, Morgie."

"Lecxa, please don't start with the Morgie."

"Well, you and Marcus had better keep me on my feet. I feel like a rag doll."

"Girl, shut up and give me a hug. How long are you here for, Lecxa?"

"I'm leaving Monday afternoon."

"Awesome! Do you wanna spend the night with me?" he asked her.

"Sure!"

"Good! I'm going to go speak to Morgan Sr. and Lillie," he told her.

"Oooh ... I bet you won't let them hear you say that," Lecxa said. "As a matter of fact, I dare you."

"Don't do dares! Okay, here goes."

"Hi, Mom and Dad." Lecxa let out a big sniggle. Morgan looked at her and then spoke to the others.

"Hi, baby," Lillie said, while hugging him.

"What about my hug, Son?"

"Oh...sorry, Dad."

"Okay, woman," Morgan Sr. "Everyone is here. Can we eat now? I'll take a piece of carrot cake first."

"Try to set an example for the kids, Morgan," Lillie responded.

"I was kidding, dear."

"Yeah, right!" she replied and shook her head. "Come on, Lecxa and Liah, let's feed the hungry."

They ate and talked and had a blissful time. Liah and Lecxa spent a lot of time together getting to know one another.

"Now, Liah, you have another daughter in college, right?"

"Yes, her name is Jayde. She's in her freshmen year. She attends the same college that you teach at."

"Get out of here!" Lecxa blurted. "What's her major?"

"Creative Writing and Graphic Designs."

"Oh, my gosh! That's what I majored in, and I'm also a Creative Writing Instructor."

"Wow! What a coincidence!"

"Wait a minute! Stay right here, Liah. I'll be right back. Hold on. Jayde Mathis—cute, precious, and petite. I don't believe it. She's my favorite student and my student helper. I have pictures. Let me grab my purse." She went in the house to get her purse. She brought out some pictures still in the package. "Okay Liah, we took these picture on a field trip when we visited the museum." She took the pictures out and handed them to Liah.

"Oh, look at her. It is my baby," Liah said proudly.

"Well, how about that. She met her auntie before she met her daddy," Lecxa blurted.

"Lecxa Michaels, don't you start," Liah said. "Anyway I have to show these to Marcus, that's if he can pull himself away from the dessert table. Well, I'll show him later."

Liah and Lecxa went for a short walk. "Liah, I am glad that Marcus met you. Until now, he hasn't showed much interest in dating."

"Marcus and I were much alike in that area. Your brother is an exceptional man. He is indeed a blessing."

"And I know that he feels the same about you. Girl, he glows like a pregnant woman."

"Come on, Liah, Dad is calling us. Whoa, it looks like Christmas," Lecxa screamed. "Who are all of these gifts for?"

"These are for the kids," Marcus answered.

"Let me guess, Mom and Dad," Lecxa said. "They finally have some children to spoil."

"Yes, we do," Lillie raved. "And that's not it." She got up and went in to get more gifts.

"It's all your mother," Morgan Sr. murmured, after Lillie went in the house.

"Dad, take that guilty look off your face," Morgan told him. "You know you were probably worse than Mom."

"Okay, but not worse, no one is worse than your Mother." Lillie came back with another arm full of gifts.

"Okay, my darlings. It's time to open gifts." She passed out gifts as if it were Christmas. And the children didn't mind at all. Lillie and Morgan were smiling from ear to ear. They also told Liah that they had gifts inside for Jayde. Liah was pleasantly surprised that they thought of Jayde.

"You all bought gifts for Jayde, too," she exclaimed.

"We sure did," Lillie responded. "We didn't know what the boys liked. But we've done college children before."

"You all are very kind," Liah said. "Thank you. And thank you for thinking of Jayde. As a matter of fact, she was just telling me that she wanted a new laptop."

"Lecxa, would you mind taking Jayde's gifts back with you," Liah asked her.

"Sure, I can do that."

"Thank you. I'm sure Jayde will be surprised. "She is not going to believe that one of her instructor's is Marcus' sister."

"I know, right!" Lecxa responded. "Well ... Mother dear, I'm going to give Liah a tour of the house."

"Alright, sweetie."

"Hold up," Marcus said. "Addie, Jeffrey, and I are going, too."

"Well come on then, Markie," Lecxa teased.

"Girl, what did I tell you about that?" he asked, pretending to take offense.

"What are you gonna do, lift me up in the air?"

"Yeah, and drop you down, too."

"Right," Lecxa responded.

"You guys are pitiful," Liah said.

"It's all Marcus' fault."

"Nope, it is not sister!" He replied. "But I'm letting it go, at least for now. So, Lecxa, which room should we tour first?"

"Let's do yours first," she replied.

"Okay. So this is my room." He had several designs of houses and buildings in frames that he had sketched when he was younger.

"Marcus," Liah said to him. "These are amazing. It seems that as a child, you had already chosen your career."

"He used to tell Mom and Dad often, that when he grew up he was going to build houses," Lecxa, conveyed. "You should have seen all the paper he wasted."

"It wasn't wasted. And besides, I paid them for it later."

"It was wasted. You used to take mine and Morgan's."

"Be quiet, Lexie. Let's show them your room."

"Marcus, you haven't called me Lexie since I left home."

"Well, you're back now."

"I've missed you, too, Marcus." He kissed her on the cheek then said, "Come on girl."

"I might as well warn you all," Lecxa said. "I still have my dolls and stuffed animals collection. They used to be my students, because Marcus and Morgan wouldn't cooperate."

"Lecxa, we used to sit for an hour listening to you," Marcus declared, in their defense.

"And the reason you all stayed that long, is because I baked you all cookies with my Easy Bake Oven."

"And they were good, too," they laughed.

"Are you guys like this all of the time?" Liah asked.

"Pretty much. It's a way of keeping our childhood alive." Liah just sighed. They walked in Lecxa's room. It was much like it was when she was home.

"Lecxa, this is so cute," Liah said. "I thought it would be more girly than this."

"Girl, how could it? I had very masculine knuckle-headed brothers around. They wouldn't let me be too feminine."

"You're funny, Lecxa," Marcus smiled. "She was a true tomboy."

"Oh—my—gosh! I don't believe it. You have a collection of the Beasley dolls. I know you weren't around when they were out. So where did you get them?"

"Mom passed them on to me."

"I used to have a few Beasley dolls. I might have some at Granny's house. However, I'm not sure, because my brother and my uncles used to take the heads off all of our dolls and bury them."

"Honey, Marcus and Morgan used to take the legs off my dolls and hide them. But, you couldn't even bribe them to look at Mom's doll collection."

"You all were a bit mischievous, huh, Marcus," Liah said.

"Here, Liah, take this one."

"You're kidding!"

"No, I'm serious."

"I can't take this doll. Your mom gave you that."

"Girl, Mom won't mind."

"She really will not" Marcus said.

"Okay, if you all are sure. Oh, wow. Thank you, Lecxa!" And then she hugged her. "Wow, I have another Beasley doll," she sang. "Lecxa, this is very kind."

"You are so welcome. Now, what happened to Addie and Jeffrey?"

"Here we are," Addie said. "We were admiring the painting."

"Yes, they are lovely paintings, I must say," Jeffrey avowed.

"Thank you Jeffrey," Marcus said.

"I like this room, Lecxa," Addie said. And look at the Beasley dolls. I didn't know there were still any around. I used to love these dolls," she whispered.

"I think all girls liked the Beasley dolls," Lecxa avowed.

"That's it," Addie said. "We should have them cloned." They all burst out laughing.

"We might as well," Lecxa replied. "They're cloning humans now."

"Well now, she does have a point," Liah said. "So I know it won't be difficult to clone the Beasley dolls."

"Excuse me, ladies," Marcus said. "Can we continue the tour?"

"We're right behind you," Lecxa replied. They continued the tour for the next fifteen minutes, then went back to join the others.

"Lillie, you have a beautiful and interesting home," Addie told her. "This could be tourist scenery."

"Well, thank you, Addie. I might just consider that. Oh, will you all excuse me for a moment, please? I'll be right back."

"I hope she's not going in to get that old photo album," Morgan mumbled.

"Are you talking about the one she calls—'my kids' date book?" Lecxa asked.

"Yeah...that's the one," Marcus replied.

"And here it comes," Morgan Sr. warned.

"Liah and Addie, come on, sit right here."

"No, Mom, not Addie, too," Marcus exclaimed.

"Hush, Marcus, she's part of the family, too. She and Jeffrey are all you had until Liah and the kids came along."

"I guess you're hush now," Lecxa murmured.

"Let's not forget, you have pictures in there, too." Morgan told her.

"Boy, I have no shame because I was cute," she said proudly. Morgan Sr. told stories behind most of the pictures. They laughed tears out of their eyes. Liah got up and put her arms around Marcus, and told him she loved him even more and he should be grateful that his mom and dad showed the photos. She went on to say, "I have learned so much about you from the stories and photos. Of course, some are a little weird." She giggled. "But, you have such a kind and loving heart, and it makes me appreciate having you in my life, even more." They embraced for a brief moment.

"That was such a sweet and precious speech," Mrs. Sandler said.

"Sounds like an invitation to a proposal to me," Mr. Sandler blurted out. They all looked at him. "What?" he asked. I'm just saying."

"You all leave him alone. I hear this often from all my friends. I am just taking this one as a compliment."

Lecxa broke the moment and uttered, "Mom and Dad, did I tell you all I might be coming home for the summer?"

"No—really, Lecxa?" Lillie replied, surprised.

"Yes, really!"

"Oh, baby, that is wonderful. I'll have all my babies here. Lord, I am so blessed," she cried.

"This is going to be a great summer," Liah said. "Lecxa, maybe we can work on those cloned dolls," Liah said seriously.

"Cloned dolls?" Morgan Sr. yelled

"Don't ask, it's a girl thing," Jeffrey told him.

322

"Yeah, Dad," Lecxa said. "You wouldn't understand."

"Then I probably wouldn't." he surrendered, like an obedient child.

"Alright, let's put this food in containers," Lillie said. "Liah, you all can take most of this stuff home."

"Make sure you leave the carrot cake and some cookies," Morgan Sr. uttered.

"I promise to leave the carrot cake and some cookies," Liah told him.

"Thank you, sweetheart," he responded.

"I'm sending food home with Marcus and Morgan, too. Lecxa, do you want to take some home too?" Lillie asked.

"I'm taking the rest of those cookies," she said.

"Cookie race," Lecxa screamed. Morgan, Marcus and Lecxa, all ran toward the cookie boxes. Marcus grabbed two boxes and took off running.

"Marcus, give me those cookies," Lecxa screamed, loudly. "Liah, help me please." Liah took off running after Marcus. Both of them cornered him. Liah jumped on Marcus' back. Then Lecxa grabbed the cookies. Marcus lost his balance and fell to the ground. Liah fell right on top of him. Even though it was a Kodak moment, it was an awkward moment for Liah.

"Do you know how much I love you?" she asked him, and then rolled off him.

He took a deep breath. "May I ask you a question before I answer?"

"Yes."

"Do you love me enough to spend an eternity with me?"

"I wouldn't have it any other way."

"Then I know exactly how much you love me."

"Hum—sneaky, but good answer," she whispered. "Now can we get off this ground?"

He let out a chuckle, "Yes, I think we should." They got up and walked back over to the dessert table.

"Did you have fun on the ground?" Morgan asked, jokingly.

"We did," Marcus answered. Liah finished helping Lillie packed up the rest of the food. She thanked Lillie and Morgan, for having them over and again for the kid's gifts.

"Lecxa, what time are you leaving on Monday?" Liah inquired.

"My plane is scheduled to leave at three forty-five Monday evening." Liah invited Lecxa, Lillie, and Morgan Sr. to join her for lunch at A'Palace. They all said yes, with no hesitation.

"Fantastic, I'll see you all around one fifteen."

"Liah, it's always a pleasure to have lunch with you," Morgan Sr. told her. "I'm looking forward to it."

"Now, Mr. and Mrs. Sandler, it was a pleasure seeing you all again," Liah said.

"Liah, dear, your Godly spirit, is exuberant," Mrs. Sandler said as she hugged her.

"Mom and Dad, thanks for everything," Morgan said. "But I have to leave. I have an appointment with a prospective client."

After Morgan left, everyone else stood outside and talked. "Liah, how many children do you have?" Mrs. Sandler asked.

"I have six children and four grandchildren."

"Liah, you barely look old enough to have older children, let alone grandchildren," Mrs. Sandler said to her.

"Thank you for the compliment. They will all be visiting soon."

"Yeah, and I can't wait to meet them," Lillie said joyfully. "Great grandbabies will be a joy to spoil."

"Oh, my goodness, she's looking for more kids to spoil," Morgan Sr. bellowed.

"Yes, I am, and I am not ashamed to say it."

"I heard that, Lillie," Mrs. Sandler smiled.

"Mom and Dad, we have to get going too," Marcus said. "Thanks for having us all over and I will see you all at church tomorrow."

"Any time, Son," Morgan Sr. said

"And the next time don't wait for an invitation," Lillie inserted.

"Okay guys … come give Auntie Lecxa a hug. Auntie … huh, I can get used to that," she said proudly.

There wasn't much conversation on the way home. Everyone seemed pretty tired. Marcus and Liah stayed outside and talked after Jeffrey, Addie and the kids went in the house. Marcus seemed to have something on his mind.

"You know, Honey, my family really likes you," he said. "No, they are crazy about you."

"I feel the same way about them."

"Do you mind if I ask you a question?"

"You know I don't mind, Marcus."

"First, let me just say this: I know it's been just you and the children for years. But how do you think the kids would respond to having someone in their lives on a daily basis?"

"Honestly, if you're referring to a father figure, I believe there would have to be some adjustments made. I'm been the only person they've depended on for years. However, I think that they would be okay with that change, especially Jas."

"That sounds fair enough. So if you ever decided to get married again, how would you feel about your husband adopting your children?"

"I would want him to. But I think it would have to be what the kids want as well."

He gently took her hand and kissed it and continued to hold it as he told her how much he loved her. He went on to say," I have reached the point in our relationship..." He paused momentarily. When I wake up in the morning, I want to wake up with you by my side. And when I close my eyes at night ... I want you in my arms."

Liah couldn't utter a word. He had rendered her speechless. She stared at him momentarily with watery eyes, trying her best not to shed a tear. "Liah, baby, what's wrong?" Tears could no longer hold back. He pulled a Kleenex out of the box and dabbed her face.

"I'm sorry, Honey, I didn't mean to make you cry."

"No, no, Marcus, I'm okay. It's just that every time you open your heart, it's kind of like you're telling me what I feel for you."

"Then you and I have a lot to think about," he told her. "So why don't we leave this on the table right now. Because we've reached the stage in our relationship where we need to look back to see how far we've come and how far we want to go." Then he told her that he wanted her to think seriously about their conversation tonight, and he would do the same. They hugged and said goodnight but were reluctant to let each other go.

"If you walk me to the door, it will give us a few more minutes together. Then again, we probably should say goodnight, now. You can watch me walk to the door. Well, you know what I mean."

After Liah got in the house, she sat in the foyer and took a moment to reflect over their conversation before going into the family room. Addie was sitting on the couch when she came in. "Are you okay?" she asked Liah.

"Yes, I'm fine. Thank you for asking. I'm just a bit emotional."

"Why? What happened?"

"Marcus and I just had a deep conversation. Let me go check on Jas first."

"He just finished his shower and now he's in his room."

"Oh—good! I'll go check on him shortly."

"So come on, talk to me."

"Well, we just feel that we have reached the stage in our relationship, where we need to decide how far we want it to go. So basically, we have some serious thinking to do. Honestly, Addie, I have prayed about this. Marcus is an amazing man. He's more than I've ever dreamed of. The kids are crazy about him, especially Jas, and I love him completely. And I know he loves me back."

"You can't go wrong with that, Liah. He is what we would refer to as a genuine man."

"Yeah, and he looks good, too," Liah blurted.

"Girl, he sure does. Now let's go watch that movie you've been trying to get me to watch."

"Okay! Let me go check on the kids. You can grab some snacks and meet me in our movie room."

"Liah."

"Yes, Addie!"

"Keep hope alive." Liah and Addie both sighed.

"Always!"

After checking on the kids, Liah put on her lounger, then went down to join Addie. "Okay I'm here, so let's get this movie going."

"What's the name of that movie again?" Addie asked.

"It's not a new-release movie, but it's a good one."

"Alright, pop it in," Addie said. They watched the movie about halfway through, and then Addie wanted to take a quick shower before continuing.

"Good idea. I need to take one, too."

"Okay, see you in a moment," Addie said.

Addie and Liah came back downstairs and cuddled back up in their throws on the sofa. Both of them fell asleep before the movie was over. They slept until the following morning.

Monday morning, Liah was back in her usual routine. She was excited about going back to work. When she walked in, they had put up a welcome banner, decorated with balloons, and the whole crew had bought her gifts. She was blown away

"Oh, wow, you guys are too much. Look at this place and all of these gifts. Guys, you all didn't have to do so. Thanks for everything. I'm going to put them in my office and open them on my break"

"Come on, Liah," Tina said. Open them now."

"Well, I'll open at least one now."

She ended up opening up all of the gifts. "These are awesome, guys. You all know how much I love my special chef outfits. This was very thoughtful of you all. I really do appreciate it. Okay, let's get to work. First of all—"

Tina cut in and told her the restaurant was going to be up for sell.

"You are kidding me," she said, totally shocked.

"Actually she's not," Louis told her. "I overheard the head boss talking to the owner. And guess who they are going to give the first shot to?"

"And who would that be?" she wiped the smile off her face.

"No one other than the great Chef, Liah Mathis," Joedi kindly stated.

"No way!" she blurted. "You all are kidding. Stop messing with me. Cut it out so we can get to work."

"We're for real," Tina said. "But don't mention it."

"For real...real. Okay, I won't. I don't believe it—I don't believe it."

"I think she's in shock, man," Joedi whispered to Louis.

"Yeah, but it will wear off soon."

"Alright, bring me up to speed. Anything else I should know?" They worked, talked, and shared stories, until it was time for the lunch rush. Liah's performance seemed to be better than before. And so was her team's. They were back in the action and were sure to keep their title of being the best restaurant in town.

"We're glad to have you back, Liah," Louis said to her. "Especially today, we are extra busy."

"Speaking of busy," Liah said, "has Liz Carrington called?"

"Yes, she just called and said she would be here around two," Mel answered.

"Thanks, Mel. Oh, and I'm expecting guests around one thirty. Marcus' parents and sister".

"Ooh, yeah. The big tipper, she screamed excitedly. I'll let you know when they get here. Girl, I am so glad you're back."

"Mel, their lunch is on me, so no bill."

"Even better, honey! Bless you, child." Liah shook her head and laughed.

"That girl likes your special clients. She knows they're big tippers," Tina said.

Well, she's right about that," Liah replied.

"Louis, what time do you want to take your break?"

"Why don't I take it after you're done with your guests?"

"Okay, that will work. Before I forget, I need you all to check your personal schedules for the night of the May tenth. The Michaels are having a party that night. I really would like it if you all could assist. Mel, I am also going to need about four or five from your team. So everyone whose available, I need you to sign the sheet on my desk, please. Okay, time to get to work."

Though the crowd seemed to be plentiful, they were done by one forty-five. The Michaels had already arrived. Liah joined them shortly before two.

"Hi, I'm sorry I had you all waiting. We have been swamped."

"No need for an apology, dear," Morgan Sr. said, "besides, we've been treated kindly."

"Well, your lunch will be served shortly."

"Liah, this is a fabulous restaurant," Lecxa told her. "And I hear you are the best chef in town."

"That's what I heard too, Lecxa, but I know a few other great chefs in town now. However, I am pleased to say that we have held the five-star title for the past four or five years."

"I can see why," Lecxa said.

"I think it's because we have a great team and we believe in team work."

"That does make a big difference," Morgan responded.

Mel came out with the serving cart. "Oh my," Lillie murmured. "Everything looks divine and I know it will taste so."

"Mel, I'll help you served," Liah said.

"Liah, please stay sitting and enjoy your lunch, girl"

"Okay, Ms. Boss."

"Thank you," Mel said. The four of them talked, ate, and had a merry time. Mel came back and asked them if they were going to have dessert. "Not me, Lecxa said. I had enough over the weekend." The others said the same.

"Liah, Liz is here," Mel told her.

"Thanks! Will you show her to the ballroom and tell her we will join her shortly?"

"Wait a minute, dear," Morgan said, "you are always so kind." He pulled out a crispy fifty dollar bill and handed it to her.

"Thank you, Mr. Michaels, Sir. Would anyone like coffee?" She knew Liah didn't drink coffee and none of the others was in the mood for it. "Then you all have a wonderful afternoon and thanks again," Mel told them.

"You too, dear," Morgan said.

"Do you all still have time to look at the ballroom?" Liah asked. Morgan looked at Lecxa. "Sure, we have at least fifteen minutes." Liz shared her ideas for the party with them. Lillie was very pleased. While she was talking to them, Marcus called. "Will you all excuse me please?" she asked them.

"By all means, go ahead, dear," Morgan said.

"Hey, Marcus, what's up?

"Hi, Liz. Hey—listen. I know Liah is probably there with you. So would you please not let her know you're talking to me?"

"O…kay," she whispered hesitantly." He chuckled. He knew from the way she responded, she thought something was wrong.

"Liz, it's not that serious. I just want you to handle her surprise birthday party."

"Marcus, don't you scare me like that again." He chuckled again and then apologized. She giggled. "You know I'll be happy to, but I have to call you back after I'm done with your parents."

"Okay, awesome! Thanks, Liz."

"Alright, I am back. I apologize. It was a client."

"Not a problem," Lillie said. She continued talking to them for a few more minutes.

"Liz, I like your ideas. I think you will do a spectacular job," Lillie told her.

"I will give you all, my best." Lillie sighed.

"We appreciate that," Morgan said. "Thank you for taking the time to share your ideas."

"Well, you're welcome, Mr. Michaels." They all said goodbye and the Michaels left. Liah walked them out to the car for a more personal goodbye to Lecxa.

When she came back in, Liz was still in the ballroom. "Liz, have you had time to eat lunch?" she asked.

"No, I haven't. I'll get something later."

"If you don't have to rush off, you should have lunch here. My treat."

"Okay, sure. You know I can't pass up an invitation to eat the great Chef Liah's, free food." Liah giggled and then asked her what she wanted.

"Okay, Mrs. Carrington, please let me show you to your table." Liz giggled and then asked her if she'd ever been a waitress before.

"Never," Liah answered.

"Why, you don't like my waitress courtesy or something?"

"Liah, I think you'll make a lot of tips," she laughed.

"Actually, I was considering doing it when Jas was a baby. I was going to put him in a pouch on my back."

"Really?"

"Girl, no!" They laughed again.

'Liah, girl, you are crazy."

"So I've been told. Anyway, Liz, make yourself comfortable. I'll be back in about ten minutes with your order."

Liz decided to call Marcus while she waited. "Hi, Marcus, this is Liz."

"Hi, Liz. Thanks for getting back with me so quickly."

"So tell me, how I can assist you?"

"Tell you what, Liz. The party is going to be at my house. So if you have some time available this evening, I would like for you to come by my house and take a look around. I'll give you the details then."

"I can do that. How about four-thirty?"

"Yea, good, that will work for me as well. Let me give you the address."

"Alright ... hold on a moment. She fumbled through her purse to find a pad and pen. Okay, give it to me."

"Liz, I really appreciate you coming on such short notice and I will see you around four-thirty."

"You bet! "I'll see you shortly." She made a couple more quick calls before her food arrived. "Liah, this looks fabulous and I am famished."

"Well, I hope you enjoy it. I wish that I could sit with you, but my sous chef has to take his break."

"Oh, Honey, I understand. I'll be fine."

"Okay. I'll check on you shortly."

"Alright, dear, and thank you for lunch."

"Anytime, honey! I got to get back to work. I'll come back to check on you in about twenty minutes." She hurried back into the kitchen to continue working.

Liah left not too long after Liz. She was beat from her first day back at work, and she wanted to get some rest before the girls' performance that evening.

After dinner, she hung out with the kids before they had to leave. Liah, Addie, Jeffrey and the kids, were meeting Marcus and the rest of the Michaels clan at the Performing Art Theater.

Liah's household arrived about forty-five minutes earlier. The girls had to get in their costumes and for a quick rehearsal before Showtime.

Liah and Liz both had blocked off two rows for all of their guests. Liah had also invited Tim, Jen, and the crew from the restaurant.

Everyone arrived at least ten minutes before Showtime. While they waited, Liah told them which performance the girls were doing. The girls were in a sports' musical called "Bound by Royalty." It was based on the story Snow White. The seven males on the football team were called the seven dorks. They were a group of geeky guys who joined the team just to meet hot girls. However, their coach did not live up to his duties as a coach. But fortunately for them, a young lady and her father had recently moved to town, and she attended the same school as the geeky guys; a school that revolved around football and cheerleading. The young lady took an interest in them and taught them what she knew about football. Later on, the young lady is noticed by the first string's star football player. Well that's when the trouble begins because she was also noticed by his ex-girlfriend.

After the play, the audience gave the casts a standing ovation.

Liah and Liz knew the kids wanted to stay and watch the other plays so they stayed and so did everyone else. Afterwards, they all stood around talking for about fifteen minutes, mostly complimenting the girls and talking about how much they enjoyed the shows. Liah and Marcus didn't get a chance to talk much. Liah was tired and ready to go home.

After Liah got home, she went right up stair to take a long bubble bath. Immediately afterwards, she got in bed and read her Bible, and then made phone calls. She was just finishing up when Marcus called. "Hi, baby," he said. "I'm sorry we didn't get a chance to talk tonight. "How was your first day back at work?"

"My first day back was good, just very busy." And no need to apologize. How was your day?"

"It was good. And before I forget, I have to go out of town on Wednesday morning."

"When will you be back?"

"I believe on Thursday."

"Okay, but I'm going to miss you."

"And I will miss you, too.

"Oh, before I forget, can you attend my lecture tomorrow night?"

"I wouldn't miss it. Is that the lecture on love?"

"Yes, it is, and I'm impressed that you remembered."

"Of course, I remembered."

"What was I thinking? I should have known you would remember."

"There you go. Sorry, Sweetheart, I have to go. I need to get back to work." Liah was pretty worn out anyway, from her first day back at work. She went right to sleep.

The next morning, Liah woke up early to review her lesson for her lecture that night, before going to work. She was expecting a big crowd.

335

After another busy day at work, she didn't have time to go home, so she called Addie, to ask her to bring the children. Liah and the crew from A'Palace, arrived thirty minutes early. Liah wanted to set up a dessert table, so she could introduce the three new pound cake recipes she had recently created. They were blueberry cream with a cream cheese glaze, lemon cranberry with lemon butter glaze, and peanut butter banana with a banana butter glaze. She had already gotten superb feedbacks from the staff at A'Palace, so she figured it would be an excellent opportunity to do a taste testing tonight.

It seemed that everyone she invited showed up at least five to ten minutes early. After a short introduction from the instructor, Liah went right into her lecture. "Good evening everyone, and thank you for coming. Tonight's lecture is about love. There are hard copies as well as CDs available for each guest. However, you must fill out a request form. You can find those in the refreshment room to my right. Also please enjoy the refreshments after the lecture. I don't need to take any home with me. I have a personal relationship with the chef. That would be me! The audience laughed after she said, "that would be me." "Our lecture for tonight is entitled 'A Love Not Broken.'"

Her lecture captivated the audience. She was an outstanding orator. After the lecture, everyone stood up for a round of applause. The instructor then came up on stage and said, "Liah Mathis, everyone." She thought it was a bit overdone; nonetheless, the audience gave her a standing ovation. Marcus and Morgan were the first ones to come up and congratulate her. Marcus was speechless, so he just hugged her. Morgan, of course, spoke for both of them.

"Liah you were astounding," Morgan told her. "I really want to get married now. That's all I have to say."

"Thank you, Morgan and Marcus, even though you couldn't speak, Marcus."

"I just wasn't ready."

"Right Marcus."

"It is a blessing that my son met you and brought you into our lives, especially Morgan. I even feel that I can love better, after all that," Lillie said.

Morgan Sr. followed with complimentary words after Lillie.

"Thank you, Morgan, I appreciate the compliment. Now if you all will kindly excuse me, I had better go mingle with the other guests before they think I like you all more."

"Then you had better, dear," Morgan Sr. said "We wouldn't want them to think that," he said as he chuckled.

"I'll catch up with you all shortly," Liah told them and then ushered them toward the desserts. She hardly made five steps before the crew from work stopped her.

"What's up, guys?" she asked.

"Hey, we're just going on about the rising star," Louis responded.

"Who—what rising star?" Liah inquired, acting coy.

"Ms. Liah Anginette Mathis," Tina answered sassily. Liah, that speech—lesson, or whatever, was awesome."

"Thank you, all of you, but I can't the take the credit. I was inspired by the Master and the Creator of love."

She continued to mingle with the guests, being showered with compliments for both her speech and cakes.

"Liah, I don't know what you put in those cakes, but it seemed that everyone is heading to the Bistro to eat," Liz said, as she crept up. "Those cakes must be something special, to be able to eat a meal after eating several pieces."

"Liz, hi! I didn't know you were here."

"I sneaked in right after your invitation to the cakes."

"You would be here for that part, girl," Liah said.

"Uh huh, and now all of the cake is gone."

"Did you get some?" Liah asked.

"Honey, you know I did. I ran in there to ration it out. I made sure I got samples of all three. By the way, they were fabulous."

"Thank you, Liz. Now I'm going to the Bistro to eat. Anyone with me?" All she heard was a lot of "I'm ins." Alright—off to the Bistro," Liah, uttered. A group of them piled up in the Bistro, stuffed themselves, and then departed. Morgan Sr. and Lillie dropped Morgan off at home. Marcus wanted to spend some time with Liah, since he was going out of town on Wednesday.

Liah carried Jas right up to bed when they got home. Marcus waited for her in the movie room, while she tucked him in and took a quick shower. Hi, honey," she said to him when she came in. "Thanks for waiting for me."

"Oh, I didn't mind a bit. By the way, I took the liberty of making you a cup of chamomile tea."

"Really?"

"Yes, really!"

"Aaah—thank you, Marcus. That was very thoughtful of you."

"You are welcome, my love. Now, come sit here by me, on this very comfortable couch—drink your tea, watch the movie, and I'm going to rub your feet."

"What? Seriously?" Wanting to scream yes, yes, please do so now... my feet are very tired, and I can't remember the last time I had them rubbed. "Sure. I don't mind. How did you …. I..."

"Yes, Addie told me where you keep your stash of downstairs foot creams."

"What else did she tell you?"

"That was it. Should I pry for more information?"

"No—you're good."

"Well, come on. Put your feet on my knee."

"Okay, here are my feet." He rubbed her feet and nearly put her to sleep. It was exactly what she needed after the long day she had had. After he was done, both of them cuddled up on the couch with a throw— him at one end and her at the other. And like always, anytime someone watched a movie with Liah, they all fall asleep. It was halfway through the night before they awakened, and realized that they'd practically slept through the entire movie and it had been over for some time.

Marcus jumped up and said, "Oh my gosh! I can't believe we almost slept through the night."

"At least halfway through it," Liah whispered. Marcus hurried out the door. Not only did he have to pack, but he also didn't want the kids to draw conclusions, if they found him there when they got up. Liah went right back to sleep as soon as he left.

~Chapter Twenty~

Liah was looking forward to Saturday morning. She had only been back to work for a week, but she was ready for an off day. She decided she would sleep in at least an hour past her normal awakening time. Since the kids were still asleep, she stayed in bed an extra thirty minutes before fixing breakfast. She had insisted that Addie sleep in this morning, instead of getting up to make breakfast.

Back to their rooms everyone went, immediately after breakfast. They had planned on going swimming later in the day. Liah got in some Bible reading, worked out, and even had time to do some writing. As she was about to get ready go swimming, her mom called. "Mommy—hi. How are you?"

"I'm doing well, baby. How are you and my grandbabies?"

"We're all good, Mom—really good."

"You finally decided to start dating again, didn't you?"

"Yes, Mom, I did," she reluctantly replied. She knew that if her mom knew a little, she would want to know more. *Here it comes*, she thought to herself.

"So come on, tell me all about him."

"Yes, ma'am," she responded like an obedient child.

She would have liked to have had just a little more time before sharing him with her mom. Of course, she knew it was too late now. She told her mother all about Marcus and his family.

"Now what was it you said he owned, honey?"

"He and his twin brother, own an architect business."

"So he designs and builds?"

"Yes, but more designing than hands on."

"And how well does he get alone with the children?"

"Very well, Mom," she answered quickly. "Especially, Jas. He's really good with him."

"Does he have any children?"

"No, he doesn't have any."

"Has he been married?"

"Yes, he has, Mom," she whispered hesitantly. "He's been divorced for several years now. And, Mom, Marcus and Morgan were sterile at birth."

"Oh, honey, I'm sorry to hear that."

"It's okay, they're fine with it."

"Well, he's sounds like a really good person."

"He really is, Mom. And you wouldn't believe this. After I was released from the hospital, he invited us to stay at his house."

"What?"

"I'm not finished, Mom. He stayed with Morgan, his brother, while we were there. We were there with his staff.

"Child, he has a staff."

"Yes, he does."

"I bet you had him investigated, didn't you?" They both giggled.

"I did."

"I knew that. But the man sounds like a real Christian man, a real saint. I'm liking this Marcus fellow."

"He is indeed."

"When are you bringing him home?"

"Maybe soon. I have to check Marcus' schedule. But, Mom, I have to be going. I'm going swimming with the kids. Be looking for your Mother's Day gift sometime today. And, Mom, try to stay home until it comes. I'll call you back later or you can call me when it arrives."

"Alright, baby. Kiss my grandbabies and tell them grandma loves them. Did I tell you that I talked to the boys and Jayde this week?"

"No, you didn't, Mother."

"I did. And I talked to the great grandbabies, too."

"They're talking much better now."

"They sure are. Well, Honey, I know you have to go. I love you. And thanks for finally telling me about Marcus. I know you just wanted to be sure before you told me."

"I did, Mom. And, Mom, thanks for being such a great Mom."

"Your father would be proud of you, baby." Liah sighed, before she told her mom she loved her.

"I love you too, Lili." Lili, was the name her dad used to call her. Her mom and her grandmother, still calls her that sometime. "You take care."

She was delighted that the conversation with her mom, about Marcus went so well, especially since she waited so long to tell her about him. But her mom also knew that Liah didn't have a bad track record for making hasty decisions, and would never put her children at risk. That's why she didn't make a fuss when Liah told her that she stayed at Marcus' after being released from the hospital.

Liah sighed and then said out loud, *I am glad I got that out of the way.* She then gathered the kids so they could go swimming. She also invited Jeffrey and Addie. She and the kids enjoyed spending time with them. They were indeed part of the family.

They all had a joyous time together. Liah even had them doing water aerobics. Believe it or not, they all seemed to have enjoyed it. Considering neither Addie, nor Jeffrey, was the least bit gung ho at first. "Liah, dear, thanks for inviting us. I believe I'm going to take a shower then a nap before the party," Jeffrey kindly uttered.

"Jeffrey, you don't have to thank me. We are glad you all joined us. But you are certainly welcome. And I am going to take a shower and catch a nap as well. Jas, you had better come, too. You might as well take a shower before you go over to Jen and Tim's." Everyone else followed suit. Liah waited until Jas was done taking his shower before she took hers.

The party was a vast success. Lillie and Morgan's niece were elated and totally surprised and they were very pleased with everything. And so were Liah and Liz. They even received a lot of feedback from the guests. "Girlfriend," Liz said to Liah, "we should go in business together."

"We do know how to hold a crowd, don't we?" Liah responded.

"Girl, you know it! Oh—Liah, here comes Marcus."

"I haven't had time to spend a moment with him all night. We had about ten minutes to talk before the party."

"Girl, you had better spend some time with that man. Didn't he just get back in town?"

"He sure did."

"Hey, you," Marcus said to Liah. "I've hardly seen you tonight."

"I know, Honey, I'm sorry."

"You don't have to apologize. You were doing your job," he said, as he hugged her."

"Hi, Liz. How are you?"

"I'm good, Marcus. Thanks for asking. How are you?"

"Really well. You know—you guys did a spectacular job on this party. I heard a lot of impressive words about you two. Maybe you all should go in business together."

"Now that's a coincidence," Liah said. "Liz just mentioned that—like right before you walked up."

"Seriously?" he replied.

"I'm serious," Liah said.

"Huh," he responded and sighed.

"Guys, I'm going to leave you love birds alone," Liz told them. "I have to go wrap things up."

"Okay, Liz. Thanks for all of your hard work. You did a really good job as always," Liah told her. Liah stood there talking to Marcus for a few minutes and then she had to go round up her crew, so they could get the place cleaned up.

Liah gathered everyone in the kitchen before cleanup. "Okay, guys, there's a lot of food left over. Please divide it equally and take it home. Now to show my appreciation for the great job you all have done tonight, everyone one is getting a bonus. So everyone gets twice your regular pay for tonight...only."

"Liah, you talking about us, too, Tina asked.

"Now, Tina, you know I'm not talking about you and Louis," she uttered with a serious expression.

"Well, it was good while it lasted." Liah started laughing.

"Why are you laughing Liah?" Louis inquired inquisitively.

"I was kidding. You all know you're getting bonuses as well. " She laughed again. "I can't believe you all did not think you would. Pitiful—just pitiful."

"Liah, why are you all always messing with me?" Tina asked.

"Cause you're funny, and I get you every time. Now you know that you, Louis, and Mel are my right-hand people."

"You're right! I'm sorry," Tina said.

"You're just pitiful," Liah said to her wittily.

"Tina, I need to go talk to Addie and Jeffrey. I'll be back in a moment." She asked Addie and Jeffrey to take the girls home. They took her car. Marcus offered to take her home. After they left, Liah went in her office to call her mom back. "Hi, Mom, I'm returning your call."

"Liah, baby, thank you ... thank you, for the lovely gift. You know I've been talking about a cruise for years."

"Yes, Mom, now you have to go. It's non-refundable."

"Don't worry, I'm going. And I can take three other people with me."

"Just don't take Tori and Paige."

"I'm not! They probably wouldn't want to go with me anyway. Now, Lili, I know you paid a lot for this cruise. You did not have to give me five-thousand dollars to go with it."

"I know, Mom. But you and dad gave us your best. And after Dad past, you continued to give us your best. Mom, so much of what you all taught us, takes care of us still today. And that, Mother, is priceless. So you deserve it. You will always be my mother of the year. I love you, Mom, and please have a magnificent time."

"I will, darling, and thank you for that beautiful speech. You've always had a way with words. And, baby, thanks again for the gift."

You're welcome, Mom. Now I have to go. I'll call you tomorrow."

"Alright ... good night sweetie."

"Mom, are you crying?

"Tears of joy, baby. I'm just blessed to have such wonderful children."

"I love you, Mom. Goodnight."

Liah leaned back in her high-back desk chair and closed her eyes. Marcus walked in and said, "There you are. Baby, are you alright?"

"Yes, Honey. I'm okay! I just finished talking to my mom. She got a little bit emotional about her Mother's Day gift."

"What did you get her?"

"Fourteen days cruise for four and five thousand dollars."

"Well, I can see why she got emotional. But I can't believe you chose a cruise. That's what the three of us got Mom, for Mother's Day."

"Are you serious?"

"Yep! I guess the saying that, 'great minds think alike' is true."

"I guess so!"

"When is your Mom leaving?" Marcus asked.

"Next weekend."

"What about your mom?"

"In two weeks."

"Wow—that's something. Our moms are going on a cruise," Marcus said.

"Yep—that's something," she yawned.

"Are you ready to leave?" he asked.

"Oh, yes, I am." He put his arm around her and they walked out together.

"You said you had something you wanted to talk to me about," Marcus, reminded her.

Oh yeah, right! Chantel is moving here on the fourteenth of this month. And they are supposed to be staying with me until she finds a house."

"Are Alisha and Shayna still coming?"

"Yes, they are. How did you know that?"

"If my memory serves me correctly, Morgan mentioned something about them coming around your birthday."

"O...kay!"

"Why you all don't move back in to my house until Chan finds her house," he suggested. "Or everyone can just stay there. And I'll move back in with Morgan. So when are you coming back?"

She giggled, and then said surreptitiously, "I haven't said yes, yet!" But yes, was written all over her face. *Hmm, he answered the question before I even asked it. I kind of like that about him*, she thought. Sometime, it seems as if he could actually read her mind. If only that was true, he would know that being with him, was home for her.

"Well?" he uttered.

"Well what?" she responded, as if she didn't know what he was talking about.

"Liah, stop it. You know what I'm talking about.

"Okay...okay. Yes, and thank you."

"You knew I wouldn't mind anyway."

"I know. But I figured I would let you think it was your idea anyway," she said sniggling. "No, seriously, I could have just let Addie and Jeffrey, come back home. But then, I truly don't know what I would do without them now."

"No, way, would they want to come back, without you. "They wouldn't have it. It would be like taking the sweet out of their sugar."

"The sweetness out of their sugar," she repeated jadedly. "Okay baby," she murmured, not quite sure what he meant, but she left it at that.

"Now when are you coming?" he asked her again.

"Probably, Wednesday."

"Good," he replied briskly. He was all gung ho about the whole idea. He loved having them there, even though he wouldn't be staying there with them.

"Marcus," she whispered.

"Yes, Honey?"

"You do know that I really appreciate everything you do, right?"

"I do, Liah." By this time they were pulling up in her driveway.

"This is the only thing I don't like about being with you," she whispered solemnly.

He looked at her puzzled and then asked, "What, baby?"

"Departing." He got out of the truck and opened her door. Then took her by the hand and walked her to her front door. Neither of them said a word as they were walking. "Let's sit here for a minute," he said to her. They sat on the bench by the door. He heaved a sigh before saying to her, "Liah, sweetheart, most of the time when I bring you home and after you walk in the house, I sit out here for a moment, feeling the same way. I love you—baby—so much; when I leave you, it feels as if I am leaving a part of my heart as well." She gazed into his eyes. She knew exactly how he felt because she felt the exact same way.

"Marcus, you are my soul mate—and when we're not together my heart throbs for you." This was indeed one of their sententious moments. At that very moment they found themselves too close for comfort. So close they could feel the warmth of each other's breath. They quickly stood up, knowing that despite how they felt about leaving each other, it was time to say goodnight. The both of them knew that if he stayed any longer, they could be opting for an unholy territory. Marcus kissed her on the cheek and then opened the door for her and they said good night. Both of them stood at the door briefly after it closed—Marcus on the outside and Liah on the inside. Coincidently, they were thinking the same thing simultaneously—that putting space between them tonight was the best choice. After all, they were both Christians and that held precedence over anyone and all things. As Liah stood there, she felt Marcus presents at the door. But she wouldn't dare peek out for verification. She hesitantly walked away and so did he.

She headed right upstairs to get undressed and into something more comfortable. Before going downstairs, she went to each of the kids' room to peek in on them. They were already in bed sleeping peacefully.

Addie was waiting for Liah when she came back downstairs. "I thought I heard you come in," Addie said. "Jeffrey and I are in the kitchen. Would you like for me to fix you some tea?"

"Thanks, Addie, but I got it. And thanks for picking up Jas and getting him to bed."

"Honey, it was no problem," Addie said. "He was asleep when we picked him up. He even had his pajamas on."

"Yeah, Jen keeps a pair over there for him," Liah responded. "Did he go right back to sleep?"

"Yes, he did," Jeffrey responded. "And I took him right up to bed."

"Thanks, Jeffrey."

"Anytime, dear."

"So, are you all ready to go back to the big house," Liah asked?

"Only if you are," Jeffrey replied.

"Why?" Addie asked. "Are you tired of us or something?"

"Hah, yeah right," with a smile on her face. "Please—we're 'til death do us part."

Jeffrey chuckled. "You're serious, aren't you?"

"About going back to Marcus' or till death do us part?"

"Well, both, I guess!"

"Isn't Ms. Harris coming here to stay?" Jeffrey inquired.

"Yes, she is, and she plans to stay here until she finds a house. Shayna and Alisha are coming too."

"You will have a full house!" Addie predicted. "Well, I know Marcus insisted you and the kids come back."

"Yes, he kind of did! But I was going to ask him anyway."

"Then I guess we're going back. So when are we going?" Jeffrey asked.

"Wednesday," Liah replied. Did I tell you'll about the remodeling that Marcus did?"

"Remodeling!" Addie exclaimed.

"No, I believe you forgot dear," Jeffrey responded.

"Right. Sorry! Honestly, it did slip my mind. But yeah, it now has a garage apartment and two of the rooms downstairs are suites with a kitchenette."

"Well, who gets the new spaces," Jeffrey asked.

"You all do."

"Wow, cool!" replied Jeffrey.

"Jeffrey, stop letting Jas rub off on you," Addie told him. "Wow, cool! You're pitiful."

"Now, Addie, dear, at least I didn't say—it's bomb diggidy fresh."

"And I hope Addie doesn't say it either," Liah declared. They all burst out laughing. "I have been trying to get that one out of Jess."

"What does it mean anyway?" Jeffrey asked.

"Simple, Jeffrey. It's a ghetto-fabulous word that kids use at school— for something being cool, that is," Liah explained.

"Well anyway, Liah, I know this was your remodeling idea," Addie said.

"Now why would you say that? Do you all not want the new space?"

"I do," both of them said at the same time. "But it has you written all over it."

"Okay, but I only put it out there. Marcus took it from there."

"I'm not complaining," Jeffrey said.

"Me either," Addie blurted.

"Alright then," Liah said. "Wednesday it is. Now I'm saying good-night. You all sleep well."

~Chapter Twenty-One~

Bright and early Sunday morning, Jeffrey and the kids fixed Addie and Liah a big Mother's Day breakfast. Addie made it downstairs shortly before Liah did. She was taken aback by the aroma coming from the kitchen.

"Something smells good in here," Addie cried out. "Of all days, this woman made a big breakfast."

Liah came in right behind her. Addie, I can't believe it, of all days. You did not have to make breakfast on Mother's Day woman."

"I didn't do it," Addie replied.

"Well, who did it?" Jeffrey and the kids stepped out of hiding, all floured down and in aprons. Surprised—they all screamed, and scared Addie and Liah into a mild shock.

"Oh—my—goodness!" Liah cried. "I don't believe it. Oh, My God. This is indeed, a shock—a welcoming one—and a blessing."

"Yes, Lord, it is ... all of the above, Addie mumbled."

"Where's Jas?"

"Here I am, Mom!" She didn't even see from where he popped out.

"There you are. Where did you come from, big boy? Did you help?"

"I was hiding. And yes, I helped. I washed the fruits."

"You did?" She was very pleased that they let him help. "I don't know about you, Addie. But I think these guys deserve hugs." They all had a group hug. Addie and Liah were beyond impressed. They thanked them several times.

"You all did an outstanding job, but I do have one question," Liah stated. "Something is not adding up. And if I know Jeffrey, he does not like wasting food. So what is all of this food for?"

"Good question, dear!" Jeffrey replied.

"And we have a good answer," Jacqlyne added. Jeffrey and the kids started counting. Addie and Liah stood there looking mystified. The next thing they heard were voices singing Happy Mother's Day in the rhythm of happy birthday.

"Wait a minute," Liah whispered, totally blown away. Now I know those voices anywhere. Those are my babies, Addie." Jayde, Joshua, and Jacob came out. Then all of the kids and Jeffrey screamed, "Surprise!" Liah was rendered speechless.

"Oh—my–God! Where? What are you all—a big breakfast and all of my babies under one roof." Her eyes filled with tears. She murmured, "Come here, you guys, and give me a hug. I am so glad you all are here. How could you all leave Kaitlyn, Miyah, and the kids?"

Before they could answer, they stepped out and screamed, "Happy Mothers' Day."

"Okay, now that one was good. You all really pulled one on me this time."

The kids ran to her screaming "Nana, Nana." Then Miyah and Kaitlyn gave her a hug.

"This day just keeps on getting better." She hugged the kids all over again. "And Jayde, look at you! You have grown into such a beautiful young lady."

"Mom, I haven't been gone that long."

"Liah," Addie, reminded her, "The food."

"Thanks, Addie. Come on, everyone. Jeffrey and the kids have prepared this wonderful breakfast feast."

"We know, and we're starving," Jacob said.

"Yes, we are, and this food does look good," Joshua stated. They all gathered around the table and held hands while Jeffrey blessed the food. As overwhelmingly happy as Liah was, she couldn't help but wish Marcus was there to share in the glorious occasion with them. Nonetheless, they all had a splendid celebration.

After breakfast, everyone hurried and got dress so that they could make it to morning service on time. Liah, of course took a moment to call Marcus to tell him about her surprise. He invited everyone over to his house for a catered Mother's Day dinner. He and Morgan had planned on taking her and their mom out today anyway. He told her that his parents were going to be thrilled to meet everyone.

Liah met everyone downstairs and told them that Marcus invited the entire family to his house for dinner.

"Oh good," blurted Jayde. "I'm looking forward to meeting this Marcus person, whom I've heard so much about. And I can't wait to meet Auntie Lecxa's, cool parents, who gave me that really nice and expensive gift."

"Who is Auntie Lecxa?" Jacob asked, puzzled. "We don't have an Auntie Lecxa!"

"She's Mr. Marcus' sister," Jas blurted

354

"Hum, well...why didn't we get gifts?" Joshua asked.

Jacob popped him and then said to him, "You are too old for gifts, boy."

"Boys," Liah said, "we have to go."

On the way to church, Liah was going about five miles over the speed limit and got pulled over by a cop. He said to her. "Ma'am, do you know you were going about five miles over the speed limit?"

"No, not really...but okay." He asked for her driver's license and insurance. She reached in the glove compartment and handed him the insurance document, and then reached in her purse to get her license. She then said to him. "Look, officer, I realize you're just doing your job, but could you hurry it up? I would like to get to church on time. I wouldn't want to miss the Lord's Supper."

"You're on your way to church?"

"Yes, I am. And if you would like to escort me to church or even follow me in, you can sit by me and write me a ticket, while I write out my contribution check." He laughed.

"I wasn't trying to be funny, officer. I really need to get to church."

"I know, Ms. Mathis. I was just thinking, I haven't been to church in— Well, I really can't remember. But I've been meaning to go."

"Well, officer—today is your blessed day because I know the way, and I'm imploring you to go. And we would be honored to have you as our guest.

"Well, it might be a sign!" he murmured.

"Okay, God is waiting." she uttered. He handed her back her license and insurance and said lead the way. "Matter of fact, give me the address and I will escort you so we can make it there on time."

"Okay," she said, surprised but yet pleased, and then gave him the address, with no hesitation. Back at the church, the boys were wondering why Liah hadn't made it there.

When she drove up and with a police escort, Jacob looked up in despair. "A cop! What has Mom done now?"

"Probably invited the man to church—after he stopped her," Joshua replied.

"Knowing Mom, you're probably right," Jacob said. When they got out, Jayde couldn't wait to tell them what happened. She ran right over to them and started babbling. Liah, Addie, and Jeffrey, along with Officer Dunkins, walked over to where they were standing. The boys looked at her. She put up her hand and said,

"Hush and let's go in. Oh, and this is Officer Richard Dunkins. Officer Dunkins, meet the family. Now let's go in."

Jacob and Joshua looked at each other sniggling until Liah gave them the eye. They all sat down, taking up two rows. Officer Dunkins sat on side of Liah, just as she had requested. Liah took her checkbook out and tore out the check she'd already made out. He saw her take the check out and whispered to her, "I'm not going to write you a ticket."

"Okay, but if you don't write one now, I'm not taking one later. And thanks." He looked at her, smiled and shook his head. He found her to be quite interesting. In ways that Marcus wouldn't take too kindly to. Nevertheless, it was all innocent. "Then it's settled," he said to her.

When the service started, Richard was wondering why there was no music involved in service. She briefly explained to him that the first century church did not use instrumental music, and then quickly showed him New Testament scriptures, pertaining to singing. She advised him to write any questions down he wanted addressed, on the note pad she gave him, and she would have one of the men address them after service. He didn't ask any questions after the sermon began. The minister had his undivided attention. The lesson was entitled "Honoring Christ." When the invitation was extended, he walked up front. He had decided to get baptized. After service, Liah walked up front and gave him a hug. He told her that stopping her was the best thing that had happened to him in a long time.

"Richard, you have made the most important and the best decision that you will ever make in your life. We are your family in Christ now and that includes everyone, who's been added to body of Christ." She took out a business card and handed it to him. "Come by A'Palace, and have lunch sometime, on me. And, by the way, thanks for not writing me a ticket."

"Thanks for inviting me to church. And, Liah, I wasn't going to write you a ticket." He looked at her and smiled and then told her he had to get back to work. "It was indeed a pleasure meeting all of you."

"Same here, man," Jacob said. "You take care."

"Alright, my brothers and sisters," Richard uttered. "I guess I'll be seeing you all on next Sunday. And, Liah, I'm taking you up on that free meal," he told her.

"I bet you are," she responded. "Have a great day, Richard."

"So, Mom, what time are we going over to Marcus'?" Joshua asked.

"About one."

"Good, I have time to beat Jas in a game of pool," Joshua declared.

"Yeah, right," Jas replied, sounding quite sure of himself. "I can beat you and Jacob"

"I don't think so, baby brother," Jacob responded.

"I wouldn't underestimate him now," Jeffrey told them. "He's pretty good."

"Bring it on," Joshua said. "I feel challenged now."

"You're right, Josh," Jayde blurted. "You are truly challenged. And I don't mean pool."

"Whatever, Jayde! I bet you can't play."

"Not a bit," she admitted.

"Probably because you're too unbalanced," Joshua mumbled.

"What, unbalanced?" She didn't have a clue as to what he was talking about.

"Yeah, that's right, unbalanced, due to the forces of your big butt working against you." Liah just shook her head. But the kids laughed hilariously, including Jayde.

"See what I'm saying, Josh," Jayde said. "It takes a challenged person to come up with something like that. But I love you just the way you are."

"I love you, too, little sister."

"Okay children, can we go now?" Liah asked.

Everyone got into something more comfortable when they got home. The males went to the game room and the females went in the kitchen to do some quick baking. Liah immediately became Chef Liah, and assigned each one a job. Of course, no one minded. They were honored to be cooking with her, even when she sometimes took over the job she had assigned them. The kids always enjoyed cooking with their mom, including the boys. The whole time they were cooking, that joyful expression never left Liah's face.

Jacob and Jas came downstairs bragging. Apparently they had teamed up against Jeffrey and Joshua and had beaten them. "That was just luck," Joshua shouted. When we get back we're on for a rematch."

"Alright, bring it on dude," Jacob replied.

"Josh and Jacque, go get your children so we can leave," Liah told them. "Jayde, will you look on my bed and bring me those five gift boxes, please?"

"Sure, Mom."

"Jeffrey, will you look in the wash room and bring me those boxes off the folding table, please?"

"Will do, dear!"

"Mom, we really like Jeffrey," Josh said to her. "He's straight and Ms. Addie, too. You all act like family or best friends."

"They're good people and yes, they are like family," she told him. "Now go get your children. Thanks, Jeffrey, for getting the boxes."

"Mom, do you want us to start loading up?" Jacob asked.

"Yes, Honey! Thanks, Jacque."

When they pulled up in Marcus' driveway, he and Lillie were outside. She was giving him pointers on having his flowerbed redone. Lillie knew that Liah was coming over. But Marcus hadn't told her that she was bringing the kids and certainly not the older ones and their families. "Marcus, I should beat you. You didn't tell me Liah was bringing the kids. And who is driving up behind Liah? I know it's not Jacqlyne." Lillie couldn't wait until they got out. She met them at the car. Jacqlyne, Jessica, and Jas got out and hugged her. She also hugged Liah, Addie, and Jeffrey. By the time Jayde was getting out Liah's car, the others walked up.

"Oh my Lord, Liah, these are my other babies. And I know this one must be Jayde. Look at you. You are beautiful just like your mother. I'm your Nana, baby," she said hugging her. Lillie and Jayde both grinned from ear to ear. "Now these handsome young men must be Josh and Jacque. And if my memory serves me, Jacque is the tallest one."

"That's right, Nana," Jacque said, "and the better looking one, too."

"Whatever, Jacque," Josh. Bellowed, "you know I'm the better looking one."

"All cut it out. You both are good looking young men" Lillie said.

"Lillie, these are my twin grandsons, Josh and Joseph, and this is Josh's wife Miyah. And this is my oldest grandson Jacob Jr. and my precious little Khila, and this is Jacob's wife, Kaitlyn. Everyone, this is Lillie, Marcus' mother and this is Marcus."

Marcus hugged Jayde first and then the others. Lillie was thrilled beyond belief to have all of them there. One would think that Liah was already Marcus' wife. Lillie didn't care. She had fallen in love with the kids, despite what the end results might be. "Now, Kaitlyn, give me this baby," Lillie told her. She took the baby and said "Come on, y'all, let's go inside."

"Mom, do you want us to take everything out?" Joshua asked.

"Yes, please! Thanks." Jacque and Joshua walked behind Liah.

"Mom!"

"Yes, Josh?"

"You didn't tell us that he lived in a mansion?"

"You didn't ask!"

"Mom!"

"Yes, Jacque?"

'This guy is loaded," he whispered.

"I know, Jacque." She looked back at them and smiled, and then told them that they were pitiful.

"Man, I thought we lived in a nice house," Josh uttered. "Man, this is a nice house."

"Yeah, this guy is doing alright," Jacob whispered.

"Would you all cut it out please," Liah said to them.

"Okay, but, Mom, this is the house you stayed in after you got out of the hospital."

"Yeah, I know, Josh. Now hush, please!"

Lillie took the liberty of introducing everyone to Morgan Sr. and Morgan Jr. Morgan Sr. was just as thrilled as Lillie was to have them all there, especially the kids. "You all are just in time," he told them. "The caterers are in the kitchen setting up the feast."

Marcus didn't bother ordering dessert. He knew Liah was bringing some. She never shows up without dessert or a few dishes when she invited to someone's home to eat.

They all gathered in the elegant Tuscan-style dining room, which was hardly ever used except for special occasions. They were served as if they were in a restaurant.

The caterers and servers were whispering amongst themselves.

"Oh, my gosh, that's Liah Mathis.

"Are you sure that's Liah Mathis, the chef from A'Palace?" one of the servers asked.

"Positively sure," the head caterer replied.

"Well, it's one way to find out, the servers muttered. I'm going to ask her." She picked up the bowl of rolls and bravely marched into the dining room. As she sat the bowl on the table, she said, "Excuse me please, but are you Liah Mathis, the chef from A'Palace restaurant?"

"Not today, honey. Today I'm only Liah Mathis. By the way, will you give a compliment to the person who prepared this fantastic feast, please?"

"Yes, I will be pleased to. And thank you for saying that. That is really an awesome compliment."

"You're quite welcome, honey."

"Wow, Mom that was a million-dollar compliment coming from you."

"What? I can give compliments when they are due."

"Yeah, she really can," Addie said in her defense.

"See! There you go. Addie has spoken! Now, who is ready for dessert?"

Everyone at the table yelled, "I am."

"Addie, would you help me please?" Liah and Addie went to the kitchen. The caterer insisted that they allow them to serve the desserts. "Okay, but only if you all enjoy some of this dessert, too."

"Aright, but you twisted our arms" the person in charge responded. They all laughed, and then Liah and Addie went back to the dining room to wait for dessert to be served.

"I thought you all were getting dessert," Morgan Jr. stated.

"And here it comes," Liah said.

"Yes, and I can't wait to get my teeth in that cheesecake," Morgan Sr. roared.

"Me either," Josh yelled. "I haven't had your cheesecake in a while."

"I like cheesecake," Jacob said, "but I'm holding out for the sweet-potato pie."

"You made sweet potato pie?" Lillie asked.

"Yes, ma'am!"

"Girl, I love sweet potato pie."

"You love sweets, period, woman," Morgan Sr. declared.

"All hush, Morgan. Honey, I'll take a piece of both," she told the server.

"See, I told you," Morgan Sr. blurted.

After enjoying Liah's delicious desserts, they went in the living room to pass out gifts. "Who is going first?" Marcus asked.

"Why doesn't Liah go first? I saw five boxes with my name on them," Lillie exclaimed.

"Lillie, were you peeking?" Liah asked.

"No! I just walked by closely," she said sniggling.

"Well, Lillie, since you already know all of these are your boxes, Addie has to open her gift first."

"Now that's just mean," Lillie grumbled.

"Serves you right," Morgan Sr. told her. Lillie sighed.

"Addie, this is for you. And let me just say that I am the blessed one to have you in my life." She handed Addie the beautifully wrapped gift, in rose-designed paper. There were three small boxes inside of one big box. The first box had earrings, the second had a matching necklace, and the third was a cashier check. Addie couldn't mumble a word. She just sat there with tears in her eyes.

"What is it? What's wrong Addie?" Lillie asked.

"I'm okay. I'm just can't believe it, wow—ten-thousand dollars, Liah. I mean...."

She got up and hugged her. And then Marcus said, "Well, since you're already emotional, I might as well give you my gift." He then handed her a flat gold box. She opened the box and there lay a check for twenty thousand-dollars.

"No, no, I can't take this, Marcus ... this is too much."

"Addie, you're taking it or you're fired," Marcus said to her.

She took a deep breath and sighed. Then she mumbled, "Since you put it that way, I guess I'll just give you a hug. You guys are the best. I mean—the best. I love you all—I mean soooo much." Everyone smiled.

"Okay, Lillie, you can open yours," Liah told her. She was acting like a happy teenager. Liah gave her a pile of boxes. The first one she opened was a picture frame.

"Look at this," she cried. "It's a beautiful framed picture of the whole family. Thank you, Liah. You all are gorgeous."

"Wait," Liah exclaimed, "don't put that box aside yet. Lift up all of that paper." She didn't have to tell her twice.

"Oh, Liah, is this what I think it is?"

"Yes, it is." Lillie pulled the suit out of the box and put it up against her.

"Ooh, this is gor...geous." She opened the rest of the boxes and was thrilled beyond belief. "Liah, tell your aunts.... No, just give me the phone number and I will call them and thank them myself. I got every outfit I wanted." She thanked Liah profusely.

"Nana, we have gifts for you too," Jacqlyne said. All the kids gave her a box each. The kids bought her jewelry to match every outfit. Addie knew how much she liked hats, so she gave her hats to match all of her outfits. By the time Lillie had finished opening all of her gifts, she was overjoyed with tears.

"Awe, woman, cut it out," Morgan Sr. told her. "Well...Liah, dear, that's leaves you." Jeffrey and Addie gave Liah their gift first. It was a canvas of her children. Jeffrey sketched it and Addie painted it.

"Will you look at this," Liah said. "This is breathtaking. You guys did this?"

"Certainly, dear, we thought it would be nice," Jeffrey responded.

"Oh, Jeffrey, this is better than nice. I've always wanted a canvas of the kids. Addie and Jeffrey, thank you all very, very much. This is beautiful."

"May we see it Mom?" Joshua asked.

"Sure, Honey!" While the painting was being passed around, Marcus handed Liah a jewelry box and an envelope. The jewelry box had a beautiful white gold ring with the birthstone of each of her children.

"Marcus, this ring is gorgeous and it has all of the kids' birthstones. I love it, and it fits perfectly. Thank you, honey!" She got up and hugged him.

"Open the envelope, Mom," Jas said.

"Okay, baby!" She opened the envelope and it had a spa day gift certificate with unlimited guests. "A spa day! Now that's what I'm talking about. My girlfriends are coming into town next week and we will be there next Saturday. Thank you, honey. Addie and Lillie, are you all up to a spa day?"

"Honey, count me in twice," Lillie said.

"You are too funny Lillie. Girl, I am there!" Addie stated.

"Look out, spa, here we come!" Liah whispered.

"Alright let's move it on," Morgan said.

"Here's a gift from us, Liah," Lillie said. They'd bought her a matching necklace and bracelet set. She was blown away. Morgan gave her a matching pair of earrings. Liah was in tears.

"Hold your tears, Mom," Jayde said. "You have one more gift to open."

"Let's give our mothers their gifts at the same time," Morgan suggested.

"Good idea," Joshua replied. Joshua and Morgan gave them the envelopes at the same time.

"Alright, Liah, let's open on the count of three," Lillie told her. Both of them counted to three at the same time. Morgan and Marcus gave Lillie a two-week cruise for four, and Liah's kids gave her two-weeks-vacation to London, England. They were both flabbergasted to the point of screaming, and they did.

"I've always wanted to go on a cruise," Lillie said excitedly.

"And I've wanted to go to London. I just haven't had the time to go."

"Well, Mom, now you have to go," Jayde insisted.

"And I plan to, baby. Children, I can't thank you all enough. This has been the best Mother's Day ever. I have so much to be thankful for. Not for the gifts but for my children and grandchildren and for each of you." Liah was emotional again.

"I feel the same way, Liah," Lillie responded. "And I thank God for all of you. I am richly blessed to have all of you to be a part of my life, and I love all of you."

"Well, I think this calls for dessert, ladies," Miyah suggested.

"Miyah, lead the way," Addie said. "Come on, ladies. Let's calm our nerves."

"Right behind you, Addie," Lillie said.

"I don't think I've ever seen mom like that before," Joshua stated.

"Yeah, Mom seems to be a bit more emotional than usual," Jacob responded.

"Marcus, did you have anything to do with that?"

"I don't know, but if that's good, I'll take credit for it."

"Oh, now, Mom really lost her composure," Morgan blurted. "She is usually the queen of composure."

366

"Ah ... it's the kids," Morgan Sr. roared. "She has been weakened. Did you see how she was carrying on—running in place like she was exercising," he said, chuckling. The others started laughing too. "I don't know if I want to give her my gift."

"What did you get her, Dad?" Marcus asked.

"I got her that black sports Mercedes that she wanted."

"Nooo, no, Dad, don't give it to her," Morgan said to him seriously. "She might start flipping out."

"Well, I got to give her something son, or I won't sleep tonight. I have the keys stuck in a box so they won't make a sound. I'll give it to her and tell her she can't open it until later."

"Yeah...right! Good luck with that," Marcus told him.

"Here they come," Jason exclaimed.

"Are you all better?" Marcus asked.

"Yes, Honey, we're fine," Liah responded. "It was just a misplacement of equanimity?"

"Equanimity—right!" Marcus replied, replicating her exact word.

"Kaitlyn and Miyah, I didn't forget about you all," Liah told them. "I was carried away with all of the excitement." She handed each of them an envelope. Kaitlyn opened hers box first but didn't look inside the envelope. She knew her mother-in-law always gave awesome gifts. Her face was glowing with excitement.

"Come on, Miyah, I want us to look at the same time."

"Okay, Kaitlyn, but I don't want to risk tearing what's inside."

"Okay, on the count of three," Kaitlyn cried. Both of them screamed, "A shopping spree." They jumped up and down like kids who'd just won trips to Disney World.

"Ooh, Mom, thank you," Miyah cried. "Kaitlyn and I were just talking about a shopping spree."

"We sure were," Kaitlyn exclaimed. "You are the best—Mom. Thanks so much."

Well, Dad, it's your turn to give Mom her Mother's Days gift," said Morgan, with a sly grin on his face.

"You didn't give me a gift, did you Morgan?" Lillie mentioned.

"Honey, I was saving the best for last." Morgan always had a way of getting himself out of tight spots with Lillie.

"Not that I believe you're telling me the truth Morgan, but okay," she said to him. He then gave her a small box.

"It sure is a small box," Morgan Jr. said, still trying to instigate.

"Baby, if I know your dad...things may seem small, but he does things big." Lillie practically tore into the first box and then through an even smaller box and finally through some wrapping tissue. "Oh, my God, this is a key. But not just any key—a key to a Mercedes. I'd know this type of key anywhere. Oh, Morgan, darling. I love you and, I thank you—yes, I do!"

"Wait, dear. You can't pick the car up until tomorrow. I'm having them personalize it for you."

"That's alright, darling. I bet it's a Sports Mercedes."

"You're right. A black one."

"Yes!" she exclaimed. She was on cloud nine. All of the males started laughing.

"I know y'all are laughing at me," Lillie cried. "But I don't care because this has been a fantastic day. And I am richly blessed."

"Lillie, you just make sure you come by and pick up Addie and me when you take it for a road test," Liah told her.

"Liah, you know I am. And I might be wearing one of those outfits your aunts made."

"Alright, people, it's about time to go back to church," roared Morgan Sr.

"Jayde, would you go in the playroom to get the little ones?" Liah asked.

"Mom, you really want me to get lost, don't you?"

"Right, you haven't been here before."

Jess, would you help her out, please?"

"Josh and Jacque, while they're rounding up the kids, y'all mind if we step outside and talk for a few minutes?" Marcus asked.

"Not at all," Jacque answered, speaking for both of them.

Marcus told them about the plans for Liah's birthday party. He also offered to fly them back out for the party, which was the upcoming weekend. "Are you serious?" Joshua asked.

"I am. As a matter of fact, if you all ever decide to move back, just let me know. And let me just say, I am not trying to take the place of your dad. I love your mom and I am here for all of you."

"You don't have to worry about it," Jacque murmured, "because he doesn't have a place."

"He's right. And we're okay. But as long as our sisters and little brother don't get caught up in any crossfire, we're cool," Josh told him.

"Besides, it would be comforting to know that they have a trusted male around."

"Yeah, man...and if our mom is happy. You're alright with us."

Marcus was pleased to hear their take on things.

"I really appreciate and respect you all's input. I'm glad you are looking out for their best interest."

"Yeah, well, my mom is a pretty good judge of character. Our dad was just an exception," Jacob stated. "Since then, our mom is very particular. She would never bring someone into our lives if she had any doubts, especially not around our sisters."

"I appreciate you all for taking the time to talk to me. I wish we had more time."

"We'll have this weekend," Joshua replied.

"Definitely!" Marcus responded. "I'll call you all on Monday with the flight reservation. And I will have the limo pick you all up at the airport. I know Jayde is flying back with Lecxa Friday evening, so she's covered"

"I have one question," Jacob said. "How are you going to get Mom out of the house?"

"That's why I gave her the spa day."

"Smarting thinking," Jacob said. "Conversation over, here they come."

"Everything okay out here?" Liah asked.

"Everything is good, Mom," Joshua replied.

"Okay, we are ready to go."

~Chapter Twenty-Two~

After her children left bright and early Monday morning, Liah was in a bit of an emotional state. She was never good at saying goodbye. As a matter of fact, she detested the word. She knew Jayde would be back by the end of the week, but she had no idea when she would be seeing the boys again. She decided to go into work early. Cooking was always a proven distraction for her.

"Addie, I'm going to work. Would you and Jeffrey get started on packing, please? If you need to call in some help, feel free. I'm going to be bringing dinner home every night this week, so we don't have to cook. And could you please have the cleaning crew come tomorrow? I'm having the carpet done on Thursday. And one more thing, Addie, please visit your mother today. This stuff can wait until you get back. Give her my love. Addie, I don't know how I got along without you all these years. I really appreciate you."

"Come here you," she said to Liah. Addie put her arms around her. She knew Liah was a bit emotional since the kids left. "Liah, they will be back before you know it."

She inhaled deeply and said, "I know. And I'll be okay. I just need to work it off. Have a good day Addie and thanks again. Oh, and if you're still here when Jeffrey comes in, would you make sure he gets that envelope on the bar."

Jeffrey walked in and said, "I'll make sure I get it, dear." Liah and Addie both were startled by Jeffrey's sudden presence. Both of them spun around and at the same time and yelled, "Jeffrey."

"Jeffrey," Liah cried out. "I declare, you are the only person I know who enters a room and doesn't make a sound."

"Yes, he is," Addie attested.

"Anyway, Jeffrey. Good morning and how are you today?"

"I am well, dear. Thank you for asking. How are you ladies this morning? Well, I know how Liah is, the children left today." Liah looked at him and smiled.

"I'm good, Jeffrey," Addie said. Liah gave Jeffrey the envelope before leaving. "Everything you need is inside, Jeffrey. Thanks a bunch. Now I have to go to work. You two have a great day."

"You too, dear."

☙❧

Wednesday, Liah didn't go in to work. She wanted to get settled in before the kids got home from school. Jen volunteered to help. Marcus and Morgan and some of the guys from the office helped them get settled in. Liah brought a lot of the kids' stuff. She wanted their rooms to look somewhat like they did at home. She even brought some of Jayde's things and fixed her up a room.

This time, Liah took a room upstairs. After settling into her new room, she went downstairs to her old room. She stood by the bed and had a retrospective moment. She thought about the zipper and earring incident. She laughed out loud. Marcus heard her laugh. He crept up behind her and slipped his arms around her. She already knew it was him. She had seen him out of her peripheral vision. "Are you thinking about the zipper and earring incident when you forced me to drop my pants to my feet?"

"Whatever, Marcus." She pulled out of his arms and turned around and gave him a disdainful look.

"So you could detach your earring from my zipper," he thought he should add. Before the reminiscing could progress, Addie yelled for Liah. I'm going to see why Addie is yelling. She smiled and walked out.

"Liah, have you seen these suites?" Addie asked.

"Not yet."

"They look just like a one-bedroom apartment. Liah, you gotta see this."

"If I like it, can I stay?"

"Girl, no, but feel free to spend the night anytime."

"Well, come on, let me see it. Marcus, would you mind unpacking that box of books and put them on the shelf in the study, please?"

"Sure, Honey!"

Liah and Addie took the elevator, which led right to Addie's door. Addie couldn't wait to open the door.

"Wow, I like it," Liah murmured. "It is gorgeous, and has a touch of eloquence. I see what you mean. And it's very spacious too. Check out this cozy little study. Wow! It has a skylight. Very nice!"

"Check out my kitchen. I'll probably just use it for warming stuff. It's too cute to cook in."

"Addie, this kitchen is beautiful. Red and olive—I like the colors. Okay, that's it. This is definitely going to be my hang out place. I'll bring the dessert."

"I'll make the sandwiches," Addie said. "We have to go shopping sometime in the next few days."

"Yes, we do. Let's make out a list tonight. But now we had better get back downstairs and supervise those men."

"Yeah, we better!" Addie confirmed.

They went back downstairs. As soon as they got off the elevator, Morgan yelled out, "You all were trying to make us do all of the work, weren't you?"

"We were not, Morgan Michaels," Liah responded. "We would not do that to you, sweetie."

"Or would we," Addie inserted.

"Hey, babe," Marcus said to Liah, "I ordered barbeque. Is that cool?"

"That's cool with me."

"Me, too," Addie said. They worked until the food came.

"Food's here," Jeffrey yelled.

"Alright, let's eat." Eating was one of Morgan's favorite things to do., .and everyone was aware of it. After they enjoyed the mini feast, they went right back to work. "Man, that barbeque was good," Morgan exclaimed.

"It was really good," Jeffrey agreed. Liah ordered them to get back to work and stop talking about food. T

"Jen, are you she still going to the spa this weekend.

"Honey, yes, I have made my plans."

374

"That's right, I'm glad you brought that up," Marcus said. "I forgot to tell you I was having the house sprayed on Friday, so we would need to be out at least ten to twelve hours. And on Saturday, I'm having the house and the carpet cleaned. I do apologize for the inconveniences. But I made reservations for all of you at the hotel, the same one you're having your spa day. I blocked off four suites. And if it's okay with you, Jas can hang out with Jeffrey and me at Morgan's."

"I'm sure he would have no problem with that," Liah said. "Well, it looks like you've thought of everything. Thank you, honey."

"You're welcome, baby. What you do think about me taking Jas horseback riding on Saturday?"

"Now I know he would like that." Marcus also offered to take Jen's little boy with them.

"What time do we check in?" Addie inquired.

"Anytime after ten o'clock." Marcus replied.

"Then I'll leave our bags downstairs," Liah told Marcus. "And when you dropped off Addie, you can bring them. Marcus, can you have the limo pick Chan and her daughter, Lisha and Shayna up from the airport, at two-thirty? Actually, that's about the time Jayne and Lecxa's flight arrives, too."

"I thought Chan was bringing the boys," Marcus said.

"They're coming on Monday."

"Okay, I'll have him pick everyone up at the airport."

"Good. I'm going to pick Jas up from school so I can spend time with him, since I'm going to be spending the night away from him. Jen, do you want me to pick up Timmy? He can go hangout with Jas and me."

"Yeah, that would work. I'll pick the girls up and meet you at the hotel."

Okay, Marcus is picking Jas up when he dropped off Addie, so he can take Timmy home." Marcus, Morgan, and the crew had to get back to work and the others finished unpacking.

Chapter Twenty-Three

Friday was the big day and all of the ladies were excited. Marcus had set the perfect plan in action in order to assure that the day he was excited about, would go well.

Liah went in to work early, since she had planned on getting off early. Mel and Tina were invited to the spa day, and they were both excited. They were also invited to stay at the hotel.

"Oh Liah, my dear, I'm not sure if I can join you all for the spa day and that night, in that luxury hotel, but I will certainly try," Mel said.

"I will put every effort in getting there, Liah," Tina said, and then burst out laughing, and so did Mel and Liah.

"You all are crazy," Liah laughed again and shook her head.

"What is the agenda for Saturday, Tina inquired?"

Saturday morning we're going shopping and we'll have lunch in between stops. And then we'll going back to the hotel for a full body makeover, including getting our hair done."

"Oooooh, child, I can't wait to be made over," Tina said enthusiastically. "My husband won't even know who I am when I get home."

"Girl, you're crazy," Mel told her, "Your husband will know you."

"No, he won't. I'm getting all of this hair cut off."

"He might not even want you after that," Mel responded.

"Mel, be quiet," Tina told her.

"You both are crazy," Liah said.

"Whatever, people! Tina murmured. "Anyway, Liah, what did you and Marcus, do for your birthday?"

"We had a picnic in the park under the moonlight."

"No expensive and extravagant gift?" Mel asked.

"No. He was forbidden to buy anything."

"By whom?" Tina questioned.

"Me! He did write me a poem and read it to me."

"Oooooh, romantic," Mel whispered, sounding like a schoolgirl.

"Ladies," Louis called out. "It's time to work."

"Sorry, Louis, we're coming," Liah yelled.

"So y'all have a girls' day out planned, huh," Louis stated.

"No, Louis, we have the whole weekend," Mel injected. "Too bad you're not a female. You could hang out with us."

"Honey, it is good that I'm not. If I was I couldn't do this."

"Mmmm—look at him ... flexing those muscles," Mel murmured. "Look pretty good, too, for a straight-up metro-sexual."

"I may be a straight-up metro-sexual, but I'm one hundred percent straight-up man. *So don't be hatin* ... because I got taste."

"I guess he told you," Tina said.

"Mel, will you go check the crowd?" Liah asked.

"Okay. Be right back!"

"Louis, I got a feeling we're going to be busy," Liah said to him.

"Liah," Mel yelled. "It's rollercoaster time. A full house!"

"Well—there you go," Liah said. "It's rollercoaster time." Rollercoaster was a system Liah used for nonstop working, especially, when they had groups.

"So, Mel, how large is the group?" Liah asked.

"At least forty. I'm going to see what they're ordering."

"I take it you weren't expecting a group that large?" Louis asked.

"Not at all!"

"Liah," Mel called out. "They want the Chef's Buffet Special."

"The Chef's Special. How did they know about that?"

"I'm thinking Jacqlyne told them. She is out there, too."

"I sure wish she would have come another day."

"Maybe she just wanted to show off her mother," Tina told her.

"She could have done that at the next play."

"Next play!" Tina exclaimed.

"Girl, yes, Jacqlyne and Jess wrote another play, so they decided to use it instead of the original one."

"Seems to me stars are in the making."

"It is pretty good. Well, I'm going to go introduce myself and then call Jeffrey to ask him if he could pick up the boys and drop them off. I'll be right back. Where's Joedi?"

"Here I am!" he said as he was walking in the kitchen.

"Good, you're here. Why don't you all get started?"

They worked nonstop until every customer was served. Jacqlyne's group stayed about an hour and a half. Liah moved them to one of the smaller party rooms. And it worked out well. Finally at about two-thirty, the restaurant was quiet. A few people were still there having coffee and dessert. The kitchen and the wait staff were beat. They all had worked through lunch. Liah suggested they all eat the leftovers. When they were done eating, they put the kitchen back in order. Shortly after Jeffrey dropped the boys off, Liah and the boys left.

~Chapter Twenty-Four~

Ladies Night Begins

Liah arrived at the hotel minutes before Marcus. They had agreed to meet down in the lobby so he could pick up the boys. By the time she made it upstairs, most of the ladies had arrived and had introduced themselves. Chantel, Alisha, and Shayna had arrived as well. The four of them were elated to see each other again. The last time they had seen each other was when Liah was ill. They were glad this time it was for a more joyous occasion. Liah looked across the room and sighed. She felt very blessed to have all of her daughters and friends there.

The girls were anxious to get their room assignment, so they could leave the adults to themselves, and get on with their night. They were pretty excited to have a suite of their own. "Now, girls," Liah said to them, "You had better keep the noise under wrap and please, don't go ordering unnecessary food. Got it?"

"Got it!" they all said in sync.

The doorbell rang. "I'll get it," Liah said. It was Tina and Mel. "You all made it. Come on in here. Everyone, introduce yourselves, please." After everyone was done introducing herself, Liah went back to the room assignments.

"Okay, as I was saying, I have three more suites." The phone rang. "Would someone get that please?" Lisha answered the phone.

"Liah, you have two more guests coming up."

"I didn't invite anyone else."

"Didn't you invite Mom and Liz?" Lecxa asked.

"Oh, yeah, they aren't here yet." There was a knock at the door.

"I'll get it," Chantel said as she was standing up. When she opened the door, the bellman came in with two bags. Everyone was looking toward the door waiting for someone to come in. Suddenly, they heard loud voices say, "Surprise."

"Tori, and Paige, Liah yelled excitedly! What are you doing here?"

"Hi, Auntie Liah."

"Hi, sweetheart! My—you have grown. Wow, you have boobs. She has boobs," she whispered again, to Tori this time. "Tori, I can't believe you're here." She reached out to hug her. "I have missed you guys so much."

"We've missed you too, big sister. And you still look good."

"What? You expect to me to look bad," she said disdainfully.

"No, but you are getting old."

"Girl, don't make me send you back home." Everyone laughed out loud.

"I'm kidding, girl. I hope I look as good as you when I get old. I mean your age."

"Everyone, as you already know, this is my little sister, Tori. Tori, meet everyone. You all can introduce yourselves. Now, Tori, how did you know we were here?"

"Someone named Marcus called me. But Mom told me that you told her about him."

"I did, but I never gave him your phone number."

"Jacqlyne gave it to him."

"Okay, that makes sense. Marcus never stops with his surprises. Well, I'm just glad you all are here—all of you. Paige, the girls are next door. Get your bag, I'll take you over."

"I'll take her, Liah," Tori volunteered, "I want to see my nieces. And where's Jas?"

"He's with Marcus."

"Oh! Well, I'll see him tomorrow."

Liah went to take a shower while the others chatted and got better acquainted. When Liah came out, they were all laughing and having a merry time. "Liah, remember to call Marcus," Lecxa told her. "He said to call him before eleven o'clock. He needs to tell you something."

"Okay, thanks, Lecxa. Are you all ready to order some food?"

"I have the list right here," Alisha yelled. "Anything you'd like to add?"

"No, I'm good with whatever! I'm going to call Marcus, and then I'll be right back." Alisha took the liberty of ordering the food. While waiting for Liah to come back, they decided to toss the pillows on the floor so they could get comfortable. When she came back in she saw bodies stretched across the floor. "What are y'all doing?"

"We are waiting for you, honey," Chantel responded.

"Yeah, Liah," Lecxa said. "We're going to eat and tell old stories."

"Liah, I know you got something juicy to tell," Mel uttered.

"Who is going first?" Shayna asked.

"Let's do alphabetical order! Seems that Addie is first in line," Tina blurted.

"Okay, but I hope you all are old enough for this story," Addie said.

"Come on—let us have it, Addie, we can take it," Tori responded.

Everyone got as quiet as a mouse when she started talking. Addie had a way with telling stories. It was like listening to a suspense story. She usually started off really low with a serious look and then took a deep breath while shaking her head and proceeded into the highlight of the story. After she was done, the next person in line shared their story. They took a brief break when the food got there. Then each of them grabbed some food and went back to the floor. After everyone was done telling the stories, they all voted on best story. Addie's story won one point over Liah's. Addie shared a story about her and some friends traveling back home after a weekend trip. Their rental vehicle nearly exploded under the hood and they were stranded on side of the road in the dark. And the worst thing was neither of their cell phones would get any service. Addie said she took out of her stilettos and gave one of her friend's a shoe so the both of them could stand guard while the other friend peed onside of the car. Now after several cars had passed by, one car actually slowed down as if it were going to stop, forcing her to abruptly stop peeing and attempt to pull up her clothes. Apparently the car didn't stop, which was in one way was a relief and another way it wasn't because they were left stranded. After being stranded in the dark for at least an hour, some bikers came by and the three of them hitched a ride to a spider-infested hotel and spent the night. According to Addie it was a really creepy night. However, it turned out to be one of the best nights for one of her friends. She met her husband of fifteen years and still today, she said, they still act as if they were newlyweds.

After the wild and humorous stories from many females, they decided to play old songs and have a karaoke contest. They cleared the floor of the pillows and covers and divided into teams and then chose group songs to sing. The singing was hilarious. Each team took turns performing. Of course when "Let's Stay Together" by Al Green, came on, they all got on the floor singing. It seemed that this song took the remaining energy out of all of them. For the rest of the night, they watched movies and played games—the kind that required sitting.

"Liah, did you call Marcus?" Lecxa enquired.

"I called him earlier, remember."

"Oh, yeah, right."

"And I'm glad that you mentioned that because Marcus invited all of us to a party tomorrow at seven o'clock. Can all of you make it?" Everyone said yes, of course. Besides they already knew about it. Liah was the only one in the dark. They all had done an excellent job at keeping it from her.

Saturday morning, Lillie came just as breakfast was being brought up. When she came in they were all over the place. "My goodness, it looks like y'all had a sailor's party. Good morning, ladies. It's time for breakfast."

"Mom, what are you doing here?" Lecxa asked.

"I'm here to get you ladies going."

"I'll go get everyone else up," Liah said.

"No, you eat. I'll get everyone else up. If you all were asleep, who ordered breakfast?" Lillie asked.

"I put in the order last night and told them what time to bring it up," Liah answered.

"Good thinking," Lillie said. "Now you all eat and get yourselves going. We have a full day ahead of us."

"Yes, we do and the car will be here in about an hour and a half," Liah said.

"The car!" Mel exclaimed. "What car?"

"The stretched HUMMER," Liah replied.

"Whoa—I'm riding in a stretched HUMMER," Mel whispered. "I'm going to get dressed."

"Girl, you have to eat first," Tina told her.

"Well, you don't have to tell me twice," Mel said.

They all enjoyed their hearty breakfast before getting dressed and made it downstairs as the limo was pulling up.

The limo ride was full of fun and laughter. They brought along the soundtrack from the Chipmunks movies. The limo driver thought it was quite hilarious when they all tried to sing just like the Chipmunks. He saw how much fun they were having, so he joined in. They thought his singing was even more hilarious than theirs, so they started egging him on. He had no shame. After the song went off, Lillie popped in Al Green's "Let's Stay Together."

"This is the song that sat us down last night," Tori uttered. "But that's alright, Ms. Lillie. Hit it!" No one said a word. "Didn't I say hit it?" Suddenly, there was lots of laughter after the second "hit it", as Tori, demanded. The song went off as they were driving up in the mall parking lot.

"It's shopping time," Lecxa screamed.

"I have an idea," Liah said. "Why don't we do at least one good deed to help or assist someone in this mall before we start shopping," she suggested. Everyone was in. "Alright, we meet back here in about forty-five minutes," Liah said. They divided up into groups and then went off in search of doing a good deed.

Jayde was the first to find one." She went to the food court and saw an elderly lady counting change to pay for her order. She bravely walked

386

up to the lady and said, "Excuse me ma'am, please allow me to pay for your order."

"Baby, that's mighty kind of you, but I can't take your money," the elderly lady replied. Jayde assured her it was no problem and insisted that she allow her to pay for it. The lady had tears of gratitude in her eyes. She took out a twenty-dollar bill and gave it to her and told her to keep the change.

"Bless you child." The elderly lady asked Jayde for her address and told her she would mail it to her when her social security check came. Jayde told her there was no need to and she was just glad she could be of some help.

Liah's group went to the children's department in Dillard's. As Jacqlyne was looking around, she overheard a lady and her children's discussion. She had two boys, probably thirteen and fourteen and a little girl, perhaps eight or nine. They were nagging her about all the things they needed. The mom sadly told them that she was fully aware of their needs, but she just couldn't afford it right now. The mom told them as honestly and as calmly as she could that things had been tough since she lost her job. She also told them that she was behind on the mortgage and, most importantly, she needed to put food on the table. She went on to tell them that she had to buy them what she could. Jacqlyne, rushed over to tell Liah. Liah, being a single parent and having gone through some struggles after her divorce, empathized with her immediately. She had strived to triumph over dilemmas. Liah called Lillie and told her. The two of them contacted the others and they all formed a plan and quickly put it in action. Lecxa and Tori were in charge of gathering money to buy a store gift card while Mel and Tina talked to the store manager. Liah and Lillie went downstairs to the bank on the first floor and got a Visa gift card for four thousand dollars and a cashier check for ten thousand dollars.

They had the manager of the store present it to the woman. They didn't want her to know where it came from. The manager told her that a customer overheard her and her children talking, but they only wanted to be known as Good Samaritans. When he presented the woman with the gift card and the check, she was bowled over. She could not believe the generosity of the people who helped her. Overwhelmed with shock, she went weak in the knees. One of the cashiers rushed to get her a chair. Liah, the others, and a few more customers were standing nearby. "I was about to lose my home because I couldn't afford to pay my mortgage. I lost my job of twenty years, due to a massive cut back," the lady disclosed in between sobs. Liah was overtaken by her emotional state. She went up to her to console her. She told her not to worry, but to put everything in God's hands, and then gave her one of her business cards, telling her to call her early next week. She would like to discuss a job opportunity with her. She also invited her to church.

"You're very kind," the lady said to her. "Thank you for inviting us." Liah wrote the address of the church on the back of the card. Everyone who had witnessed the incident was deeply touched.

Lillie insisted they all go in the lobby and take a breather. It seemed that all of them were emotionally affected. "The plan didn't go as we had planned," Lillie said, "it went better. And I give all that glory to God."

"You're right, Lillie, Liah avowed. God places us where he needs us to be. So we should feel even more blessed than the lady we helped. Now, is anyone still in the mood for shopping?" Everyone looked at her as if she'd called the entire day off. "Okay, evil looking people, I got it. Let's go shopping."

They all divided up again and were off to search for bargains and the perfect outfit for tonight's occasion.

They were back at the hotel in enough time to drop off their bags and make it to their spa treatment.

"Good, we made it right on time," Lillie said. "And I want the works— face, nails, feet, body massage, and hair."

"I think we all want that," Lecxa agreed. The spa staff gave them a royal treatment. They were pressed for time and had to get dressed right after their spa treatment. When they stepped into the lobby, they looked as if they were dressed for the runway. They took lots of pictures before loading in the limousine.

Upon arriving at Marcus' house, Liah was surprised to see so many vehicles there. "Wow, there sure are a lot of vehicles here. I assumed since it was job-related it was going to be a small party."

"Honey, Marcus doesn't know how to do small parties," Lillie told her. "Come on let's just go in and blend." When they walked in the house it was completely quiet. Liah instantly thought something was peculiar.

"I guess the party must be outback," Lillie whispered. "Come on, we should walk through the house," she suggested." Lillie walked out first. She tried to give Marcus a signal that Liah was behind her. Just as soon as Liah stepped out on the patio, everyone screamed, "surprise." Then they started singing Happy Birthday. Liah was speechless and totally in shock. Marcus came forward, showing his dimples as always, and looked pleased that he had actually pulled this off.

"I got you, didn't I?" Liah just sighed and then put her arms around him and thanked him.

"My, you are quite sly, Mr. Michaels. I can't believe you pulled this off without me knowing."

"It wasn't easy, believe me. But I have more surprises."

"Marcus, what more could there be?"

"Come on out, guys," he yelled. Within seconds she heard voices singing.

"Wait a minute. I'd know those voices anywhere." The boys came through the crowd singing the happy birthday song that Joshua had composed, especially for this occasion. Her grandsons broke through running and screaming, "Happy birthday, Nana." After hugging and kissing the boys and grandchildren, Kaitlyn, and Miyah, she looked at Marcus with tears in her eyes and gently pressed her face against his, then whispered to him, "I love you."

"Mom, were you surprise?" Jas asked.

"I sure was, sweetie. And I missed you last night, big boy."

"I missed you, too, Mom." She leaned down and kissed him. "Okay, I had better go mingle with the guests." She got the baby from Kaitlyn. "Well happy birthday, Ms. Liah," Liz smiled, pleasingly.

"Liz, I might have known, this setup has you written all over it."

"Honey, I am glad Marcus called me. Besides, don't anyone know your party style better than yours truly." Liah smiled and agreed. "Anyway, girl, I do wish I could have made it to the ladies night out."

"So do I. Girl, we had a marvelous time."

"Well when you get some time, I want to hear all about it."

"I will. Talk to you a little later." Liah walked out in the crowd to mingle with her guests. Just as soon as she started talking, Marcus yelled,

"Excuse me, everyone. May I have your attention please?"

The servers started serving the special made non-alcoholic beverages. Marcus asked Liah to come up to the platform to join him. He took her by the hand and looked into her eyes. He then said to her, "Liah, before

I met you I was going about my life as if I had no hope of finding real love, ever. From the very first day I met you, it was as if the love in your heart was so full that it spilled over in mine. From that moment, I couldn't get you out of my mind. Honestly, I was afraid to love again. You reminded me that God said, 'There is no fear in love because love is from Him. And the one who fears is not made perfect in love.' Now I understand how to love with the love of God. And I know that kind of love is real. The truth is that, I've been in error by waiting for someone to teach me how to love. God's word teaches all how to love. When I gave you the promise ring, we vowed to give this relationship a chance to grow. And I loved you then. But I don't love you like that anymore. He paused for a brief moment. I love you with the love of the Lord. And that love is inseparable. And if you love me that way, our love will be inseparable. You are the most amazing woman I've ever met."

He picked up the microphone and started singing to her. A well-chosen song, I must say. "Amazing" by Elliot Yamin. It was as if he had written the song himself, for this very moment. Liah was in tears and so was Marcus. When he finished singing, he said to her. "Liah, as I stand here before God, our familes, and friends, with your permission, I'd like to remove this promise ring from your finger and place a ring symbolizing our everlasting love."

She whispered to him, "Hold that thought for a moment. Kids, what do you all think?" Her children came up on the platform.

"Marcus, do you mind if we remove the promise ring?" Joshua asked.

"No, not at all. By all means, please do so." Joshua held her hand and Jacob removed the ring. He gave the ring to Jason and Jason gave it to Marcus. Then Jacob placed her hand back in Marcus' hand. Marcus kneeled down on one knee and said to her passionately, "Liah Anginette

Cunningham Mathis. God said, 'A man who findest a wife, findest a good thing.' You are my good thing. Will you be my wife?"

She sighed momentarily. "Mom," Jas cried, "say yes, so he can be my dad." The guests started laughing. Jeffrey cleared his throat to quiet the laughing.

"Yes, yes, yes, Marcus Adrian Michaels," Liah answered with a whimper. "I will marry you. But only if you always remember that I am your good thing." He said' I promise to always remember and then slipped the one-carat rock on her finger. Liah was dazzled by its beauty. "Marcus this is the most beautiful ring I've ever seen. Almost too beautiful to wear, and I did say, almost. Marcus kissed her hand.

Morgan Sr. proudly said, "Everyone raise your glass to my son and his bride to be." From then on there were congratulations, eating, and mingling.

Finally, Marcus and Liah had a private moment to themselves, before she left to go back to the hotel. The boys and their families stayed at Marcus' house.

After returning to the hotel, the wedding plans discussion began. Chantel grabbed a pen and pad. "Okay, let's do the maid of honor first." They worked on wedding plans for at least an hour or better. They planned to meet at the bridal shop on Tuesday to look at dresses.

"Okay, I'm beat," Liah said. "I'm going to bed."

"It's probably that's rock weighing you down," Mel laughed. They all giggled.

"Stop it, children, it's time to go to sleep," Liah told them.

"Alright, grumpy," Chantel mumbled. "But wasn't that a beautiful proposal?"

"Girl, yes, it was," Alisha responded. "I've never seen anything like it. But he really got me when he started singing. I wanted to say yes, myself. I've never had a man to sing to me before."

"Honey, I was entirely blown away," Shayna blurted.

"Yeah, me too," Tori uttered. "You're amazing, so amazing," Tori sang.

Lecxa thought she would pick up where Tori left off and sang a line. "Amazing to me, one word!"

"You all are crazy. Can we please go to sleep now?" Liah asked. "Y'all are going to thank me for sending you to bed when you get up at six-thirty in the morning." Everyone went back to their room and went right to bed.

~Chapter Twenty-Five~

Thursday morning, Alisha, Chantel, Liah and Shayna, got together for a departing breakfast. It was the last time they would see each other until the final fitting. Marcus planned on joining them before they were done with breakfast. "Liah, I am so overjoyed that you and Marcus found each other," Alisha told her.

"I am, too, Lisha.

"Liah," Chantel pointed, "here come your soon-to-be hubby."

"Hi, honey," Liah said. I'm so glad you could make it."

"How's everyone doing?" Marcus gave Liah a quick kiss on the cheek.

"We're having a wedding discussion, Chantel responded."

"Is it safe to ask if you've found a dress?"

"I sure have, and I found your tux, too"

"Seriously? What color?"

"Yes, and it is chocolate."

"Chocolate! I like that color. Where did you find it?"

"In a magazine! We have to fly everyone back for the fitting. The designer has to fly in as well."

"Marcus, would you believe that she went through about twenty dresses between three bridal shops?" Chantel said. "And that's when she picked up the magazine and saw the dress she wanted. It's one of her aunts' newest designs."

"And I am the only one who will have one like it. I made sure of it. Of course, they don't know I'm wearing it."

"I still don't believe you tried on twenty dresses," Chantel said again.

"Yep, Chantel, I do. She's just like my mom. Can I see?"

"Sure, sweetie—at the altar."

"Don't tell me you're superstitious!"

"I'm not. But you're still not seeing my dress."

"Okay. Well let's get on with the wedding planning." They worked on wedding plans until the limo showed up to take the boys and their families, Tori, Paige, Alisha, and Shayna to the airport.

After everyone left, including Marcus, Liah and Chantel went back in the house. Liah had to get ready for work and Chantel had to go meet the movers at Liah's house.

Liah decided she would pick out her outfit for her date with Marcus before she left for work. *Hum*, she said out loud, *I haven't worn this in a while*. It was the outfit she had worn on her first date with Marcus.

Addie knocked at the door. "Liah, it's me," she yelled.

"Come in, Addie," she yelled outside the closet door. Addie came in. "I'm in the closet."

"Are you working today?" Addie asked.

"Uh huh! Why? What's up?"

"Nothing, I just asked.

"Why don't you and Jeffrey get out of the house today," Liah suggested. "It's a beautiful day."

"I might get out for a few hours," Addie said. "I like that outfit. Is that what you're wearing on your date tonight?"

"I am. I wore this on my first date with Marcus."

"Was that the time you thought he was Morgan?"

"Uh huh."

"Good choice."

"I hope it is. And he had better remember it."

"Knowing him, he might. But don't get mad if he doesn't."

"I'm not. But I gotta get a little fun out of it." They laughed. "Well, I need to get out of here. Are you cooking tonight or would you like for me to bring something home?"

"No, I'll cook."

"Okay, but if you have a change of mind just call or you can order something."

"Alright, I will." Addie responded.

As Liah was walking down the stairs, her phone rang. She didn't bother answering it. After she got in the car, she checked her missed call. It was Marcus. *Let me put this blue tooth on first*, she said to herself. *I don't know how people wear these things. They are so annoying.* "Hi, honey," she said with a huge smile on her face.

"Hello, Mrs. Michaels."

"I think I like the sound of that," she said.

"It feels like you're my wife already."

"Then I have a lot to look forward to."

"Yes, you do. But let's discuss that tonight, sweetie. As much as I would like to talk to you, I have to get to a meeting. Actually, I have several to get through. But the reason I called is to ask you if I send the car for you tonight, can you meet me at Jenos?"

"I would be delighted to."

"Great, I gotta go, love. See you tonight." Before Marcus put his phone down, Faith called. "Faith—hi what's going on?"

"Hi Marcus. How are you?"

"I'm good. I'm in a bit of a hurry."

"I understand. I'll get right to the point. Is it possible for us to get together this evening? I really need to talk to you about something."

"What about, Faith?"

"I'll tell you when I see you."

"It would definitely have to be before six, and very short. I'm having dinner with Liah at six."

"That's fine."

"Alright, meet me at Jenos," he said hurrying her off the phone. He had a very uncomfortable feeling about meeting Faith, especially after the stunt she pulled at the banquet. Marcus, being the kind-hearted person he is, was willing to hear her out.

Marcus arrived at the restaurant shortly after five. He spotted Faith as soon as he walked in the restaurant. He went over to her table. She got up and kissed him on the cheek. "I really appreciate you meeting me."

"No problem. So what's going on Faith?" He wanted to hear what she had to say and get her out before Liah arrived. He knew exactly how Liah felt about her. Faith sedately began saying what was on her mind.

After about five minutes, she started stumbling over her words. Not sure how to ask Marcus for the help she needed. "Faith, just take a deep breath and tell me what's on your mind." It didn't take much encouraging for her to blurt out what she wanted. She told Marcus what she needed, which was money. "He pulled out his checkbook and wrote her a check.

"Thank you, Marcus." When she looked up, she saw Liah talking to the hostess. She got up out of her chair, went over to Marcus, bent down and hugged him. He returned the hug out of kindheartedness. When she rose, she brought her hands to his cheeks and kissed him. He put his hands on top of hers, with the intention of removing them from his face. He furiously asked her what she was doing, as if he didn't know. Unfortunately for her, she lost her balance when he pushed her away and fell to the floor. But most unfortunately, Liah saw her kiss him and him putting his hands on Faith's. Immediately after Liah saw that incident she stepped out of sight, before seeing Marcus pushed Faith away. She walked back in the lounge as composed as she could be, considering the circumstance. *What am I doing?* Liah thought. *I am his fiancé, and I am not walking out again in this outfit. Besides his explanation had better be as good as it was the very first time I walked out of here.* She quickly turned around and walked back in with every intention of giving him the chance to explain. Be that as it may, she saw Marcus holding Faith in his arms. Despite how innocent it was, at this point it wasn't good for Marcus. Marcus was actually helping Faith up. As he was pulling her up by one hand, he innocently slipped one hand around her waist for support. It appeared to be something more than what it was. Marcus was too engulfed in apologizing to Faith to notice that his arm was still around her waist.

Since Liah didn't see the entire incident, she was left to her own conclusion. She stood there for a moment, stunned. Being the serene person she was, she walked out of the restaurant and got in the limo. She refused to let her anger get the best of her. She took out her phone and called Marcus and told him she was not feeling well and that she was going home to go straight to bed. He asked her if she needed anything. Of course she told him no and she would talk to him tomorrow.

When she got home, she checked on the kids and then got ready for bed. She read her Bible until she fell asleep.

The next morning, she told Addie and Jeffrey what happened. Jeffrey told her she did the right thing by not causing a scene. He also told her in a comforting voice that the whole incident was surely not what it appeared. He knew Marcus was a faithful man, and would do nothing to risk what he has with her.

Liah agreed with him. "I have every intention of giving him the opportunity to explain. Considering how conniving Faith is, I would not be surprised if she set the whole thing up. I know Marcus wouldn't risk what we have. But he does have a tendency to allow Faith to manipulate him. He likes to give her the benefit of a doubt when he knows she seems to always have an agenda. Besides, I know by now, she's heard about the engagement."

"Well, for what it's worth," Jeffrey added, "I am certain that he would not risk losing you. However, he has to cut ties with that girl. She means nothing but trouble."

"Regardless of Marcus' innocence, I need him to be able to come to me and tell me what happened, rather than me bringing it to his attention. Anyway, thanks for listening. I have to go meet Liz at the bakery so we can pick out the wedding cakes."

"Liah, you're right to continue on with your wedding plans and not leave any room for doubt," Addie advised.

"Don't worry, Addie, I have no doubts. I'm just a bit disappointed in him."

Liah went right to work after she left the bakery. Tina told her that Marcus had called and he also had tried to reach her on her cell, but didn't get an answer.

"I turned my phone off when Liz and I were meeting with the cake designer. I'll call him back. Thanks, Tina." Liah went to her office to call him. "Hi, sweetie. Are you better?" he asked.

"Yes, I'm better. How are you?"

"I'm good. I missed you last night."

"Did you really?" she whispered softly.

"Yeah, baby. You know I did."

"What did you do after I didn't show up?" she asked fishing for a favorable answer.

"I stayed there and had dinner and then went home and worked on the proposal with Morgan." Well, that wasn't quite the answer she was hoping for. But it was a partial truth. He did stay there to have dinner, he just didn't mention with whom he had dinner. "Are you sure you're okay?" I don't hear that cheerful spark in your voice."

"Well, I didn't sleep well last night," she murmured.

"I'm going to come by there in about thirty minutes, so I can see for myself."

"I'll be here. But right now I need to get to work."

"Alright, I'll see you shortly." She went in the kitchen and started working.

"Liah, what's wrong honey?" Louis asked. "You miss those kids already, don't you?"

"I do miss them already. But I just have a lot going on right now."

"If anyone really knows you, and I do," Louis said to her, "you have something troubling on your mind."

"I do but I don't want to discuss it right now."

"Liah, Marcus is here," Mel said."

"Thanks, Mel. Could you sit him at a private table and tell him I will be right out, please?"

"Okay, you okay?"

"Yes!" she answered with a sigh.

Despite how disenchanted she was with Marcus at the moment, she was still happy to see him. "Hi, sweetheart," he said to her as he got up and kissed her on the forehead.

"Hi. How are you?" she responded, trying to keep a straight face. They sat and talked for a while. She showed Marcus pictures of the cakes and the sets of China that they had to choose from for the reception. Both of them chose the Italian cream cake and coincidently, they also chose the same China.

Marcus invited Liah to dinner at Jenos at six o'clock that evening. She was hoping he was going to mention the incident between him and Faith, since they had spent almost an hour together and he didn't breathe a word about it. Liah was even more disappointed in him. She knew this was no way to start a marriage, though he might have a good reason for not telling her. Nonetheless, he was far from being off the hook.

Liah went right back to work right after Marcus left. Tina had a strange look on her face. "What's wrong, Tina?" Liah asked.

"Can we go in your office for a moment?"

"Sure. Come on." They went in the office and Liah closed the door behind them. "Okay, what's going on?"

"Remember my friend, the one who owns the newspaper?"

"Yes, I do."

"Well, he just called me. Can we sit down?" Tina asked.

"Of course, sure."

"Anyway, he told me he was emailing me some pictures, he thought I needed to see." He didn't tell her much but he did say they would not be pleasing to Liah.

"Here, come around her and pull them up on my computer, please." She got up out of her chair so Tina could sit down. When she pulled up the pictures, there were three of Faith and Marcus. One in a kissing position, one in a hugging position, and the other was of them having dinner together.

"Liah, you don't want to see this," Tina told her.

"Leave it up, please."

"Liah, I am so sorry."

"Don't be, all you did was open an email." Liah looked at the pictures. She had a bit of a vague response.

"From your response, I assume you knew about this, or are you just in shock?"

"Somewhat! But what I would like to know is how he got these pictures?"

"Hold up, Liah! What do you mean by' somewhat?"

"Remember I was supposed to meet Marcus for dinner at Jenos around six o'clock yesterday?"

"Yeah, right."

"Well, when I showed up, I saw Faith bending over and her lips were on Marcus'. It seemed like a kiss to me. So I walked back into the lounge. But then I thought to myself, this is Faith and the circle she encompasses exhales trouble. So I decided I would go back in to give Marcus a chance to explain what I had seen. I walked back in and there were both of them standing closely and he was holding her hand and had his other arm around her waist. So I took out my phone and took a quick snapshot for my own proof. But then I left."

"This is not good," Tina declared. "But it doesn't make any sense. Marcus wouldn't invite you there just so you could witness something like that."

"Exactly," Liah murmured. "He has too much integrity for that. Did he say how he got the pictures?

"Someone sold them to him," Tina replied.

"It has Faith written all over it."

'Faith, she's the ex wife, right? Girl, you want me to beat her down for you?" Liah and Tina both giggled.

"Thanks, but no thanks."

"Girl, you got too much honor."

"Violence is not the answer. It only causes more violence. God knew what he was doing when said, 'vengeance is mine.' He knew we would make things worse. But thanks to God, he gave man the good sense to do the intelligent thing ... which is what I intend to do."

"And what is that?"

"First, I want ownership of all photos and negatives. I have to protect Marcus' reputation as a Christian. I truly believe that he was set up. Men can be blind under a woman's spell. We are deceptive by nature. Look what Eve did to Adam. Don't get me wrong, all of us don't choose to do evil things to men just because we're good at deception."

"Girl, God brought one man into this world without a woman's help.

"Yeah, but women brought the rest of them in, painfully and with his help. So I guess we're supposed to have their best interest at heart."
"God is good—isn't he?

And wise too," Tina said.

"Yes, he is. But let's get back to the situation at hand. I need you to print off a copy of those pictures and then delete the email. Then call your friend and thank him for me and ask him for the negative or any other copies he might have lying around. I know he would have made big money off of these pictures. After all, Marcus Michaels is an icon. So if he needs to put a price on them, by all means, do so. Just get me those photos ASAP."

"That price could be big. Are you going to pay for it?"

"No, this is Marcus' mess. He's going to pay the cost. I'm just blue printing it for him."

"Girl, you are something else," Tina told her. "So I take it you're going to show them to Marcus when you bring it to his attention."

"Not quite. Although I know he's innocent and he hasn't a clue that anything is wrong. But his little incident with Faith is not something he should be keeping from his wife to be. They were in a public place, so he should know that I would eventually hear about it. I'm going to take a shower. Tina, thanks for all your help." Liah smiled and walked off. "Oh, and if he gives you any problem about those pictures, please give him my number and have him call me."

"I will, honey, and you know there won't be a problem."

While Liah was taking a shower, Tina was handling the business with the pictures.

When she came back in, Tina had printed the pictures off and had them in an envelope. She handed them to Liah and then assured her that there was no problem with getting the originals or the negatives. As a matter of fact, she told her that he would personally bring them over to her tomorrow.

"I just have one more question," Tina said.

"What's that?"

"What if he doesn't mention it to you?"

"Then I will leave him with these pictures in the restaurant—alone and give him some time to ponder over what he stands to lose. I will not start a marriage off with secrets.

"I heard that."

"Sweetie, I have to go. I'm going to stop by the kitchen first." "Alright, good luck."

When Liah arrived at the restaurant, Marcus was waiting for her in the lounge. He stood up gazing at her with his usual contagious smile. He passionately wrapped her in his masculine arms. "Hi, sweetheart! You look great."

"Thank you," she whispered and for a brief moment she melted into his arms. Suddenly there was an inviting interruption by the hostess. Well, on Liah's part anyway.

"Mr. and Mrs. Michaels, your table is ready," the hostess said. They didn't bother correcting her. They just followed her to the table. While they were sitting waiting to be served, Marcus got a really un-easy feeling from Liah.

"Honey, are you okay?" he asked.

"I will be."

"Anything you would like to talk about?"

"Not at moment." He didn't bothering pushing her. He knew that when she was ready to talk she would. The waitress came over to take their order.

"Do you mind if I order for you?" he asked. "I want to test myself."

"No, please do so."

"She will have the special of the day with broccoli and cheese, and mushroom soup, and a medium raspberry lemonade with a twist of lime. And I'll have the same."

She looked at him and couldn't help but smile. "I'm impressed," she told him.

"Yeah, not bad, huh."

"Not at all. Actually, it's exactly what I would have ordered." He sighed with a pleased look on his face. "Now, what do I want for dessert?" she asked him.

He looked at her and smiled. "I bet you're in the mood for something smooth and delightful."

"And that would be?"

"Cheesecake with whipped cream only."

"Wow, that—that's remarkable and scary. No one knows me that well but myself."

"Yeah, I impressed myself."

"Do I detect a bit of arrogance?"

He glanced at her hand and noticed how beautiful the ring looked on her finger. "We should elope and get married in a few days and still have the wedding as planned." Liah was thinking she would like to do just that, except there was a small matter that needed clearing up first. However, she told him it was a nice gesture, but the vows should go on as planned. "Besides, why spoil building up to the very moment we say I do."

"Okay, if you insist."

"I do," she replied.

The hostess came back with their food. "Aren't you the chef from A'Palace?" she asked her. *Maybe in the future I should wear a disguise*, she thought. *But then again it is really a blessing and great for A'Palace.*

"Yes, I am."

"Do you know how popular you are?"

"Popular, no, not really. I wouldn't say that. I'm just a well-known chef," she said modestly.

"Are you kidding me?" You're somewhat of a celebrity."

"Now I certainly wouldn't say that. But thank you. That was very kind of you."

The hostess smiled and said, "I'm going to let you all eat."

"This soup is really good," Liah commented.

"I agree. And the melody is not bad either. What is this, Whitney Houston night?" Marcus asked.

"They have been playing a lot of Whitney Houston's songs, Liah responded. But I like her. She's one of my favorite artists."

"Yeah, I like her, too." For a moment, there was a brief silence. "So anyway, you must really like this place. You ate dinner here last night," Liah said, giving him another opportunity to tell her about Faith. Again he did not take the bait. They continued talking through dinner and halfway through dessert, and still he mentioned nothing of the sort.

407

Finally she'd had enough. By this time, she knew he had no intention of telling her.

As she was about to reach in her purse, Marcus asked her, "What was the most interesting or unusual thing that had happened to her in the last twenty-four hours?"

"I went first the last time, why don't you go first," she suggested. He shared with her about something happening at work. When he was done, he told her it's was her turn.

"Are you sure you're done?"

"I'm sure."

Why don't I just show you what happened to me? She pulled the envelope out of her purse and handed it to him. She looked at her watch. "And I'll give you five more minutes to explain. Especially, since you've had over twenty-four hours to tell me." He opened the envelope and took the pictures out. He sat there momentarily with a stunned look on his face. "The clock is ticking, Marcus."

"Liah, I don't know—baby, this is not what you think it is. I'm sorry you had to see this."

"Still ticking!" He started trying to explain. But he was doing a real bang up job of it. "Marcus," she said cutting in. "Let's say you're telling the truth. Because I have no problem believing that Faith mastered minded the whole thing. So that will explain pictures one and two. But why don't you explain picture three—the one with you and Faith smiling and having dinner together, even after that little kissing scene. And then you can tell me why you didn't bother sharing the little incident with me. I might have gotten a laugh out of it as well."

408

"Well, since you couldn't make it, Faith said she hadn't had dinner and asked if she could have dinner with me."

"And you said yes!" And then you stayed after she pulled her latest stunt. And you didn't bother mentioning it to me.

"Honey, I am sorry."

"You know what, Marcus, I've heard enough." She stood up.

"What are you doing?"

"I'm leaving. Marcus, I love you with everything that I am. But this is no way to start a marriage."

"Liah, I don't understand."

"Okay, let me make it clear for you. I was here last night. I saw Faith kiss you. I walked out and when I came right back in, I saw you holding her hand with your arm around her, and then the picture of the two of you having dinner together. I suggest you take some time to decide if Faith and I both can fit into this relationship. Because, Marcus, from where I'm looking, there is not enough room for the three of us. And don't get me wrong. I am in no way jealous. Faith is trouble and you don't seem to see it. But most importantly, you kept something important from me. Not only did you risk our relationship, you risked your reputation. Now I'm leaving." He attempted to follow her. She told him, "Don't."

"Liah," he said, reaching out to grab her hand.

"Not now, Marcus." As she was walking off away, "I Have Nothing" by Whitney Houston was playing. Coincidently, when Marcus said,

"Please don't go," the song was at the part that says "don't you dare walk away from me; I've got nothing, nothing if I don't have you." Liah and Marcus both had tears in their eyes. Liah walked out of the restaurant and Marcus sat back down. Fortunately, for them, they were in a private area, so no one had seen nor heard them. Marcus pulled himself together and then got the waitress's attention so he could pay the bill.

Marcus was on his way back to Morgan's house. But then he thought to himself, *I don't need to decide what I want. I was wrong. I should have told her and I should have sent Faith on her way right after I wrote her that check. And I didn't tell her about that. I have to go find her. Man—Faith is trouble and I'm not about to lose the love of my life over this.*

He was hoping Liah had gone home. When he drove up, she was sitting on the bench by the flowerbed. "Good, you're still here. And before you say anything please hear me out. Liah, I don't need time to decide what I want or who I want in my life. I already made that decision when I asked you to be my wife. So that's settled. I should have told you. I just didn't want to bother you with Faith's pettiness. But I made a bad call and I am truly sorry. Faith called just as I was hanging up from talking to you. She said she needed to talk to me so I told her I would meet her. She said that she was in a financial bind. So I wrote her a check. And you know the rest.

"Marcus, I don't have a problem with you helping her if she needs it. But you have got to see that Faith is trouble. Do you think she planted that kiss on you because she was grateful? I wouldn't be surprised if she didn't see me before I saw the two of you. And I wouldn't have a problem with her if she weren't breathing evil. I will not tolerate this disrespectfulness from her or you. So as of now, I think it may be in your best interest to put some distance between you and Faith. But that's your choice."

Marcus took a deep sigh. "You're right and I will talk to her about her behavior. Do you think she had something to do with the pictures?"

"I wouldn't be surprised. But I don't want to dislike Faith any more than I do right now. So I just want to get past it, forgive her, and move on. But I did mean what I said earlier."

"Does that mean you will still marry me?"

"I never said I wouldn't marry you. I said you need to decide what you wanted," she said sarcastically.

"I wasn't sure what you meant, especially after Whitney told you not to walk away from me and you did."

"What? What are you talking about? Oh, the song. Did you also hear her when she told you that, 'you have nothing, nothing, if you don't have me'?"

"I did, baby, and that's why I'm here now." He pulled her in his arms and told her he loved her. And she told him that she loved him.

Marcus brought up the subject about adopting the kids. He and Liah had talked about it a while back. Liah told him she thought it was a good idea, but she wanted to talk to all of the kids together when the boys came back. She told him that the boys would be back in two weeks.

"Remember, I will be leaving for Africa in two weeks."

"I know, and I know it's for a good purpose."

"Yeah, honey, missionary work."

"I know that. I just don't have a good feeling about it."

"If it was a business trip I would cancel it, but I can't cancel God's work."

"And I wouldn't ask you too. Because neither would I."

"I do wish I could be here working on the wedding plans with you."

"No, you don't." He laughed.

"You're right, but I do wish I could be here."

"So do I." she said, yawning.

"You're tired so I'm going to go."

"I am pretty tired too." Marcus walked her to the door and they said good night.

~Chapter Twenty-Six~

For the next two weeks, they worked on wedding plans and getting Liah moved in the house permanently. A few days before Marcus was due to leave, he had his lawyer draw up documents, leaving all of his assets to Liah in case something happened. He told her the night before his departure that he was giving her open access to the bank accounts and he had added her name to the deed on the house. He didn't tell her about the other documents.

The day had finally arrived for him to leave. He and Liah both were tired from practically staying up all night. He was with her until the very moment he left for the airport. He knew Liah wasn't good at saying good-bye, so he had the limo pick him up at the house. She had no problem with that. The limo picked up Morgan and his parents before picking up Marcus. Lillie and Morgan Sr. wanted to see them off. Liah was glad Morgan was going on the mission trip with Marcus.

Chantel knew that Liah would be a bit emotional that day, so she planned a girls' night. Jeffrey and Tim took all the boys out. The ladies had a spa treatment, dinner, and a movie. Liah seemed more cheerful by the time they made it back. They all ended up spending the night.

Marcus called as soon as they arrived to tell Liah that they had arrived safely and he wouldn't be able to call for a days. At least for now, she was just glad to have heard his voice.

Liah kept herself busy for the next few days— with the kids, work, wedding plans, and anything that could keep her mind occupied. A few days had gone by and neither Liah, nor Lillie, had heard from Marcus or Morgan. She convinced herself that they were just unable to call.

Another day had gone by, and still no call, so Liah called Lillie to talked to her about the uneasy feeling she had. Lillie also had a bad feeling. But she didn't tell Liah about it.

Another few days went by, and still no call. The next day Morgan came home. He gave his parents and sister the news. Lillie and Lecxa immediately broke down. Morgan and his dad tried to console them even though they were upset as well. After an hour or so they went to tell Liah.

Liah was sitting downstairs reading when the doorbell rang. When she answered the door, Morgan walked in first. She screamed Morgan's name with exhilaration and then hugged him. Then she saw Lillie, Morgan Sr. and Lecxa. She hugged all the three of them and then asked, "Where's Marcus?" Morgan had an unusual look on his face when she asked.

"Liah," he whispered.

"Morgan, where's Marcus?" she asked again, this time without a hint of enthusiasm in her voice. He reached in his pocket and pulled out Marcus' ring.

"Morgan, what are you doing with Marcus' ring?" she asked sedately. Lillie and Lecxa put their arms around her. "No, I don't want to hear it," she said, still speaking sedately and then pulling away from them.

"Liah, a riot started while we were doing field work. Marcus and his partner took off together, as did the rest of us, seeking a safe place." She cut him off before he could finish telling her what happened.

"No," she screamed and then ran outside screaming in complete refutation. "Marcus, this is not funny. You can come out now."

Addie, Jeffrey, and the kids were in the kitchen when they heard all the commotion. They came out just as the others were going outside after Liah and went out as well—all wondering what was going on. Morgan Sr. stepped in. He grabbed hold of Liah and held her in his arms. "Liah, sweetheart, I'm sorry. But they found the body and they took the ring off and found his wallet right next to his body."

Jeffrey came up to her. "Jeffrey," she cried, with rain drop tears flowing down her eyes "he's not gone. I know he's not. I just can't accept that. If I don't hear anything else by tomorrow, I will be leaving for Africa on the next available flight." She looked at them and said, "I will bring him home."

The kids and Addie came over to her and all hugged her. "Liah, what do you need to me do?" Addie asked.

"If I have to leave, will you take care of the kids?"

"Honey, you know I will."

"Morgan," Lillie said "I'm with Liah. Liah, whatever you need me to do, you have my full support."

First of all," Morgan Sr. said. "Let's us all pray...right now." They all held hands and Morgan and Jeffrey both offered up a prayer each.

"Why don't we all go inside and worked out the details." They went into the kitchen and sat at the bar. "Alright, Liah," Morgan Sr. said, "Tell us the plan."

She got up from the bar and started to talk. "Morgan, I need you to give me every possible detail you can remember. Lecxa, I need you to locate every hotel, hospital, clinic, halfway house, and anything pertinent within a hundred-mile radius. Jeffrey, will you work on booking me on the next available flight.

"Liah, Morgan said," the company has a private jet. "Marcus is not here and I'm not going to need it. We usually used it for emergencies."

She looked at him and said, "Really? Okay—well if Jeffrey can't get me on a flight, then I will be glad to take the jet."

"Jeffrey, make reservation for two, please," Lecxa told him. "I'm coming, too."

"For real," Liah exclaimed.

"Yes, you can't go way to Africa by yourself." Liah went over and hugged her.

"Now, Lillie and Morgan will you all solicit prayers and help out with the kids?"

"Now, Liah, you know we will be delighted to," Lillie said.

"Yes, we will be," Morgan Sr. added.

"Girls, I expect you all to help out with Jas and please don't tell your brothers. They will be trying to leave their families and come to Africa. You know how they are."

"Morgan, can you and Jeffrey spend a little extra time with Jas, as well?"

"Yeah, we can go horseback riding. Right, champ?"

"Right, Uncle Morgan."

Liah went upstairs to make phone calls after Morgan Sr. and Lillie left. Morgan and Lecxa spent the night with Liah. She called all of her friends to tell them what happened. And of course they wanted to come to be by her side; but she told them she would probably be leaving for Africa in a day or so.

The attorney called the next day to set up a meeting with Liah about the legal documents Marcus left for her. Marcus had given him precise instructions to follow. He also warned the attorney that Liah was stubborn and she wouldn't hear anything he had to say until she had absolute proof. And she told him just that when he called her. She also told him she promised to talk to him after she returned from Africa.

Liah and Lecxa left the next day. They had a long flight ahead of them.

~Chapter Twenty-Seven~
Africa, The Pursuit

Despite the long flight, as soon they settled into the hotel Liah and Lecxa went out in search of Marcus. They started off searching the hospitals and clinics. Within two days, they had searched almost every hotel and clinic within a hundred-mile radius and no sight of Marcus. The third day, they were told about a free clinic that mostly serviced Jane and John Does. "Lecxa, I believe he's there."

"Are you sure," she asked.

"Yes. I know it's weird. But I believe he's there." They went to that clinic and were told about four men who were brought in around the same time of the riot. The nurse told them they had to wait until the doctor got in.

Finally, it seemed that things were looking up. "Liah, why don't we go back to the hotel and get some of Marcus' things," Lecxa suggested. Both of them were near exhaustion by the time they got back to the hotel.

"I am so tired, Lecxa, I'm going to rest for a moment."

"I think I am, too." Lecxa crawled into bed and the both of them slept until morning.

They got up bright and early feeling invigorated. They stopped by a little breakfast shop before heading to the clinic. When they arrived at the clinic, the nurse told them the doctor was in the room examining the men. Eagerly, they sat in the waiting room, waiting for the nurse to come back, which seemed to them, hours.

As she walked in the waiting room she could see the anticipation on their faces. "Right this way, please!" At first the doctor was hesitant to give them much information. He was taking precautions due to a past experience with one of his patients. They sat down with the nurse and Doctor Jhehi, who owned the clinic. They explained to them what had happened and who they were looking for. After hearing their story, Doctor Jhehi took them to the room. He gave them full access to the entire hospital. Liah hired private nurses to come in around the clock to take care of the men.

Liah gave the men an earnest speech. She said to them, "Alright, guys, my name Liah and I know one of you is Marcus Michaels. I am his fiancé' and Lecxa is sister. Say hi, Lecxa."

"Hi, guys."

"Since I don't know which one of you is Marcus, all four of you have to hear our voices daily until your bandages off. We will sit beside you and read the Bible, poetry, and talk to you and sing to you. I know you are probably hoping that we can at least sing a little bit. I have to warn you, we cannot. No, seriously, I think we have that covered. We might even lie beside you. Now Marcus is a Christian man, so for those of you who don't know Jesus, you will know him by the time you come back to the land of the living. So I guess you can say this is the beginning of a new relationship for all of us. Just keep in mind, there's only one man in this room for me. But don't feel bad, although we came here for Marcus, we found all of you. Therefore we're taking all of you under our wings. We will make sure that you all get the best help possible. Right now we are what you have until someone comes to claim you. And when that happens, I want you all to be out of these mummy suits and ready to live again. Don't disappoint me. It's time for you all to decide to either get busy living or get busy dying."

Lecxa blurted out and said to them, "So awaken, you sleepers, and rise back to life." Liah started laughing at her. Lecxa laughed, too.

"Well—there you have it, Lecxa has spoken. Anyway, guys, I have babies to get back to and a wedding to finish planning and I don't plan on postponing it. Okay, then let's get busy." She took out her Bible and started reading to the man in the first bed from the left and Lecxa started with the first bed from the right.

After they were done reading, they told them stories. Lecxa told them about some of Marcus' childhood experiences and Liah talked about some of the not-so-personal highlights of their relationship, like the first time they went horseback riding and she fell in the manure. For some reason, both Liah and Lecxa seemed to be more drawn to the man in the third bed to the right of Liah. "You know, Liah," Lecxa said, "it would be helpful if they had more of their mouths showing. That was the only way people could tell Marcus and Morgan apart."

"That would certainly make it easier," Liah said. "Nonetheless, I still believe he's in here. My bet is on bed three."

"Me too! You really love my big-headed brother, don't you?"

"Yes, I really do."

"And I already knew that. But when I saw how you were when Morgan first gave you the news about Marcus. It just confirmed it even more, that you were the kind of woman he needed in his life. I just hope that one day I'm blessed to be loved like that. Love is the most powerful thing that ever existed."

"You're right. It is very powerful. It reads in John: 13, there is no greater love than for a friend to lay down his life for you."

"And Marcus is blessed have that from you."

"We're both blessed to have each other. I've never met anyone like him before." Liah and Lecxa both sighed. Then Lecxa told Liah it was about time for them to say good night. They told Marcus they loved him and would see him tomorrow. Then they told the other guys good night. Liah told them she expected a little more response out of them the next day.

They stopped by a small restaurant on their way back to the hotel and ordered a to-go meal. Lecxa was almost halfway done by the time they got there.

Before going back to bed, Liah called to talk to the kids. Lecxa called her mom and dad to give them an up-date.

The next day they went through the routine again. The doctor told them that they had more brain activity than before. He told them that whatever they were doing to keep it up, especially with bed thice. Their hope spun into a higher level. He also told them they would be removing their bandages in a few days. Liah and Lecxa were both thrilled and nervous. He warned them that there would still be some swelling, but assured them that it will subside. "I don't care," Lecxa cried. "Most importantly they're alive. I just want my brother back."

"Dr. Jhehi, thank you for all you've done and all that you do for your patients. I know that this is a nonprofit organization, so before we leave I'd like to discuss what we can do to help you continue your work."

"I would like that very much." After Dr. Jhehi left the room, Liah and Lecxa lay next to the guys when they read to them that day. By the end of the day, there was still no response from any of them. They left the clinic a little early. They wanted to get in to make phone calls.

Another day had come, and Liah and Lecxa still remained hopeful. Liah sat on bed three that day and read the poem she wrote the night before. "Marcus, I know this is you. I can feel it when I'm close to you. I need you, Marcus. We still have a wedding to plan—together. I need you to fight, my love."

"Liah, here comes Dr. Jhehi," Lecxa told her.

"Good morning, ladies." Both of them said good morning. "I believe I have some good news." Liah and Lecxa's faces lit up.

"What do you mean?" Liah asked.

"Well, the nurse told me that she came shortly after you all left and checked in on the guys, and bed three's bandages were damp around the eyes." Liah's hope increased. She was a firm believer in hope.

"Thank you, Lord," she whispered. "I knew it was Marcus."

"Oh, my God! Liah he can hear us," Lecxa exclaimed. "He can hear us, right, Dr. Jhehi?"

"Yes, he can dear. His vitals are normal and he responded the only way he could. This is good news. I wish I had more volunteers like you all. You all keep doing whatever you've been doing. It's working. I have to go check on the other patients."

"I have to go call Mommy," Lecxa uttered excitedly.

"No, Lecxa. Not until we see his face. They would only be wondering from afar."

"Yeah, you're probably right."

"Did you hear that, Marcus? You all are on your way back."

"Come on, Liah," Lecxa said, "you heard the man. We got to keep doing what we're doing."

"Okay, why don't we play Uno?" Liah suggested.

"Alright, I'm good at Uno. Just don't get mad when I whip you."

"Lecxa, get real. I'm the one who created this game."

"Yeah right, whatever! I'm all over it. Come on so I can whip you." They played at least four games and both won two each. After the game, they had lunch in the room. The nurse was kind enough to pick it up for them.

After lunch, Lecxa and Liah watched TV. Liah lay down at the end of bed three and dozed off until she felt a touch on her hand. "What is it, Lecxa?" she asked. She thought Lecxa had touched her hand.

"Liah, wake up, you're dreaming." Lecxa said to her.

"I'm not dreaming. You touched my hand. I thought you wanted something."

"Liah, what are you talking about?" I didn't touch your hand."

"Come on, Lecxa, stop playing."

"I'm not. I'm serious." Liah jumped out of the bed and told Lecxa to get Dr. Jhehi. Dr. Jhehi ran in.

"What's wrong?" he asked.

"He touched me," Liah exclaimed. "I was lying beside him and I felt a touch on my hand. I thought Lecxa touched me but she didn't"

"Alright, I'll examine him. Would you step out for a moment and will you ask the nurse to come in?" After about ten minutes, the nurse called them back in. Dr. Jhehi told them that it could have been an involuntary movement, but he might know more tomorrow. He also told them that he could have another response. "Did you hear that Marcus? You are coming back to us. What about the others?"

"They all seemed to be doing well. I'm going to check them at the end of the day. I'll see you all later."

"Thank you, Dr. Jhehi," Liah said. They were in such high spirit, they decided to leave a little earlier and go site seeing.

"Well Liah," Lecxa said, tomorrow is the big day."

"I know, and I am ready—and nervous."

"Yeah, me too." Both of them agreed to try to put it out of their minds and try to enjoy the rest of their evening. "Okay, but I have one question."

"What?" Let's say it is him."

"It is Lecxa, I'm sure of it."

"Okay. But what if his face is disfigured?"

"As long as it's him. It will take some adjusting seeing his face like that. But I love him now and I will love him even more. The person I love is still inside of that body. It will take death to depart me from him. So we will take our life together one day at a time. And besides, I would be a fool to ever let a man like Marcus get away. There's not very many like him around."

"Wow, I see why people love you so much. You have a beautiful heart." Liah looked at her and sighed.

"And so do you, Lecxa Michaels."

The doctor and the nurses were in the room waiting on them when they came back. "Good morning, ladies," Dr. Jhehi said. "We've been waiting for you. Are you all ready?" he asked. Liah and Lecxa both took deep breaths and held hands.

"Okay, let's do it," Lecxa whispered.

They started with bed one first. He didn't look so bad but he wasn't Marcus. The second guy wasn't Marcus. When they got to the third guy, Liah yelled, "Wait." She took a deep breath and then asked him to do bed four next. "Can you give me a moment with these two before you proceed?"

"Sure," Dr. Jhehi responded.

She sat on the end of bed two and said, "Guys, you have all have come a long ways to be where you are today. You have been truly blessed to have such an outstanding medical team taking care of you. Although you haven't spoken a word to me, I feel like I know you. So no matter what happens next, I want you all to know that you have helped me just as much as we've have helped you. I like to believe that I am a better person, a stronger person and more appreciative. But most importantly, I've grown more spiritually. I came here in search of my missing soul-mate but I found so much more. I understand even more what it means to love someone you're never seen. Because I love each of you and I will never forget you. So I want to thank you all. Because of you I've had the opportunity to grow in God's love. Okay, Dr. Jhehi, I'm ready." He took the bandages off bed four and it was not Marcus.

"Okay, ladies, it's time. This is the moment you've been waiting for." He proceeded to bed three. Liah, Lecxa, and two of the nurses held hands. As he was cutting the bandage, Liah and Lecxa closed their eyes. "This is amazing," he avowed.

"What? What's amazing?" Lecxa asked.

"Well, you have to open your eyes." His eyes were open with tears rolling down his face. Liah and Lecxa and the nurses were all in tears.

"It's him," Liah whispered. "It's him Lecxa. He's alive." They hugged and said, "Thank you Lord, thank you Lord." Both of them were frozen in their spot, starring at Marcus in shock.

"Liah and Lecxa are you okay?" the nurse questioned.

"Yes," Liah murmured, "we're okay." She walked over to the bed and climbed in with him and pressed her lips against his and then wiped the tears from his face. "It is so good to see your face again. I love you, baby. I love you, Marcus Adrian Michaels. Thank you, God, for bringing him back to us." Lecxa came over, and then Liah got off the bed.

"Hey big head," she said with a big grin on her face. "You look pretty good for a guy that's been in a coma and bandaged up for almost two weeks. But you still don't look better than me," she said in a childish way. "Plastic surgery couldn't even make that happen for you."

"Dr. Jhehi, how long will it be before he can talk?" Liah asked. By this time Marcus had closed his eyes.

"It could be anytime now or it could be a while. We have to do more testing. I can tell you that he's going to need quite a bit of therapy. If not for learning to talk, definitely, learning to walk. For now, I have to ask you all to leave for a few hours. We need to get the rest of the bandages off and get them cleaned up."

"Okay," Lecxa, "come on, Liah, we can come back later." She didn't want to leave him but she knew she needed to let them finish their work. She went over to Marcus and kissed him and told the others that they would be back soon. On the way out the door, Dr. Jhehi called out to Liah.

"I've got a feeling Mr. Michaels will be talking soon. He just made a slight lip movement." Liah and Lecxa both, looked overjoyed.

They picked up something to eat on the way back to the hotel. They could barely wait to call home to give everyone the good news.

Lecxa called home to tell her parents and Liah called home to tell Jeffrey and Addie. Lillie answered the phone. Lecxa was so excited, she screamed, "Mommy, he's alive. We found him."

Lillie started, yelling, "Morgan, Morgan."

"What is it, dear?"

"Morgan, he's alive. Our baby is alive. They found him."

Morgan Sr. sat down in his chair. "Thank you, Jesus, thank you, Jesus, thank you, Jesus."

Morgan walked in and asked, "What's all the excitement?"

"Morgan, Morgan," Lillie yelled. "He's alive! Your brother is alive. Liah and Lecxa found him." Morgan kneeled down beside his mom and put his arms around her.

"Mom, he's alive?" He asked with tears in his eyes. "My brother is alive. Thank you, Jesus. You brought him back to us. Mom, how is he? Is he okay?"

"How is he, Lecxa?" Lillie questioned.

"He looked good, Mom. He can't move or speak, but he knows we're there. He had tears in his eyes."

"Don't worry, sweetie," she told Lecxa. He'll be back and then you all can carry on talking about each other. How's Liah? Where's Liah."

"She's talking to Addie and Jeffrey."

"I want to talk to her when she's done."

"Liah, Mom wants to speak to you."

"Okay, tell her to give me a moment. I'm talking to my babies."

"Mom, she's talking to the kids right now. She said give her a moment. Oh, she's done." Here she is."

"Hi, Lillie, how are you?"

"Thanks to you and Lecxa, I'm on cloud nine. Honey, I can't thank you enough for not letting us give up on him. And I will be eternally grateful to you for bringing him back to us. We all thank you. You said you would bring him back and you all did."

"God brought him back to us. And, Lillie, thank you all for helping out with the kids. Now how my wedding is plans going?"

"Everything is going well. Liz is doing a remarkable job, as you knew she would. I think she had one question about the groom's cake." Liah wanted it to have eight layers, four chocolate layers and four German-chocolate layers in the design of a tower.

"Okay, I'll call her tonight." The nurse called while Liah was still talking to Lillie.

"Liah, the nurse is on the phone, Lecxa said, she said they have to take Marcus up for some testing and it will take a while, so if we wanted to see him we need to come back to the hospital right away."

"Oh—okay. Lillie, I have to go. We have to get back to the hospital before they take Marcus for more tests." Lillie told her to give him their love.

When they got back to the hospital, they had hospital gowns on the men and had the head of their beds' up. Liah and Lecxa were able to spend at least an hour with them. Marcus opened his eyes twice while they were there, but only for a few minutes each time. He even made lip movements. When they came to take him for testing, Liah and Lecxa left the hospital and went shopping. They did some more sites seeing and enjoyed an early dinner. They bought Marcus and the other guys some clothes. Liah bought Marcus a silk pajama set. She knew how he liked his silk pajamas. They shopped until they were tired.

As soon as they were wheeling Marcus out the door, the nurse thought she heard him say Liah's name. They didn't call her back in because they needed to get him to testing. After they got him settled back in the room, Dr. Jhehi examined him again. While he was examining Marcus, he said two words, "Where's Liah?"

By this time, Liah and Lecxa were back at the hotel resting. The nurse called and asked them to come back to the hospital. She didn't tell them why, but assured them that it was good news.

Liah and Lecxa rushed back to the hospital, not knowing what to expect. They went straight to the room. When they walked in, Marcus had his eyes opened. Liah went right to his bed. He was able to move his arms some. "Marcus, you can move," she said slowly and surprisingly. She sat on side of the bed and took both his hands to her cheeks. "I love you, Liah."

"What? Lecxa—did you hear that? You can talk, Marcus."

"I did hear him. Oh, my God. This is what she was talking about."

"I said I love you, Liah Mathis," he whispered again.

"I love you, too, baby." She crawled into bed with him and pressed her face to his. "You have no idea how much I've needed to hear those words come from you."

"I tried to talk," he whispered. "I could hear your voices, Lecxa. Lecxa is here."

"Yes, I am big head. Come here, you." Lecxa climbed into bed with them and hugged him. "I'm glad you're back with us, Markie. You better not scare us again."

"I'm sorry. I heard talking. I thought I was dreaming. The voices sounded far away." Then he said, "Morgan, what happened? Where's Morgan?"

"Marcus, Morgan is fine," Liah, told him trying to quickly calm him. "He's back at home, honey."

"Did they think I was...?"

"Yes, and I wouldn't hear of it."

"I'm glad you didn't. When did you all get here?"

"About a week ago." After she had finish answering his questions, he told her he had something else to ask her.

"What is it, honey?"

"Will you marry me?"

"I've already said yes."

"No—marry me now. Life is too short. I don't want to go another day without you being my wife. We can still have the wedding as planned. We don't even have to tell anyone. Please—marry me now."

She looked at Lecxa as if she needed her approval.

"You might as well."

Liah sighed momentarily, before saying yes." She then said to him, "only if Dr. Jhehi says you're up to it and we're not consummating it until after the real wedding."

He chuckled and said, "Whatever you say."

"I'm serious, Marcus."

"I know you are, and I'm fine with it."

"Uh huh," Lecxa thought she would add. "Well anyway, I guess it's time to go shopping for a wedding dress." Getting married," Lecxa screamed.

Dr. Jhehi came in the room as Lecxa was screaming, "getting married."

"Well, I guess you all have been reunited again. What is this I hear about a getting married?"

"Marcus and Liah are getting married. She's his fiancée."

"We're getting married today," Marcus said. "That's if it's okay with you."

"Well, I would rather you wait at least one day. You need to regain some of your strength."

"She is my strength, Dr. Jhehi."

"Now that, I believe," he responded.

"Marcus, honey, we can wait until tomorrow."

"Okay, if you insist, but I don't want you all to leave. Can you all stay here tonight?"

"I think I can arrange that," Dr. Jhehi responded.

"Okay, Liah, let's go shopping," Lecxa urged her.

"Just a moment, Lecxa." She started talking to the guys. "Alright, guys, we're having a wedding tomorrow so you all need to wake up so you can see it."

They heard a voice whisper, "I'm awake." They all looked toward bed two.

"Oh—my—God," Lecxa exclaimed. "He's awake and can speak."

"Well, hello there, bed two. Welcome back to the land of the living," Dr. Jhehi said. "I'm Dr. Jhehi."

"I'm Lecxa."

"And I'm Liah."

"You were all in my dream and so were some guy named Marcus." "It wasn't a dream, man. I'm Marcus."

"Hey, man, I'm Drake." Drake was a light-tone African American. "Who is the poet?"

Marcus didn't waste any time answering that question.

"That would be my wife-to-be."

"It's Liah. Right?"

"That's right." Marcus replied. Dr. Jhehi asked Drake if he had a last name. "Cunningham," he replied proudly.

"Cunningham," Lecxa blurted. "Liah, that's your last name."

"It sure is," she responded curiously. "Wait a minute. Before you all start comparing DNA, I need to examine Mr. Cunningham." They all laughed at him.

"Do I detect a sense of human?" Liah asked.

"What can I say? You all bring out the wittiness in me." They all laughed again. Lecxa and Liah were about to leave the room but Dr. Jhehi told them they could stay. He was only checking vitals. They sat on Marcus' bed until he was done. Marcus touched Liah's arm. She looked at him and knew he wanted her closer. And then he asked her if he'd told her how much he loved her. For a quick moment she thought about how much she'd missed him pulling her into his arms and how blessed she felt to be back in his arms again.

"Tell me," she whispered. He told her as much as he loved his own life. And then he said to her, "You don't have to tell me how much you love me, because you being here tell me that." She relaxed in her arms and told him she loved him.

"Alright, you two need to break it up," Lecxa demanded. "You have the rest of your lives for that. Right now, we need to get a dress."

"Don't we need a minister?" Marcus asked.

"I'm a minister," Dr. Jhehi blurted.

"More sense of humor, huh?" Liah mumbled.

"No, I'm serious. I've been the minister of Shanghai church of Christ for seventeen years."

"You're serious," Liah repeated.

432

"Yes."

"Well, Markie, looks like we have a minister," Lecxa smirked. "Now come on, Liah."

"Hold on, ladies," Dr. Jhehi bellowed. "What time tomorrow?"

"Whatever time is good for you," Liah responded.

"Eleven is good for me."

"Wonderful," Marcus whispered.

"Okay, we're out of here. See you all later," Lecxa said.

Liah and Lecxa were up early the next morning. Lecxa was just as excited as Liah. She was happy that Marcus had finally found true love.

After a hefty breakfast, they went back to the hotel to get dressed. Liah wore a cute ivory full-length wedding dress she found at one of the local boutiques. She even found a bouquet of white roses. Lecxa had a similar dress except hers was chocolate. When Liah and Lecxa had gone on their shopping spree, Liah bought Marcus an ivory shirt, not knowing he was going to propose, again. Who would have thought he would insist on them getting married right away. Liah found herself thinking about how close she came to losing Marcus. She knew that was his reason for not wanting to wait to get married. She also knew he wanted to marry her because he loved her and that's what mattered. With that in mind, a smile obliterated the frown upon her face, forcing her to heave a sigh.

"Liah," Lecxa called out. "What?" she answered briskly.

"Where are you? It's time to go."

"I'm sorry, Lecxa?"

"Are you okay?" Lecxa asked her.

"Yes, I'm fine. I just let myself get overwhelmed with the thought of almost losing Marcus."

"I know how you feel, but he's back with us. Now let's go. They're waiting."

They made it to the hospital about ten minutes early. Liah stayed outside the room while Lecxa went in to see if they were ready. She stood patiently waiting for Lecxa to come out. What was only a moment seemed much longer. Lecxa stepped outside the door to tell Liah it was time.

Lecxa walked in first with her bouquet and Liah followed behind her. Marcus was sitting up in bed looking freshly groomed with his to-die-for dimple flexed, leaving Liah breathless. She sashayed her way to Marcus's bed with a smiled so bright it lit up the room. Marcus reached out to hold her hand at the same time telling her how beautiful she looked, not losing a moment of her beauty.

"I don't blame Marcus. I wouldn't take my eyes off her either," Drake uttered.

"Alright, kids," Dr. Jhehi hissed. "It's show time. I take it Mr. Drake is your best man," he assumed.

"Yes, he is," Marcus answered. Liah, Lecxa, and Dr. Jhehi stood in between Marcus and Drake's bed. Two of the nurses stood on the opposite side of Drake's bed. The ceremony was short, sweet, and simple. Marcus and Liah didn't want to use their original vows. They wanted to save them for the day when they confessed their love in the presence of their families and friends.

"You are now husband and wife," he pronounced, and then told Marcus to kiss his bride. Liah and Marcus shared their first real kiss as Mr. and Mrs. Marcus Adrian Michaels. "I love you, Mrs. Michaels."

"And I love you, Mr. Michaels, she whispered.

"What about the honey moon?" Drake inquired.

"We decided the honeymoon will wait until the original wedding date," Liah responded.

"You're okay with that, man?" Drake asked.

"Yep, I am. Good things come to those to who wait," Marcus replied.

"You're a wise man," Drake told him. "I think I'm going to like you. Congratulation, guys." Everyone else congratulated them, and Lecxa welcomed her to the family.

Liah wanted to know when Marcus would be able to travel. Dr. Jhehi told her in a few days but he would need to check right into the hospital when he arrived home. She told him that she would make sure of it, and Marcus expressed to Dr. Jhehi, his appreciation.

"I can never repay you," Marcus said to him. And then he asked Liah if she had the checkbook with her.

"Yes, I do." She whispered in his ear. She took the checkbook out of her purse and handed it to him, and he made out a check and handed it to Dr. Jhehi.

"I hope this will help you continue to provide the care for others as you have for us.

Dr. Jhehi looked at the check and his eyes widened. "I think I need to check your eyes. You put too many zeros on here."

"No, my eyes are fine, Dr. Jhehi!"

"But these numbers read five million dollars."

"They're correct, Dr. Jhehi," Lecxa assured him. He sat on Drake's bed nearly in shock.

"Let me see the check," Drake insisted. He handed him the check. Drake looked at it.

"Well, if I know my numbers right, and I'm an accountant, it is five million dollars. I don't believe it. I was a millionaire's best man," he uttered comically.

Dr. Jhehi was still somewhat a bit besieged. "Do you know how many people I can service with this kind of contribution? We get regular donations but this—thank you—thank you. This is a great blessing."

"Thank you, Dr. Jhehi. I'm glad I ended up here."

"Me too." Everyone looked around.

"Well this day just keeps on getting better," Dr. Jhehi declared. "Welcome back, bed one."

They all were glad to see him awake and speaking. "Did someone just get married?" he asked. They all stated talking to him. He thanked Liah and Lecxa for reading the Bible stories. They all were engrossed in conversation and forgot to ask him his name.

"By the way," he said to them, "my name is Matthew Kendrick. Matthew is a Euro American, in his mid-forties.

"Well, Matthew Kendrick," Dr. Jhehi uttered, knowing your name is a good sign and I know you all would like to get better acquainted, but I need to exam you."

Liah, Lecxa, Drake, and Marcus talked while he was examining Matthew. They were trying to talk Drake into going back to the States. He finally agreed to go, if he was able to travel.

After Dr. Jhehi finished examining Matthew, he told Marcus he was going to have him transferred to a private room so Liah could stay with him. He also had them fix up a room for Lecxa.

Before he left, Drake asked him if was able to travel. If so he said, "I'm going back to the states." He told him that it was very possible but he wanted to run some more test on him before he could be sure.

Liah and Lecxa left out with Dr. Jhehi so the guys could do some male bonding. After all, the tragedy that they all had endured brought them together. Liah and Lecxa stepped outside the clinic to talk.

The nurse came out to get them when they were ready to take them to their rooms. This time instead of wheeling Marcus out on a bed they put him in a wheelchair. The room was beautifully decorated, somewhat like a hotel room. "You guys," Liah, said to the nurses, "this is beautiful. Thank you all. You all did well. I was expecting a regular hospital room. But you all made it so much more."

"You all deserve it," the nurse told them. "Besides, this is the first day of the rest of your lives together. Now we're going to go and let you all have some private time. At least until it's time to check Marcus' vital signs again." Lecxa decided to hang out with the guys before going to her room.

~Chapter Twenty-Eight~

The Homecoming

"Alright, Americans, it's time for you all to get out of here," Dr. Jhehi told them, still savoring the humor that Liah so adored. Everyone was somewhat emotional. They were glad to be going back home but sad that they had to leave their new friends. Shortly before they left for the airport, the last guy woke up. They had only a short time to spend with him. Liah and Marcus invited everyone to attend their wedding ceremony, if it was possible. Marcus, of course, volunteered to take care of their airfare.

Back in the States the Michaels, Chantel, Addie, Jeffrey, and the kids were awaiting their arrival. As soon as Liah spotted her children, she ran toward them. Then Jas spotted her. He ran screaming, "Mommy" and jumped in her arms. The girls were right behind him. It was a glorious day for Liah to be back with her children again.

"It feels like I've been gone for such a long time. I'm sorry, babies," she said to them. "I've missed you all so much."

Lecxa was walking with the nurses that Liah hired to accompany them back to Santa Barbara. They were pushing Marcus and Drake in wheelchairs. By the time they caught up with Liah and the kids, everyone

438

else was standing with them waiting, overjoyed with tears in their eyes. It was a blissful reunion for them all. Lecxa introduced Drake to them. She didn't mention his last name. Liah had asked them not to. She knew there would be questions neither she nor Drake could answer. They all loaded into the stretch Hummer and headed straight to the hospital, just as Dr. Jhehi had ordered.

Their rooms were ready when they arrived at the hospital. Everyone sat in the waiting room until Marcus and Drake got settled in.

Morgan went in first so he could talk to Marcus. He apologized for coming back home without him. "I should have stayed longer," he said. Marcus told him he had nothing to apologize for and he was glad that he went home. Marcus also told Morgan that he counted it all a blessing for what had happened to him. He went on to say, "sometimes man we see things at its worse when bad things happen, but man's worse happenings are sometimes his best teacher." Morgan was so touched by Marcus' wisdom—he hugged him and walked out of the room with tears in his eyes.

Lillie and Morgan Sr. went in after Morgan left out and then Addie and Jeffrey. Liah, Lecxa, Chantel, and the kids were visiting with Drake.

~Chapter Twenty-Nine~

For the next few weeks, Marcus and Drake were in therapy. Marcus was determined to walk down the aisle at his wedding. Both of them were making satisfactory progress. Liah and Liz were working around the clock to insure that everything would be ready for the August 16th wedding. Liah also had her hands full working with the design team on redesigning her newly purchased restaurant. In addition to that, she was getting settled into her new home and redesigning Marcus' and her bedroom. Marcus suggested she temporarily close A'Palace while in the process of redesigning, so she could free up some time for herself, the kids, and everything she had going on. He offered to compensate the employees for any lost wages. Thanks to all his help, she was able to stay afloat.

Two days before the big day, the guests started arriving. It was the night of the rehearsal dinner—the night when both Liah and Marcus' families came together. Liah called Marcus to remind him that he was picking up her mother, grandmother, and aunts from the airport. He told her not to forget about his Aunt Roxy and Uncle Sonny. He also reminded her that they were not the easiest people to deal with. She said to him," Sweetie, I'm not at all worried. I'll be fine. Besides if they don't like me, so what. I'm not marrying them anyway. And you should feel the same about my relatives."

"But what if your mom doesn't like me?"

"Marcus, honey! What is there not to like?

"I don't know," he responded.

"Marcus, don't worry. She'll like you. Now I have to go. I have to meet with Liz. I'll see you tonight, Mr. Michaels, my wonderful walking husband."

"And so blessed to be walking," he added." He was overcome by a sudden shiver. He knew that he was blessed to even be alive, let alone, being able to walk. No matter how much he wanted to be able to walk down the aisle, he knew that being alive and being able to be with the love of his life was bountiful blessing. "I love you, Mrs. Michaels— more than words can ever say."

She heaved a sigh and said, "Marcus, I am just as blessed as you are, to be able to hear those words from you, and feel the profundity of your love, and to say that there's no end to my love for you. I love you, my love...forever. Now I really have to go. Talk later!"

Marcus was left with her words, pulsating through his mind. He held the phone in his hand for at least a minute or so before hanging up.

Liah's phone rang as soon as she hung up. "All, man! Who's calling now? Liz! Hi Liz, I am parking as we speak."

"Oh yea, you're here. I was calling to ask you if you brought your guests list."

"Yes, I brought it."

"Good." She replied with relief.

"Liz, have Chantel, Alisha, and Shayna made it?

"They just walked in."

"Wonderful, I'll see you in a moment. I have to stop by the kitchen and talk to Louis."

"All right, hon." Liah walked through the dining room instead of going through the side door. She stood looking for a moment, reminiscing about the very first time she walked into the restaurant. That day marked the beginning of a new chapter in her life. She thought about how far she'd come and how blessed she was. And now she was the owner. *Man, God is good all the time*, she said out loud.

"And all the time God is good," another voice said.

"Tina, hi, how long have you been standing there?"

"Long enough to hear the beginning of your quote. Were you thinking about the first time you came here?"

"Yes, I was. Who would have thought that I would be the owner of this place?"

"Girl, you have been running the place ever since you walked through the door."

"We have been running the place," Liah corrected her. "Now did you all remember to bring your clothes?"

"Yes, we did, but don't we have to serve the guests first?"

"Tina, rehearsal dinner. You all are a part of the wedding, remember?"

"Right. I don't know what I was thinking about." Liah shook her head and smiled at her.

"We hired servers and they should already be here," And here they are. Would you excuse me for a minute, Tina, please?"

She went over to greet the serving crew then brought them over to meet Tina and then the kitchen staff. "Louis, I have to be leaving here shortly to head to the airport. I need you all, if you will, to show them what to do and get them familiar with the kitchen. Then you all can get dressed. Okay, I must get to the ballroom. Liz is waiting for me. I'll see you all at the rehearsal dinner." She thanked them and headed to the ballroom.

"Well, it's about time you show yourself," Chantel said to her.

"Oh, be quiet, Chan. I had to take care of something. And I'm not done yet. Lisha and Shayna, hi, I am so glad to see you guys. The three of them hugged as usual. Hi, Liz. Girl, you have out done yourself. Outstanding, spectacular! I don't know why you need my help."

"Place settings," Liz replied.

"And that's all I see to do," Liah said. "Liz, everything is so elegant."

"You really like it?"

"I really do. Now, come on. Let's do the place setting. I have to go pick up Marcus' aunt and uncle from the airport. Hey, Liz, if you get Uncle Arthur's card, please sit him between my mom and Drake. That should keep his mouth occupied." They all knew what she was talking about, so they burst out laughing.

"Liah is he that bad?" Liz questioned.

"No," she answered comically, "he's a sweetheart and very bold—if you can put those two together."

"Kind of like you huh, Liah," Lisha uttered.

"I'm not that bad, I have tact."

"Yes, you are, but you do have tact," Shayna said. "You have come such a long ways, and have triumphed over more obstacles than I can remember. Now here you are today, a restaurant owner and you have truly found your soul mate. You traveled all the way to Africa and brought your man back home alive."

"I can't take all the responsibility for that. Lecxa was right there with me all the way. And I have to give God, all the credit for leading us to him."

"I can't argue with you there, but, Shayna, you should have saved that speech for the toast," Chantel told her.

"It was good, wasn't it?" Liah said. Everyone agreed. Liah looked at the clock on the wall and then said, "Guys, I have to get to the airport to pick up Marcus' relatives. Would anyone like to ride with me? I don't want to be alone with Aunt Roxy and Uncle Sonny. Marcus warned me about them."

"I can't believe you're worried about them," Shayna said to her.

"Me either, that's a first," Lisha blurted.

"Hey, I just need a backup plan in case I'm bored, stupid. Sorry Lecxa." They looked at Liah and laugh.

"Whatever, come on, Chan. Liz, I can't thank you enough for all that you have done. I'm sorry I haven't been much help."

"Girl, you brought your husband back from the dead. I would say that counts."

Louis walked in. "Liah, a minute, please," he said.

"Yes, Mr. Manager," she replied.

"Mr. Manager. What do you mean?"

"Oh—I didn't tell you. I'm crowning you as the new restaurant manager."

"You're kidding me, right?"

"No. What did you think I was going to do? Go out and hire some-one else?"

"No—I knew better."

444

"Well, I have to go. Would you tell Tina that she's being bumped up to kitchen manager, and tell Mel she's taking Tina's place and Joedi is taking your position?"

"I will be glad to, boss."

"Don't call me boss."

"Right. I'm sorry." Both of them laughed and then Liah left.

~Chapter Thirty~

Rehearsal Dinner

Liah and Marcus showed up early for the rehearsal dinner. Marcus made it a few minutes earlier than Liah. They hadn't seen each other since the day before so they showed up early so they could have some alone time before the guests arrived.

Liah walked in wearing the very same dress she wore when she and Marcus were married in Africa. Marcus couldn't take his eyes off her. She looked even more beautiful than the day they married. He walked over to her. "Well, hello there, Mrs. Michaels. You are breathtaking."

She smiled and took a deep breath. He was wearing the suit he'd worn when she first met him. "That suit represents the beginning of our relationship. And you look as good in it now as you did the first time I saw you in it, if not better, Mr. Michaels."

"This dress symbolizes the ending of our courtship, and began our day as husband and wife … and you look as stunning tonight, as you did when I married you, Mrs. Michaels." He took her into his arms and kissed her.

"Okay, enough of that for now," she told him.

"I have waited our whole relationship to kiss you, until I made you my wife. And I'm glad I did. But now I get to cherish, and savor every kiss we share."

"Yes, you do, in two more days."

"You're hard core. But I love you anyway, baby."

"And I love you, Mr. Impatient. So tell me. How did things go with my relatives?"

"Really well! I really like your mom. I think she likes me, too. And your grandmother is beautiful and exemplifies great wisdom, and I see a lot of you in her. And your aunts are funny and cool."

"People always tell me I'm a lot like my grandmother. That's a great compliment." Liah's grandmother is her heart. She has the utmost respect for her.

"Tonight, sweetie, is the night to merge two families," Marcus declared. "Are you ready for it?"

"As ready as I will ever be."

He took her by the hand and said, "Come here. Sit down with me for a moment. And before I forget to ask, how are things with Liz and her husband?"

"They're good. He told her the truth and now they're in marriage counseling. She seems much happier now."

"I am so glad to hear that. That's really good. Now you tell me how things went with my relatives."

"We had a good conversation. We found out we had some common interests. I really liked them both. They had us laughing constantly."

"Us!" Marcus responded.

"I took Chan with me in case I needed a backup plan." They got quiet for a moment. Then Liah said, "you know, honey, tonight will be the last time we will see each other until our wedding day."

"Then we should have one last kiss before you officially become Mrs. Michaels, known to society. We are allowed to kiss in the eyes of God now," he pleaded in his defense. Then he took her into his arms and kissed her passionately. Suddenly, a clearing of a throat interrupted the moment. It was Lecxa.

"Hey, you all better break it up ... unless you want to explain to mom and dad, why you all are kissing like that. They're right behind me." Marcus quickly took out his handkerchief and wiped the lipstick from his lips. He had barely finished wiping the lipstick off when Lillie and Morgan Sr. walked in.

"Hello, my favorite couple," Lillie yelled. You all are looking joyful." Liah and Marcus looked at her with a guilty smile.

"I'm going to put the guest book out," Lecxa said making a quick exit. "I'll be right back."

"Hi, Mom and Dad," Marcus smiled.

"Hi, my parents-to-be," Liah said with a pleasing smile.

"Ooh, look at you. You look gorgeous. Where did you get that dress?"

"Thank you. I picked it up in a little boutique in Africa. You look incredible in that suit, Lillie," Liah, complimented, trying to take the focus off her dress. She didn't want her inquiring any further, especially since the dress looked similar to a wedding dress.

"Yes, it does," she responded, without a hint of modesty. "And please thank your aunts for me because, honey, I am liking all those outfits."

"Why don't you thank them? You will meet them tonight."

"Make sure you introduce me."

"I will be delighted to. Would you all excuse me? I need to speak to Liz." When Liah walked off, Lillie looked at Marcus and asked him what was wrong.

"I'm good, Mom," he replied. "I'm just ridiculously happy. And I have so much to be happy for. I am marrying the most awesomeness woman in the world, well at least for me. Do you know she wouldn't let my lawyer read my will?"

"Yes, I know, son. She said nothing in the will would replace or bring you back, and a will would mean you weren't coming back. She wouldn't even let us tell her you were gone. She wouldn't hear of it."

"Mom, if it wasn't for her and Lecxa, I might not have come back," he murmured emotionally.

"But you are back, Marcus, and that's what matters," Lillie said to him.

"Your mother is right, son," his dad told him. "You're back here with your family and you and Liah are together."

"Until death do us part," Marcus whispered, "and even then the legacy of our love will touch the lives of others."

"Son, you are becoming a real poet," his dad roared.

"That's because Liah brings out the best in him," Lillie said. Liah came back and joined them. They stood talking until they heard a voice from behind her saying.

"Hello, my darling child."

Liah spun around and screamed, "Mommy, Grandma Aliah." She eagerly rushed over to them and went right into a hug.

"You look as beautiful as always, darling," her mom said to her.

"My beautiful, Lili," her granny said, hugging her again. "And she has a glow." Her aunts walked in with Lecxa and Morgan.

"Aunties," Liah, yelled as she walked toward them, and hugged them both at the same time. Hi, Morgan, you look good," she told him.

"So do you, sis, so do you," he said, as if he knew they were already married. Marcus hadn't mentioned that he had told Morgan, but she figured he had since they were pretty close.

"Come on over so you all can meet Marcus' parents." She hurried them over, eager to introduce them to the Michaels. "Mom, Granny, and Aunties, these are the parents, Lillie and Morgan, and this duplicate, is Marcus' twin brother, Morgan." After the introduction, they all hugged.

"Lili, where's my grandchildren?" her mom asked.

"They should be here soon."

"Here they come now," Marcus said.

"There are my beautiful grandchildren and the great grand, too." She looked toward Lillie and then said, "I'm sorry Lillie and Morgan. I meant our grand and great-grandchildren."

"Now, that's better," Lillie replied. All of the children came over to hug them.

"Mom, where's Uncle Arthur and Tori?" Liah asked.

"They were right behind us," Jacob told them.

"Liah, I saw Drake standing nearby, so they probably introduced themselves," Lecxa mentioned.

"Are you talking about the young man you all met in the hospital?" Amelia asked.

"Yes, Mom, your nephew."

"Well, I would like to meet this young man. Come on, Mom," Amelia said, "so you can meet your grandson. Would you all excuse us, please?"

Liah walked out with her mom and Grandma Aliah. They found Drake, Tori, and Uncle Arthur, talking in the dining room. They sat down with them, and talked until Liz came to tell them it was time for the rehearsal to start. Arthur and Drake continued talking. They seemed to be getting along quite well.

During rehearsal, Liah and Marcus seemed to be mesmerized by each other. They found themselves having flashbacks of their wedding in Africa. It was as if they were the only people in the room. Lecxa whispered to them and told them to snap out of it. They smiled. Nonetheless, the rehearsal went off without a glitch. Liz gave them about a ten minute intermission before the dinner.

"Everyone," she exclaimed, "it's about time for dinner. I need everyone to please sit where you see your nameplate. Thank you for your cooperation."

The ballroom was designed somewhat like the wedding reception ballroom would be. Liah had specifically asked Liz to do so. It was very elegantly designed.

After everyone took their seats, the servers served Liah's special made non-alcoholic beverage. Morgan stood up tapping his glass. "Alright everyone, it's time for the toast. Marcus and Liah, you all are a star example of real love. I've watched your relationship flourish from the start. Liah talked about a love not broken, in one of her lessons. She enlightened and inspired all those who were blessed to have heard her speak. She knows God's love, and how he commanded us to love. Liah, your love brought Marcus back to us, and for that we are eternally grateful. Everyone—raise your glass to Liah and Marcus."

Next, Shayna stood up and made a toast, followed by Amelia, Lillie, and then Jacob. Liah had asked Jeffrey to say the blessing before dinner. The last toast of the night was from Morgan Sr., welcoming Liah into the family. He then ended with a prayer.

~Chapter Thirty-One~

The Bachelor Party and Wedding Shower

The bachelor party was at Morgan's and the wedding shower was at Liah and Marcus' house.

The wedding shower started off with a traditional keepsake ceremony. It was something the women in Liah's family did the night before a female in the family got married. Lillie, Amelia, and Granny wanted to have the ceremony first, so they could leave early. "Alright y'all," Lecxa said, "let's get this party started.

"Amelia, would you like to go first?" Lillie asked her.

"Yes, sure, thank you." She pulled a gold box out of her purse and handed it to Liah.

"Mom! The gloves," Liah exclaimed. "I used to always want to play with these gloves when I was a little girl. These were the forbidden gloves."

"Yeah," Tori blurted. "Every time Mom caught us looking at them she gave us the eye."

"Uh huh, and you got in big trouble, too," Liah reminded her. "Remember?"

"Yep. I remember. But those gloves looked good with the play dress."

"I remember that, too," Amelia said. "That play dress went on punishment for a whole month and Ms. Tori was on punishment for two weeks."

"Yeah, and it was the worst two weeks of my life." Amelia looked at her and shook her head and then continued with her story.

"Anyway, these gloves have been in our family for fifty-one years. Mom's father had these specially designed for her when she was getting married. We send them out to be cleaned twice a year."

"They are beautiful," Lillie said. "And they look new."

"Those are real pearls, too," Granny murmured.

"They are indeed," Amelia concurred. "Now, Liah, these are yours to wear on your wedding day, and you get to pass them on to your sister or your daughter. Or whoever gets married first." Liah hugged her and told her that she would take care of them just as she had. Amelia said to her, "I'm holding you to that, honey."

Liah smiled and whispered, "I know, but I love you and thank you."

"Okay, Lillie," Amelia said, "it's on you." Lillie took out a silver box and handed it to Liah. She opened the box.

"Oh, my, Lillie, this is gorgeous."

"Yes, it is ... and thank you, dear." She then proceeded with her story. "Now this bracelet has been in our family for four generations. It was my great grandmother's. Her husband gave it to her on their wedding day. She had a fascination with diamonds and pearls. So he used the diamonds his grandmother left him and a string of his mother's favorite pearls and had them made into a bracelet. I would love to give these to you but Lecxa is next in line for these and she gets to pass them to her child or any of her nieces. Now one of your girls will probably be getting it."

"Lillie, I will be honored to wear it and thank you for loaning it to me. You all have such beautiful love stories to share. I hope I can share my own story with my grandchildren. My girls seem to already know the story."

"Okay, moving right along," Lisha said. "Now you have something borrowed, something old, and I'm giving you something blue."

"Wait," Liah yelled. "Let me guess. The garter I bought you, right?"

"Yep." She handed her a shiny sky-blue gift bag.

"All right! Thank you, Lisha. It still looks new."

"Glad I could be of some help. Alright, who's got something new?"

"I got that covered," Lecxa yelled. "Well, actually Marcus has that covered. He asked me to present this gift to you." Lecxa reached in a huge gift bag and pulled out a bouquet of multicolored roses. Look at this, he chose all of the colors we're using in the wedding.

"There's a box in the middle, Liah," Lecxa told her. She reached in the middle and pulled out the white box and opened it. Her eyes widened.

"Wow," Addie whispered, "would you look at those pearls."

"Pass it around, Liah," Lecxa ordered.

"Okay, okay!" He'd bought her a three-string choker with matching earrings. "Is this a twist of fate or did you all get together on these pearl tokens?" Liah inquired, curiously.

'I don't think any of us had a clue as to what the other one was giving," Amelia responded.

"Well—I am pleased with the way it worked out."

"They all do complement each other quite well," Lillie said. Everyone agreed. "Alright, ladies, who's going first with the gift?"

"I'll go first," Kaitlyn blurted. "Mom," she said, "you know it's hard buying you a gift. So, Miyah and I decided we'd give you something that would touch your heart, and capture the memorable moment that brought us to this very day." They gave her a picture capturing the proposal in a beautiful handcrafted frame. And she loved it. Her eyes filled with tears as she thanked them.

"This gift is priceless," she said, before hugging them.

"Okay, enough of that," Jayde yelled. "Mom, we couldn't find anything that you really needed and we didn't feel comfortable buying you any lingerie." Everyone burst out laughing.

"Good choice, baby."

"Soooo, Uncle Morgan helped us with this project. We hope you like it." Jacqlyne handed her the large wrapped package. Liah tore into the paper excitedly, not wasting a moment getting the paper off.

"Ah, I'm going to kill you guys. But it is kind of cute. No, it's really beautiful. But I can't believe you guys would do this to me. I'm your mother, honey," she said giggling."

"What is it?" Shayna asked. Liah turned the picture around. Everyone screamed laughing. It was a portrait of her when she fell off the horse in the poop.

"Wait a minute, we're not done yet," Jess exclaimed. She handed her another package.

"I don't know if I want to open this one." But she quickly tore in it anyway. This time she started laughing. And so did everyone else, after she showed it to them. This one was a portrait of Marcus helping her up off the ground with the poop on her. "Now I just have one question," Liah said. How did you all get these pictures?"

"The ranch is surrounded by cameras, Liah," Lecxa told her. She shook her head and the sniggling continued.

"Well, I have to give it to you girls. This was definitely something I didn't have. You all are pitiful, but I really like these paintings. Come here, crazy kids." She hugged and thanked them.

"Alright," Jayde announced, we're going to go upstairs with the little ones, so we can let you old folks do whatever y'all do at a wedding shower."

"And who are you calling old, young lady," Tori asked in a playful sarcastic way.

"I'm sorry, Aunt Tori." She left, laughing.

"Liah, that's your daughter," Granny said to her.

After the teens and the younger kids went upstairs, Liah continued opening her gifts. "You know, why don't we take a break and eat?" Liah suggested.

"I am kind of hungry," Granny said.

They didn't waste any time going to the kitchen. While they were eating, the doorbell rang. Lillie volunteered to answer it. "Liz, I'm glad you could make it."

"I'm sorry I'm late. I got a last-minute call about the reception setup. Don't be alarmed. It's all good. It was just a mix up."

"Glad to hear that. Come on, we're in the kitchen."

"Liz, I am so glad you didn't miss this one."

"Me too, girl." After their intermission, they finished with the gifts then the older women left. Only minutes after they left, Liah's surprise for the ladies showed up. A whole crew of people came in, even a photographer. "Ladies, I know how well you all enjoyed the spa treatment, so I brought them to you."

"Yes, you did," Chantel cried, "and thank you. Come on, y'all, it is spa time."

"Hold on, Chan, let's give them a moment to set up," Liah told her. The massage crew set up in the living room and people were scattered all over the place.

The others set up in the downstairs library. They were queens for at least two hours or more. They got everything done but their hair. Liah had scheduled the stylists to come in around noon the next day. After the spa treatment, they all gathered in the den to watch a movie. They figured they would all fall asleep so everyone grabbed a sleeping bag. They were all over the floor.

Marcus wanted to keep the bachelor party simple. He specifically told everyone no strippers, no alcohol, and no wild party. No one but Morgan knew, that he was already a married man. So they did as he requested and kept it simple. They ate unhealthy foods, watched old Super Bowl games, played cards and dominoes.

~Chapter Thirty-Two~

The Final Day

The next morning Liah sat out on the balcony with her mind deep in thoughts. Tori came out to check on her. "Well, big sister, this is your day. In just a short time now, you will become Mrs. Marcus Michaels." Little did Tori know, she was already Mrs. Marcus Michaels, she just hadn't began her life with him.

"I know, and I am ready to begin my life with him." She was tempted to tell stories but she didn't think it was important enough. After all, the premature wedding was about her and Marcus. "Have you talked to Mom today?" Liah asked her.

"Now, Liah, you know she called. She said that she, Lillie, and Grandma will meet us in the bridal dressing room."

"The talk before the vows, right?"

"Right! Plus you get one from grandma, too."

"I don't think hers is as intense as Mom's." Liah stated.

"Remember the talk before I married Brannon?"

"Honey, I would like to forget it," Tori said, sniggling.

"You are bad," Liah told her, sniggling as well.

"Oh—Liah!"

"What, girl?"

"I came up here to tell you that the stylists are here." Liah looked at her and just started laughing. They got up and went inside.

Lillie, Amelia, and Grandma Aliah, were waiting in the bridal dressing room just as Tori said they would be. When Liah and Tori walked in, Amelia said, "There are my girls. Baby, are you ready for this big day?"

"Yes, ma'am." She sat down beside her and took her hand, and said to her. "Mom, this is the wedding day I've dreamt about. Not because of the attributes of the wedding but because this day signifies the beginning of spending the rest of my life with one of the most wonderful men in the world. Mom and Granny, I know if you could choose a man for me, Marcus, would be him. And, Lillie, I have you and Morgan to thank for this wonderful man with such a beautiful soul. Lillie, you've been in my life for only a short time but it feels like a lifetime. I thank you for making my family feel a part of yours. And most of all, I have God to thank for all of you and for all of his bountiful blessings"

"Honey," Lillie said to her. "You and your beautiful children have been a great blessing to my family. Please know that we couldn't love you all anymore...if you were our very own. And, Amelia and Mom, and you, too, Tori, thank you for sharing your family with ours." They all held hands together and Grandma Aliah said a prayer.

After the prayer, Amelia said to Liah, "Daughter, my darling, I had this speech all planned for you, but now I don't think it's necessary. What about you, Mom?"

"Baby, you turned out to be such a beautiful, bright, successful and godly woman, there's not much to say. Just keep doing what you've been doing — keeping your hands in God's hand." Everyone left the room. Tori went to get the rest of the ladies so they could all get dressed. Liah was left to her thoughts, until a knock on the door. She didn't open the door. She asked who was there.

"It's me, baby. I'm not trying to see you. I just needed to hear your voice and say, I love you, Mrs. Michaels."

"I love you, too, Marcus, very much. Now, go back to your room, please."

"Okay, honey." He chuckled as he walked away.

~Chapter Thirty-Three~
The Wedding
Final Chapter

The wedding took place in the lobby of the Michaels building. The lobby was elegantly decorated with style and sophistication and with a touch of tradition. The lighting reflected a romantic ambiance, and magnified the snow-white-like doves that hung from the ceiling, adding an even more enchanting ambiance, while esteeming the beautiful doves. The seating was arranged to form a wide center aisle to allow extra space for the wedding march. Akito white roses mixed with greenery and baby's breath sat at the end of each row in a beautifully crafted white vase, with dove designs. Akito roses were Liah's favorite. She found them fascinating because of the abundance of dazzling large star-shaped blossoms. She thought they would go well with the doves because of the pure whiteness.

An exquisitely designed heart-shaped ice sculpture, with the shape of the bride and groom's hands in a praying position were centered in the middle of the heart. In the center of the lobby, between the stairs, was a fascinating and alluring mountain-shaped waterfall, with four beautiful areca palm trees sitting at each corner. It was a sight that would warm any heart.

Morgan Sr. made a last minute visit to Marcus' dressing room. "Son," he said to him. "I am so proud of you. You have chosen a beautiful woman to be your bride. I truly believe this one will last a lifetime. Well, are you ready?"

"Dad, I believe I've been ready for this since the day I met her. Yes, sir, I am ready to begin my life as a husband and a father." Morgan walked in. "Hey man, Liz said it is show time. Are you ready?"

"As I will ever be!"

"Marcus, Morgan, I'll see you boys downstairs."

As the guests were being seated, they were captivated by the beautiful ambiance. Many of them were whispering to each about how amazing everything looked, and how much thought and effort must have been put in to it, and how it reminded them of a fairytale, and whether or not they used a designer, or came up with the theme themselves. They were all marveled.

After the guests were seated, the close family members were escorted to the reserved seating. The minister walked up and took his place in front of the ice sculpture, the wedding march began.

Liah's granddaughter was the flower girl. She sat in a white heart-shaped wagon with two handles filled with satin akito roses. The roses accentuated the beautiful ivory lacy dress she was wearing. She was also wearing a tiara made of roses. Liah's twin grandsons, Joshua and Joseph, pulled the wagon. Her other grandson, Jacob Jr., was the ring bearers. He walked behind the twins and Khila.

The wedding party walked across the indoors bridge which led to both sides of the stairs. The females in the wedding party walked down the stairs on the right, leading down to the lobby and the males from the left. The view of the stairs was hidden about a fourth of the way down, then opened up to a full view of the lobby. The stairs curved toward the huge waterfall, which captivated the attention of those coming down.

Chantel and Morgan led the bridesmaids and the groomsmen down the aisle. Some of the bride maids wore champagne-colored gowns, accentuated with long ivory satin wraps and some with long satin chocolate wraps dropping midways the back, and draped across the arms. Each bridesmaid carried a bouquet of akito white roses mixed with greenery and a different color rose in the center. Each rose symbolized the uniqueness of Liah and Marcus' relationship. Morgan wore a chocolate tux with an ivory shirt and a matching champagne tie and vest, as all of the males wore. The maidens of honor wore ivory gowns—Alisha with a long satin chocolate wrap, and Shayna, a long satin champagne wrap that dropped midway their backs, and draped across the arms. They carried a bouquet of akito roses, accentuated with greenery.

The moment that everyone had been waiting for was only moments away. Only the wedding party and the wedding planner knew what to expect at the wedding. It was definitely not your traditional wedding.

When the bride and groom's music began to play, everyone stood. Marcus walked halfway down the stairs. He stood watching and waiting to cast his eyes on his bride. He inhaled deeply, knowing that in a moment, the woman he would spend the rest of his life with would soon be on his arm.

Liah wore a full-length stunning strapless ivory wedding gown, made from the matte duchess bridal satin and alencon lace. It had a v-cut corset back and a heart-cut neckline that blossomed into a full-shaped heart, with the point stopping just below the waistline. Each rose was bejeweled with one-half karat in the center and a pearl on each petal. The second heart began the skirt. It blossomed into a complete heart, beginning right below the point of the first heart, accentuating the hips with the point splitting about two inches or so above the ankles, capturing the mermaid look. The split blossomed into a complete beautiful heart-shaped train, made out of Italian organza lace to give it a fuller look. The beautifully blossomed heart stretched about twelve feet in length. The train was trimmed with the same diamond and rose designed as the upper portion of the gown. The gown also had a matching wrap. Liah carried a dazzling hand-crafted bouquet made out of akito roses, mixed with greenery and about twelve inches of ivory-colored satin ribbons that hung from it. It rested on a Bible covered with ivory colored lace. And last but not least, to accentuate the immaculate designed gown, she wore the gloves and jewels she received at the bachelorette party.

Stepping into full view, she paused and gazed at Marcus with a smile that could light up the midnight sky. He, as well as the guests, was mesmerized by her exquisiteness. Marcus eyes pursued her as she began to gracefully walk down the stairs. She stopped about halfway down. As she fixed her eyes on him she began to sing "I Believe in You and Me" by Whitney Houston. It was one of her favorite love songs. Marcus was breathless. He did not expect her to be the one singing a song.

After she was done Marcus sang to her. He sung, "You are the One" by the Elliot Yamin. He was one of Marcus' favorite artists. As he sang to her, his eyes never left her sight, and they didn't from the moment he first saw her on the stairs. Liah was also taken by surprise and totally blown away. *I cannot believe we had the same idea,* she thought to herself. As overwhelmed as she was, she wouldn't dare allow tears to fill her eyes and destroy her well done make-up job. She felt light on her feet as if she could float into his arms. She took a deep breath and managed to push the rush of tears of joy back.

Wow, his voice is as comforting as an angel's, she whispered to herself. Marcus and Liah both had powerful voices. The two voices blended together would be mystical.

The guests were as astonished as Liah and Marcus were of each other, when they sang. The guests didn't have any complaints, but why would they, it was perfect. Well, except for Uncle Arthur. "Hey, Amelia, what is this? A bride and groom concert," he whispered.

"Arthur, be quiet, please."

After Marcus' finished singing, he walked to the bottom of the stairs. Jacqylne and Jayde were waiting to escort him to the other stairs, to get a closer view of his bride walking down. There, at the bottom of the stairs, were Marcus and all six of Liah's children. When Liah reached the bottom of the stairs, Marcus took the veil from her face and kissed her on each cheek. Then he took her by the hand and led her in front of the waterfall. The march began when the song "Inseparable" by Natalie Cole started to play. Jayde and Jacqlyne escorted Marcus down first; Jason escorted Jessica, and finally Joshua and Jacob escorted Liah.

The minister announced before the ceremony began, that Liah and Marcus wanted to present the members of the wedding party with tokens of appreciation. Liz brought out a basket filled with white—gold bracelets with a one-carat charm. She instructed the males to place one around the wrist of the females they escorted down the aisle. Of course Marcus would place one on Jacqlyne and Jayde's wrist. Then she brought out a basket of watches and instructed the females to do the same. No one in the wedding party was aware of the token ceremony. However, they were quite marveled by it.

When everyone was back in place, the minister asked, "Who gives this bride's hand in marriage?" All six of the children answered, "We do."

The boys took one of her hands and placed it in Marcus' hand and the girls took the other hand and placed it in his hand.

Marcus looked at her and whispered, "I love you," and she whispered the same.

~The Vows~

"Dearly beloved, we are gathered here today to join this man and this woman in holy matrimony. Shall we lift Marcus and Liah up in prayer?" After the prayer, the minister read scriptures from the Bible.

Ephesians 5:22-31 reads, "Wives, be subject to your own husbands, as to the Lord; For the husband is the head of the wife, as Christ also is the head of the church, He himself being the savior of the body. But as the church is subject to Christ, so also wives ought to be to their husbands in everything. Husbands, love your wives, just as Christ also loved the church and gave Himself up for her; that He might sanctify her, having cleansed her by the washing of water with the word, that He might present to Himself the church in all her glory, having no spot or wrinkle or any such thing; but that she should be holy and blameless. So husband ought to also love their own wives as their own bodies. He who loves his own wife loves Himself; for no one ever hated his own flesh, but nourishes and cherishes it, just as Christ also does the church, because we are members of His body. FOR THIS CAUSE A MAN SHALL LEAVE HIS FATHER AND MOTHER, AND CLEAVE TO HIS WIFE, AND THE TWO SHALL BECOME ONE FLESH (NAS)." And in Colossians 3:18-19, "Wives, be subject to your husbands, as is fitting in the Lord. Husband, love your wives, and do not be embittered against them (NAS)."

"Liah, do you understand what I've just read to you?"

"Yes."

"Liah, do you promise to hold true to these words?"

"I do."

"Marcus, do you understand?"

"Yes, I do?"

"Marcus, do you promise to hold true to these words?"

"I do."

After the minister had finished this part of the ceremony, he informed the guests that Liah and Marcus had a poem they would like to recite to one another. Marcus and Liah recited the poem at the same time, as they gazed into each other eyes.

Inseparable

Inseparable is our love at best

A love within a treasure chest

Together forever you and I

In God's love our hearts will sigh

As we face the world together we'll walk in righteous through trials

Reaching far above and beyond that extra mile

In our hearts, our souls, our minds

Our love will remain in God's hand for a lifetime

Through hope and faith our love abides

Holding true to God victoriously in our hearts God's love resides

In God's love we face no fears

An inseparable union for an eternity of years

468

Inseparable our will be
Together forever, you and me'

"Liah, do you take Marcus to be your husband in the sight of God?"

"I do."

"Marcus, do you take Liah to be your wife in the sight of God?"

"I do." The minister asked for the rings. Jacob handed Marcus the ring. Marcus placed the ring on Liah's finger and said, "With this ring, I thee wed."

Jacob then gave Liah the ring and she stated, "With this ring, I thee wed."

"By the power invested in me, I now pronounce you husband and wife."

"Whatever therefore God has joined together, let no man separate (Matthew 19:6). You may kiss your bride." Marcus stood there for a moment.

"Marcus," Morgan murmured. "What are you waiting for?"

"I'm just savoring the moment," he responded. He then placed his hands on Liah's faced and kissed her. And then they embraced.

Jacob noticed a familiar face standing in front of the waterfall so he stepped over and touched Liah on the shoulders and said to her.

"Mom, Dad is here."

"What? Jacque, what are you talking about?"

"He's standing in front of the waterfall." Marcus and Liah both looked toward the waterfall.

"What is he doing here?" Liah wondered. "And after all of these years, why on our wedding day?" Brannon Mathis certainly knew how to put a damper on things.

"Mom, Josh and I will handle this," Jacob told her.

"No, I will handle this," Liah whispered.

"No, Liah, we will handle this—together," Marcus told her. The guests had no idea that anything was going on. What could be Brannon Mathis's reason for showing up on his ex-wife's wedding day?

Bonus Section

Spiritual Lessons

Desserts

Poetry Section

A Love Not Broken

The Bible says "**love never fails**." Just how many of us believe that, since we have either witnessed or heard about marriages and relationships around the world, crashing every day. What exactly does God means when he said "Love never fails" (1Co. 13:8, NIV®)?" It is important for us first to understand God's Love; because His love teaches us the true meaning of love and how to love.

This is how God showed his love toward us: *He sent his one and only Son into the world that we might live through him (1 John 4:9, NIV®).*

This verse along is an excellent example of true love. Fortunately for us, He provided the original recipe on how to love, so his love will be perfected in us. God's love is perfect.

No one has ever seen God; but if we love one another, God lives in us and his love is made complete in us (1 John 4:12, NIV®).

But why do we find it so hard to express love? Why do we practically destroy the ones we profess to love? Is it due to our lack of understanding of love? We are the ones who fail love. It has never failed us. We already know that God says, "love never fails." Perhaps it could it be due to the fear of love? God also says that there is no fear in love.

There is no fear in love. *But perfect love casteth out fear, because fear hath torment. He that fear is not made perfect in love (1 John 4:18, KJV).*

God's love is the love that sustains all and any relationship. He is the master of love. As a matter of fact, if you are looking for a good love story, read your Bible. It is the love story of all love stories. You will not be disappointed. You will find love expressed in various forms in the Bible. There are no other examples of love that could compare to those shown in the Bible. Real true love is not expressed in feelings or just saying "I love you." In this sense, feelings are just emotions: anyone could breathe out those words. Real true love is expressed in actions.

Dear Children, let us not love with words or tongue but with actions and in truth (1 John 3:18, NIV®).

When you love with God's love...you are able to put forth that love before you are aware of any flaws or downfalls. You are able to feel empathy or sympathy for someone by just hearing about another's tragedy, pain or heartache; it reaches out to someone in need and cares and continues to care regardless of circumstances. To love with the love of the Lord, we have to love unconditionally. The best description of this love is found in 1 Corinthian 13:

If I speak in tongues of men and of angels, but have not love, I am only a resounding gong or a clanging cymbal. If I have the gift of prophesy and can fathom all mysteries and all knowledge, and if I have a faith that move mountains, but have not love, I am nothing. If I give all I possess to the poor and surrender my body to the flames, but have not love, I gain nothing (1 Co. 13:1-3, NIV®).

God's command to love applies to all...even the angels in heaven. No one is exempt from God's love. His love is exalted to the highest level. If I may, let me point out the significant amount of emphasis that is placed on love by using examples of faith. As Jesus was talking to his disciples, the Bible reads:

Faith and Hope: *He replied, "Because you have so little faith. I tell you the truth, if you have faith as small as a mustard seed, you can say to this mountain, Move from here to there' and it will move. Nothing will be impossible for you (Matt. 17:20, NIV®).*

Now make no mistakes, what Paul said in (1st Co. 13:2, ISV) "If I have the gift of prophesy and can understand all secrets and every form of knowledge, and I have absolute faith, so to move mountains, but don't have love, I am nothing." This scripture does not emasculate the importance of faith, because faith is *essential* to salvation. As a matter of fact the Bible reads in *"...without faith it is impossible to please God (Hebrew 11:6, ISV)."*

Though this lesson is not about faith, nor hope, however, I feel that it is imperative to exemplify the importance of faith and hope in order to elucidate the importance of love. Therefore I implore you to read the following scriptures pertaining to faith and hope.

Faith: Matthew 17:20; Romans 10:17; 2 Corinthians 5:7; Galatians 5:7; Ephesians 2:8; Ephesians 6:16; 2 Thessalonians 3:2; Hebrews 11:1; Hebrews 11:6; James 5:15

Hope: Ephesians 4:4; 1 Peter 1:3; Colossian 1:27; Colossian 1:5; 1 Timothy 1:1; Hebrew 6:18; 19; 1 Corinthians 13:13; Psalms /1:5; Jeremiah 14:8; Lamentations 3:26; Romans 5:5

With these verses in mind, I entreat you to take to heart the seriousness of love. There is no place in heaven for us if we don't honor God's commandments.

In (John 13:34, KJV) Jesus gave a new commandment. He said, *"A new commandment I give to you, that ye love one another; as I have loved you, that ye also love one another."*

What Lies Beneath Your Giving: As I was reading the story in Matthew (19:16-22) about the rich man I felt compelled to use it as an example in this lesson. The rich young man asked Jesus what things he would have to do to have eternal life. Jesus said to him, "if you want to enter into life, keep the commandments." He then asked, "which ones." Jesus gave him a list of commandments. The young man told him he had kept all of those from his youth. He then said to Jesus, *"What do I still lack?" Jesus said to him, "If you want to be perfect, go, sell everything you have and give to the poor, and you will have treasure in heaven; and come follow me" (Matt. 19:17-21, NIV®).* It is safe to conclude that his possessions meant more to him than God's commandments, because according to the Bible, "he went away sorrowful" (19:22). I'm not going to say that giving up *all* of ones possessions, even for the needy, will be an effortless task. Never the less, I would like to think that, if Jesus were to say to me, sell all your possessions and give to the poor and follow me I would not hesitate to do as he suggested, and out of the goodness of my heart. Moreover, it may be my only chance to follow. What about you? What do you think would be your reaction, if you were in the rich man's place? After all, we know that if the giving is not out of love it means nothing anyway (1st Co. 13:3).

We are taught by God to love one another (1st Thess. 4:9). The love that God teaches, teaches us to respect his commandments; it does not deny the needy, it does not destruct. It lifts up, it builds up, and it inspires goodness.

What we do for or give to someone holds little significance, compared to how or why we give. God doesn't care about quantity of your giving...it's the quality of your giving that counts. He is not impressed with what we give or how much we give.

A good man out of the good treasure of his heart brings forth good things, and an evil man out of the evil treasure brings forth evil things (Matt. 12:35, KJV).

How many people can we name who gives big out of their bank account, rather than their heart because they can, and is acclaimed by

God? Now let me show you a person who gave what they had from their heart and was exalted by God. Take heed to the example of the widow who gave two mites, which is barely a fraction of a penny. She gave all she had to give.

The Bible says in (Mark 12:41-44, NKJ) *"Now Jesus sat opposite the treasury and saw how the people put money into the treasury. And many who were rich put in much. Then one poor widow came and threw in two mites, which make a quadrans. So He called His disciples to Himself and said to them, "Assuredly, I say to you that this poor widow has put in more than all those who have given to the treasury; for they all put in out of their abundance, but she out of her poverty put in all that she had, her whole livelihood."*

There is no need to do as the scribes, who went around doing flamboyant deeds to be noticed by men. We need to resolve to be more like the widow. We need to resolve to more like Christ. We need to resolve to love with the love of the Lord. Love is the face of many expressions but those expressions stream from one root, the heart of love.

What Inspire Ones' Giving?

Resolve to Love with the love of God: *Love is **patient**, love is **kind**, it does not **boast**, it is not **proud**. It is not **rude**, it is not **self-seeking**, it is not **easily angered**, it **keeps** no record of **wrong**. Love does not delight in evil but **rejoices** with truth. It always **protects**, always trusts,* *always* **hopes**, *always* **preserves**. *Love* **never fails**... *(1 Cor. 13:4-8, NIV®)*

If I may, let me just insert, that even though love is exalted above hope, and faith, yet, it does not lessen either of their importance.

And now these three things remain: **faith**, **hope** *and* **love**. *But the* **greatest** *of these is* **love** *(1 Cor. 13:13).*

The love that is described in (1 Corinthian 13) is Agape love. It is the love that teaches how to love in every type of relationship, whether it's neighbors, friends, co-workers, loved ones, spouses and even those whom you don't know or have never seen. It teaches unconditional love. This is the most powerful love you will ever know. It surrounds the world. It is the love that will sustain the love for loved ones known as (storge), friendship (Philia, Phileo or

Philos) a relationship united mainly by commonality. Friendship does not stem from natural love, like family love. However, in time, a strong bond can form into something just as wonderful as a family member.

"Greater love has no one than this, that he lay down his life for his friends" (John 15:13, NIV®).

It is the love that will sustain emotional or romantic love (Eros); the love for ones' spouse. Agape love is charitable love; it yields compassion in spite of circumstance. This type of love holds its own. It is an unwavering love. Most importantly, because of this love, (God's love) we were given a savior, by the shedding of His blood.

When Christ came as a high priest of good things that are already here, he went through the greater and more perfect tabernacle that is not manmade, that is to say not a part of this creation. He did not enter by means of the blood of goats and calves: but he entered the Most Holy Place once for all by his own blood. Having obtained eternal redemption. The blood of goats and bulls and the ashes of a heifer sprinkled on those who are ceremonially unclean, sanctify them so that they are outwardly clean. How much more, then, will the blood of Christ, who through the eternal spirit offered himself unblemished to God, cleanse our conscience from acts that lead to death, so that we may serve the living God! For this reason, Christ is the mediator of a new covenant, that those who are call may receive the promise eternal inheritance-now that he has died as ransom to set them free from the sins committed under the first covenant (Heb. 9:11- 15, NIV®).

This new covenant came out of God's love for the world.

For God so loved the world that he gave his only begotten Son, that whosoever believeth in him should not perish, but have everlasting life (John 3:16, KJV).

We need to learn to love with the love of the Lord in order that we will be able to express love to the fullest, especially in our personal relationships. Therefore when we are faced with challenges in our relationships, we have God's love (Agape) to look to that we may be renewed. And, that we will have the courage to persevere, in spite of any obstacles. *God's love is a love that can't be broken.* Paul conveys to us in Romans 8:39.

Yet in all these things we are more than conquerors through Him who loved us. For I am persuaded that neither death nor life, nor angels not principalities, nor powers, not things present, nor things to come, nor height, nor depth, nor any created thing, shall be able to separate us from the love of God which in Christ Jesus our Lord (Romans 8:37- 39, NKJ). I don't know about you, but I say that this is a love unbreakable. Why wouldn't anyone want to receive that kind of love in his relationships, in his daily living? Why would anyone want to settle for counterfeit love? Because *perfect love drives out fear (1st John 4:18), Love never fails (1st Cor. 13:8).*

If we learn to love like God, it will be manifested in our lives and in our personal relationships. When a relationship fails, someone, if not both parties, are guilty of failing the relationship: Why? Because someone fail to love as God has commanded. I've watched many relationships around me fail, including my own, and I used to often ask myself, why? If God's love is perfected in us, then what's wrong, what is the real problem? Love is the foundation that holds the world together. I truly believe that if more of God's love was shown in the world less people will suffer from the hands of evil predators, fewer people would be homeless; fewer people will be suffering from starvation; fewer people would be sick or dying from lack of medical treatment and so on. Everything we have in the world belongs to God and he can zap us of it at any time and without any warning. You see, God does not show favoritism. He does not love anyone more because they're rich or less because they're poor, and it doesn't make anyone more blessed. Money only buys material things. It can't buy love and it certainly can't buy one's way into heaven. You see, "salvation is free." Christ has already paid the price for it.

For God so love the world that He gave His only begotten Son (John 3:16, KJV).

Money is good to one only while they live. And even then, if it's in the possession of an unrighteous mind and heart, its earthly purpose could hold no heavenly treasure for them.

Inseparable

In Matthew 19:23-24, the Bible reads, "Then Jesus said to His disciples, Assuredly, I say to you that it is hard for a rich man to enter the kingdom of heaven. And again I say to you, it is easier for a camel to go through the eye of a needle than for a rich man to enter the kingdom of God (NKJ)."

We are accountable for our own actions and that accountability cannot be passed on to anyone else. Our accountability began in our lives the moment we were able to comprehend and understand the sincerity of God's words. That moment we were able to make accountable decisions, from that day until the Day of Judgment. Unfortunately, if we wait until the last stage, the "Day of Judgment," it is far too late.

Love is what makes a person rich. I don't know about you, but I don't think love gets any deeper than that. What we are asked to do, seems pretty simple, love one another. Let us all resolve to communicate with God's love to each other the way He communicates it to us.

Communication serves as a catalyst for any relationship. We communicate to God through prayer. And the love that's in between God and us is Christ. He is the mediator, for He is our Savior and it is because of God's love for us that we have Christ as a mediator and Savior.

God is Love: Love does not get any better than that. Now if we just use Christ, as a mediator in our relationships (all of our relationships) because he "He is Love," there shouldn't be anything that we can't resolve, even if it's a matter of agreeing to disagree. Though relationships are indeed the most challenging of all our encounters, one can withstand with God's plan. While each relationship is different, they all must be rooted from the same foundation—God's love. I tell you it is unshakeable, unmovable, unalterable, it is stanch and steadfast. Why wouldn't we want to love and be loved with God's love?

God's love teaches us how to communicate to one another, whether in our personal relationships or with a stranger. *Love is not rude (1*st *Co. 13:5)*. And it is essential that a good line of communication is open and flowing, especially in our personal relationships, and most importantly, in marital relationships.

There must be a superb line of communication between a husband and wife. This will not only enhance the relationship, but will prevent one from feeling as if one is living with a stranger, especially at a time when it is possible to share so much.

Love bridges the mode of communication. One thing I can promise you is that in relationships there will be trials and errors and while so, there will be a great need for understanding, permissiveness, and communication will be absolutely imperative to the outcome. I can guarantee you that if you love with God's love, when these times arise, it will keep those boxing gloves out of the discussions. After all, it's a discussion, not a boxing match. Allow God's love to pave the way for communicating with openness, respect, honesty, trust and understanding, and allow it to build a stronger relationship.

Hear what I'm saying— no relationship can survive without real true love. Love gives that reason to dream of all those things that are possible. When true love is manifested in a relationship, it is easier to express sentiments of love, whether it's with tears, laughter, joy, a smile or even tokens. When two people are able to share these things together, it can strengthen the ties of a relationship. Love exemplifies the true meaning of riches.

Where Love Lies: Let me ask you a question. When someone is seeking a person to share one's life with, what do you think should be a priority? Do you think it's more important to marry a millionaire or someone who makes you feel like a millionaire and likewise? God said the love of money is the root of all kinds of evils.

"For the love of money is the root of all evil: while which some coveted after, they have erred from the faith, and pierced themselves through with many sorrows." (1st Timothy 6:10, KJV).

People kill because they don't have it and want it or because they do have it and want to keep it. Either way God is not pleased.

In this the children of God and the children of the devil are manifest: Whoever does not practice righteousness is not of God, nor is he who does not love his brother. For this is the message that you heard from the beginning, that we should love one another, (1st John 3:10-11, KJV).

We have here two totally different foundations. Love is the foundation that holds the world together. Evil is the foundation that rips the world apart. Love builds—Evil annihilates; love exalts—evil disparages; love respects—evil disrespects; love safeguards—evil devastates, and love magnifies—evil restricts. God's love is everlasting. Evil is eternal damnation. *Jesus said in (John 14:15, NKJ).*

"If you love Me, keep My commandments,"and in (John 14:21, NKJ) He who has My commandments and keep them, it is he who loves Me; and he who loves Me shall be loved by My Father, and I will love him and disclose Myself to him."

Our God is all powerful, Lord, God Almighty—He is Omnipotent; He is always present in all places and at the same time—He is Omnipresent; He knows the mind of your heart, for he is all knowing—He is Omniscient; He is the remarkable Creator of this world and all the immeasurable wonderful things in it, He is the creator of the wonderful minds and hearts—He is Omnificent. He is the God of promises and guarantees, and we should love him and esteem Him to the highest—He is always giving; no one can beat it. He is Ombenevolence (my word).

Love the LORD your God with all your heart and with all your soul and with all your strength. These commandments that I give you today are to be upon your hearts. Impress them on your children. Talk about them when you sit at home and when you walk along the road, when you lie down and when you get up. Tie them as symbols on your hands and bind them on your foreheads. Write them on the doorframes of your houses and on your gates. When the LORD your God brings you into the land he swore to your fathers, to Abraham, Isaac and Jacob, to give you—a land with large, flourishing cities you did not build, houses filled with all kinds of good things you did not provide, wells you did not dig, and vineyards and olive groves you did not plant— then when you eat and are satisfied, be careful that you do not forget the LORD, who brought you out of Egypt, out of the land of slavery. Fear the LORD your God, serve him only and take your oaths in his name. Do not follow other gods, the gods of the peoples around you; for the LORD your God, who is among you, is a jealous God and his anger will burn against you, and he will destroy you from the face of the land (Deut 6:5-15, NKJ);

You shall diligently keep the commandments of the Lord your God, His testimonies, and His statures which He has commanded you. And you shall do what is right and good in the sight of the Lord, that it may be well with you, and that you may go in and possess the good land of which the Lord swore to your fathers (Deut 6:17,18, NAS);

"You shall love the Lord your God with all your heart, with all your soul, and with all your mind. This is the first and great commandment. And the second is like it: You shall love your neighbor as yourself; On these two commandments, hang all the Law and the Prophets (Matt 22:37-40 NKJ,)." If we keep God's Commandments, there is nothing we have to need for.

And my God shall supply all your need according to His riches in glory by Christ Jesus (Phil 4:19, NKJ). If we keep God's commandments there is no need to worry.

Therefore I say to you, do not worry about your life, what you will eat or what you will drink: nor about your body, what you will put on (Matt 6:25, NKJ). Also consider reading Matthew 6:26-34.

Let us resolve to obey God's commandments. Let us be victorious in His love. **God's** love is ***A Love Not Broken.***

Why Honor the Oneness in Christ

God gave us a simple plan of salvation to follow. If only some of us follow that plan, that means someone is either following his own plan, someone else's plan or simply ignoring it all.

"for God is not a God of confusion, but of peace, as in all churches of the saints (1 Cor. 14:33, NAS)."

I warn everyone who hears the words of prophesy of this book: If anyone adds anything to them, God will strike him with the plagues that written in this book. And if anyone takes words away from this book of prophesy, God will take away his portion of the tree of life and the holy city that are described in this book (Rev. 22:18-19, ISV).

God is the Father and creator of all mankind. No one, not even the angels in heaven, have the authority to change God's word.

Just as an earthly father expects his children to obey him, God expects us to honor his words, without any changes. Just like an earthly father punishes his children for disobedience. There are also consequences for those who disobey God (2 John 9; Matt. 7:21). The difference is, if one fails to obey God's words, they cannot enter into the kingdom of Heaven.

For if after they have escaped the pollutions of the world through the knowledge of the Lord and Saviour Jesus Christ, they are again entangled therein, and overcome, the latter end is worse with them than the beginning. For it had been better for them not to have known the way of righteousness, than, after they have known it, to turn from the holy commandment delivered unto them (2 Pet. 2:20-21, KJV). You see, no one who is able to understand is excluded from obedience. God knows all who are able to understand.

The Lord is one: *Hear O Israel: The Lord our God, the Lord is one (Due.6:4).*

There is one body and one spirit—just as you were called to one hope when you were called—one faith, one baptism; one God and father of all who is over all and through all and in all (Eph. 4:4-6).

I pray also that the eyes of your heart be enlightened in order that you may know **the hope** *(one hope) to which he has called you, the riches of his glorious inheritance in the saints (Eph. 1:1),*

[11]*Therefore, remember that formerly you who are Gentiles by birth and called "uncircumcised by those who called themselves the circumcision" (that done in the body by the hands of men)*[12] *remember at that time you were separate from Christ, excluded from citizenship in Israel and foreigners to the covenants of the promise, without hope and without God in the world.*[13] *But now in Christ Jesus you who once were far away have been brought near through the blood of Christ.*[14] *For he himself is our peace, who has made the two* **one** *and has destroyed the barriers, the dividing wall of hostility*[15] *by abolishing in his flesh the law with its commandments and regulations. His purpose was to create in himself* **one** *new man out of the two making peace*[16] *and in this* **one** *body to reconcile both of them to God through the cross by which he put to death their hostility.*[17] *He came and preached peace to those who were far away and to those who were near.*[18] *For through him we both have access to the Father by one spirit.*[19] *Consequently you are no longer foreigners and aliens, but fellow citizens with God's people and members of God's household,*[20] *built on the foundation of the apostles and*

prophets, with Christ Jesus himself as the chief cornerstone.[21] *In Him the whole building is joined together and rises to become a holy temple in the Lord.*[22] *And in him you too are being built together to become a dwelling in which God lives by his Spirit (Eph. 2:11-22).*

So then about eating food sacrificed to idols: We know that an idol is nothing at all in the world and there is no God but **one.** *For even if there are so-called gods, whether in heaven or on earth (as indeed there are many gods and many lords), yet for us there is but* **one** *God, the Father from whom all things came and for whom we live; and there is but* **one** *Lord, Jesus Christ through whom all things came and through whom we live (1*[st] *Cor. 8:4-6).*

[12] *The body is a unit, though it is made up of many parts; and though all its parts are many, they form* **one** *body. So it is with Christ.*[13] *For we were all baptized by* **one** *Spirit into* **one** *body whether Jews or Greeks, slaves or free— and we were all given the* **one** *Spirit to drink (1 Cor. 12:12-13).*

*(***KJV***) Neither pray I for these alone, but for them also which shall believe on me through their word; That they all may be* **one** *in us: that the world may believe that thou hast sent me. And the glory which thou gavest me I have given them; that they may be* **one**, *even as we are one: I in them and thou in me, that they may be made perfect in* **one**; *and that the world may know that thou hast sent me, and hast loved them as thou hast love me. Jesus prayed that all believers be* **one** *(John 17:20-23);*

Paul accentuated on oneness the by using the symbolism of oneness in a marital relationship. The husband and wife joined together as one was God's plan from the beginning. It is still God's plan, just as Christ and the church is one, the Father, Son and the Holy Spirit are one.

Therefore shall a man leave his father and his mother, and shall cleave to his wife, and they shall be one flesh (Gen. 2:24, KJV)

Inseparable

For this cause shall a man leave his father and mother, and shall be joined unto his wife, and they two shall be one flesh. This is a great mystery: but I speak concerning Christ and the church (Eph. 5:31-32, KJV).

When a man takes a woman as his bride they have become one, (unified) to take another woman within that marriage, goes against God's plan for oneness (unity) in marriages. For oneness is their foundation. To be one signifies unity. It is impossible to be unified when everyone is doing his own thing. The old saying still applies, today. "Together we stand and divided we fall". The United States is one nation with many states, a state is one state with many cities, a business is one business with many employees, a family is one family with many members. The church (Christ's bride) is one church with many members. Let us keep in mind that God is not the author of confusion. God's plan for us is simple. It only becomes confusing when we start adding to or taking away from it. God did not need our help with the creation. He did not need our help with the resurrection. His plan was intact long before our existence.

God's Plan for the Church: *And it shall come to pass in the last days, that the mountain of the Lord's house shall be established in the top of the mountains, and shall be exalted above the hill; and all nations shall flow into it (Isaiah 2:2, KJV).*

And they shall bring all your brethren for an offering unto the Lord out of all nations upon horses and in chariots, and in litters and upon mules, and upon swift beasts, to my holy mountain in Jerusalem, saith the Lord, as the children of Israel bring offering in a clean vessel into the house of the Lord (Isaiah 66:20, KJV).

Except the Lord build the house, they labour in vain that build it: except the Lord keep the city, the watchmen waketh but in vain (Ps. 127:1, KJV).

For we are labourers together with God: ye are God's husbandry, ye are God's building. According to the grace of God which is given to me, as a wise masterbuilder, I have laid the foundation, and another buildeth thereon. But let everyman take heed how he buildeth thereupon. For other foundation can no man lay than that is laid which is Jesus Christ (1 Cor. 3:9-11, KJV)

*And I say also unto thee, That thou art Peter, (Christ is saying "Peter, I am going to build my church") and upon this rock I will build my church; and the gates of hell shall not prevail against **it** (Matt. 16:18, KJV). **"It,** specifies **one** and **my,** signifies **ownership."***

Christ is the head of the only church and the only one whom God gave the authority to build a church; for He is the only Bridge to heaven." The church Christ built refers to a spiritual church; consisting of members He and only He, adds to it. The buildings we worship in are not the church; the people inside of it make up the church. If you take the people away from that building; all you have left is a building, because the church is not present. Therefore the actual building itself holds little importance. Now the important question is this, whose church is inside of the building when people are present? Is it Christ's church or man's? Now it makes sense to specify who is on the inside by identifying them on the outside. Surely one would not post the Jones name on their door or mailbox when the Smiths live there. There are many members in Christ's family all over the world. Although we are all one family, we are not all in one place. Therefore each family member

490

has a church home. For example, let us say that Ridgeview church of Christ... Ridgeview is identifying the location and church of Christ is giving recognition to Christ and his body—the body that is made up of the people He added to His church. Therefore the body is the church.

Praising God, and having favour with all the people. And the Lord added to the church daily such as should be save (Acts 2:47, KJV).

If you have a sign posted outside that reads Ridgeview Baptist church, you've identified location and have given recognition to a Baptist church in which Christ has no part. He has been left out of the loop. Christ should be given full recognition inside and outside in spirit and in truth. Many have said it doesn't matter what name we wear or how our service is conducted. God's word says:

But in vain they do worship me, teaching for doctrines the commandments of men (Matt. 15:9, KJV)But the hour cometh, and now is, when the true worshipers shall worship the Father in spirit and in truth: for the Father seeketh such to worship him. God is a Spirit: and they that worship him must worship him in spirit and in truth (John 4:23-24, KJV).

Christ is the head—He is the builder—He has been given all authority. He deserves all respect. We have no authority to choose what religious name we wear—there is only one. Nor what name to call Christ's church—it has already been given. Baptist is a name, but it does not associated with the Christian name in the, Bible, neither is

491

Methodist, nor Presbyterian, nor Protestant and so on. The members of Christ's body, the church of Christ—are given the name, Christian. It is the only name that will be given recognition to by our Father, God. "The Father who spared not his own Son, for us all."

We cannot justify using any other names. The name Christian was first given at Antioch. According to (Acts 11:26). If we refer to Christ's church as the church of the living God, it is still Christ's church, because he is and is recognized as the Living God. If it is called the church of God, it is still Christ's church, because He is God in the flesh. Man has chosen many names for Christ's church. The simple fact is that Christ' has been given all authority...that means identifying him by Bible names, Jesus, Messiah, The One, Alpha and Omega, Immanuel, Holy One, Christ, Son of Man, The Amen, etc. and identifying His church by the Bible name—church of Christ (Roman 16:16); church of God (Acts 20:28; 1Cor. 1-2); household of God (Ehp.2:19); the body, the church (Col. 1:18; Eph. 1:22-23); the church (1 Th. 1:1; Eph. 5:23); house of God, church of the living God (1 Tim. 3:15); church of the Firstborn (Heb. 12:23); God's building (1 Cor. 3:9); the Flock (1 Pet. 5:3; Acts 20:28), because it belongs to him, and identifying his people by the name given (Christians) that He added to His church, the church that He built. Therefore, giving honor to him as the head of the church and moreover, giving recognition to his church by calling it, nothing other than "the church of Christ." Nothing more—nothing less. At the conclusion of reading all of these scripture, it all sums up to this ... Christ have been given all authority over **everything**.

Salute one another with a holy kiss. The churches of Christ salute you (Ro.16:16, KJV). You will not find salvation in any other name.

Neither is there salvation in any other: for there is none other name under heaven given among men, whereby we must be saved (Acts 4:12, KJV).

Wherefore God also hath highly exalted him, and given him a name which is above every name. That at the name of Jesus every knee should bow, of things in heaven, and in earth, and things under the earth (Phi. 2:9-10, KJV).

There is no way around it. There's no under-cutting it. There is no making it better. It has already been made better.

Behold, the days comes, saith the Lord that I will make a new a covenant with the house of Israel, and with the house of Judah: Not according to the covenant that I made with their fathers in the day that I took by the hand to bring them out of the land of Egypt: which my covenant they brake, although I was an husbandman unto them, saith the Lord (Jer. 31:31 32, KJV):

But now hath he obtained a more excellent ministry, by how much also he is the mediator of a better covenant, which was established upon a better promise (Heb. 8:6, KJV).

God made it better when He sacrificed his son.

For God so loved the world, that he gave his only begotten Son, that whosoever believeth in him should not perish, but have everlasting life (John 3:16, KJV).

And he is the head of the body, the church: who is the beginning, the firstborn from the dead; that in all things he may have the preeminence (Col. 1:18, KJV).

For the husband is the head of the wife, even as Christ is the head of the church: and he is the Savior of the body (Eph. 5:23, KJV).

Thou madest him a little lower than the angels; though crownedst him with glory and honour, and didst set him over the works of thou hands: Thou hast put all things under his feet. For in that he put all things in subjection under him, he left nothing that is not put under him. But now we see not yet all things put under him (Hebrews 2:7-8, KJV).

Thou madest him to have dominion over the works of thy hands, thou hast put all things under his feet (Psalm 8:6, KJV).

And hath put all things under his feet, and gave him to be the head over all things to the church (Eph. 1:22, KJV).

For he hath put all things under his feet. But when he saith all things are put under him, it is manifest that he is expected, which did put all things under him. And when all things shall be subdued unto him, then shall the Son also himself be subject unto him that put all things under him, that God may be all in all ((1 Cor. 15:27-28, KJV).

There is one body, and one spirit, even as ye are called into one hope of your calling: One Lord, one faith, one baptism, One God and Father of all, who is above all, and through all, and in you all (Eph. 4:4-6, KJV).

So we, being many, are one body in Christ, and every one members one of another (Romans 12:5, KJV).

It pleases the Lord when we are walking worthy.

"That ye might walk worthy of the Lord unto him all pleasing, being fruitful in every good work, and increasing in the knowledge of God (Col 1:10, KJV);

"For it pleased the Father that in him should all fullness dwell (Col. 1:19,KJV);

One cannot walk worthy of the Lord if one is abiding by something other than His biblical teaching. One cannot please the Lord nor be fruitful if he is mixing manmade doctrine with the Holy Bible's teaching.

Paul said, "*Only let your conversation be as it becometh the gospel of* **Christ**: *that whether I come and see you, or else be absent, I may hear of your affairs, that ye stand fast in* **one** *spirit, with* **one** *mind striving together for the faith of the gospel. (Phil. 1:27, KJV);*

Paul also said, *"Furthermore then we beseech you, brethren, and exhort you by the* **Lord Jesus** *that as ye have received of us how ye ought to walk and please* **God***, so ye would abound more and more" (1 Thess. 4:1, KJV)."* Let us keep in mind that through His word, God offers all men deliverance from the power of darkness. Manmade doctrine cannot deliver anyone from darkness. If we allow ourselves to partake in the distorted truth of man, then what was the purpose of Christ's sacrifice? God does not know sin. At the time of the sacrifice, Christ took on the sins of the world. When the world was covered with darkness, God forsook His own Son.

And about the ninth hour Jesus cried with a loud voice, saying, E-li, E-li la'-ma sa-bach'-tha-ni? that is to say, My god, my God, why hast thou forsaken me (Matthew 27:46, KJV)? Forsaken is defined as abandoned, to leave, and to dessert. Tell me...how would you feel if you had to stand by and watch a loved one or even your child be brutally tortured, and you were unable to help or save him/her? God made the greatest sacrifice for us all. He allowed his one and only son to suffer for the *sins* of the world.

Paul's Warning: *Take heed therefore unto yourselves, and to all the flock, over the which the Holy Ghost had made you overseers, to feed the church of God which he hath purchased with his own blood. For I know this, that after my departing shall grievous wolves enter in among you, not sparing the flock. Also of your own selves shall men arise, speaking perverse things (distorting the truth) to draw away disciples after them (Acts 20:28-30, KJV).*

Who hath delivered us from the power of darkness, and hath translated us into the kingdom of his dear Son. In whom we have redemption through his blood, even the forgiveness of sins (Col.1:13-14, KJV):

I marvel that ye are so soon removed from him that called you into the grace of Christ unto another gospel: Which is not another; but there be some that trouble you, and would pervert the gospel of Christ. But though we, are an angel from heaven, preach any other gospel unto you, than that which we have preached unto you, let him be accursed. As we said before, so say I now again, If any man preach any other gospel unto you than that ye have received, let him be accused (Gal. 1:6-9, KJV).

I know that, whatsoever God doeth, it shall be for ever: nothing can be put to it, nor anything taken from it: and God doeth it, that men should fear before him (Eccl. 3:14, KJV).

Whosoever transgresseth, and abideth not in the doctrine of Christ, hath not God. He that abideth in the doctrine of Christ, he hath both the Father and the Son. If there come any unto you, and bring not this doctrine, receive him not into your house, neither bid him God speed (II John 9-10, KJV):

But I tarry long, that thou mayest know how thou oughtest to behave thyself in the house of the God, which is the church of the living God (Christ), the pillar and ground of truth (1 Tim. 3:15, KJV).

Wherefore God also hath highly exalted him, and given him a name which is above every name (Phil. 2:9, KJV).

Who is the image of the invisible God (Christ), the firstborn of every creature (Col.1:15, KJV):

Many will say they love God; many will say they believe in God; many will confess that they believe that Jesus Christ is the Son of God: however, it doesn't stop there.

Not everyone that saith unto me, Lord, Lord, shall enter into the Kingdom of heaven; but he that doeth the will of my Father which is in heaven. Many will say to me in that day, Lord, Lord, have we not prophesied in thy name? And in thy name have cast out devils? And in thy name done many wonderful works? And then will I profess unto them, I never knew you: depart from me, ye that work iniquity. Therefore whosoever hearth these sayings of mine, and doeth them, I will liken him unto a wise man, which built his house upon a rock: And the rain descended, and the floods came, and the wind blew and beat upon that house; and it fell not: for it was founded upon a rock. And everyone that heareth these sayings of mine, and doeth them not, shall be likened unto a foolish man, which built his house upon the sand: And the rain descended, and the floods came, and the winds blew and beat upon that house; and it fell: and great was the fall of it (Matt 7:21-27, KJV).

God said prove all things. The only way to prove God's words is go to His source, the "Bible."

Prove all things; hold fast that which is good (1 Thess. 5:21,KJV). It comes down to this simple fact, the truth. Christ is the only bridge to heaven.

For by him were all things created, that are in heaven, and that in earth, visible and invisible, whether they be thrones, or dominions or principalities, or powers: all things were created by him, and for him: And he is before all things and by him all things consist (Col. 1:16-17, KJV).

All things were made by him; and without him was not any thing made that was made (John 1:3, KJV).

And having made peace through the blood of his cross, by him to reconcile all things unto himself, by him, I say, whether they be things in earth, or things in heaven (Col. 1:20, KJV). I will not say who will or who will not enter into the kingdom of heaven. Nonetheless, I will refer you to Matt. 7:21.

Even him, whose coming is after the working of Satan with all power and signs and lying wonders, And with all deceivableness of unrighteousness in them that perish; because they received not the love of the truth, that they might be saved. And for this cause God shall send them strong delusion, that they should believe a lie: That they all might be damned who believe not the truth, but had pleasure in unrighteousness (II Thess. 2:9-12, KJV). **Will you accept God's word or will you be lead astray by man's word?**

Inseparable

The Holy Bible, King James Version Copyright 1984, 1977 by Thomas Nelson, Inc.

Poetry

<u>*Love Is*</u>

Love exceeds those feelings

You feel in side,

Love is something you cannot hide.

Love brings happiness

though sometimes you maybe sad,

but love is the best thing a person ever had.

It's a lot richer than money,

you can't spend it all in one day

If the love is real it will never go away.

Not every moment will be joyous,

sometimes things will seem down

Keep holding on, love always hangs around.

When your heart is burdened by life's troubles,

there's no greater comfort that will sustain,

love will bring sunshine in fog and rain.

When sometimes happiness seems far away

love's joy is here to stay.

When you can't find laughter

from the best of rhymes

Love is there to comfort those times.

When troubled hearts are broken,

love has a healing token.

Love is'

From a Mothers Heart

My darling child, you are a blessing from above

another way God has shown me his love.

He reached out to me through you, I believe,

and joy and laughter to my life I received

A child whose faith and hope help me to grow

in a Godly way this I know.

You're overflowing with compassion, love and concern

from this many others could learn.

You're such an overachiever,

a giver rather than a receiver.

You've been that way from the start

I used to always say, she's too smart.

My child, you mean to me, more than words can say.

I'm so thankful that God has blessed us to be here this day.

No matter how old you are, young lady,

you, my dear, will always be my baby.

A special tribute to my daughter Tyrica

Way Back When

Way back when I was a young girl,

living a block down from my grandmother's house.

I often walked through the narrow trail,

hoping I wouldn't see a mouse.

Two by fours stuck in the ground,

held together by barb wire and nails.

Clothes hanging on the line

with the fresh smell of Tide,

hoping they'll dry before dark on time.

Mixed with the a fresh smell of the country air inhaling the outside

Granny always sat in her rocking chair,

on the long closed-in back porch.

Brushing every strand of her gray and black hair,

hoping the garden and roses the sun won't torch.

Granny always had a serious look.

She treated everyone better than they deserved,

especially when she cooked.

My Granny, she means the world to me.

She's always had a listening ear that served

And her love overflowed, a love everyone could see.

Harboring Resentment

The moment you find yourself resenting,

turn back or else become a slave by consenting.

It controls your dream and absorbs your digestion

it causes you to lose directions.

Deprives you of your peaceful mind and good will,

takes away the gratification of pleasures with laughter and thrill.

It ruins your religion and nullifies your prayer,

Get rid of it for it goes everywhere.

It destroys the goodness of your heart and hounds you wherever

you go,

there is no escaping because you resent so.

It is with you when you're awake

even on vacation, for God's sake.

It is with you when you're asleep

and still present when you're eat.

While you're on your job and driving your car,

you can bet, it's not very far.

You can't be efficient, nor have happiness,

as long as resenting exist.

It influences even the tone of your voice

guides you in your every choice.

You'll find yourself taking medicine for different reasons,

and you'll lose yourself between seasons.

It'll rob you of your pleasant thoughts,

no one is the blame, it's all your fought.

Looking Through a Mirror

When I look through a mirror, what do I see?

I see myself looking at me.

When I close my eyes,

I see a portrait of myself in demise.

My outer self I see no more.

It's the inner appearance I saw not before.

Looking through the mirror of my heart, leaving the mirrored

face behind.

I heave a sigh into the deepness of my mind.

Undulating through the glass of my heart

as did in the mirror from the start.

A different face I now see

the face I need to be.

Where would my soul reside,

except in Christ I abide?

Redemption I know I must face,

to receive the reward of God's amazing grace.

Voice

A man of Christ

I've been blessed to know

The love in his heart

Gives a spiritual glow

The changes he brought to many lives

Men, women, children, husbands and wives

The knowledge to take what belongs to us

Our souls, indeed we must

Oh what a wonderful man

He gave us courage to open our spirits and to trust again

Those closed by pain, suffering and sin

The wisdom to allow Christ to work within

He taught us how to be whole

Never to trade right for wrong, never to roll the dice

The price could be our soul

A man after Christ

Once with us and now far away

But his presents remain with us

Still today

A voice to wake up his fellow men

Given sound gospel to deter from a life of sin

How could we not take these words to heart

When we know that being born again

Is a brand new start

If I hear not his voice again and in life lies many years ahead

I'll hold dear in my heart the things he have said If in this world he was near

These words I'd want him to hear

Thank you for reminding us

That God is the Beginning and the End

And only Satan is in a life of sin

A special dedication in memory a dear friend and brother in Christ

Journey to Success

We often think we fail because we don't succeed

in the things in which we attempt.

Success is not determined by a close-ended question,

But rather individually characterized

For some success means,

having the money to fulfill all their material dreams,

financial independency, educational achievement,

overcoming fear or breaking a bad a habit,

completing an important exam or a semester in school

or as simple as completing a daily task.

Success ranges from personal to professional achievement,

success is climbing the ladder to advance, to overcome,

to endure, to achieve, to fulfill, to love, and to be loved.

If you have a plan for success

and your success foundation is built on your dreams

or your desired accomplishments,

and you journey with determination, confident, honesty

and believe in yourself.

If it's about who you are and what you want to become,

then your success is your own.

Your success journey is

achieved with one step at a time,

Sometime success is found in your genuine effort.

Most importantly, seek success in Christ.

Where success is eternally guaranteed.

Keep your journey in God's hand

and always strive for the success in keeping His commands.

Cakes and Pound Cakes

Note: Extra virgin, unrefined coconut oil can be used in place of butter.

Pineapple Pound Cake

3 cups unbleached flour (sifted)

2 cups sugar

3 sticks unsalted butter

2 tsp. baking powder

½ tsp. salt

5 large eggs

1 cup buttermilk (low-fat)

2 tsp. pineapple extract

1 tsp. pure vanilla extract

1-20 ounce can crushed pineapples in juice (drain juice and reserve)

Preheat oven on 350 degrees F (175 C). Grease and flour a 10-tube cake pan.

1) Measure flour and sift three times; re-measure, add baking powder and salt and sift one time and set aside.
2) Whip butter until light and fluffy; add sugar and beat until light and creamy. Separate egg whites from yokes. Put whites in a medium size bowl and set aside.
3) Add yolks to butter mixture one at a time, beating 30 seconds after each egg. Beat until fluffy. Alternate with flour and milk; continue beating on low until all ingredients are incorporated.
4) Add flavor and beat on medium for about 2 minutes.

5) Remove ¼ cup to add in the bottom of tube pan. Fold the remaining into batter.

6) Beat egg white for about 30 seconds, continue beating while adding 1 tablespoon of sugar along the side of the bowl; beat until fluffy and peak forms.

7) Fold into cake mixture with large spoon or spatula. Don't beat. Spread pineapples in the bottom of tube pan and sprinkle lightly with light brown sugar. Pour into tube cake pan.

8) Bake on 350 for 70 to 75 minutes. Baking time may vary depending on stove. Remove from oven and let cool for 15 minutes. Transfer to a plate or platter and drizzle with pineapple glaze.

9) Tip: I usually can tell if my cake is ready by checking to see if the cake has slightly pulled away from the sides of the pan.

Pineapple Glaze

15 ounces crushed pineapples

10 ounces powdered sugar

1 stick unsalted butter

2 packed tablespoons light brown sugar

---

1) In a small saucepan melt butter and stir in pineapples, juice and brown sugar. Cook on medium low heat for 10 to 15 minutes (stir to prevent scorching).

2) Remove from heat and pour in mixing bowl. Beat in powdered sugar. Use reserved pineapple juice for thinner glaze. Let set for 5 to 7 minutes and pour across the top of cake.

Lemon Cranberry Pound Cake

2 cups sugar	*1 cup buttermilk (low-fat)*
3 sticks unsalted butter	*2 teaspoons pure lemon extract*
3 cups unbleached flour	*1 teaspoon pure vanilla extract*
2 tsps. baking powder	*1 cup frozen cranberries (chopped)*
½ tsps. sea salt	*zest of 1 lemon*
5 large eggs	

Preheat oven on 350.

1) Spray or grease and flour a 10 inch tube cake pan.
2) Measure flour and sift three times; re-measure, add baking powder and salt and sift one time and set aside.
3) Whip butter on high speed until light and fluffy; add sugar and beat until light and creamy. Separate egg whites from yokes. Put whites in a medium size bowl and set aside.
4) Add yolks to butter mixture one at a time, beating for 30 second after each egg. Beat on high speed until fluffy.
5) Add flavors and 2 tablespoons of the flour, beating for about 30 seconds.
6) Gradually add flour and milk alternating between the two (adding about ¾ cup of flour at a time); continue beating on low speed until all ingredients are well incorporated.
7) Mix chopped cranberries, lemon zest and fold into batter.
8) Beat egg white for about 30 seconds, continue beating while adding 1 tablespoon of sugar along the side of the bowl; beat

until opaque and soft peak forms. Fold into cake mixture with large spoon or spatula. Don't beat. Pour into tube cake pan.

9) Bake on 350 for 70 to 75 minutes. Baking time may vary depending on stove. Remove from stove and let cool for 15 minutes. Transfer to a plate or platter, let rest for 15 minutes and drizzle well with lemon glaze. Tip: I usually can tell if my cake is ready by checking to see if the cake has slightly pulled away from the side of the pan.

Lemon Glaze

2 cups powdered sugar

2 ½ tablespoons fresh lemon juice

2 tablespoons melted butter

2 tablespoons grated lemon zest

1 small drop yellow food coloring (optional)

1) Add all ingredients to a bowl and whip until smooth.

Peanut Butter Pound Cake

3 cups unbleached flour (sifted)

2 cups sugar

3 sticks unsalted butter

2 tsps. baking powder

1/8 tsp. baking soda

½ tsp. salt

5 large eggs

1 cup buttermilk

1 tsp. banana flavor

1 tsp. pure vanilla extract

1 cup creamy honey roasted peanut butter (preference)

Preheat oven on 350 F.

1) Grease and flour a 10 inch tube cake pan.
2) Measure flour and sift three times; re-measure, add baking powder and salt and sift one time and set aside.
3) Whip butter and peanut butter on high speed until light and fluffy; add sugar and beat until light and creamy. Separate egg whites from yokes. Put whites in a medium size bowl and set aside.
4) Add yolks to butter mixture one at a time, beating for 30 second after each egg. Beat on high speed until fluffy.
5) Add flavors and 2 tablespoons of the flour, beating for about 30 seconds.
6) Gradually add flour and milk alternating between the two (adding no more than ¾ cup of flour at a time); continue beating on low speed until all ingredients are well incorporated.
7) Beat egg white for about 30 seconds, continue beating while adding 1 tablespoon of sugar along the side of the bowl; beat

until opaque and soft peak forms. Fold into cake mixture with large spoon or spatula. Don't beat. Pour into tube cake pan.

8) Bake on 350 for 70 to 75 minutes or until toothpick comes out clean. Baking time may vary depending on stove. When the cake releases from the sides of the pan is an indication that it is ready or very near. Remove from stove and let cool for 15 minutes. Transfer to a plate or platter and drizzle well with glaze.

Peanut Butter Glaze

¼ cup creamy peanut butter	½ teaspoon banana flavor
¼ cup low-fat milk	10 ounces powdered sugar

1) Add all ingredients to a mixing bowl and beat with a mixer until smooth and well blended. Drizzle over cake after cooling, but still warm. I like a piece with a scoop of ice cream and whipped cream on top, with drizzles of the glaze. Enjoy

Desserts

Carrot Cake

2 cups unbleached flour (sifted 3 times)	*1 ½ cup unsalted butter*
2 teaspoon baking soda	*4 large eggs*
½ to ¾ teaspoon salt	*½ cup pecans (chopped)*
2 teaspoons ground cinnamon	*½ cup walnuts (chopped)*
½ teaspoon ground ginger	*2 teaspoons pure vanilla extract*
1 ½ cups fine granulated sugar	*2 teaspoon freshly squeezed lemon juice*
3 cups grated carrots	

Preheat oven on 350 degrees F (175 C)

1) Grease or spray and flour 3-9 inch round cake pans.
2) Measure 2 cups of flour after sifting 3 times. Add baking soda, cinnamon, ginger and salt to sifter. Sift through and set aside.
3) In a large mixing bowl, using an electric mixer, whip butter. Add sugar and beat until creamy.
4) Separate egg whites and yolks. Put yolks in a small bowl and whites in a medium size-mixing bowl. Lightly beat yolks with a fork and set aside.
5) Add dry ingredients to cream mixture, alternating with egg yolks, beating well after each addition. Add vanilla extract and lemon juice and beat for a minute. Add carrots to mixture and beat on medium speed until well incorporated, about 2 minutes.
6) Fold in walnuts and pecans.
7) Beat egg whites until foamy and then add 1 tablespoon of sugar along the side of bowl and beat until fluffy. Fold egg

whites into mixture. Pour evenly into cake pans and bake for 25-30 minutes.

8) Hint: Cakes are usually ready when they separate from sides of pans. You can also use 2 toothpicks held together and insert in the middle of cakes to check for doneness. After taking cakes from oven, let cool for at least 10 minutes. Lay a piece of parchment paper on top of cakes and turn each cake onto paper. Let cool for 10 to 15 minutes and then frost. Brush off any crumbs before frosting. Place the first layer on cake plate and frost. Make sure each layer is evenly frosted.

Cream Cheese Frosting

1-8 ounce pack low-fat cream cheese (room temperature) *1 stick butter (room temp)*	**4 to 5 cups powdered sugar (more for thicker frosting)** **1 teaspoon pure vanilla extract**

1. In a large bowl add cream cheese and butter and then beat with a mixer until creamy.

2. Slowly beat in powdered sugar; a small amount at a time, and add in vanilla extract. Beat until light and fluffy.

Yvonne Taylor, has held a lifelong passion for writing and cooking, and pours her creativity into short stories, poems, songs and creating tantalizing dishes. She has a passion for writing Christian romance, children's and young adult literature, and futuristic crime stories.

She was born and raised in Arkansas and educated at the University of Arkansas at Little Rock, where she majored in Criminal Justice and Psychology, with coursework in creating writing and techniques of writing. She began writing her first novel, *Inseparable*, while working as a life skill counselor for mentally challenged adults and children.

Her first published work is *Inseparable*, a Christian romance novel, and her first published cookbook is the *Madd Batter*. She is also the author of the Madd Chicken on a Budget cookbook and a second romance novel, Hearts.

As an avid researcher on natural health, she is dedicated to healthy living. She serves others by sharing her research and advocating the importance of using natural health treatments, cooking and eating healthy. She is a dedicated Christian, and believes that nothing is worthy without Christ. Taylor lives in Central Texas with her family.

www.ingramcontent.com/pod-product-compliance
Lightning Source LLC
Chambersburg PA
CBHW030752260626
47169CB00001B/8